Praise for
THE RETRIEVAL ARTIST SERIES

The SF thriller is alive and well, and today's leading practitioner is Kristine Kathryn Rusch.

—*Analog*

[The Anniversary Day Saga is] one of the top science fiction sagas in recent years.

—*Midwest Book Review*

Instant addiction. You hear about it—maybe you even laugh it off— but you never think it could happen to you. Well, you just haven't run into Miles Flint and the other Retrieval Artists looking for The Disappeared. ...I am hopelessly hooked....

—Lisa DuMond
MEviews.com on *The Disappeared*

An inventive plot and complex, conflicted characters increases the appeal of Kristine Kathryn Rusch's *Extremes*. This futuristic tale breaks new ground as a space police procedural and should appeal to science fiction and mystery fans.

—*RT Book Reveiws* on *Extremes*

Part science fiction, part mystery, and pure enjoyment are the words to describe Kristine Kathryn Rusch's latest Retrieval Artist novel.... This is a strong murder mystery in an outer space storyline.

—*The Best Reviews* on *Consequences*

An exciting, intricately plotted, fast-paced novel. You'll find it difficult to put down.

—*SFRevu* on *Buried Deep*

A science fiction murder mystery by one of the genre's best.... A book with complex characters, an interesting and unpredictable plot, and timeless and universal things to say about the human condition.

—*The Panama News* on *Paloma*

Rusch continues her provocative interplanetary detective series with healthy doses of planet-hopping intrigue, heady legal dilemmas and well-drawn characters.

—*Publishers Weekly* on *Recovery Man*

...the mystery is unpredictable and absorbing and the characters are interesting and sympathetic.

—*Blastr* on *Duplicate Effort*

Anniversary Day is an edge-of-the-seat thriller that will keep you turning pages late into the night and it's also really good science fiction. What's not to like?

—*Analog* on *Anniversary Day*

The latest Retrieval Artist science fiction thriller is an engaging investigative whodunit starring popular Miles Flint on a comeback mission. The suspenseful storyline is fast-paced and filled with twists as the hero comes out of retirement to confront his worst nightmare.

—*Midwest Book Reviews* on *Blowback*

Fans of Rusch's Retrieval Artist universe will enjoy the expansion of the Anniversary Day story, with new characters providing more perspectives on its signature events, while newcomers will get a good introduction to the series.

—*Publishers Weekly* on *A Murder of Clones*

This new Retrieval Artist Universe novel is action-packed and continues where *A Murder of Clones* leaves off. These must be read in order to fully appreciate the suspense and mystery that is taking place.

—*RT Book Reviews* on *Search & Recovery*

The Anniversary Day Saga just keeps getting more interesting and more complicated. Each addition is eagerly anticipated and leaves the reader anxious to discover what will happen next, who the bad guys are and what it is they are hoping to achieve.

—*RT Book Reviews* on *The Peyti Crisis*

THE RETRIEVAL ARTIST SERIES:

The Disappeared
Extremes
Consequences
Buried Deep
Paloma
Recovery Man
The Recovery Man's Bargain (Novella)
Duplicate Effort
The Possession of Paavo Deshin (Novella)

The Anniversary Day Saga:

Anniversary Day
Blowback
A Murder of Clones
Search & Recovery
The Peyti Crisis
Vigilantes
Starbase Human
Masterminds

Other Stories:

The Retrieval Artist (Novella)
The Impossibles (A Retrieval Artist Universe Short Story)

STARBASE HUMAN

A RETRIEVAL ARTIST UNIVERSE NOVEL

KRISTINE KATHRYN RUSCH

wmg PUBLISHING

Starbase Human

Book Seven of the Anniversary Day Saga

Published 2015 by WMG Publishing
www.wmgpublishing.com
Parts of this book appeared in different form in *Asimov's SF Magazine,*
March/April 2015, and in *Fiction River: Pulse Pounders,* January 2015
Cover and Layout copyright © 2015 by WMG Publishing
Cover design by Allyson Longueira/WMG Publishing
Cover art copyright © Nicholas Burningham/Dreamstime
ISBN-13: 978-1-56146-622-1
ISBN-10: 1-56146-622-0

For Annie Reed
Thanks for watching my back
(and for giving the College Kid such a great home)

Acknowledgements

I could not have done any of this project without the help of dozens of people. It has truly taken a village to finish the project—sometimes simply to keep me on track.

I owe a huge debt to Dean Wesley Smith for helping me with the plotting, to Allyson Longueira for her patience and attention to detail, to Colleen Kuehne who makes sure the details are accurate, and to Annie Reed for making sure I'm consistent from book to book (and for her eagle eye).

With this book, I also owe Sheila Williams and Kevin J. Anderson a rousing thank you. Sheila bought a novella for *Asimov's SF Magazine* that I wrote to figure out some details in this book, and Kevin bought the opening as a standalone short for *Fiction River: Pulse Pounders.* He helped the pulse pound even more.

Most of all, I want to thank the readers. You have stayed with me throughout, and I'm very grateful. Thank you, all.

Author's Note

Dear Readers,

Parts of Starbase Human *should be familiar to those of you who track down every little story in the Retrieval Artist universe. I wrote one full novella and a short story to explain what happened with a few characters before I realized that the novella and the short story belong in the longer Anniversary Day Saga.*

These, and the story of someone I hadn't written about since Blowback *were those elements I kept trying to shoehorn into earlier books, and they weren't shoeing (or horning, or whatever the right word actually is).*

It's time for a short explanation. Those of you who have faithfully bought the new books I've been releasing in the saga since January, thank you! You know what I'm going to say next because you've seen it in the previous author notes. Skip a few paragraphs, if you like.

Those of you who picked up this book without ever having read a novel in the Retrieval Artist universe, well, I'm sorry to tell you that you bought book seven in an eight-book saga. Usually the Retrieval Artist novels stand alone. But these eight books don't. Go back to Anniversary Day, *and start there. There's a list in each of the books that'll tell you which one to read next.*

Those of you who regularly read the Retrieval Artist books, but some-how missed the first four books released in 2015, you have some catching up to do. The book to read after Blowback *is* A Murder of Clones. *Then follow the list to see which book comes next.*

Starbase Human *is the last book before the big finale. A few loose threads get tied up here, and a lot of characters get to do what I intended them to do all along. You should have some a-ha! moments and a few what-the? moments.*

All will be revealed in the final chapter of the saga, Masterminds, *coming in June.*

—*Kristine Kathryn Rusch*
Lincoln City, Oregon
July 27, 2014

STARBASE HUMAN

A RETRIEVAL ARTIST UNIVERSE NOVEL

OVER THIRTY-FIVE
YEARS AGO

TAKARA HAMASAKI CROUCHED BEHIND THE HALF-OPEN DOOR, HER HEART pounding. She stared into the corridor, saw more boots go by. Good God, they made such a horrible thudding noise.

Her mouth tasted of metal, and her eyes stung. The environmental system had to be compromised. Which didn't surprise her, given the explosion that had happened not three minutes before.

The entire starbase rocked from it. The explosion had to have been huge. The base's exterior was compensating—that had come through her desk just before she left—but she didn't know how long it would compensate.

That wasn't true; she knew it could compensate forever if nothing else went wrong. But she had a hunch a lot of other things would go wrong. Terribly wrong.

She'd had that feeling for months now. It had grown daily, until she woke up every morning, wondering why the hell she hadn't left yet.

Three weeks ago, she had started stocking her tiny ship, the crap-ass thing that had brought her here half her life ago. She would have left then, except for one thing:

She had no money.

Yeah, she had a job, and yeah, she got paid, but it cost a small fortune to live this far out. The base was in the middle of nowhere, barely in what the Earth Alliance called the Frontier, and a week's food alone cost as much as her rent in the last Alliance place she had stayed. She got paid well, but every single bit of that money went back into living.

Dammit. She should have started sleeping in her ship. She'd been thinking of it, letting the one-room apartment go, but she kinda liked the privacy, and she really liked the amenities—entertainment on demand, a bed that wrapped itself around her and helped her sleep, and a view of the entire public district from above.

She liked to think it was that view that kept her in the apartment, but if she was honest with herself, it was that view and the bed and the entertainment, maybe not in that order.

And she was cursing herself now.

While the men—they were all men—wearing boots and weird uniforms marched toward the center of the base. Thousands of people lived or stayed here, but there wasn't much security. Not enough to deal with those men. She would hear that drumbeat of their stupid boots in her sleep for the rest of her life.

If the rest of her life wasn't measured in hours. If she ever got a chance to sleep again.

Her traitorous heart was beating in time to those boots. She was breathing through her mouth, hating the taste of the air.

If nothing else, she had to get out of here just to get some good clean oxygen. She had no idea what was causing that burned-rubber stench, but something was, and it was getting worse.

More boots stomped by, and she realized she couldn't tell the difference between the sound of the boots that had already passed her and those that were coming up the corridor.

She only had fifty meters to go to get to the docking ring, but that fifty meters seemed like a light-year.

And she wouldn't even be here, if it weren't for her damn survival instinct. She had looked up—before the explosion—saw twenty blond-haired men, all of whom looked like twins. Ten sets of twins—two sets of decaplets?—she had no idea what twenty identical people, the same age, and clearly monozygotic, were called. She supposed there was some name for them, but she wasn't sure. And, as usual, her brain was busy solving that, instead of trying to save her own single individual untwinned life.

She had scurried through the starbase, utterly terrified. The moment she saw those men enter the base, she left her office through the service corridors. When that seemed too dangerous, she crawled through the bot holes. Thank the universe she was tiny. She usually hated the fact that she was the size of an eleven-year-old girl and didn't quite weigh 100 pounds.

At this moment, she figured her tiny size might just save her life.

That, and her prodigious brain. If she could keep it focused instead of letting it skitter away.

Twenty identical men—and that wasn't the worst of it. They looked like younger versions of the creepy pale guys who had come into the office six months ago, looking for ships. They wanted to know the best place to buy ships in the starbase.

There was no place to buy new ships on the starbase. There were only old and abandoned ships. Fortunately, she had managed to prevent the sale of hers, a year ago. She'd illegally gone into the records and changed her ship's status from delinquent to paid in full, and then she had made that paid-in-full thing repeat every year. (She'd checked it, of course, but it hadn't failed her, and now it didn't matter. Nothing mattered except getting off this damn base.)

Still those old creepy guys had gotten the names of some good dealers on some nearby satellites and moons, and had left—she thought forever—but they had come back with a scary fast ship and lots of determination.

And, it seemed, lots of younger versions of themselves.

(Clones. What if they were clones? What did that mean?)

The drumbeat of their stupid boots had faded. She scurried into the corridor, then heard a high-pitched male scream, and a thud.

Her heart picked up its own rhythm—faster, so fast, in fact, that it felt like her heart was trying to get to the ship before she did.

She slammed herself against the corridor wall, felt it give (cheap-ass base), and caught herself before she fell inward on some unattached panel coupling.

She looked both ways, saw nothing, looked up, didn't see any movement in the cameras—which the base insisted on keeping obvious so that all kinds of criminals would show up here. If the criminals knew where the monitors were, they felt safe, weirdly enough.

And this base needed criminals. This far outside of the Alliance, the only humans with money were the ones who had stolen it—either illegally or legally through some kind of enterprise that was allowed out here, but not inside the Alliance.

This place catered to humans. It accepted non-human visitors, but no one here wanted them to stay. In the non-Earth atmosphere sections, the cameras weren't obvious.

She thanked whatever deity was this far outside of the Alliance that she hadn't been near the alien wing when the twenty creepy guys arrived and started marching in.

And then her brain offered up some stupid math it had been working on while she was trying to save her own worthless life.

She'd seen more than forty boots stomp past her.

That group of twenty lookalikes had only been the first wave.

Another scream and a thud. Then a woman's voice:

No! No! I'll do whatever you want. I'll—

And the voice just stopped. No thud, no nothing. Just silence.

Takara swallowed hard. That metallic taste made her want to retch, but she didn't. She didn't have time for it. She could puke all she wanted when she got on that ship, and got the hell away from here.

She levered herself off the wall, wondering in that moment how long the gravity would remain on if the environmental system melted. Her nose itched—that damn smell—and she wiped the sleeve of her too-thin blouse over it.

She should have dressed better that morning. Not for work, but for escape. Stupid desk job. It made her feel so important. An administrator at 25. She should have questioned it.

She should have questioned so many things.

Like the creepy older guys who looked like the baked and fried versions of the men in boots, stomping down the corridors, killing people.

She blinked, wondered if her eyes were tearing because of the smell or because of her panic, then voted for the smell. The air in the corridor had a bit of white to it, like smoke or something worse, a leaking environment from the alien section.

She was torn between running and tiptoeing her way through the remaining forty-seven meters. She opted for a kind of jog-walk, that way her heels didn't slap the floor like those boots stomped it.

Another scream, farther away, and the clear sound of begging, although she didn't recognize the language. Human anyway, or something that spoke like a human and screamed like a human.

Why were these matching people stalking the halls, killing everyone they saw? Were they trying to take over the base? If so, why not come to her office? Hers was the first one in the administrative wing, showing her lower-level status—in charge, but not in charge.

In charge enough to see that the base's exterior was compensating for having a hole blown in it. In charge enough to know how powerful an explosion had to be to break through the shield that protected the base against asteroids and out-of-control ships and anything else that bounced off the thick layers of protection.

A bend in the corridor. Her eyes dripped, her nose dripped, and her throat felt like it was burning up.

She couldn't see as clearly as she wanted to—no pure white smoke any more, some nasty brown stuff mixed in, and a bit of black.

She pulled off her blouse and put it over her face like a mask, wished she had her environmental suit, wished she knew where she could steal one right now, and then sprinted toward the docking ring.

If she kept walk-jogging, she'd never get there before the oxygen left the area.

Then something else shook the entire base. Like it had earlier. Another damn explosion.

She whimpered, rounded the last corner, saw the docking ring doors—closed.

She cursed (although she wasn't sure if she did it out loud or just in her head) and hoped to that ever-present unknown deity that her access code still worked.

The minute those doors slid open, the matching marching murderers would know she was here. Or rather, that someone was here.

They'd come for her. They'd make her scream.

But she'd be damned if she begged.

She hadn't begged ever, not when her dad beat her within an inch of her life, not when she got accused of stealing from that high-class school her mother had warehoused her in, not when her credit got cut off as she fled to the outer reaches of the Alliance.

She hadn't begged no matter what situation she was in, and she wouldn't now. It was a point of pride. It might be the last point of pride, hell, it might mark her last victory just before she died, but it would be a victory nonetheless, and it would be *hers*.

Takara slammed her hand against the identiscanner, then punched in a code, because otherwise she'd have to use her links, and she wasn't turning them back on, maybe ever, because she didn't want those crazy matching idiots to not only find her, but find her entire life, stored in the personal memory attached to her private access numbers.

The docking ring doors irised open, and actual air hit her. Real oxygen without the stupid smoky stuff, good enough to make her leap through the doors. Then she turned around and closed them.

She scanned the area, saw feet—not in boots—attached to motionless legs, attached to bleeding bodies, attached to people she knew, and she just shut it all off, because if she saw them as friends or co-workers or other human beings, she wouldn't be able to run past them, wouldn't be able to get to her ship, wouldn't get the hell out of here.

She kept her shirt against her face, just in case, but her eyes were clearing. The air here looked like air, but it smelled like a latrine. Death—fast death, recent death. She'd used it for entertainment, watched it, read about it, stepped inside it virtually, but she'd never experienced it. Not really, not like this.

Her ship sat at the far end of this ring, the cheap area, where the ceiling of the base bent downward and would have brushed the top of some bigger ship, something that actually had speed and firepower and *worth*.

Then she mentally corrected herself: her ship had worth. It would get her out of this death trap. She would escape before one of those tall blond booted men found her. She would—

—she flew forward, landed on her belly, her elbow scraping against the metal walkway, air leaving her body. Her shirt went somewhere, her chin banged on the floor, and then the sound—a whoop-whamp, followed by a sustained series of crashes.

Something was collapsing, or maybe one of the explosions was near her, or she had no damn idea, she just knew she had to get out, get out, get out—

She pushed herself to her feet, her knees sore too, her pants torn, her stomach burning, but she didn't look down because the feel of that burn matched the feel of her elbow, so she was probably scraped.

She didn't even grab her shirt; she just ran the last meter to her ship, which had moved even with its mooring clamps—good God, something was shaking this place, something bad, something big.

Her ship was so small, it didn't even have a boarding ramp. The door was pressed against the clamps, or it should have been, but there was a gap between the clamps and the ship and the walkway, and it was probably tearing something in the ship, but she didn't want to think about that so she didn't.

Instead, she slammed her palm against the door four times, the emergency enter code, which wasn't a code at all, but was something she thought (back when she was young and stupid and new to access codes) no one would figure out.

What she hadn't figured out was that no one wanted this cheap-ass ship, so no one tried to break into it. No one wanted to try, no one cared, except her, right now, as the door didn't open and didn't open and didn't open—

—and then it did.

Her brain was slowing down time. She'd heard about this phenomenon, something happened chemically in the human brain, slowed perception, made it easier (quicker?) to make decisions—and there her stupid brain was again, thinking about the wrong things as she tried to survive.

Hell, that had helped her survive as a kid, this checking-out thing in the middle of an emergency, but it wasn't going to help her now.

She scrambled inside her ship, felt it tilt, heard the hull groan. If she didn't do something about those clamps, she wouldn't have a ship.

She somehow remembered to slap the door's closing mechanism before she sprinted to the cockpit. Her bruised knees made her legs wobbly or maybe the ship was tilting even more. The groaning in the hull was certainly increasing.

The cockpit door was open, the place was a mess, as always. She used to sleep in here on long runs, and she always meant to clean up the blankets and pillows and clothes, but never did.

Now she stood in the middle of it, and turned on the navigation board. She instructed the ship to decouple, then turned her links on— not all of them, just the private link that hooked her to the ship—and heard more groaning.

"Goddammit!" she screamed at the ship, slamming her hands on the board. "Decouple, decouple—get rid of the goddamn clamps!"

Inform space traffic control to open the exit through the rings, the ship said in its prissiest voice.

Tears pricked her eyes. Crap. She'd be stuck here because of some goddamn rule that ship couldn't take off if there was no exit. She'd die if there was another explosion.

"There's no space traffic control here," she said. "Space traffic control is dead. We have to get out. Everyone's dead."

Her voice wobbled just like the ship had as she realized what she had said. *Everyone.* Everyone she had worked with, her friends, her co-workers, the people she drank with, laughed with, everyone—

We cannot leave if the exit isn't open, the ship said slowly and even more prissily, if that were possible.

"Then ram it," she said.

That will destroy us, the ship said, so damn calmly. Like it had no idea they were about to be destroyed anyway.

Takara ran her fingers over the board, looking for—she couldn't remember. This thing was supposed to have weapons, but she'd never used them, didn't know exactly what they were. She'd bought this stupid ship for a song six years ago, and the weapons were only mentioned in passing.

She couldn't find anything, so she gambled.

"Blow a damn hole through the closed exit," she said, not knowing if she could do that, if the ship even allowed that. Weren't there supposed to be failsafes so that no one could blow a hole through something on this base?

That will leave us with only one remaining laser shot, the ship said.

"I don't give a good goddamn!" she screamed. "Fire!"

And it did. Or something happened. Because the ship heated, and rocked and she heard a bang like nothing she'd ever heard before, and the sound of things falling on the ship.

"Get us out of here!" she shouted.

And the ship went upwards, fast, faster than ever.

So fast she could hear the engines screaming—

Which meant she didn't have to.

2

As the ship screamed its way out of the base, Takara tumbled backwards. The attitude controls were screwed or the gravity or something, but she didn't care.

"Visuals," she said, and floating on the screens that appeared in front of her was the hole that the ship had blown through the exit, and debris heading out with them, and bits of ship—and then she realized that there were bits of more than ship. Bits of the starbase and other ships and son of a bitch, more bodies and—

"Make sure you don't hit anything," she said, not knowing how to give the correct command.

I will evade large debris, the ship said as if this were an everyday occurrence. *However, I do need a destination.*

"Far away from here," Takara said.

How far?

"I don't know," she said. "Out of danger."

She was pressed against what she usually thought of as the side wall, with blankets and smelly sheets and musty pillows against her.

"And fix the attitude controls and the gravity, would you?" she snapped.

The interior of the ship seemed to right itself. She flopped on her stomach again, only this time, it didn't hurt.

She stood, her mouth wet and tasting of blood. She put a hand to her face, realized her nose was bleeding, and grabbed a sheet, stuffing it against her skin.

She dragged the sheet with her to the controls. The images had disappeared (had she ordered that? She didn't remember ordering that) and so she called them up again, saw more body parts, and globules of stuff (blood? Intestines?) and shut it all off—consciously this time.

God, she was lucky. She had administration codes. She had a sense that things were going bad. She had her ship ready. And, most important of all, she had been close enough to the docking ring to get out of there before anyone knew she even existed.

She sank into the chair and closed her eyes, wondering what in the bloody hell was going on.

She'd met those men, the creepy older ones, and asked her boss what they wanted with ships, and he'd said, *Better not to ask, hon.*

He always called her hon, and she finally realized it was because he couldn't remember her name. And now he was dead or would be dead or was dying or something awful like that. He'd been inside the administration area when the twenty clones had come in—or the forty clones—or the sixty clones, God, she had no idea how many.

It was her boss's boss who'd answered her, later, when she mentioned that the men looked alike.

Don't ask about it, Takara, he'd said quietly. *They're creatures of someone else. Designer criminal clones. They need a ship for nefarious doings.*

They're not in charge? she'd asked.

He'd shaken his head. *Someone made them for a job.*

Her eyes opened, saw the mess that her cockpit had become. A job. They'd had to find fast ships for a job.

But if the creepy older ones were made for a job, so were the younger versions.

She called up the screens, asked for images of the starbase. It was a small base, far away from anything, important only to malcontents and criminals, and those like her, whose ships wouldn't cross the great distance between human-centered planets without a rest-and-refueling stop.

The starbase was glowing—fires inside, except where the exterior had been breached. Those sections were dark and ruined. It looked like a volcano that had already exploded—twice. More than twice. Several times.

Ship, her ship said, and for a minute, she thought it was being recursive. "What?" she asked.

Approaching quickly. Starboard side.

She swiveled the view, saw a ship twice the size of hers, familiar too. The creepy older men had come back to the starbase in a ship just like that.

"Can you show me who is inside?" she asked.

I can show you who the ship is registered to and who disembarked from it earlier today, her ship sent. *I cannot show who is inside it now.*

Then, on an inset screen floating near the other screens, images of the two creepy older men and five younger leaving the ship. They went inside the base.

"Did anyone else who looked like them—"

The other clones disembarked from a ship that landed an hour later, her ship answered, anticipating her question for once. Did ships think?

Then she shook her head. She knew better than that. Ships like this one had computers that could deduce based on past performance, nothing more.

That second ship has been destroyed, the ship sent, *along with the docking ring.*

"What?" Takara asked. She moved the imagery again, saw another explosion. The docking ring about five minutes after she left.

She was trembling. Everyone gone. Except her. And the creepy men, and maybe the five young guys they had brought with them.

Bastards. Filthy stinking horrible asshole bastards.

"You said we have one shot left," she said.

Yes, but—

"Target that ship," she said. "Blow the hell out of it."

Our laser shot cannot penetrate their shields.

Her gaze scanned the area. Other ships whirling, twirling, looping through space, heading her way.

Their way.

She ran through the records stored in her links. She'd always made copies of things. She was anal that way, and scared enough to figure she might need blackmail material.

One thing she did handle as a so-called administrator: requests to dock for ships with unusual fuel sources. She kept them on the far side of the ring.

Right now, she scanned for them and their unusual size, saw one, realized it had a huge fuel cell, still intact.

"Can you shoot that ship?" she asked, sending the image across the links, "and push it into the manned ship?"

What she wanted to say was "the ship with the creepy guys," but she knew her ship wouldn't know what she meant.

Yes, her ship sent. *But it won't do anything to the ship except make them collide.*

"Oh, yes it will," Takara said. "Make sure the fuel cell hits the manned ship directly."

That will cause a chain reaction that will be so large it might impact us, her ship sent.

"Yeah, then get us out of here," Takara said.

We have a forty-nine percent chance of survival if we try that, her ship sent.

"Which is better than what we'll have if that damn ship catches up with us," Takara said.

Are you ordering me to take the shot? Her ship asked.

"Yes!"

Her ship shook slightly as the last laser shot emerged from the front. The manned ship didn't even seem to notice or care that she had fire-power. Of course, from their perspective, she had missed them.

The shot went wide, hit the other ship, and destroyed part of its hull, pushing it into the manned ship.

And nothing happened. They collided, and then bounced away, the manned ship's trajectory changed and little else.

Then the other ship's fuel cell glowed green, and Takara's ship sped up, again losing attitude control and sending her flying into the back wall.

An explosion—green and gold and white—flashed around her.

She looked up from the pile of blankets at the floating screens, saw only debris, and asked, "Did we do it?"

Our shot hit the ship. It exploded. Our laser shot ignited the fuel cell—

"I know," she snapped. "What about the manned ship?"

It is destroyed.

She let out a sigh of relief, then leaned back against the wall, gathering the pillows and blanket against her. The blood had dried on her face, and she hadn't even noticed until now. Her elbow ached, her knees stung, and her stomach hurt, and she felt—

Alive.

She felt alive and giddy and sad and terrified and...

Curious.

She scanned through the information on the creepy men. They didn't have names, at least that they had given to the administration. Just numbers. Numbers that didn't make sense.

She saw some imagery: the men talking to her boss, saying something about training missions for their weapons, experimental weapons, and something about soldiers—a promise of a big payout if the experiment worked.

And if it doesn't? her boss asked.

The creepy men smiled. *You'll know if it doesn't.*

Practice sessions. Soldiers. A failed experiment.

Had her boss realized that the destruction of everything he had known was a *practice session*? Had that become clear to him in his last moment of life?

And the men, heading off to report the failure to someone.

But they hadn't gotten there. She had stopped them.

But not the someone in charge.

She ran a hand over her face. She would send all of this to the Alliance. There wasn't much more she could do. She wasn't even sure what the Alliance could do.

This was the Frontier. It was lawless by any Alliance definition. Each place governed itself.

She had liked that when she arrived. She was untraceable, unknown, completely alone.

Then she'd made friends, realized that every place had a rhythm, every place had good and bad parts, and she had decided to stay. Become someone.

Until she got that feeling from the creepy men, and had planned to leave.

"Fix the attitude and gravity controls, would you?" she asked the ship, only this time, she didn't sound panicked or upset.

The ship righted itself. Apparently when it sped up, it didn't have enough power for all of its functions. She was going to need to get repairs.

Maybe in the Alliance. She had enough fuel to get there.

She'd been stockpiling. Food, fuel, everything but money.

She could get back to a place where there were laws she understood, where someone didn't blow up a starbase as an experiment with creepy matching soldiers.

She'd let the authorities know that someone—a very scary someone—was planning something. But what she didn't know. She didn't even know if it was directed against the Alliance.

She would guess it wasn't.

It would take more than twenty, forty, sixty, one hundred matching soldiers to defeat the Alliance. No one had gone to war against it in centuries. It was too big.

Something like this had to be Frontier politics. A war against something else, or an invasion or something.

And it had failed.

All of the soldiers had died.

Along with everyone else.

Except her, of course.

She hadn't died.

She had lived to tell about it.

And she would tell whoever would listen.

Once she was safe inside the Alliance.

A place too big to be attacked. Too big to be defeated.

Too big to ever allow her to go through anything like this again.

7.5 YEARS BEFORE
ANNIVERSARY DAY

3

DETECTIVE NOELLE DERICCI OPENED THE TOP OF THE WASTE CRATE. THE stench of rotting produce nearly hid the faint smell of urine and feces. A woman's body curled on top of the compost pile as if she had fallen asleep.

She hadn't, though. Her eyes were open.

DeRicci couldn't see any obvious cause of death. The woman's skin might have been copper colored when she was alive, but death had turned it sallow. Her hair was pulled back into a tight bun, undisturbed by whatever killed her. She wore a gray-and-tan pantsuit that seemed more practical than flattering.

DeRicci put the lid down and resisted the urge to remove her thin gloves. They itched. They always itched. Because she used department gloves rather than buying her own, and they never fit properly.

She rubbed her fingers together, as if something from the crate could have gotten through the gloves, and turned around. Nearly one hundred identical containers lined up behind it. More arrived hourly from all over Armstrong, the largest city on Earth's moon.

The entire interior of the warehouse smelled faintly of organic material gone bad. She was only in one section of the warehouse. There were dozens of others, and at the end of each was a conveyer belt that took the waste crate, mulched it, and then sent the material for use in the Growing Pits outside Armstrong's dome.

The crates were cleaned in a completely different section of the warehouse and then sent back into the city for reuse.

Not every business recycled its organic waste for the Growing Pits, but almost all of the restaurants and half of the grocery stores did. DeRicci's apartment building sent organic food waste into bins that came here as well.

The owner of the warehouse, Najib Ansel, stood next to the nearest row of crates. He wore a blue smock over matching blue trousers, and blue booties on his feet. Blue gloves stuck out of his pocket, and a blue mask hung around his neck.

"How did you find her?" DeRicci asked.

Ansel nodded at the ray of blue light that hovered above the crate, then toed the floor.

"The weight was off," he said. "The crate was too heavy."

DeRicci looked down.

"I take it you have sensors in the floor?" she asked.

"Along the orange line."

She didn't see an orange line. She moved slightly, then saw it. It really wasn't a line, more like a series of orange rectangles, each long enough to hold a crate and too short to measure anything beside them.

"So you lifted the lid..." DeRicci started.

"No, sir," Ansel said, using the traditional honorific for someone with more authority.

DeRicci wasn't sure why she had more authority than he did. She had looked him up on her way here. He owned a multimillion dollar industry, which made its fortune charging for waste removal from the city itself, and then reselling that waste at a low price to the Growing Pits.

She had known this business existed, but she hadn't paid a lot of attention to it until an hour ago. She had felt a shock of recognition when she saw the name of the business in the download that sent her here: Ansel Management was scrawled on the side of every waste container in every recycling room in the city.

Najib Ansel had a near monopoly in Armstrong, and had warehouses in six other domed communities. According to her admittedly cursory research, he had filed for permits to work in two new communities just this week.

So the fact that he was in standard worker gear, just like his employees, amazed her. She would have thought a mogul like Ansel would be in a gigantic office somewhere making deals, rather than standing on the floor of the main warehouse just outside Armstrong's dome.

Even though he used the honorific, he didn't say anything more. Clearly, Ansel was going to make her work for information.

"Okay," DeRicci said. "The crate was too heavy. Then what?"

"Then we activated the sensors, to see what was inside the crate." He looked up at the blue light again. Obviously that was the sensor.

"Show me how that works," she said.

He rubbed his fingers together—probably activating some kind of chip. The light came down and broadened, enveloping the crate. Information flowed above it, mostly in chemical compounds and other numbers. She was amazed she recognized that the symbols were compounds. She wondered where she had picked that up.

"No visuals?" she asked.

"Not right away." Ansel reached up to the holographic display. The numbers kept scrolling. "You see, there's really nothing out of the ordinary here. Even her clothes must be made of some kind of organic material. So my people couldn't figure out what was causing the extra weight."

"You didn't find this, then?" she asked.

"No, sir," he said.

"I'd like to talk with the person who did," she said.

"She's over there." He nodded toward a small room off to the side of the crates.

DeRicci suppressed a sigh. Of course he'd cleared the employee off the floor. Anything to make a cop's job harder.

"All right," DeRicci said, not trying to hide her annoyance. "How did your 'people' discover the extra weight?"

"When the numbers didn't show anything non-organic causing the extra weight," he said, "they had the system scan for a large piece. Sometimes, when crates come in from the dome, someone dumps something directly into the crate without paying attention to weight and size restrictions."

Those were hard to ignore. DeRicci vividly remembered the first time she had tried to dump something of the wrong size into a recycling crate. She had dumped a rotted roast she had never managed to cook (back in the days when she actually believed she could cook). She'd put it into the crate behind her then-apartment building. The damn crate beeped at her, and when she didn't remove the roast fast enough for the stupid thing, it actually started to yell at her, telling her that she wasn't following the rules.

There was a way to turn off the alarms, but she and her building superintendent hadn't known it. Clearly, someone else did.

"So," DeRicci said, "the system scanned, and…?"

"Registered something larger," he said somewhat primly. "That's when my people switched the information feed to visual, and got the surprise of their lives."

She would wager. She wondered if they thought the woman was sleeping. She wasn't going to ask him that question; she'd save it for the person who actually found the body.

"When did they call you?" DeRicci asked.

"After they visually confirmed the body," Ansel said.

"Meaning what?" she asked. "They saw it on the feed or they actually lifted the lid?"

"On the feed," he said.

"Where was this?" she asked.

He pointed to a small booth that hovered over the floor. The booth clearly operated on the same tech that the aircars in Armstrong used. The booth was smaller than the average car, however, and was clear on all four sides. Only the bottom appeared to have some kind of structure, probably to hide all the mechanics.

"Is someone in the booth?" she asked.

"We always have someone monitoring the floor," he said, "but I just put someone new up in the booth, so that the team that discovered the body can talk to you."

DeRicci supposed he had put the entire team in one room, together, so that they could align their stories. But she didn't say anything like that. No sense antagonizing Ansel. He seemed to be trying to help her.

"We're going to need to shut down this part of your line," DeRicci said. "Everything in this part of the warehouse will need to be examined."

To her surprise, he didn't protest. Of course, if he had protested, she would have had him shut down the entire warehouse.

Maybe he *had* dealt with the police before.

"So," she said, "who actually opened the lid on this container?"

"I did," he said quietly.

She hadn't expected that. "Tell me about it."

"The staff contacted me after they saw the body."

"On your links?" she asked. She would wager that the entire communication system inside Ansel Management was on its own dedicated link.

"Yes," he said. "The staff contacted me on my company link."

"I'd like to have copies of that contact," she said.

"Sure." He wasn't acting like someone who had anything to hide. In fact, he was acting like someone who had been through this before.

"What did your staff tell you?" she asked.

His lips turned upward. Someone might have called that expression a smile, but it wasn't. It was rueful.

"They told me that there was a woman in crate A1865."

DeRicci made a mental note about the number. Before this investigation was over, she'd learn everything about this operation, from the crate numbering system to the way that the conveyer operated to the actual mulching process.

"That's what they said?" she asked. "A woman in the crate?"

"Crate A1865," he repeated, as if he wanted that detail to be exactly right.

"What did you think when you heard that?" DeRicci asked.

25

He shook his head, then sighed. "I—we've had this happen before, Detective. Not for more than a year, but we've found bodies. Usually homeless people in the crates near the port, people who came into Armstrong and can't get out. Sometimes we get an alien or two sleeping in the crates. The Oranjanie view rotting produce as a luxury, and they look human from some angles."

Member species of the Earth Alliance had to stop at the Port of Armstrong first before traveling to Earth. Some travelers never made it into Earth's protected zone, and got stuck on the Moon itself.

Right now, however, she had no reason to suspect alien involvement in this crime. She preferred working human-on-human crime. It made the investigation so much easier.

"You've found human bodies in your crates before," she clarified.

"Yeah," he said.

"And the police have investigated?"

"All of the bodies, alien and human," he said. "Different precincts, usually, and different time periods. My grandmother started this business over one hundred years ago. She found bodies even way back then."

DeRicci guessed it would make sense to hide a body in one of the crates. Or someone would think it made sense.

"Do you think that bodies have gotten through the mulching process?" It took her a lot of strength not to look at the conveyer belt as she asked that question.

"I don't think a lot got through," Ansel said. "I know some did. Back in my grandmother's day. She's the one who set up the safeguards. We might have had a few glitches after the safeguards were in place, before we knew how well they worked, but I can guarantee nothing has gone through since I started managing this company twenty-five years ago."

DeRicci tried not to shudder as she thought about human flesh serving as compost at the Growing Pits. She hated Moon-grown food, and she had a hunch she was going to hate it more after this case.

But she had to keep asking questions.

"You said you can guarantee it," she repeated.

He nodded.

"What if someone cut up the body?" she asked.

He grimaced. "The pieces would have to be small to get past our weight and size restrictions. Forgive me for being graphic, but no full arms or legs or torsos or heads. Maybe fingers and toes. We have nano-probes on these things, looking for human DNA. But the probes are coating the lining of the crates. If someone buried a finger in the middle of some rotting lettuce, we might miss it."

She forced herself to swallow back some bile and wished she had some savings. She wanted to go home and purge her refrigerator of anything grown on the Moon and buy expensive, Earth-grown produce.

But she couldn't afford that, not on a detective's salary.

"Fair enough," she said, surprised she could sound so calm when she was so thoroughly grossed out. "No full bodies have gone through in at least twenty-five years. But you've seen quite a few. How many?"

"I don't know," he said. "I'd have to check the records."

That surprised her. It meant that enough had gone through to make it hard to keep track. "Any place where they show up the most often?"

"The port," he said. "There's a lot of homeless in that neighborhood."

Technically, they weren't homeless. They were people who lived on the city's charity. A lot of small, cubicle-sized rooms existed on the port blocks, and anyone who couldn't afford their own home or ended up stranded and unemployable in the city could stay in one of the cubicles for six months, no questions asked.

After six months, they needed to move to long-term city services, which were housed elsewhere. DeRicci wanted to ask if anyone had turned up dead in those neighborhoods, but she'd do that after she looked at his records.

"I'm confused," she said. "Do these people crawl into the crates and die?"

The crate didn't look like it was sealed so tightly that the person couldn't get oxygen.

"Some of them," he said. "They're usually high or drunk."

"And the rest?" she asked.

"Obviously someone has put them there," he said.

"A different someone each time, I assume," she said.

He shrugged. "I let the police investigate. I don't ask questions."

"You don't ask questions about dead people in your crates?"

His face flushed. She had finally gotten to him.

"Believe it or not, Detective," Ansel snapped, "I don't like to think about it. I'm very proud of this business. We provide a service that enables the cities on the Moon to not only have food, but to have *great* food. Sometimes our system gets fouled up by crazy people, and I *hate* that. We've gone to great lengths to prevent it. That's why you're here. Because our systems *work*."

"I didn't mean to offend you," she lied. "This is all new to me, so I'm going to ask some very ignorant questions at times."

He looked annoyed, but he nodded.

"What part of town did this crate come from?" she asked.

"The port," he said tiredly.

She should have expected that after he had mentioned the port a few times.

"Was the body in the crate when it was picked up at the port?" she asked.

"The weight was the same from port to here," he said. "Weight gets recorded at pick-up but flagged near the conveyer. The entire system is automated until the crates get to the warehouse. Besides, we don't have the ability to investigate anything inside Armstrong. There are a lot of regulations on things that are considered garbage inside the dome. If we violate those, we'll get black marks against our license, and if we get too many black marks in a year, we could lose that license."

More stuff she didn't know. City stuff, regulatory stuff. The kinds of things she always ignored.

And things she would probably have to investigate now.

"Do you know her?" DeRicci asked, hoping to catch him off balance.

"Her?" Ansel looked confused for a moment. Then he looked at the crate, and his flush grew deeper. "You mean, *her*?"

"Yes." Just from his reaction, DeRicci knew his response. He didn't know the woman. And the idea that she was inside one of his crates upset him more than he wanted to say.

Which was probably why he was the person talking to DeRicci now.

"No," Ansel said. "I don't know her, and I don't recognize her. We didn't run any recognition programs on her either. We figured you all would do that."

"No one touched her? No one checked her for identification chips?"

"I'm the one who opened the crate," he said. "I saw her, I saw that her eyes were open, and then I closed the lid. I leave the identifying to you all."

"Do you know all your employees, Mr. Ansel?"

"By name," he said.

"By look," she said.

He shook his head. "I have nearly three hundred employees in Armstrong alone."

"But you just said you know their names. You know all three hundred employees by name?"

He smiled absently, which seemed like a rote response. He'd responded to this kind of thing before.

"I have an eidetic memory," he said. "If I've seen a name, then I remember it."

"An eidetic memory for names, but not faces? I've never heard of that," DeRicci said.

"I haven't met all of my employees," he said. "But I go over the pay amounts every week before they get sent to the employees' accounts. I see the names. I rarely see the faces."

"So you wouldn't know if she worked here," DeRicci said.

"Here?" he asked. "Here I would know. I come here every day. If she worked in one of the other warehouses or in transport or in sales, I wouldn't know that."

"Did this crate go somewhere else before coming to this warehouse?" DeRicci asked.

29

"No," Ansel said. "Each crate is assigned a number. That number puts it in a location, and then when the crate fills, it gets swapped out with another. The crate comes to the same warehouse each time, without deviation. And since that system is automated, as I mentioned, I know that it doesn't go awry."

"Can someone stop the crate in transit and add a body?"

"No," he said. "I can show you if you want."

She shook her head. That would be a good job for her partner, Rayvon Lake. Rayvon still hadn't arrived, the bastard. DeRicci would have to report him pretty soon. He had gotten very lax about crime scenes, leaving them to her. He left most everything to her, and she hated it.

He was a lazy detective—twenty years in the position—and he saw her as an upstart who needed to be put in her place.

She wouldn't have minded his attitude if he did his job. Well, that wasn't exactly true. She would have minded. She hated people who disliked her. But she wouldn't be considering filing a report on him if he actually did the work he was supposed to do.

She would get Lake to handle the transport information by telling him she wasn't smart enough to understand it. It would mean that she'd have to suffer through an explanation later in the case, but maybe by then, she'd either have this thing solved or she'd have a new partner.

A woman could hope, after all.

"One of the other detectives will look into the transport process," DeRicci said. "I'm just trying to cover the basics here, so we start looking in the right place. Can outsiders come into this warehouse?"

"And get into one of our crates?" Ansel asked. "No. Look."

He touched the edge of the lid, and she heard a loud snap.

"It's sealed shut now," he said.

She didn't like the sound of that snap.

"If I were in there," she asked, "could I breathe through that seal?"

"Yes," Ansel said. "For about two days, if need be. But it doesn't seal shut like that until it leaves the transport and crosses the threshold here at the warehouse. So there's no way anyone could crawl in here at the warehouse."

"All right," DeRicci said. "So, let me be sure I understand you. The only place that someone could either place a body into a crate or crawl into it on their own is on site."

"Yes," Ansel said. "We try to encourage composting, so we allow by-passers to stuff something into a crate. We search for non-organic material at the site, and flag the crates with non-organic material so they can be cleaned."

"Clothing is organic?" DeRicci asked.

"Much of it, yes," Ansel said. "Synthetics aren't good hosts for nanoproducts, so most people wear clothing made from recycled organic material."

DeRicci's skin literally crawled. She hadn't known that. She wasn't an organic kind of woman. She preferred fake stuff, much to the dismay of her friends, what few of them she had.

"All right," she said. "I'm going to talk with your people in a minute. I'll want to know what they know. And I'll need to see your records on previous incidents."

She didn't check to see if he had sent her anything on her links. She didn't want downloads to confuse her sense of the crime scene. She liked to make her own opinions, and she did that by being thorough.

Detectives like Rayvon Lake gathered as much information as possible, multitasking as they walked through a crime scene. DeRicci believed they missed most of the important details while doing that, and that led to a lot of side roads and wasted time.

And, if she could prove it, a lot of false convictions. She had caught Lake twice trying to close a case by accusing an innocent person who was convenient, rather than doing the hard leg work required of a good investigator.

Ansel fluttered near her for a moment. DeRicci inclined her head toward the room where the staff had gathered, knowing she was inviting him to contaminate her witnesses even more, but she had a hunch none of them were going to be useful to the investigation anyway.

"Before you go," she said, just in case he didn't take the hint, "could you unseal this crate for me?"

"Oh, yes, sorry," he said, and ran his fingers along the side again. It snapped one more time, then popped up slightly.

DeRicci thanked him and pulled back the lid. The crate was tall—up to DeRicci's ribs—and filled with unidentifiable bits of rotting food. The woman lay on top of them, hands cradled under her cheek, feet tucked together.

DeRicci couldn't imagine anyone just curling up here, even at the bidding of someone else. But people did strange things for strange reasons, and she wasn't going to rule it out.

She put the lid down and then looked at the warehouse again. She would need the numbers, but she suspected thousands of crates went through Ansel's facilities around the Moon daily.

Done properly, it would be a perfect way to dispose of bodies and all kinds of other things that no one wanted to see. She wondered how many others knew about this facility and how it worked.

She suspected she would have to find out.

4

GETTING THE CRIME SCENE UNIT TO A WAREHOUSE OUTSIDE OF THE DOME took more work than Ethan Brodeur liked to do. Fortunately, he was a deputy coroner, which meant he couldn't control the crime scene unit. Someone with more seniority had to handle requisitioning the right vehicle from the police department yards outside the dome, and making certain the team had the right equipment.

Brodeur came to the warehouse via train. The ride was only five minutes long, but it made him nervous.

He had been born inside the dome, and he hated leaving it for any reason at all, especially for a reason involving work. So much of his work had to do with temperature and conditions, and if the body had been in an airless environment at all, it had an impact on every aspect of his job.

He was relieved when he arrived at the warehouse and learned that the body had never gone outside of an Earth Normal environment. However, he was annoyed to see that he would be working with Noelle DeRicci.

She was notoriously difficult and demanding, and often asked coroners to redo something or double-check their findings. She'd caught him in several mistakes, which he found embarrassing.

Then she'd had had the gall to tell him that he should probably double-check all of his work, considering its shoddy quality.

She stood next to a crate, the only one of thousands that was open. She was rumpled—she was always rumpled—and her curly black hair looked messier than usual.

When she saw him approach, she glared at him.

"Oh, lucky me," she said.

Brodeur bit back a response. He'd been recording everything since he got off the train inside the warehouse's private platform, and he didn't want to show any animosity toward DeRicci on anything that might go to court.

"Just show me the body and I'll get to work," he said.

DeRicci raised her eyebrows at the word "work," and she didn't have to add anything to convey her meaning. She didn't think Brodeur worked at all.

"My biggest priority at the moment is an identification," she said.

And his biggest priority was to do this investigation right. But he didn't say that. Instead he looked at the dozens of crates spread out before him.

"Which one am I dealing with?" he asked, pleased that he could sound so calm in the face of her rudeness.

DeRicci placed a hand on the crate behind her. He was pleased to see that she wore gloves. He had worked with her partner, Rayvon Lake, before, and Lake had to be reminded to follow any kind of procedure.

But Brodeur didn't see Lake anywhere.

"Have you had cases involving the waste crates before?" DeRicci asked Brodeur.

"No," he said, not adding that he tried to pass anything outside the dome onto anyone else, "but I've heard about cases involving them. I guess it's not that uncommon."

"Hmm," DeRicci said looking toward a room at the far end of the large warehouse. "And here I thought they were uncommon."

Brodeur was going to argue his point when he realized that DeRicci wasn't talking to him now. She was arguing with someone she had already spoken to.

"Can you get me information on that?" DeRicci asked Brodeur.

He hated it when detectives wanted him to do their work for them. "It's in the records."

DeRicci made a low, growly sound, like he had irritated her beyond measure.

So he decided to tweak her a bit more. "Just search for warehouses and recycling and crates—"

"I know," she said. "I was hoping your office already had statistics."

"I'm sure we do, Detective," he said, moving past her, "but you want me to figure out what killed this poor creature, right? Not dig into old cases."

"I think the old cases might be relevant," she said.

Brodeur shrugged. He didn't care what was or wasn't relevant to her investigation. His priority was dealing with this body.

"Excuse me," he said, and slipped on his favorite pair of gloves. Then he raised the lid on the crate.

The woman inside was maybe thirty. She had been pretty too, before her eyes had filmed over and her cheeks had sunk in.

She had clearly died in an Earth Normal environment, and she hadn't left that environment, as advertised. He would have to do some research to figure out if the presence of rotting food had an impact on the body's decomposition, but that was something to worry about later.

Then Brodeur glanced up. "I'll have information for you in a while," he said to DeRicci, trying to dismiss her.

"Just give me a name," she said. "We haven't traced anything."

He didn't want to move the body yet. He didn't even want to touch it, because he was afraid of disturbing some important evidence.

The corpse's hands were tucked under her head, so he couldn't just run the identification chips everyone had buried in their palms.

So he used the coroner's office facial recognition program. It had a record of every single human who lived in Armstrong, and was constantly updated with information from the arrivals and departures sections of the city every single day.

"Initial results show that her name is Sonja Mycenae. She was born here, and moved off-Moon with her family ten years ago. She returned one month ago to work as a nanny for…."

He paused, stunned at the name that turned up.

"For?" DeRicci pushed.

Brodeur could feel the color draining from his face.

"Luc Deshin," he said quietly. "She works for Luc Deshin."

5

Luc Deshin.

DeRicci hadn't expected that name.

Her gaze met Ethan Brodeur's. Brodeur looked scared. He immediately turned his attention to the poor dead woman in the compost.

DeRicci tugged on her gloves, thinking about what Brodeur had just told her.

With Deshin's involvement, everything changed.

Luc Deshin ran a corporation called Deshin Enterprises that the police department flagged and monitored continually. Everyone in Armstrong knew that Deshin controlled a huge crime syndicate that trafficked in all sorts of illegal and banned substances. The bulk of Deshin's business had moved off-Moon, but he had gotten his start here as an average street thug, rising, as those kids often do, through murder and targeted assassination into a position of power, using the deaths of others to advance his own career.

Then DeRicci realized what was bothering her. It wasn't that Deshin might have killed the woman. DeRicci firmly believed that was possible.

It was something else entirely. "Luc Deshin needed a nanny?"

"He married a few years ago," Brodeur said, as he ran some kind of scanner slightly above the body. He watched what he was doing. He didn't look at DeRicci. "I guess he and the wife had kids."

KRISTINE KATHRYN RUSCH

"And didn't like the nanny." DeRicci whistled. "Talk about a high stress job."

She glanced at that room filled with the employees who had found the body. There was a lot of work to be done here, but none of it was as important as catching Deshin by surprise with this investigation.

If he killed this Sonja Mycenae, then he would be expecting the police's appearance. But he might not expect the police so soon.

Or maybe he had always used the waste crates to dump his bodies. No one had ever been able to pin a murder on him.

Perhaps this was why.

She needed to leave. But before she did, she sent a message to Lake. Only she sent it using the standard police links, not the encoded link any other officer would use with her partner. She wanted it on record that Lake hadn't shown up yet.

Rayvon, you need to get here ASAP. There are employees to interview. I'm following a lead, but someone has to supervise the crime scene unit. Someone sent Deputy Coroner Brodeur and he doesn't have supervisory authority.

She didn't wait for Lake's response. Before he said anything, she sent another message to her immediate supervisor, Chief of Detectives Andrea Gumiela, this time through an encoded private link.

This case has ties to Deshin Enterprises, DeRicci sent. *I'm going there now, but we need a good team on this. It's not some random death. This case needs to be done perfectly. Between Brodeur and Lake, we're off to a bad start.*

She didn't wait for Gumiela to respond either. In fact, after sending that message, DeRicci shut off all but her emergency links.

She didn't want Gumiela to tell her to stay on site, and she didn't want to hear Lake's invective when he realized she had essentially chastised him in front of the entire department.

"Make sure no one leaves," DeRicci said to Brodeur.

He looked up, panicked. "I don't have the authority."

"Pretend," she snapped, and walked away from him.

She needed to get to Luc Deshin, and she needed to get to him now.

38

6

Luc Deshin grabbed his long-waisted overcoat and headed down the stairs. So a police detective wanted to meet with him. He wished he found such things unusual. But they weren't.

The police liked to harass him. Less now than in the past. They'd had a frustrating time pinning anything on him.

He always found it ironic that the crimes they accused him of were crimes he'd never think of committing, and the crimes he had committed—long ago and far away—were crimes they had never heard of. Now, all of his activities were legal. Just-inside-the-law legal, but legal nonetheless.

Or so his cadre of lawyers kept telling the local courts, and the local judges—at least the ones he would find himself in front of—always believed his lawyers.

So, a meeting like this, coming in the middle of the day, was an annoyance, and nothing more.

He used his trip down the stairs to stay in shape. His office was a penthouse on the top floor of the building he'd built to house Deshin Enterprises years ago. He used to love that office, but he liked it less since he and his wife Gerda brought a baby into their lives.

He smiled at the thought of Paavo. They had adopted him—sort of. They had drawn up some legal papers and wills that the lawyers assured him would stand any challenge should he and Gerda die suddenly.

But Deshin and Gerda had decided against an actual adoption given Deshin's business practices and his reputation in Armstrong. They were worried that some judge would deem them unfit, based on Deshin's reputation.

Plus, Paavo was the child of two Disappeareds, making the adoption situation even more difficult. The Earth Alliance's insistence that local laws prevailed when crimes were committed meant that humans were often subjected to alien laws, laws that made no sense at all. Many humans didn't like being forced to lose a limb as punishment for chopping down an exotic tree, or giving up a child because they'd broken food laws on a different planet.

Those humans who could afford to get new names and new identities did so rather than accept their punishment under Earth Alliance law. Those people Disappeared.

Paavo's parents had Disappeared within weeks of his birth, leaving him to face whatever legal threat that the aliens his parents had angered could dream up.

Paavo, alone, at four months.

Fortunately, Deshin and Gerda had sources inside Armstrong's family services, which they had cultivated for just this sort of reason. Both Deshin and Gerda had had difficult childhoods—to say the least. They knew what it was like to be unwanted.

Their initial plan had been to bring several unwanted children into their homes, but after they met Paavo, a brilliant baby with his own special needs, they decided to put that plan on hold. If they could only save Paavo, that would be enough.

But they were just a month into life with the baby, and they knew that any more children would take a focus that, at the moment at least, Paavo's needs wouldn't allow.

Deshin reached the bottom of the stairwell, ran a hand through his hair, and then walked through the double doors. His staff kept the detective in the lobby.

She was immediately obvious, even though she wasn't in uniform. A slightly disheveled woman with curly black hair and a sharp, intelligent face, she wasn't looking around like she was supposed to be.

Most new visitors to Deshin Enterprises either pretended to be unimpressed with the real marble floors, the imported wood paneling, and the artwork that constantly shifted on the walls and ceiling. Or the visitors gaped openly at all of it.

This detective did neither. Instead, she scanned the people in the lobby—all staff, all there to guard him and keep an eye on her.

She would be difficult. Deshin could tell that just from her body language. He wasn't used to dealing with someone from the Armstrong Police Department who was intelligent *and* difficult to impress.

He walked toward her, and as he reached her, he extended his hand.

"Detective," he said warmly. "I'm Luc Deshin."

She wiped her hands on her stained shirt, and just as he thought she was going to take his hand in greeting, she shoved her hands into the pockets of her ill-fitting black pants.

"I know who you are," she said.

She deliberately failed to introduce herself, probably as a power play. He could play back, ask to see the badge chip embedded in the palm of her hand, but he didn't feel like it.

She had already wasted enough of his time.

So he took her name, Noelle DeRicci, from the building's security records, and declined to look at her service record. He had it if he needed it.

"What can I do for you then, Detective?" He was going to charm her, even if that took a bit of strength to ignore the games.

"I'd like to speak somewhere private," she said.

He smiled. "No one is near us, and we have no recording devices in this part of the lobby. If you like, we can go outside. There's a lovely coffee shop across the street."

Her eyes narrowed. He watched her think: did she ask to go to his office and get denied, or did she just play along?

"The privacy is for you," she said, "but okay...."

She sounded dubious, a nice little trick. A less secure man would then invite her into the office.

Deshin waited. He learned that middle managers—and that was what detectives truly were—always felt the press of time. He never had enough time for anything and yet, as the head of his own corporation, he also had all the time in the universe.

"I'm here about Sonja Mycenae," she said.

Sonja. The nanny he had fired just that morning. Well, fired wasn't an accurate term. He had deliberately avoided firing her. He had eliminated her position.

Deshin and Gerda had decided that Sonja wasn't affectionate enough toward their son. In fact, she had seemed a bit cold toward him. And once Deshin and Gerda started that conversation about Sonja's attitudes, they realized they didn't like having someone visit their home every day, and they didn't like giving up any time with Paavo.

Both Gerda and Deshin had worried, given their backgrounds, that they wouldn't know how to nurture a baby, but Sonja had taught them that training mattered a lot less than actual love.

"I understand she works for you," the detective said.

"She work*ed* for me," Deshin said.

Something changed in the detective's face. Something small. He felt uneasy for the first time.

"Tell me what this is about, Detective," he said.

"It's about Sonja Mycenae," she repeated.

"Yes, you said that. What exactly has she done?" he asked.

"Why don't you tell me why she no longer works for you," the detective said.

"My wife and I decided that we didn't need a nanny for our son. I called Sonja to the office this morning, and let her know that, effective immediately, her employment was terminated through no fault of her own."

"Do you have footage of that conversation?" the detective asked.

"I do, and it's protected. You'll need permission from both of us or a warrant before I can give it to you."

The detective raised her eyebrows. "I'm sure you can forgo the formalities, Mr. Deshin."

"I'm sure that many people do, Detective," he said, "however, it's my understanding that an employee's records are confidential. You may get a warrant if you like. Otherwise, I'm going to protect Sonja's privacy."

"Why would you do that, Mr. Deshin?"

"Believe it or not, I follow the rules." He managed to say that without sarcasm.

The detective grunted as if she didn't believe him. "What made you decide to terminate her position today?"

"I told you," Deshin said, keeping his voice bland even though he was getting annoyed. "My wife and I decided we didn't need a nanny to help us raise our son."

"You might want to share that footage with me without wasting time on a warrant, Mr. Deshin," the detective said.

"Why would I do that, Detective? I'm not even sure why you're asking about Sonja. What has she done?"

"She has died, Mr. Deshin."

The words hung between them. He frowned. The detective had finally caught him off guard.

For the first time, Deshin did not know how to respond. He probably needed one of his lawyers here. Any time his name came up in an investigation, he was automatically the first suspect.

But in this case, he had nothing to do with Sonja's death. So he would act accordingly, and let the lawyers handle the mess.

"What happened?" he asked softly.

He had known Sonja since she was a child. She was the daughter of a friend. That was one of the many reasons he had hired her, because he had known her.

Even then, she hadn't turned out as expected. He remembered an affectionate, happy girl. The nanny who had come to his house didn't seem to know how to smile at all. There had been no affection in her.

And when he last saw her, she'd been crying and pleading with him to let her keep her job. He actually had to have security drag her out of his office.

43

"We don't know what happened," the detective said.

That sentence could mean a lot. It could mean that they didn't know what happened at all or that they didn't know if her death was by natural causes or by murder. It could also mean that they didn't know exactly what or who caused the death, but that they suspected murder.

Since Deshin was facing a detective and not a beat officer, he knew the police suspected murder.

"Where did it happen?" Deshin asked.

"We don't know that either," the detective said.

Deshin snapped, "Then how do you know she's dead?"

Again, that slight change in the detective's face. Apparently he had finally hit on the correct question.

"Because workers found her in a waste crate in a warehouse outside the dome."

"Outside the dome…?" That didn't make sense to him. Sonja hadn't even owned an environmental suit. She had hated them with a passion. "She died outside the dome?"

"I didn't say that, Mr. Deshin," the detective said.

He let out a breath. "Look, Detective, I'm cooperating here, but you need to work with me. I saw Sonja this morning, eliminated her position, and watched her leave my office. Then I went to work. I haven't gone out of the building all day."

"But your people have," the detective said.

Deshin felt a thin thread of fury, and he suppressed it. Everyone assumed that his people murdered other people according to some whim. That simply was not true.

"Detective," he said calmly. "If I wanted Sonja dead, why would I terminate her employment this morning?"

"I have only your word for that," the detective said. "Unless you give me the footage."

"And I have only your word that she's dead," he said.

The detective pressed her hands together, then separated them. A hologram appeared between them—a young woman, looking as if she had fallen asleep in a meadow. Until he looked closely, and saw that the "meadow" was bits of food, and the young woman's eyes were open and filmy.

It was Sonja.

"My God," he said.

"If you give me the footage," the detective said, "and it confirms what you say, then you'll be in the clear. If you wait, then we're going to assume it was doctored."

Deshin glared at her. The detective was good—and she was right. The longer he waited, the less credibility he would have.

"I'm going to consult with my attorneys," he said. "If they believe that this information has use to you and it doesn't cause me any legal liabilities, then you will receive it from them within the hour."

The detective crossed her arms. "I suggest that you send it to me now. I will promise you that I will not look at anything until you or your attorneys say that I can."

It was an odd compromise, but one that *would* protect him. If she believed he would doctor the footage, then having the footage in her possession wouldn't harm him.

But he didn't know the laws on something this arcane.

"How's this, Detective," Deshin said. "My staff will give you a chip with the information on it. You may not put the chip into any device or watch it until I've consulted with my attorneys. You will wait here while I do so."

"Seems fine to me," the detective said. "I've got all the time in the world."

7

SHE DIDN'T HAVE ALL THE TIME IN THE WORLD, OF COURSE. DERICCI WAS probably getting all kinds of messages on her links from Lake and Gumiela and Brodeur and everyone else, telling her she was stupid or needed or something.

She didn't care. She certainly wasn't going to turn her links back on. She was close to something.

She had actually surprised the Great Luc Deshin, Criminal Mastermind.

He pivoted, and moved three steps away from her. He was clearly contacting someone on his links, but using private encoded links.

He was a much more formidable man than she had expected. She had never stood up close to him before. He was taller, broader, and more animated. His eyes were warm, and he had a charm that she hadn't expected.

It made sense, of course. The man had run a large group of people, and convinced them to continually break the law.

And he never got caught, which meant that he had charmed his way out in one fashion or another.

Hell, he'd even charmed her, just a minute ago. This claim he'd made about following the rules—she would have believed it, if she hadn't known his history.

The building itself added to his charm. The lobby was impressive, designed to distract—art rotating on the walls, showing the history of ancient Earth art on one wall, Frontier art on another. The high ceilings made the place feel cavernous, and the small furniture groupings allowed anyone who was feeling overwhelmed to find a cozy place to sit down.

DeRicci was determined not to let the lobby distract her. She watched the employees work or walk through, all with that vaguely I'm-so-happy-to-be-here expression many corporations required of their staff.

A woman approached DeRicci. The woman was enhancement-thin, with hints of the fat she didn't want lurking in her arms. She was dressed in a black suit that made her seem even thinner.

The woman extended a hand covered with gold rings. "If you'll come this way, Detective DeRicci…"

DeRicci shook her head. "Mr. Deshin promised me a chip. I'm staying here until I get it."

The woman opened her other hand. In it was a chip case the size of a thumbnail. The case was clear, and inside, DeRicci saw another case—blue, with a filament thinner than an eyelash.

"Here is your chip, Detective," the woman said. "I've been instructed to escort you—"

"I don't care," DeRicci said. "I'll take the chip, and I'll wait right here. You have my word that I won't open either case, and I won't watch anything until I get the okay."

The woman's eyes glazed slightly. Clearly, she was seeing if that was all right.

Then she focused on DeRicci, and bowed her head slightly.

"As you wish, Detective."

She handed DeRicci the case. It was heavier than it looked. It probably had a lot of protections built in, so that she couldn't activate anything through the case.

Not that she had the technical ability to do any of that, even if she wanted to.

She sighed. She had a fluttery feeling that she had just been outmaneuvered.

Then she made herself watch Deshin. He was standing several meters away from her, clearly having a discussion through his links.

He seemed truly distressed at the news of Sonja Mycenae's death. If DeRicci had to put money on it, she would say that he hadn't known she was dead and he hadn't ordered the death.

But DeRicci had already let him charm her once. She wasn't going to trust her gut when it came to him. She was going to assume this man was guilty until he proved himself innocent.

She closed her fist around the chip case, clasped her hands behind her back, and waited, watching Luc Deshin the entire time.

8

DESHIN STOPPED BY A GROUPING OF COUCHES, NEXT TO SOME TALL, LEAFY plants. He wanted to keep an eye on the detective. He'd learned in the past that police officers had a tendency to wander and observe things they shouldn't.

He had staff in various parts of the lobby to prevent the detective from doing just that.

Through private, encoded links, he had contacted his favorite attorney, Martin Oberholst. For eight years, Oberholst had managed the most delicate cases for Deshin—always knowing how far the law could bend before it broke.

Before I tell you what to do, Oberholst was saying on their link, *I want to see the footage.*

It'll take time, Deshin paced slightly as he worked the links. He hated standing still.

Ach, Oberholst sent. *I'll just bill you for it. Send it to me.*

I already have, Deshin sent.

I'll be in contact shortly, Oberholst sent, and signed off.

Deshin walked to the other side of the lobby. He didn't want to vanish because he didn't want the detective to think he was doing something nefarious.

But he was unsettled. That meeting with Sonja had not gone as he expected.

49

Over the years, Deshin had probably fired two hundred people personally, and his staff had fired even more. And that didn't count the business relationships he had terminated.

Doing unpleasant things didn't bother him. They usually followed a pattern. But the meeting that morning hadn't followed a pattern that he recognized.

He had spoken quite calmly to Sonja, telling her that he and Gerda had decided to raise Paavo without help. He hadn't criticized Sonja at all. In fact, he had promised her a reference if she wanted it, and he had complimented her on the record, saying that her presence had given him and Gerda the confidence to handle Paavo alone.

He hadn't said that the confidence had come from the fact that Sonja had years of training and yet she missed the essential ingredient—affection. He had kept everything as neutral and positive as possible, given that he was effectively firing her without firing her.

Midway through his little speech, her eyes had widened. He had thought she was going to burst into tears. Instead, she had put a shaking hand to her mouth, looking like she had just received news that everything she loved in the world was going to be taken away from her.

He had a moment of confusion—had she actually cared that much about Paavo?—and then he decided it didn't matter; he and Gerda really did want to raise the boy on their own, without any outside help.

"Mr. Deshin," Sonja had said when he finished. "Please, I beg you, do not fire me."

"I'm not firing you, Sonja," he had said. "I just don't have a job for you any longer."

"Please," she said. "I will work here. I will do anything, the lowest of the low. I will do jobs that are disgusting or frightening, anything, Mr. Deshin. Please. Just don't make me leave."

He had never had an employee beg so strenuously to keep her job. It unnerved him. "I don't have any work for you."

"Please, Mr. Deshin." She reached for him and he leaned back. "Please. Don't make me leave."

That was when he sent a message along his links to security. This woman was crazy, and no one on his staff had picked up on it. He felt both relieved and appalled. Relieved that she was going nowhere near Paavo again, and appalled that he had left his beloved little son in her care.

His office door had opened as security responded to his request. A security team of four entered.

Sonja screamed "No!" at the top of her lungs.

She grabbed at Deshin, and his security people pulled her away.

She kicked and fought and screamed and cried all the way through the door. It closed behind her, leaving him alone, but he could still hear her yelling all the way to the elevator.

The incident had unsettled him.

It still unsettled him.

And now, just a few hours later, Sonja was dead.

That couldn't be a coincidence.

It couldn't be a coincidence at all.

9

Luc Deshin paced the lobby, his expression grim. For a while, DeRicci could tell that he wasn't on his links. He appeared to be waiting for a response to something, which surprised her.

She would have thought that he would vanish until he had news for her. Instead, he remained.

However, he never looked at her. It was as if she weren't there, as if he had planned to be in this lobby all along, that being here was an essential part of his day.

It was taking so long for him to actually get back to her that DeRicci almost turned on her own links. Then she remembered that she'd probably have a screaming message from Lake, some complaint from Gumiela, and some misinformation from Brodeur, and so DeRicci did nothing.

Except watch Luc Deshin.

It took nearly fifteen minutes for him to look at her. He nodded once, as if he hadn't been sure she would wait for him.

But she had.

He walked over to her, his strides long, a few employees working hard to get out of his way.

His expression remained grim as he nodded at the chip in her hand.

"You may watch it, Detective," he said. "In fact, you may log it in as evidence in this case."

"Thank you," DeRicci said. She started to leave, when Deshin held up one finger, silently commanding her to stay, as if she worked for him as well.

For the first time, his charm didn't work with her.

"I want this on the record as well," he said. "You have all the information we have about this morning's meeting on that chip. In addition to the meeting in my office, you'll see Sonja's arrival and her departure. You'll also see that she left through that front door. After she disappeared off our external security cameras, no one on my staff saw her again."

He was being very precise. DeRicci figured his lawyer had told him to do that.

"Thank you," she said, closing her fingers around the case. "I appreciate the cooperation."

"You're welcome," Deshin said, then walked away.

She watched him go. Something about his mood had darkened since she originally spoke to him. Because of the lawyer? Or something else?

It didn't matter. She had the information she needed, at least for the moment.

She would deal with Deshin later if she needed to.

10

DESHIN TOOK THE STAIRS BACK TO HIS OFFICE. HE NEEDED TO THINK, AND he didn't want to run into any of his staff on the elevator. Besides, exercise kept his head clear.

He had thought Sonja crazy after her reaction in his office. But what if she knew her life was in danger if she left his employ? Then her behavior made sense.

He wasn't going to say that to the detective, nor had he mentioned it to his lawyer. Deshin was going to investigate this himself.

As he reached the top floor, he sent a message to his head of security, Otto Koos: *My office. Now.*

Deshin went through the doors and stopped, as he always did, looking at the view. He had a 360-degree view of the City of Armstrong. Right now, the dome was set at Dome Daylight, mimicking midday sunlight on Earth. He loved the look of Dome Daylight because it put buildings all over the city in such clear light that it made them look like a beautiful painting or a holographic wall image.

He crossed to his desk and called up the file on Sonja Mycenae, looking for anything untoward, anything his staff might have missed.

He saw nothing.

She had worked for a family on Earth, who had filed monthly reports with the nanny service that had vetted her. The reports were excellent.

Sonja had then left the family to come to the Moon, because, apparently, she had been homesick.

He couldn't find anything in a cursory search of that file that showed any contradictory information.

The door to his office opened, and Koos entered. He was a short man, with broad shoulders and a way of walking that made him look like he was itching for a fight.

Deshin had known him since they were boys, and trusted Koos with his life. Koos had saved that life more than once.

"Sonja was murdered after she left us this morning," Deshin said.

Koos glanced at the door. "So that was why Armstrong PD was here."

"Yeah," Deshin said, "and it clarifies Sonja's reaction. She knew something bad would happen to her."

"She was a plant," Koos said.

"Or something," Deshin said. "We need to know why. Did anyone follow her after she left?"

"You didn't order us to," Koos said, "and I saw no reason to keep track of her. She was crying pretty hard when she walked out, but she never looked back and as far as I could tell, no one was trailing her."

"The police are going to trace her movements," Deshin said. "We need to as well. But what I want to know is this: What did we miss about this woman? I've already checked her file. I see nothing unusual."

"I'll go over it," Koos said.

"Don't go over it," Deshin said, feeling a little annoyed. After all, he had just done that, and he didn't need to be double-checked. "Vet her again, as if we were just about to hire her. See what you come up with."

"Yes, sir," Koos said. Normally, he would have left after that, but he didn't. Instead, he held his position.

Deshin suppressed a sigh. Something else was coming his way. "What?"

"When you dismissed her and she reacted badly," Koos said, "I increased security around your wife and child. I'm going to increase it again, and I'm going to make sure you've got extra protection as well."

Deshin opened his mouth, but Koos put up one finger, stopping him.

"Don't argue with me," Koos said. "Something's going on here, and I don't like it."

Deshin smiled. "I wasn't going to argue with you, Otto. I was going to thank you. I hadn't thought to increase security around my family, and it makes sense."

Koos nodded, as if Deshin's praise embarrassed him. Then he left the office.

Deshin watched him go. As soon as he was gone, Deshin contacted Gerda on their private links.

Koos might have increased security, but Deshin wanted to make sure everything was all right.

He used to say that families were a weakness, and he never wanted one. Then he met Gerda, and they brought Paavo into their lives.

He realized that families *were* a weakness, but they were strength as well.

And he was going to make sure his was safe, no matter what it took.

11

IT HAD TAKEN MORE WORK THAN BRODEUR EXPECTED TO GET THE BODY back to the coroner's office. Just to get the stupid crate out of the warehouse, he'd had to sign documentation swearing he wouldn't use it to make money at the expense of Ansel Management.

"Company policy," Najib Ansel had said with an insincere smile.

If Brodeur hadn't known better, he would have thought that Ansel was just trying to make things difficult for him.

But things had become difficult for Brodeur when DeRicci's partner, Rayvon Lake, arrived. Lake had been as angry as Brodeur had ever seen him, claiming that DeRicci—who was apparently a junior officer to Lake—had been giving him orders.

Lake had shouted at everyone, except Brodeur. Brodeur had fended off a shouting match by holding up his hands and saying, "I'm not sure what killed this girl, but I don't like it. It might contaminate everything. We have to get her out of here, now."

Lake, who was a notorious germophobe (which Brodeur found strange in a detective), had gulped and stepped back. Brodeur had gotten the crate to the warehouse door before Ansel had come after him with all the documentation crap.

Maybe Ansel had done it just so that he wouldn't have to talk with Lake. Brodeur would have done anything to avoid Lake—and apparently just had.

Brodeur smiled to himself, relieved to be back at the coroner's office. *Office* was a misnomer—the coroners had their own building, divided into sections to deal with the various kinds of death that happened in Armstrong.

Brodeur had finally left the alien section after two years of trying. He'd tested out, rather than relying on a supervisor's recommendation. If he'd waited for that, he might never have left.

He hated working in an environmental suit, like he'd so often had to. Weirdly (he always thought), humans started in the alien section and had to get a promotion to work on human cadavers. Probably because no one really wanted to see the interior of a Sequev more than once. No human did, anyway.

There were more than a dozen alien coroners, most of whom worked with human supervisors since many alien cultures did not investigate cause of death. Armstrong was a human-run society on a human-run Moon, so human laws applied here, and human laws always needed a cause of death.

Which often caused all kinds of problems with cultures that had differing views of death—particularly the Disty, who controlled Mars.

Brodeur never wanted to work a Disty Vengeance Killing ever again, and not because of the gruesome way that the Disty spread out the entrails. It was because the Disty seemed to go a little crazy around corpses, in a way he didn't ever want to deal with again.

A nice human body, served up on its own bed of lettuce, was just about perfect.

He smiled to himself at that thought. He couldn't make jokes like that to anyone. Everyone—including his colleagues—thought his sense of humor was inappropriate.

Even his friends shied away from his comments most of the time. And women—he was considered a player in the department because he dated so many, but that wasn't because he was a love-'em-and-leave-'em kinda guy. It was because around date three he'd relax and make a joke, and he'd get one of those what-the-hell? looks. Too many humorous comments and he wouldn't be able to reach the woman on her links.

So he'd try again.

Even with his reputation, he'd never dated a woman as beautiful as Sonja Mycenae. He had placed her on the autopsy table, carefully positioning her before beginning work, and he'd been startled at how well proportioned she was.

Most people had obvious flaws, at least when a coroner was looking at them. One arm a little too long, a roll of fat under the chin, a misshapen ankle.

He hadn't removed her clothing yet, but as far as he could tell from the work he'd done with her already, nothing was unusual.

Which made her unusual all by herself.

He also couldn't see any obvious cause of death. He had noted, however, that full rigor mortis had already set in. Which was odd, since the decomposition, according to the exam his nanobots had already started, seemed to have progressed at a rate that put her death at least five hours earlier.

By now, under the conditions she'd been stored in, she should have still been pliable—at least her limbs. Rigor began in the eyes, jaw, and neck, then spread to the face and through the chest before getting to the limbs. The fingers and toes were always the last to stiffen up.

That made him suspicious, particularly since livor mortis also seemed off.

He would have thought, given how long she had been curled inside that crate, that the blood would have pooled in the side of her body resting on top of the compost heap. But no blood had pooled at all.

He decided to have bots move the autopsy table into one of the more advanced autopsy theaters. He wanted every single device he could find to do the work.

He suspected she'd been killed with some kind of hardening poison. They had become truly popular with assassins in the last two decades, and had just recently been banned from the Moon. Hardening poisons killed quickly by absorbing all the liquid in the body and/or by baking it into place.

It was a quick death, but a painful one, and usually the victim's muscles froze in place, so she couldn't even express that pain as it occurred.

He'd have to put on a high-grade environmental suit in an excess of caution. Some of the hardening poisons leaked out of the pores and then infected anyone who touched them.

What he had to determine was if Sonja Mycenae had died of one of those, and if her body had been placed in a waste crate not just to hide the corpse, but to infect the food supply in Armstrong.

Because the Growing Pits inspections looked at the growing materials—the soil, the water, the light, the atmosphere, and the seeds. The inspectors would also look at the fertilizer, but if it came from a certified organization like Ansel Management, then there would only be a cursory search of materials.

Hardening poisons could thread their way into the DNA of a plant— just a little bit, so that, say, an apple wouldn't be quite as juicy. A little hardening poison wouldn't really hurt the fruit of a tree (although that tree might eventually die of what a botanist would consider a wasting disease), but a trace of hardening poison in the human system would have an impact over time. And if the human continued to eat things with hardening poisons in them, the poisons would build up until the body couldn't take it anymore.

A person poisoned in that way wouldn't die like Sonja Mycenae had; instead, the poison would overwhelm the standard nanohealers that everyone had, that person would get sick, and organs would slowly fail. Armstrong would have a plague but not necessarily know what caused it.

He double-checked his gloves, worried that he'd touched her at all. Then he let out a breath. Yes, he knew he was being paranoid. But he thought about these things a lot—the kinds of death that could happen with just a bit of carelessness, like sickness in a dome, poison through the food supply, the wrong mix in the air supply.

He had moved from working with living humans to working with the dead primarily because his imagination was so vivid. Usually working with the dead calmed him. The regular march of unremarkable deaths reminded him that most people would die of natural causes after 150 or more years, maybe longer if they took good care of themselves.

Working with the dead usually gave him hope.

But Sonja Mycenae was making him nervous.

And he didn't like that at all.

12

DESHIN HAD JUST FINISHED TALKING WITH GERDA WHEN KOOS SENT HIM
an encoded message:

Need to talk as soon as you can.

Now's fine, Deshin sent.

He moved away from the windows, where he'd been standing as he
made sure Gerda was okay. The Dome Daylight seemed to reveal everything and nothing. He looked at the light on the buildings, wondering
what was actually going on in the city.

At least Gerda had sounded happy, which she hadn't since Paavo
moved in. She said she no longer felt like her every move was being judged.

She said that Paavo seemed happier too. He wasn't crying as much,
and he didn't cling as hard to Gerda. Instead, he played with a mobile
from his bouncy chair and watched her cook, cooing most of the time.

Just that one report made Deshin feel like he had made the right
choice with Sonja.

Not that he had had a doubt—at least about her—after her reaction
that morning. But apparently a tiny doubt had lingered about whether
or not he and Gerda needed the help of a nanny.

Gerda's report on Paavo's calmness eased that. Deshin knew they
would have hard times ahead—he wasn't deluding himself—but he also
knew that they had made the right choice to go nanny-free.

He hadn't told Gerda what happened to Sonja, and he wouldn't until he knew more. He didn't want to spoil Gerda's day.

The door to Deshin's office opened, and Koos entered, looking upset. "Upset" was actually the wrong word. Something about Koos made Deshin think the man was afraid.

Then Deshin shook that thought off; he'd seen Koos in extremely dangerous circumstances and the man had never seemed afraid.

"I did what you asked," Koos said without preamble. "I started vetting her all over again."

Deshin leaned against the desk, just like he had done when he spoke to Sonja. "And?"

"Her employers on Earth are still filing updates about her exemplary work for them."

Deshin felt a chill. "Tell me that they were just behind in their reports."

Koos shook his head. "She's still working for them."

"How is that possible?" Deshin asked. "We vetted her. We even used a DNA sample to make sure her DNA was the same as the DNA on file with the service. And we collected it ourselves."

Koos swallowed. "We used the service's matching program."

"Of course we did," Deshin said. "They were the ones with the DNA on file."

"We could have requested their file sample, and then run it ourselves."

That chill Deshin had felt became a full-fledged shiver. "What's the difference?"

"Depth," Koos said. "They don't go into the same kind of depth we would go into in our search. They just look at standard markers, which is really all most people would need to confirm identity."

His phrasing made Deshin uncomfortable. "She's not who she said she was?"

Koos let out a small sigh. "It's more complicated than that."

More complicated. Deshin shifted. He could only think of one thing that would be more complicated.

Sonja was a clone.

And that created all kinds of other issues.

But first, he had to confirm his suspicion.

"You checked for clone marks, right?" Deshin asked. "I know you did. We always do."

The Earth Alliance required human clones to have a mark on the back of their neck or behind their ear that gave their number. If they were the second clone from an original, the number would be "2."

Clones also did not have birth certificates. They had day of creation documents. Deshin had a strict policy for Deshin Enterprises: every person he hired had to have a birth certificate or a document showing that they, as a clone, had been legally adopted by an original human and therefore could be considered human under the law.

When it came to human clones, Earth Alliance and Armstrong laws were the same: clones were property. They were created and owned by their creator. They could be bought or sold, and they had no rights of their own. The law did not distinguish between slow-grow clones, which were raised like any naturally born human child, and fast-grow clones, which reached full adult size in days, but never had a full-grown human intelligence.

The laws were an injustice, but only clones seemed to protest it, and they, as property, had no real standing.

Koos's lips thinned. He didn't answer right away.

Deshin cursed. He hated having clones in his business and didn't own any, even though he could take advantage of the loopholes in the law.

Clones made identity theft too easy, and made an organization vulnerable.

Deshin always made certain his organization remained protected.

Or he had, until now.

"We did check like we do with all new hires." Koos's voice was strangled. "And we also checked her birth certificate. It was all in order."

"But now you're telling me it's not," Deshin said.

Koos's eyes narrowed a little, not with anger, but with tension.

"The first snag we hit," he said, "was that we were not able to get Sonja Mycenae's DNA from the service. According to them, she's currently employed and not available for hire, so the standard service-subsidized searches are inactive. She likes her job. I looked: the job is the old one, not the one with you."

Deshin crossed his arms. "If that's the case, then how did we get the service comparison in the first place?"

"At first, I worried that someone had spoofed our system," Koos said. "They hadn't. There was a redundancy in the service's files that got repaired. I checked with a tech at the service. The tech said they'd been hit with an attack that replicated everything inside their system. It lasted for about two days."

"Let me guess," Deshin said. "Two days around the point we'd hired Sonja." Koos nodded.

"I'm amazed the tech admitted it," Deshin said.

"It wasn't their glitch," Koos said. "It happened because of some government program."

"Government?" Deshin asked.

"The Earth Alliance required some changes in their software," Koos said. "They made the changes and the glitch appeared. The service caught it, removed the Earth Alliance changes, and petitioned to return to their old way of doing things. Their petition was granted."

Deshin couldn't sit still with this. "Did Sonja know this glitch was going to happen?"

Koos shrugged. "I don't know what she knew."

Deshin let out a small breath. He felt a little off-balance. "I assume the birth certificate was stolen."

"It was real. We checked it. I double-checked it today," Koos said.

Deshin rubbed his forehead. "So, was the Sonja Mycenae I hired a clone or is the clone at the other job? Or does Sonja Mycenae have a biological twin?"

Koos looked down, which was all the answer Deshin needed. The Sonja Mycenae he had hired was a clone.

"She left a lot of DNA this morning," Koos said. "Tears, you name it. We checked it all."

Deshin waited, even though he knew.

He knew, and he was getting furious.

"She had no clone mark," Koos said, "except in her DNA. The telomeres were marked."

"Designer criminal clone," Deshin said. A number of criminal organizations, most operating outside the Alliance, made and trained designer criminal clones for just the kind of thing that had happened to Deshin.

The clone, who replicated someone the family or the target knew casually, would slide into a business or a household for months, maybe years, and steal information. Then the clone would leave with that information on a chip, bringing it to whoever had either hired that DCC or had grown and trained the clone.

"I don't think she was a DCC," Koos said. "The markers don't fit anyone we know."

"A new player?" Deshin asked.

Koos shrugged. Then he took one step forward. "I'm going to check everything she touched, everything she did, sir. But this is my error, and it's a serious one. It put your business and more importantly your family in danger. I know you're going to fire me, but before you do, let me track down her creator. Let me redeem myself."

Deshin didn't move for a long moment. He had double-checked everything Koos had done before they hired Sonja Mycenae. *Everything.* Because Sonja Mycenae—or whatever that clone was named—was going to work in his home, with his family.

"Do you think she stole my son's DNA?" Deshin asked quietly.

"I don't know. Clearly she didn't have any with her today, but if she had handlers—"

"She wouldn't have had trouble meeting them, because Gerda and I didn't want a live-in nanny." Deshin cursed silently. There was more than enough blame to go around, and if he were honest with himself, most of it belonged to him. He had been so concerned with raising his son that he hadn't taken the usual precautions in protecting his family.

"I would like to retrace all of her steps," Koos said. "We might be able to find her handler."

"Or not," Deshin said. The handler had killed her the moment she had ceased to be useful. The handler felt he could waste a slow-grow clone, expensive and well-trained, placed in the household of a man everyone believed to be a criminal mastermind.

Some mastermind. He had screwed up something this important.

He bit back anger, not sure how he would tell Gerda. *If* he would tell Gerda.

Something had been planned here, something he hadn't figured out yet, and that planning was not complete. Sonja (or whatever her name was) had confirmed that with her reaction to her dismissal. She was terrified, and she probably knew she was going to die.

Deshin sighed.

"I will quit now if you'd like me to," Koos said.

Deshin wasn't ready to fire Koos.

"Find out who she answered to. Better yet, find out who made her," Deshin said. "Find her handler. We'll figure out what happens to you after you complete that assignment."

Koos nodded, but didn't thank Deshin. Koos knew his employer well, knew that the thanks would only irritate him.

Deshin hated to lose Koos, but Koos was no longer one hundred percent trustworthy. He should have caught this. He should have tested Sonja's DNA himself.

And that was why Deshin would put new security measures into place for his business and his family. Measures he designed.

He'd also begin the search for the new head of security.

It would take time.

And, he was afraid, it would take time to find out what exactly Sonja (or whatever her name was) had been trying to do inside his home.

That had just become his first priority.

Because no one was going to hurt his family.

No matter what he had to do to protect them.

13

Brodeur hated working in the more sophisticated autopsy theater. Nothing was in its usual place. All of the standard equipment was hard to reach.

The specialized stuff, the things he had come in here for, were right near his triple-gloved hands.

And the gloves really didn't help. They made his fingers feel fat. Plus, he was sweating in the environmental suit. It didn't matter how cold he set the internal temperature, environmental suits always made him sweat.

He wanted this autopsy to end, but he also knew this one was going to take three times longer than the standard autopsy, just because of all of the things he had to check to make certain this woman's body wasn't a contaminant in its own right.

Brodeur had six different nanoprobes digging into various places on the dead woman's skin, when a holographic computer screen appeared in front of him, a red warning light flashing.

He moaned slightly. He hated the lights. They got sent to his boss automatically, and often the damn lights reported something he had done wrong.

Well, not wrong, exactly, but not according to protocol.

The irony was, everything he had done in this autopsy so far had been exactly according to protocol.

The body was on an isolated gurney, which was doing its own investigation; they were in one of the most protected autopsy chambers in the coroner's office; and Brodeur was using all the right equipment.

He even had on the right environmental suit for the type of poison he suspected killed the woman.

He cursed, silently and creatively, wishing he could express his frustration aloud, but knowing he couldn't, because it would become part of the permanent record.

Instead, he glared at the light and wished it would go away. Not that he could make it go away with a look.

The light had a code he had never seen before. He put his gloved finger on the code, and it created a whole new screen.

This body is cloned. Please file the permissions code to autopsy this clone or cease work immediately.

"The hell...?" he asked, then realized he had spoken aloud, and he silently cursed himself. Some stupid supervisor, reviewing the footage, would think he was too dumb to know a cloned body from a real body.

But he had made a mistake. He hadn't taken DNA in the field. He had used facial recognition to identify this woman, and he had told De-Ricci who the woman was based not on the DNA testing, but on the facial recognition.

Of course, if DeRicci hadn't pressed him to give her an identification right away, he would have followed procedure.

Brodeur let out a small sigh, then remembered what he had been doing. There was still a way to cover his ass. He had been investigating whether or not this woman died of a hardening poison, and if that poison had gotten into the composting system.

He would use that as his excuse, and then mention that he needed to continue to find cause of death for public health reasons.

Besides, someone should want to know who was killing clones and putting them into the composting.

Not that it was illegal, exactly. After all, a dead clone was organic waste, just like rotted vegetables were.

He shuddered, not wanting to think about it. Maybe someone should tell the Armstrong City Council to ban the composting of any human flesh, be it original or cloned.

He sighed. He didn't want to be the one to do it. He'd slip the suggestion into his supervisor's ear and hope that she would take him up on it.

He pinged his supervisor, telling her that it was important she contact him right away.

Then he bent over the body, determined to get as much work done as possible before someone shut this investigation down entirely.

14

DeRicci sat in her aircar in the part of Armstrong Police Department parking lot set aside for detectives. She hadn't used the vehicle all day, but it was the most private place she could think of to watch the footage Deshin had given her.

She didn't want to take the footage inside the station until she'd had a chance to absorb it.

She wasn't sure how relevant it was, and she wasn't sure what her colleagues would think of it.

Or, if she were being truthful with herself, she didn't want Lake anywhere near this thing. He had some dubious connections, and he might just confiscate the footage—not for the case, but for reasons she didn't really want to think about.

So she stayed in her car, quietly watching the footage for the second time, taking mental notes. Because something was off here. People rarely got that upset about being fired from a job, at least not in front of a man known to be as dangerous as Luc Deshin.

Besides, he had handled the whole thing well, made it sound like not a firing, more like something inevitable, something that Sonja Mycenae's excellent job performance helped facilitate.

The man really was impressive, although DeRicci would never admit that to anyone else.

When DeRicci watched the footage the first time, she had been amazed at how calmly Deshin handled Mycenae's meltdown. He managed to stay out of her way, and he managed to get his security into the office without making her get even worse.

Not that it would be easy for her to be worse. If DeRicci hadn't known that Sonja Mycenae was murdered shortly after this footage was taken, DeRicci would have thought the woman unhinged. Instead, DeRicci knew that Mycenae was terrified.

She had known that losing her position would result in something awful, mostly likely her death.

But why? And what did someone have on a simple nanny with no record, something bad enough to get her to work in the home of a master criminal and his wife, bad enough to make her beg said criminal to keep the job?

DeRicci didn't like this. She particularly did not like the way that Mycenae disappeared off the security footage as she stepped outside of the building. She stood beside the building and sobbed for a few minutes, then staggered away.

No nearby buildings had exterior security cameras, and what DeRicci could get from the street cameras told her little.

Um, Detective?

DeRicci sighed. The contact came from Brodeur, on her links. He was asking for a visual, which she was not inclined to give him.

But he probably had something to show her from the autopsy.

So she activated the visual in two dimensions, making his head float above the car's control panel. Brodeur wore an environmental suit, but he had removed the hood that should have covered his face. It hung behind his skull like a half-visible alien appendage.

News for me, Ethan? DeRicci asked, hoping to move him along quickly. He could get much too chatty for her tastes.

Well, you're not going to like any of it. He ran a hand through his hair, messing it up. It looked a little damp, as if he'd been sweating inside the suit.

DeRicci waited. She didn't know how she could like or dislike any news about the woman's death. It was a case. A sad and strange case, but a case nonetheless.

She died from a hardening poison, Brodeur sent. *I've narrowed it down to one of five related types. I'm running the test now to see which poison it actually is.*

Poison. That took effort. Not in the actual application—many poisons were impossible to see, taste, or feel—but in the planning.

Someone wanted this woman dead, and then they wanted to keep her death secret.

That's a weird way to kill someone, DeRicci sent.

Brodeur looked concerned. Over the woman? He usually saw corpses as a curiosity, not as someone to empathize with.

That was one of the few things DeRicci liked about Brodeur. He could handle a job as a job.

It is *a weird way to kill someone,* Brodeur sent. Then he glanced over his shoulder as if he expected someone to enter his office and yell at him. *The thing is, one of these types of poisons could contaminate the food supply.*

What? DeRicci sent. Or maybe she said that out loud. Or both. She felt cold. Contaminate the food supply? With a body?

She wasn't quite sure of the connection, but she didn't like it.

She hadn't liked the corpse in the compost part of this case from the very first.

Brodeur took an obvious deep breath and his gaze met hers. She stabilized the floating image, so she wasn't tracking him as he moved up, down, and across the control panel.

If the poison leaked from the skin and got into the compost, he sent, *then the poison would be layered onto the growing plants, which would take in the poison along with the nutrients. It wouldn't be enough to kill anyone, unless someone'd been adding poison for a long time.*

DeRicci shook her head. *Then I don't get it. How is this anything other than a normal contamination?*

If a wannabe killer wants to destroy the food supply, he'd do stuff like this for months, Brodeur sent. *People would start dying mysteriously. Generally, the old and the sick would go first, or people who are vulnerable in the parts of their bodies this stuff targets.*

Wouldn't the basic nanohealers take care of this problem? DeRicci was glad they weren't doing this verbally. She didn't want him to know how shaken she was.

If it were small or irregular, sure, he sent. *But over time? No. They're not made to handle huge contaminations. They're not even designed to recognize these kinds of poisons. That's why these poisons can kill so quickly.*

DeRicci suppressed a shudder.

Great, she sent. *How do we investigate food contamination like that?*

That's your problem, Detective, Brodeur sent back, somewhat primly. *I'd suggest starting with a search of records, seeing if there has been a rise in deaths in vulnerable populations.*

Can't you do that easier than I can? She sent, even though she knew he would back out. It couldn't hurt to try to get him to help.

Not at the moment, he sent, *I have a job to do.*

She nearly cursed at him. But she managed to control herself. A job to do. The bastard. *She* had a job to do too, and it was just as important as his job.

This was why she hated working with Brodeur. He was a jerk.

Well, she sent, *let me know the type of poison first, before I get into that part of the investigation. You said there were five, and only one could contaminate the food supply. You think that's the one we're dealing with?*

I don't know yet, Detective, he sent. *I'll know when the testing is done.*

Which will take how long?

He shrugged. *Not long, I hope.*

Great, she sent again. She wanted to push him, but pushing him sometimes made him even more passive/aggressive about getting work done.

Well, you were right, she sent. *I didn't like it. Now I'm off to investigate even more crap.*

Um, not yet, Brodeur sent.

Not yet? Who was this guy and why did he think he could control everything she did? She clenched her fists. Pretty soon, she would tell this idiot exactly what she thought of him, and that wouldn't make for a good working relationship.

Um, yeah, he sent. *There's one other problem.*

She waited, her fists so tight her fingernails were digging into the skin of her palm.

He looked down. *I, um, misidentified your woman.*

You what? DeRicci sent. He had been an idiot about helping her, and then he told her that he had done crappy work?

This man was the absolutely worst coroner she'd ever worked with (which was saying something) and she was going to report him to the chief of detectives, maybe even to the chief of police, and get him removed from his position.

Yeah, Brodeur sent. *She's, um, not Sonja Mycenae.*

You said that, DeRicci sent. Already, her mind was racing. Misidentifying the corpse would cause all kinds of problems, not the least of which would be problems with Luc Deshin. *Who the hell is she, then?*

Brodeur's skin had turned gray. He clearly knew he had screwed up big time. *She's a clone of Sonja Mycenae.*

A what? DeRicci rolled her eyes. That would have been good to know right from the start. Because it meant the investigation had gone in the wrong direction from the moment she had a name.

A clone. I'm sorry, Detective.

You should be, DeRicci sent. *I shouldn't even be on this investigation. This isn't a homicide.*

Well, technically, it's the same thing, Brodeur sent.

Technically, it isn't, DeRicci sent. She'd had dozens of clone cases before, and no matter how much she argued with the Chief of Detectives, Andrea Gumiela, it didn't matter. The clones weren't human under the law; their deaths fell into the category of property crimes, generally vandalism or destruction of valuable property, depending on how much the clone was worth or how much it cost to create.

But, Detective, she's a human being…

DeRicci sighed. She believed that, but what she believed didn't matter. What mattered was what the law said and how her boss handled it. And she'd been through this with Gumiela. Gumiela would send DeRicci elsewhere.

Gumiela hadn't seen the poor girl crying and begging for her life in front of Deshin. Gumiela hadn't seen the near-perfect corpse, posed as if she were sleeping on a pile of compost.

Wait a minute, DeRicci sent. *You told me about the poisoning first because…?*

Because, Detective, she might not be human, but she might have been a weapon or weaponized material. And that would fall into your jurisdiction, wouldn't it?

Just when DeRicci thought that Brodeur was the worst person she had ever worked with, he manipulated a clone case to keep it inside DeRicci's detective division.

I don't determine jurisdiction, she sent, mostly because this was on the record, and she didn't want to show her personal feelings on something that might hit court and derail any potential prosecution.

But check, would you? Brodeur sent. *Because someone competent should handle this.*

She wasn't sure what "this" was: the dead clone or the contamination. Still, despite herself, she felt vaguely flattered that Brodeur thought she was competent.

She rubbed a hand on her knee. Wow, she was hard up for something positive in her life if she was preening over compliments from Brodeur.

Just send me all the information, DeRicci sent, *and let me know the minute you confirm which hardening poison killed this clone.*

I'll have it soon, Brodeur sent and signed off.

DeRicci leaned back in the aircar seat, her cheeks warm. She had gone to Luc Deshin for nothing.

Or had she?

Which Sonja Mycenae had Deshin fired that morning? The real one? Or the clone?

DeRicci let herself out of the aircar. She had to talk to Gumiela. But before she did, she needed to find out where the real Mycenae was—and fast.

15

DESHIN WASN'T CERTAIN HOW TO TELL GERDA THAT SONJA HAD BEEN placed in their home for a reason he didn't know yet.

He wandered his office, screens moving with him as he examined the tracker he had placed in Sonja. Then he winced. Every time he thought of the clone as Sonja, he felt like a fool. From now on, he would just call her the clone, because she clearly wasn't Sonja.

So he examined the information from the tracker he had place in the clone's palm the moment she was hired. She hadn't known he had inserted it. He had done it when he shook her hand, using technology that didn't show up on any of the regular scans.

He wished he had been paranoid enough to install a video tracker, but he had thought—or rather, Gerda had thought—that their nanny needed her privacy in her off time.

Of course, that had been too kind. Deshin should have tracked the clone the way he tracked anyone he didn't entirely trust.

Whenever the clone had been with Paavo, Deshin had always kept a screen open. He'd even set an alert in case the clone took Paavo out of the house without Gerda accompanying them. That alert had never activated, because Gerda had always been nearby when the clone was with Paavo.

Deshin was grateful for that caution now. He had no idea what serious crisis they had dodged.

He was now searching through all the other information in the tracker—where the clone had gone during her days off, where she had spent her free time. He knew that Koos had been, in theory, making sure the clone had no unsavory contacts—or at least, Deshin had tasked Koos with doing that.

Now, Deshin was double-checking his own head of security, making certain that he had actually done his job.

The first thing Deshin had done was make sure that the clone hadn't gone to the bad parts of town. According to the tracker, she hadn't. Her apartment was exactly where she had claimed it was, and as far as he could tell, all she had done in her off hours was shop for her own groceries, eat at a local restaurant, and go home.

He had already sent a message to one of the investigative services he used. He wanted them to search the clone's apartment. He wanted video and DNA and all kinds of trace. He wanted an investigation of her finances and a look at the things she kept.

He also didn't want anyone from Deshin Enterprises associated with that search. He knew that his investigative service would keep him out of it. They had done so before.

He had hired them to search before he had known she was a clone. He had hired them while he was waiting for his attorney to look at the footage he had given that detective.

With luck, they'd be done with the search by now.

But Deshin had decided to check the tracker himself, looking for anomalies.

The only anomaly he had found was a weekly visit to a building in downtown Armstrong. On her day off, she went to that building at noon. She had also been at that building the evening Deshin had hired her.

He scanned the address, looking for the businesses that rented or owned the place. The building had dozens of small offices, and none of the businesses were registered with the city.

He found that odd: usually the city insisted that every business register for tax purposes.

So he traced the building's ownership. He went through several layers of corporate dodges to find something even stranger: the building's owner wasn't a corporation at all.

It was the Earth Alliance.

Deshin let out a breath, and then sank into a nearby chair.

Suddenly everything made sense.

The Earth Alliance had been after him for years, convinced he was breaking thousands of different Alliance laws and not only getting away with it, but making billions from the practice.

Ironically, he had broken a lot of Alliance laws when he started out, and he still had a lot of sketchy associates, but *he* hadn't broken a law in years.

Still, it would have been a coup for someone in Alliance government to bring down Luc Deshin and his criminal enterprises.

The Alliance had found it impossible to plant listening devices and trackers in Deshin's empire. The Alliance was always behind Deshin Enterprises when it came to technology. And Deshin himself was innately cautious—

Or he had thought he was, until this incident with the clone.

They had slipped her into his home. They might have had a hundred purposes in doing so—as a spy on his family, to steal familial DNA, to set up tracking equipment in a completely different way than it had been done before.

And for an entire month, they had been successful.

He was furious at himself, but he knew he couldn't let that emotion dominate his thoughts. He had to take action, and he had to do so now.

He used his links to summon Ishiyo Cumija to his office. He'd been watching her for some time. She had been Koos's second in command in the security department. She had set up her own fiefdom, and she had once mentioned to Deshin that she worried no one was taking security seriously enough.

At the time, Deshin had thought she was making a play for Koos's job. Deshin *still* thought she was making a play for Koos's job on that day, but she might have been doing so with good reason.

Now, Cumija would get a chance to prove herself.

While Deshin waited for her, he checked the clone's DNA and found that strange clone mark embedded into her system. He had never seen anything like it. The designer criminal clones he'd run into had always had a product stamp embedded into their DNA. This wasn't a standard DCC product stamp.

It looked like something else.

He copied it, then opened Cumija's file, accessed the DNA samples she had to give every week, and searched to see if there was any kind of mark. His system always searched for the DCC product stamps, but rarely searched for other examples of cloning, including shortened telomeres.

Shortened telomeres could happen naturally. In the past, he'd found that searching for them gave him so many false positives—staff members who were older than they appeared, employees who had had serious injuries—that he had decided to stop searching for anything but the product marks.

He wondered now if that had been a mistake.

His search of Cumija's DNA found no DCC product mark, and nothing matching the mark his system had found in the clone's DNA.

As the search ended, Cumija entered the office.

She was stunningly beautiful, with a cap of straight hair so black it almost looked blue, and dancing black eyes. Until he met Cumija, he would never have thought that someone so very attractive would function well in a security position, but she had turned out to be one of his best bodyguards.

She dressed like a woman sexually involved with a very rich man. Her clothing always revealed her taut, nut-brown skin and her fantastic legs. Sometimes she looked nearly naked in the clothing she chose. Men and women watched her wherever she went, and dismissed her as someone decorative, someone being used.

One rather memorable afternoon, she had killed a man who was coming after Deshin with a laser pistol. She had disarmed the man with a blow to the elbow, and then, when he grabbed a knife and threatened her with it, she kicked him in the leg. The point of her high heel punctured his femoral artery, and he couldn't contain the bleeding.

No one helped him do so, either.

On this day, she wore a white dress that crossed her breasts with an X, revealing her sides and expanding to cover her hips and buttocks. Her matching white shoes looked as deadly as the shoes that had killed the man that afternoon.

"That nanny we hired turns out to have been a clone," Deshin said without greeting.

"Yes, I heard." Cumija's voice was low and sexy, in keeping with her appearance.

"Has Koos made an announcement?" Deshin asked. Because he would have recommended against it.

"No," Cumija said curtly, and Deshin almost smiled. She monitored everything Koos did. It was a great trait in a security officer, a terrible trait in a subordinate—at least from the perspective of someone in Koos's position.

Deshin said, "I need you to check the other employees—*you*, and you *only*. I don't want anyone to know what you're doing. I have the marker that was in the cloned Sonja Mycenae's DNA. I want you to see if there's a match. I also want a secondary check for designer criminal clone marks, and then I want you to do a slow search of anyone with abnormal telomeres."

Cumija didn't complain, even though he was giving her a lot of work. "You want me to check everyone."

"Yes," Deshin said. "Start with people who have access to me, and then move outward. Do it quickly and quietly."

"Yes, sir," she said.

"Report the results directly to me," he said.

"All right," Cumija said.

She nodded, thanked him, and left the office.

Deshin stood there for a moment, feeling a little shaken. If the Alliance was trying to infiltrate his organization, then he wouldn't be surprised if there were other clones stationed in various areas, clones he had missed.

After Cumija checked, he would have Koos do the same check, and see if he came up with the same result.

Deshin went back to his investigation of that building that the clone had visited regularly. He had no firm evidence of Earth Alliance involvement. Just suspicions, at least at the moment.

And regular citizens of the Alliance would be stunned to think that their precious Alliance would infiltrate businesses using slow-grow clones, and then disposing of them when they lost their usefulness.

But Deshin knew the Alliance had done all kinds of extra-legal things to protect itself over the centuries. And somewhere, Deshin had been flagged as a threat to the Alliance.

He had known that for some time.

He had always expected some kind of infiltration of his business.

But the infiltration of his home was personal.

And it needed to stop.

16

BRODEUR STOOD IN THE OUTER OFFICE OF THE AUTOPSY THEATER, STARING at floating computer screens. He had pulled his environmental suit's hood back to talk to DeRicci (*that* had been fun), and he hadn't put it back on yet. He was still too hot.

But now, he didn't care.

He was looking at the information pouring across his screen, and, after a moment, he let out a sigh of relief.

The hardening poison wasn't one of the kinds that could leach through the skin. He still had to test the compost to see if the poison had contaminated it, but he doubted that.

The livor mortis told him that she had died elsewhere, and then been placed in the crate. And given how fast this hardening poison acted, the blood wouldn't have been able to pool for more than a few minutes anyway.

He stood and walked back into the autopsy room. Now that he knew the woman had died of something that wouldn't hurt him if he came in contact with her skin or breathed the air around her, he didn't need the damn environmental suit.

Hers was the only body in this autopsy room. He had placed her on her back before sending the nanobots into her system. They were still working, finding out even more about her.

He knew now that she was a slow-grow clone, which meant she had lived some twenty years, had hopes, dreams, and desires. As a forensic pathologist who had examined hundreds of human corpses—cloned and non-cloned—the *only* difference he had ever seen were the telomeres and the clone marks.

Slow-grow clones were human beings in everything but the law.

He could make the claim that fast-grow clones were too, that they had the mind of a child inside an adult body, but he tried not to think about that one. Because it meant that all those horrors visited on fast-grow clones meant those horrors were visited on a human being that hadn't seen more than a few years of life, an innocent in all possible ways.

He blinked hard, trying to focus on something else. Then he stopped beside the woman's table. Lights moved along the back of it, different beams examining her, trying to glean her medical history and every single story her biology could tell.

Now that it was clear that the poison that killed her wouldn't contaminate the dome, no one would investigate this case. No one would care.

No one legally *had* to care.

He sighed, then shook his head, wondering if he could make one final push to solve her murder.

Detective DeRicci had asked for a list of bodies found in the crates. Brodeur would make DeRicci that list after all, but before he did, he would see if those bodies were "human" or clones.

If they were clones, then there was a sabotage problem, some kind of property crime—hell, it wasn't his job to come up with the charge, not when he gave her the thing to investigate.

But maybe he could find something to investigate, something that would have the side benefit of giving some justice to this poor woman, lying alone and unwanted on his autopsy table.

"I'm doing what I can," he whispered, and then wished he hadn't spoken aloud.

His desire to help her would be in the official record. Then he corrected himself: There would be no official record, since she wasn't officially a murder victim.

He was so sorry about that. He'd still document everything he could. Maybe, in the future, the laws would change.

Maybe, in the future, her death would matter as more than a statistic.

Maybe, in the future, she'd be recognized as a person, instead of something to be thrown away like leftover food.

17

The Chief of Detectives, Andrea Gumiela, had an office one floor above DeRicci's, but it was light years from DeRicci's. DeRicci's office was in the center of a large room, sectioned off with dark, movable walls. She could protect her area by putting a bubble around it for a short period of time, particularly if she was conducting an interview that she felt wouldn't work in one of the interview rooms, but there was no real privacy and no sense of belonging.

DeRicci hated working out in the center and hoped that one day she would eventually get an office of her own.

The tiny aspirations of the upwardly mobile, her ex-husband would have said. She couldn't entirely disagree. He'd had the unfortunate habit of being right.

And as she looked at Gumiela's office, which took up much of the upper floor, DeRicci knew she would never achieve privacy like this. She wasn't political enough. Some days she felt like she was one infraction away from being terminated.

Most days, she didn't entirely care.

Andrea Gumiela, on the other hand, was the most political person DeRicci had ever met. Her office was designed so that it wouldn't offend anyone. It didn't have artwork on the walls, nor did it have floating imagery. The décor shifted colors when someone from outside the department entered.

When someone was as unimportant as DeRicci, the walls were a neutral beige, and the desk a dark, wood-like color. The couch and chairs at the far end of the room matched the desk.

But DeRicci had been here when the governor-general arrived shortly after her election, and the entire room shifted to vibrant colors—the purples and whites associated with the governor-general herself.

The shift, which happened as the governor-general was announced, had disturbed DeRicci, but Gumiela managed it as a matter of course. She was going to get promoted someday, and she clearly hoped the governor-general would do it.

"Make it fast," Gumiela said as DeRicci entered. "I have meetings all afternoon."

Gumiela was tall and heavyset, but her black suit made her look thinner than she was—probably with some kind of tech that DeRicci didn't want to think about. Gumiela's red hair was piled on top of her head, making her long face seem even longer.

"I wanted to talk with you in person about that woman we found in the Ansel Management crate," DeRicci said.

Gumiela, for all her annoying traits, did keep up on the investigations.

"I thought Rayvon Lake was in charge of that case," Gumiela said.

DeRicci shrugged. "He's not in charge of anything, sir. Honestly, when it comes to cases like this, I don't even like to consult him."

Gumiela studied her. "He's your partner, Detective."

"Maybe," DeRicci said, "but he doesn't investigate crimes. He takes advantage of them."

"That's quite a charge," Gumiela said.

"I can back it with evidence," DeRicci said.

"Do so," Gumiela said, to DeRicci's surprise.

DeRicci frowned. Had Gumiela paired them so that DeRicci would bring actual evidence against Lake to the Chief's office? It made an odd kind of sense. No one could control Lake, and no one could control De-Ricci, but for different reasons.

Lake had his own tiny fiefdom, and DeRicci was just plain contrary.

"All right," DeRicci said, feeling a little off balance. She hadn't expected anything positive from Gumiela.

And then Gumiela reverted to type. "I'm in a hurry, remember?"

"Yes, sir, sorry, sir," DeRicci said. This woman always set her teeth on edge. "The woman in the crate, she was killed with a hardening poison. For a while, Brodeur thought she might have been put there to contaminate the food supply, but it was the wrong kind of poison. We're okay on that."

Gumiela raised her eyebrows slightly. Apparently she hadn't heard about the possible contamination. DeRicci had been worried that she had.

"Good…" Gumiela said in a tone that implied …*and*…?

"But I got a list from him, and sir, someone is dumping bodies in those crates all over the city, and has been for at least a year, maybe more."

"No one saw this pattern?" Gumiela asked.

"The coroner's office noticed it," DeRicci said, making sure she kept her voice calm. "Ansel Management noticed it, but the owner, Najib Ansel, tells me that over the decades his family has owned the business, they've seen all kinds of things dumped in the crates."

"Bodies, though, bodies should have caught our attention," Gumiela said. Clearly, DeRicci had Gumiela's attention now.

"No," DeRicci said. "The coroner got called in, but no one called us."

"Well, I'll have to change this," Gumiela said. "I'll—"

"Wait, sir," DeRicci said. "They didn't call us for the correct legal reasons."

Gumiela turned her head slightly, as if she couldn't believe she had heard DeRicci right. "What reasons could those possibly be?"

"The dead are all clones, sir." DeRicci made sure none of her anger showed up in the tone of her voice.

"Clones? Including this one?"

"Yes, sir," DeRicci said. "And they were all apparently slow-grow. If they had been considered human under the law, we would have said they were murdered."

Gumiela let out an exasperated breath. "This woman, this poisoned woman, she's a clone?"

"Yes, sir." DeRicci knew she only had a moment here to convince Gumiela to let her continue on this case. "But I'd like to continue my investigation, sir, because—"

"We'll send it down to property crimes," Gumiela said.

"Sir," DeRicci said. "This pattern suggests a practicing serial killer. At some point, he'll find legal humans, and then he'll be experienced—"

"What is Ansel Management doing to protect its crates?" Gumiela said.

DeRicci felt a small surge of hope. Was Gumiela actually considering this? "They have sensors that locate things by weight and size. They believe they've reported all the bodies that have come through their system in the last several years."

"They believe?" Gumiela asked.

"There's no way to know without checking every crate," DeRicci said.

"Well, this is a health and safety matter. I'll contact the Armstrong City Inspectors and have them investigate all of the recycling/compost plants."

DeRicci tried not to sigh. This wasn't going her way after all. "I think that's a good idea, sir, but—"

"Tell me, Detective," Gumiela said. "Did you have any leads at all on this potential serial before you found out that the bodies belonged to clones?"

DeRicci felt her emotions shift again. She wasn't sure why she was so emotionally involved here. Maybe because she knew no one would investigate, which meant no one would stop this killer, if she couldn't convince Gumiela to keep the investigation in the department.

"She worked as a nanny for Luc Deshin," DeRicci said. "He fired her this morning."

"I thought this was that case," Gumiela said. "His people probably killed her."

"I considered that," DeRicci said. "But he wouldn't have gone through the trouble of firing her if he was just going to kill her."

Gumiela harrumphed. Then she walked around the furniture, trailing her hand over the back of the couch. She was actually considering DeRicci's proposal—and she knew DeRicci had a point.

"Do you know who the original was?" Gumiela asked.

DeRicci's heart sank. She hadn't wanted Gumiela to ask this question. DeRicci hadn't recognized the name, but Lake had. He had left a message on DeRicci's desk—a message that rose up when she touched the desk's surface (the bastard)—which said, *Why do we care that the daughter of an off-Moon crime lord got murdered?*

DeRicci then looked up the Mycenae family. They were a crime family and had been for generations, but Sonja herself didn't seem to be part of the criminal side. She had attended the best schools on Earth, and actually had a nanny certificate. She had renounced her family both visibly and legally, and was trying to live her own life.

"The original's name is Sonja Mycenae," DeRicci said.

"The Mycenae crime family." Gumiela let out a sigh. "There's a pattern here, and one we don't need to be involved in. Obviously there's some kind of winnowing going on in the Earth-Moon crime families. I'll notify the Alliance to watch for something bigger, but I don't think you need to investigate this."

"Sir, I know Luc Deshin thought she was Sonja Mycenae," DeRicci said. "He didn't know she was a clone. That means this isn't a crime family war—"

"We don't know what it is, Detective," Gumiela said. "And despite your obvious interest in the case, I'm moving you off it. I have better things for you to do. I'll send this and the other cases down to Property, and let them handle the investigation."

"Sir, please—"

"Detective, you have plenty to do. I want that report on Rayvon Lake by morning." Gumiela nodded at her.

DeRicci's breath caught. Gumiela was letting her know that if she dropped this case, she might get a new partner. And maybe, she would guarantee that Lake stopped polluting the department.

Much as DeRicci wanted this case, there was nothing she could do. This battle was lost.

"Thank you, sir," she said, not quite able to keep the disappointment from her voice.

Gumiela had already returned to her desk.

DeRicci headed for the door. As it opened, Gumiela said, "Detective, one last thing."

DeRicci closed the door and faced Gumiela, expecting some kind of reprimand or so type of admonition.

"Have you done the clone notification?" Gumiela asked.

Earth Alliance law required any official organization that learned of a clone to notify the original, if at all possible.

"Not yet, sir." DeRicci had held off, hoping that she would keep the case. If she had, she could have gone to the Mycenae family, and maybe learned something that had relevance to the case.

"Don't," Gumiela said. "I'll take care of that too."

"I don't mind, sir," DeRicci said.

"The Mycenae require a delicate touch," Gumiela said. "It's better if the notification goes through the most official of channels."

DeRicci nodded. She couldn't quite bring herself to thank Gumiela. Or even to say anything else. So she let herself out of the office.

And stopped in the hallway.

For a moment, she considered going back in and arguing with Gumiela. Because Gumiela wasn't going to notify anyone about the clone. Gumiela probably believed that crime families should fight amongst themselves, so the police didn't have to deal with them.

DeRicci glanced at the closed door.

If she went back in, she would probably lose her job. Because she would tell Gumiela exactly what she thought of the clone laws, and the way that Property would screw up the investigation, and the fact that *people* were actually dying and being placed in crates.

But if DeRicci lost her job, she wouldn't be able to investigate anything.

The next time she got a clone case, she'd sit on that information for as long as she could, finish the investigation, and maybe make an arrest. Sure, it might not hold up, but she could get one of the other divisions to search the perpetrator's home and business, maybe catch him with something else.

This time, she had screwed up. She'd followed the rules too closely. She shouldn't have gone to Gumiela so soon.

DeRicci would know better next time.

And she'd play dumb when Gumiela challenged her over it.

Better to lose a job after solving a case, instead of in the middle of a failed one.

DeRicci sighed. She didn't feel better, but at least she had a plan.

Even if it was a plan she didn't like at all.

18

DESHIN'S RESTLESSNESS CONTINUED WHILE HE WORKED. HE MOVED AROUND his large office, letting the screens move with him. Every now and then, he noted how the Dome's fake sunlight remained the same. At Dome Twilight, it would suddenly get darker. No sunlight program managed to mimic Earth's sun exactly—parts of the Dome were too old for that.

He usually loved the consistency. Today, it made him feel as if the hours crawled by.

Of course, he was buried in research he hadn't planned on doing when he got up that morning. He was still digging into information on the person the clone had visited the most.

That person, named Cade Faulke, ran a one-man business near the port. Ostensibly, Faulke owned an employment consulting office, one that helped people find jobs or training for jobs. But it didn't take a lot of digging to discover that that was a cover for a position with Earth Alliance Security.

From what little Deshin could find, it seemed that Faulke worked alone, with an android guard—the kind that usually monitored prisons. Clearly, no one expected Faulke to be investigated: the android alone would have been a tip-off to anyone who looked deeper than the thin cover that Faulke had over his name.

Deshin wondered how many other Earth Alliance operatives worked like that inside of Armstrong. He supposed there were quite a few, monitoring various Earth Alliance projects.

Projects like, apparently, his family.

Deshin let out a sigh. His office suddenly felt like a cage. He clenched and unclenched his fists.

Sometimes he hated the way he had restrained himself to build his business and his family. Sometimes he just wanted to go after someone on his own, squeeze the life out of that person, and then leave the corpse, the way someone had left that clone.

Spying on Deshin's family. Gerda and five-month-old Paavo had done nothing except get involved with him.

And he would wager that Sonja Mycenae's family would say the same thing about her.

He stopped. He hadn't spoken to the Mycenae family in a long time, but he owed them for an ancient debt.

He sent an encoded message through his links to Aurla Mycenae, the head of the Mycenae and Sonja's mother, asking for a quick audience.

Then Deshin got a contact from Cumija: *Five low-level employees have the marker. None of them have access to your family or to anything important inside Deshin Enterprises. How do you want me to proceed?*

Get me a list, he sent back.

At that moment, his links chirruped, announcing a massive holomessage so encoded that it nearly overloaded his system. He accepted the message, only to find out it was live.

Aurla Mycenae appeared, full-sized, in the center of his floor. She wore a flowing black gown that accented her dark eyebrows and thick black hair. She had faint lines around her black eyes. Otherwise she looked no older than she had the last time he saw her, at least a decade ago.

"Luc," she said in a throaty voice that hadn't suited her as a young woman, but suited her now. "I get a sense this isn't pleasure."

"No," he said. "I thought I should warn you. I encountered a slow-grow clone of your daughter Sonja."

He decided not to mention that he had hired that clone or that she had been murdered.

Mycenae exhaled audibly. "Damn Earth Alliance. Did they try to embed her in your organization?"

"They succeeded for a time," he said.

"And then?"

So much for keeping the information back. "She turned up dead this morning."

"Typical," Mycenae said. "They've got some kind of operation going, and they've been using clones of my family. You're not the first to tell me this."

"All slow-grow?" Deshin asked.

"Yes," Mycenae said. "We've been letting everyone know that anyone applying for work from our family isn't really from our family. I never thought of contacting you because I thought you went legit."

"I did," Deshin lied. He had gone legit on most things. He definitely no longer had his fingers in the kinds of deals that the Mycenae family was famous for.

"Amazing they tried to embed with you, then," Mycenae said.

"She was nanny to my infant son," he said, and he couldn't quite keep the fury from his voice.

"Oh." Mycenae sighed. "They want to use your family like they're using mine. We're setting something up, Luc. We've got the Alliance division that is doing this crap tracked, and we're going to shut it down. You want to join us?"

Take on an actual Earth Alliance division? As a young man, he would have considered it. As a man with a family and a half-legitimate business, he didn't dare take the risk.

"I trust you to handle it, Aurla," he said.

"They have your family's DNA now," she said, clearly as a way of enticement.

"It's of no use to them in the short term," he said, "and by the time we reach the long term, you'll have taken care of everything."

"It's not like you to trust anyone, Luc."

And, back when she had known him well, that had been true. But now, he had to balance security for himself and his business associates with security for his family.

"I'm not trusting you per se, Aurla," he said. "I just know how you operate."

She grinned at him. "I'll let you know when we're done."

"No need," he said. "Good luck."

And then he signed off. The last thing he wanted was to be associated in any way with whatever operation Aurla ran. She was right: it wasn't like him to trust anyone. And while he trusted her to destroy the division that was hurting her family, he didn't trust her to keep him out of it.

Too much contact with Aurla Mycenae, and Deshin might find himself arrested as the perpetrator of whatever she was planning. Mycenae was notorious for betraying colleagues when her back was against the wall.

At that moment, Cumija sent the list. She had been right: the employees were low-level. He didn't recognize any of the names and had to look them up. None of them had even met Deshin.

Getting the clone of Sonja embedded into his family must have been some kind of coup.

He wouldn't fire anyone yet. He wanted to see if Koos came up with the same list. If he did, then Deshin would move forward.

But these employees were tagged, just like Sonja's clone had been. He decided to see if they had been visiting Faulke as well.

And if they had, Faulke would regret ever crossing paths with Deshin Enterprises.

19

DETECTIVE DERICCI LEFT ANDREA GUMIELA'S OFFICE, AND GUMIELA FELT herself relax. DeRicci was trouble. She hated rules and she had a sense of righteousness that often made it difficult for her to do her job well. There wasn't a lot of righteousness in the law, particularly when Earth Alliance law trumped Armstrong law.

Gumiela had to balance both.

She resisted the urge to run a hand through her hair. It had taken a lot of work to pile it just so on top of her head, and she didn't like wasting time on her appearance, as important as it was to her job.

Of course, the days when it was important were either days when a major disaster hit Armstrong or when someone in her department screwed up.

She certainly hoped this clone case wouldn't become a screw-up.

She put a hand over her stomach, feeling slightly ill. She had felt ill from the moment DeRicci mentioned Mycenae and Deshin. At that moment, Gumiela had known who had made the clone and who was handling it.

She also knew who was killing the clones—or at least, authorizing the deaths.

DeRicci was right. Those deaths presaged a serial killer (or, in Gumiela's unofficial opinion, already proved one existed). Or worse, the deaths suggested a policy of targeted killings that Gumiela couldn't countenance in her city.

Technically, Gumiela should contact Cade Faulke directly. He had contacted her directly more than once to report a possible upcoming crime. She had used him as an informant, which meant she had used his clones as informants as well.

And those clones were ending up dead.

She choked back bile. Some people, like DeRicci, would say that Gumiela had hands as dirty as Faulke's.

But she hadn't known until a few minutes ago that he was killing the clones when they ceased being useful or when they crossed some line. She also hadn't known that he had been poisoning them using such a painful method. And he hadn't even thought about the possible contamination of the food supply.

Gumiela swallowed hard again, hoping her stomach would settle.

Technically, she should contact him and tell him to cease that behavior.

But Gumiela had been in her job a long time. She knew that telling someone like Faulke to quit was like telling an addict to stop drinking. It wouldn't happen, and it couldn't be done.

She couldn't arrest him either. Even if she caught him in the act, all he was doing was damaging property. And that might get him a fine or two or maybe a year or so in jail, if the clone's owners complained. But if DeRicci was right, the clone's owners were the Earth Alliance itself. And Faulke worked for the Alliance, so technically, *he* was probably the owner, and property owners could do whatever they wanted with their belongings.

Except toss them away in a manner that threatened the public health.

Gumiela sat in one of the chairs and leaned her head back, closing her eyes, forcing herself to think.

She had to do something, and despite what she had said to DeRicci, following procedure was out of the question.

Gumiela needed to get Faulke out of Armstrong, only she didn't have the authority to do so.

But she knew who did.

She sat up. Long ago, she'd met Faulke's handler, Ike Jarvis. She could contact him.

Maybe he would work with her.

It was worth a try.

20

OTTO KOOS LED HIS TEAM TO THE BUILDING HOUSING CADE FAULKE'S FAKE business. The building was made of some kind of polymer that changed appearance daily. This day's appearance made it seem like old-fashioned red brick that Koos hadn't seen since his childhood on Earth.

Five Ansel Management crates stood in their protected unit in the alley behind the building. They had a cursory lock with a security code that anyone in the building probably had.

It was as much of a confession as he needed.

But the boss would need more. Luc Deshin had given strict orders for this mission—no killing.

Koos knew he was on probation now—maybe forever. He had missed the Mycenae clone, and, after he had done a quick scan of the employees, discovered he had missed at least five others. At least they hadn't been anywhere near the Deshin family.

The Mycenae clone had. Who knew what kind of material the Alliance had gathered, thanks to her.

Faulke knew. Eventually, Koos would know too. It just might take some time.

He had brought ten people with him to capture Faulke. The office had an android guard, though, the durable kind used in prisons. Koos either had to disable it or get it out of the building.

He'd failed the one time he'd tried to disable those things in the past. He was opting for getting it out of the building.

Ready? he sent to two of his team members.

Yes, they sent back at the same time.

Go! he sent.

They were nowhere near him, but he knew what they were going to do. They were going to start a fight in front of the building that would get progressively more violent. And then they'd start shooting up the area with laser pistols.

Other members of his team would prevent any locals from stopping the fight, and the fight would continue until the android guard came down.

Then Koos would sneak in the building the back way, along with three other members of his team.

They were waiting now. They had already checked the back door— unlocked during daylight hours. They were talking as if they had some kind of business with each other.

At least they weren't shifting from foot to foot like he wanted to do.

Instead, all he could do was stare at that stamp for Ansel Management.

It hadn't been much work to pick up the Mycenae clone and stuff her into one of the crates.

If Deshin hadn't given the no-kill order, then Koos would have stuffed Faulke into one of the crates, dying, but alive, so that he knew what he had done.

Koos would have preferred that to Deshin's plan.

But Koos wasn't in charge. And he had to work his way back into Deshin's good graces.

And he would do that.

Starting now.

21

GUMIELA HAD FORGOTTEN THAT IKE JARVIS WAS AN OFFICIOUS PRICK. HE ran intelligence operatives who worked inside the Alliance. Generally, those operatives didn't operate in human-run areas. In fact, they shouldn't operate in human-run areas at all.

Earth Alliance Intelligence was supposed to do the bulk of its work *outside* the Alliance.

Gumiela had contacted him on a special link the Earth Alliance had set up for the Armstrong Police Department, to be used only in cases of Earth Alliance troubles or serious Alliance issues.

She figured this counted.

Jarvis appeared in the center of the room, his three-dimensional image fritzing in and out, either because of a bad connection or because of the levels of encoding this conversation was going through.

He looked better when he appeared and disappeared. She preferred it when he was slightly out of focus.

"This had better be good, Andy," Jarvis said, and Gumiela felt her shoulders stiffen. No one called her Andy, not even her best friends. Only Jarvis had come up with that nickname, and somehow he seemed to believe it made them closer.

"I need you to pull Cade Faulke," Gumiela said.

"I don't pull anyone on your say so." Jarvis fritzed again. His image came back just a little smaller, just a little tighter. So the problem was on his end.

If she were in a better mood, she would smile. Jarvis was short enough without doctoring the image. He had once tried to compensate for his height by buying enhancements that deepened his voice. All they had done was ruin it, leaving him sounding like he had poured salt down his throat.

"You pull Faulke or I arrest him for attempted mass murder," she said, a little surprised at herself.

Jarvis moved and fritzed again. Apparently he had taken a step backwards or something, startled by her vehemence.

"What the hell did he do?" Jarvis asked, not playing games any longer.

"You have Faulke running slow-grow clones in criminal organizations, right?" she asked.

"Andy," he said, returning to that condescending tone he had used earlier, "I can't tell you what I'm doing."

"Fine," she snapped. "I thought we had a courteous relationship, based on mutual interest. I was wrong. Sorry to bother you, Ike—"

"Wait," he said. "What did he do?"

"It doesn't matter," she said. "You get to send Earth Alliance lawyers here to talk about the top-secret crap to judges who might've died because of your guy's carelessness."

And then she signed off.

She couldn't do anything she had just threatened Jarvis with. The food thing hadn't risen to the level where she could charge Faulke, and that was if she could prove that he had put the bodies into the crates himself. He had an android guard, which the chief of police had had to approve—those things weren't supposed to operate inside the city—and that guard had probably done all the dirty work. The Earth Alliance would just claim malfunction, and Faulke would be off the hook.

Jarvis fritzed back in, fainter now. The image had moved one meter sideways, which meant he was superimposed over one of her office chairs. The chair cut through him at his knees and waist. Obviously, he had no idea where his image had appeared, and she wasn't about to tell him or move the image.

"Okay, okay," Jarvis said. "I've managed to make this link as secure as I possibly can, given my location. Guarantee that your side is secure."

Gumiela shrugged. "I'm alone in my office, in the Armstrong Police Department. Good enough for you?"

She didn't tell him that she was recording this whole thing. She was tired of being used by this asshole.

"I guess it'll have to be. Yes, Faulke is running the clones that we have embedded with major criminal organizations on the Moon."

"If the clones malfunction—" She chose that word carefully "— what's he supposed to do?"

"Depends on how specific the clone is to the job, and how important it is to the operation," he said. "Generally, Faulke's supposed to ship the clone back. That's why Armstrong PD approved android guards for his office."

"There aren't guards," she said. "There's only one."

Jarvis's image came in a bit stronger. "What?"

"Just one," she said, "and that's not all. I don't think your friend Faulke has sent any clones back."

"I can check," Jarvis said.

"I don't care what you do for your records. According to ours—" and there she was lying again "—he's been killing the clones that don't work out and putting them in composting crates. Those crates go to the Growing Pits, which grow fresh food for the city."

"He *what?*" Jarvis asked.

"And to make matters worse, he's using a hardening poison to kill them, a poison our coroner fears might leach into our food supply. We're checking on that now. Although it doesn't matter. The intent is what matters, and clearly your man Faulke has lost his mind."

Jarvis cursed. "You're not making this up."

It wasn't a question.

"I'm not making this up," she said. "I want him and his little android friend out of here within the hour, or I'm arresting him, and I'm putting him on trial. Public trial."

"Do you realize how many operations you'll ruin?"

"No," she said, "and I don't care. Get him out of my city. It's only a matter of time before your crazy little operative starts killing legal humans, not just cloned ones. And I don't want him doing it here."

Jarvis cursed again. "Can I get your help—"

"No," she said. "I don't want anyone at the police department involved with your operation. And if you go to the chief, I'll tell her that you have thwarted my attempts to arrest a man who threatens the entire dome. Because, honestly, Ike *baby*, this is a courtesy contact. I don't have to do you any favors at all, especially considering what kind of person you installed in my city. Have you got that?"

"Yes, Andrea, I do," Jarvis said, looking serious.

Andrea. So he had heard her all those times. And he had ignored her, the bastard. She made note of that too.

"One hour," she said, and signed off.

Then she wiped her hands on her skirt. They were shaking just a little. Screw him, the weasely bastard. She'd send someone to that office now, to escort Jarvis's horrid operative out of Armstrong.

She wanted to make sure that asshole left quickly, and didn't double back.

She wanted this problem out of her city, off her Moon, and as far from her notice as possible.

And that, she knew, was the best she could do without upsetting the department's special relationship with the Alliance.

She hoped her best would be good enough.

22

KOOS LED THE RAID UP THE BACK STAIRS, INTO THE NARROW HALLWAY THAT smelled faintly of dry plastic, his best team members behind him. They fanned out in the narrow hallway, the two women first, signaling that the hallway was clear. Koos and Hala, the only other man on this part of the team, skirted past them and through the open door of Faulke's office.

It was much smaller than Koos expected. Faulke was only three meters from him. Faulke was scrawny, narrow-shouldered, the kind of man easily ignored on the street.

He reached behind his back—probably for a weapon—as Koos and Hala held their laser rifles on him.

"Don't even try," Koos said. "I have no compunction shooting you."

Faulke's eyes glazed for a half second—probably letting his android guard know he was in trouble—then an expression of panic flitted across his face before he managed to control it.

The other members of Koos's team had already disabled the guard.

"Who are you?" Faulke asked.

Koos ignored him, and spoke to his team. "I want him bound. And make sure you disable his links."

One of the women slipped in around Koos and put light cuffs around Faulke's wrists and pasted a small rectangle of Silent-Seal over his mouth.

You can't get away with this, Faulke sent on public links. *You have no idea who I am—*

And then his links shut off.

Koos grinned. "You're Cade Faulke. You work for Earth Alliance Intelligence. You've been running clones that you embed into businesses. Am I missing anything?"

Faulke's eyes didn't change, but he swallowed hard.

"Let's get him out of here," Koos said.

They encircled him, in case the other tenants on the floor decided to see what all the fuss was about.

But no one opened any doors. The neighborhood was too dicey for that. If anyone had an ounce of civic feeling, they would have gone out front to stop the fight that Koos had staged below, and no one had.

He took Faulke's arm, surprised at how flabby it was. Hardly any muscles at all.

No wonder the asshole had used poison. He wasn't strong enough to subdue any living creature on his own.

"You're going to love what we have planned for you," Koos said as he dragged Faulke down the stairs. "By the end of it all, you and I will be old friends."

This time Faulke gave him a startled look.

Koos grinned at him and led him to the waiting aircar that would take them to the port.

It would be a long time before anyone heard from Cade Faulke again. If they ever did.

23

DESHIN ARRIVED HOME, EXHAUSTED AND MORE THAN A LITTLE UNSETTLED. The house smelled of baby powder and coffee. He hadn't really checked to see how the rest of Gerda's day alone with Paavo had gone.

He felt guilty about that.

He went through the modest living room to the baby's room. He and Gerda didn't flash their wealth around Armstrong, preferring to live quietly. But he had so much security in the home that he was still startled the clone had broken through it.

Gerda was sitting in a rocking chair near the window, Paavo in her arms. She put a finger to her lips, but it did no good.

His five-month-old son twisted, and looked at Deshin with such aware eyes that it humbled him. Deshin knew that this baby was twenty times smarter than he would ever be. It worried him, and it pleased him as well.

Paavo smiled and extended his pudgy arms. Deshin picked him up. The boy was heavier than he had been just a week before. He also needed a diaper change.

Deshin took him to the changing table and started, knowing just from the look on her face that Gerda was exhausted, too.

"Long day?" he asked.

"Good day," she said. "We made the right decision."

"Yes," he said. "We did."

He had decided on the way home not to tell her everything. He would wait until the interrogations of Cade Faulke and the five clones were over. Koos had taken all six of them out of Armstrong in the same ship.

And the interrogations wouldn't even start until Koos got them out of Earth Alliance territory, days from now.

Deshin had no idea what would happen to Faulke or the clones after that. Deshin was leaving that up to Koos. Koos no longer headed security for Deshin Enterprises in Armstrong, but he had served Deshin well today. He would handle some of the company's work off Moon.

Not a perfect day's work, not even the day's work Deshin had expected, but a good one, nonetheless. He probably had other leaks to plug in his organization, but at least he knew what they were now.

His baby raised a chubby fist at Deshin as if agreeing that action needed to be taken. Deshin bent over and blew bubbles on Paavo's tummy, something that always made Paavo giggle.

He giggled now, a sound so infectious that Deshin wondered how he had lived without it all his life.

He would do everything he could to protect this baby, everything he could to take care of his family.

"He trusts you," Gerda said with a tiny bit of amazement in her voice.

Most people never trusted Deshin. Gerda did, but Gerda was special.

Deshin blew bubbles on Paavo's tummy again, and Paavo laughed.

His boy did trust him.

He picked up his newly diapered son, and cradled him in his arms. Then he kissed Gerda.

The three of them, forever.

That was what he needed, and that was what he had ensured today.

The detective could poke around his business all she wanted, but she would never know the one thing that calmed Deshin down.

Justice had been done.

His family was safe.

And that was all that mattered.

JUST BEFORE
THE PEYTI CRISIS

24

Acting Marshal in Charge Elián Nuuyoma stared at the coordinates displayed on the screens before him. Then he looked out the windows of the observation deck on the *EAFS Stanley*.

Nothing except stars, off in the distance.

He should have expected it. He *had* expected it.

Intellectually, he had known that the starbase known as *Strangers' Paradise, Starbase Human,* and *Danger Zone,* depending on which star map he consulted, had been destroyed over thirty-five years ago, but part of him hadn't believed it.

Part of him was still incredibly naïve. He had hoped that something that remained on the Alliance's star maps would still exist, maybe rebuilt after the massive explosions he had seen in a grainy old vid nearly six months ago.

He stood with his hands clasped behind his back. He could see himself, reflected in the windows, the soft light behind him obscuring the childhood scarification on his face from religious rituals that his parents practiced. He could have repaired those scars, but he didn't. The scars scared some aliens he came across—and a few humans, as well.

He liked having a slightly scary appearance. It made up for his tall, reedy build. A friend in school once described him as a man who could hide behind a twig. Nuuyoma was a little thicker now, but not much—certainly not enough to be imposing without the scars.

He sighed, staring at the unfamiliar stars glowing against the blackness. Usually he loved the observation deck. It housed not just windows on all sides, but also the hydroponics bay. If he moved far enough back, he could feel the warmth of the fake sunlight used for some of the plants.

He'd been on ships for so long that he actually preferred ship-grown food to food grown planetside. The planetside food had a different flavor, often depending on growing region. Ship-grown food had a consistency he welcomed.

He liked consistency in shipboard life. Because his day-to-day existence was anything but consistent.

He had assumed the job of acting marshal on the *Stanley* when Judita Gomez took a year's leave, in advance of a probable retirement—or so she told her bosses, mostly so that she could promote Nuuyoma into her position and leave the rest of the staff intact. Otherwise, everyone would have gone through evaluations and been shuffled to other ships. The marshal in charge of the *Stanley* would have been someone who had downloaded the ship's history, but hadn't lived it.

And, if that were the case, Nuuyoma would have asked for a transfer. He had served on the *Stanley* since he left the academy. He loved this ship as if she were his own.

He let out a small sigh. He was treating her as if she were his own as well. The *Stanley* really didn't belong out here. The starbase—whatever it was called or had been called—had been at the far edge of the Frontier when the base was destroyed. No Alliance ship had ever docked at it, as far as he could tell.

Now, it wasn't quite at the edge of the Frontier, but it was close. It had taken the *Stanley* five months of travel (with some important stops in between) to get here.

He had lied to his crew about the reason for the visit: he had said he'd been ordered to investigate the incorrect Alliance maps.

But he hadn't been ordered by anyone, not even Gomez. He had done this on his own. In fact, he had told Gomez he was going to do it, and she had tried to talk him out of it.

Not that she had a chance of doing so. He couldn't talk her out of investigating the clones who had bombed the Moon on Anniversary Day. She was taking her leave to do that—and she really didn't plan on retiring after it was all done, although she said that she would.

Sometimes, he thought she said that because she wasn't sure if she would have a career when she was done and/or still be alive.

She suspected—and so did he—that the Alliance was somehow involved in that bombing, and several other things. Which was why she had stepped down.

Once Nuuyoma had learned what was going on, he wasn't surprised that she was investigating this. In her shoes, he would have done the same thing.

She'd let him into the early parts of the investigation, back when she was running the *Stanley*. Both she and Lashante Simiaar had been shocked by the Anniversary Day bombings—not just because of the destruction, but because of the bombers themselves.

Apparently, the *Stanley* had run into a different group of clones from the same source almost sixteen years ago. The clones and the *Stanley* had had a strange, memorable, and deadly interaction, and three of clones had been shipped into the Alliance.

Gomez and her team had believed that the Alliance would investigate the clones' origins and then put a stop to the illegal practices. It was only after Anniversary Day that they discovered no one had ever investigated the clones.

And after Gomez interviewed one of them herself, all three clones either disappeared or died.

Nuuyoma had been present for that part, at least. And if he hadn't been suspicious of the situation before, (he had), he would have been suspicious afterwards.

Something was definitely off, which he said to Gomez as they had their own argument about his role in the investigation.

Gomez had told him she didn't want him to come with her.

You have a career, Elián. I'm at the end of mine. I have enough money saved to last five lifetimes if I need it. But you, you're just starting out, and you're good. *You shouldn't risk your future for my quest.*

He had argued with her. Three others from the *Stanley* had gone with her—Charlie Zamal, probably the best pilot the *Stanley* had ever had; Neil Apaza, a researcher whom Nuuyoma had never gotten a sense of; and Lashante Simiaar, the chief forensic examiner, who was absolutely cranky and absolutely brilliant.

All but Apaza had had long careers. And Apaza was not a good fit for Frontier Security. He had trouble remaining in shape, and Nuuyoma had a sense that Apaza missed the Alliance more than he wanted to admit.

Gomez had taken him, not just because she needed him, but also because he probably would have tested out of the service in the next year or so.

Nuuyoma wasn't going to test out. He had always known this would be his career. He loved the first contacts and the strange encounters. And he loved being away from all the familiar things. He loved the way this ship became the real world for everyone on board, and he loved the way that it forged its own future.

That was why he thought he could get away with this particular investigation. He had told Gomez that.

No one cares what direction we travel in. I'll make sure we answer any requests for assistance, but I'll also head in the direction of the starbase. You don't have time to go there. It'll take more than a year to get there and back, especially since you want to go to the middle of the Alliance when you've finished. Let me do this job, Judita. Not even the staff will know what's going on.

She had studied him for a long time after he said that. He'd worked with her long enough to know that she contemplated while studying people like that.

Finally, she had nodded.

He had the sense she didn't believe there was much to learn out here. The destruction of that starbase looked like a practice run for the destruction on the Moon. The fact that the destruction had come thirty-five years before Anniversary Day made sense; the bad guys, as Gomez had started calling them, needed time to make slow-grow clones and to test them, like they had done on Epriccom.

Nuuyoma slowly walked around observation deck, sticking to the path along the windows, looking at the area where the starbase had been. The coordinates for the base put the *Stanley* right on top of the center of the base.

Unlike historical sites on planets, there was no way to see even a remnant of the destruction and death that had happened here. The emptiness made it look like the *Stanley* was the first ship to ever come to this part of space.

He knew better—there was a long history in this sector. It just wasn't an Alliance history. Humans who had come this far out were running *from* the Alliance. They didn't want to be part of it.

That was the other side of work on the Frontier. The humans who were out here were mostly anti-Alliance and anti-Earth. They didn't like humans in uniform showing up and telling them what to do. They really didn't like it when the Frontier Security Service started asking various cultures if they were interested in joining the Alliance.

Footsteps resounded behind him, clip-clopping their way toward him. He didn't turn around, but he watched the reflections in the windows. He saw the form first, and realized that Chepi Verstraete was joining him.

She wasn't wearing her uniform. Instead, she was wearing her day-off clothing—a white, gauzy, flowing pants-and-shirt thing that always made him think she could fly away. She was tiny to begin with, and the clothing seemed to give her wings.

The white did set off her ebony skin and made it seem even darker. It added a depth to her dark eyes, as well. She had gathered her black hair in the back, but left it down. It flowed to her waist.

Verstraete was the only other person on the *Stanley* who knew why they were out here. She also knew about the clones, and wanted to investigate. Gomez hadn't given her the same speech, but a similar one—Gomez hadn't wanted Verstraete to ruin her career, either, by going on "this crazy mission."

So Verstraete remained on the *Stanley*, and Nuuyoma had promoted her to his number one deputy. He had done so because she was good, but he had also done so because they shared a secret.

"I kinda thought maybe there'd be something here," she said by way of greeting.

He nodded. "Me, too."

She stopped beside him. The scents of teak and green bamboo teased his nose. Verstraete designed perfumes in her free time, usually using materials she found on their journeys. But for herself, she always wore a scent her grandmother had designed. Verstraete had had to tell him what the scents were, and now he would always associate them with her.

"That report threw me off," she said.

Report was the wrong word, but he knew what she meant. Someone had actually written about the starbase just a few years ago, as if that person had stayed at the base recently.

His entire team had tried to trace the author. Apaza was also working on it, or he had been when Nuuyoma last saw him. They all had found nothing. It was a deliberate misdirection, one Nuuyoma still didn't entirely understand.

Just like he didn't understand who had made the Alliance maps of this sector, and why those maps still included the starbase—and had included the starbase for the past 35 years.

He had done a cursory investigation of that in his spare time, but he wasn't as good at ferreting out information as Apaza was. And Nuuyoma had to be careful, too; he didn't want to tip off whoever was in the Alliance, trying to keep the base's destruction a secret.

That was the one thing that had worried Gomez about their trip here. She knew—they all knew—that their presence would show someone in the Alliance that the maps were wrong.

Nuuyoma figured he'd deal with that by not reporting that they had ever come to these coordinates. One nice thing about being the head of this ship was that he could control what information he sent to FSS headquarters.

He wouldn't send their exact route to headquarters. And he certainly wouldn't do so before he sent information he gathered—if it was valuable—to Gomez herself.

She needed time to finish her work, and he was determined to give that to her.

"The maps threw me off more," he said.

Verstraete stood beside him, mimicking his posture, hands clasped behind her back, chin out, staring at the field of stars before them. She looked younger when she wasn't in uniform.

"Hmm," she said. "The maps didn't bother me much. I've always figured that Alliance maps of the Frontier had mistakes in them."

"I've been thinking a lot about it." More than he wanted to admit, actually, although it felt good to talk to her. "And I'm still confused by it all. I mean, if no Alliance ships have been out this far, how did we get the maps in the first place?"

"No *official* Alliance vessels," she said. "I'm sure that members of the Alliance have come out here."

"And sent maps back?" He looked at her. She had to raise her head to meet his gaze.

She shrugged. "Why would that be unusual?"

"Most humans who come out here don't want anything to do with the Alliance," he said.

"Maybe the maps came from one of the non-human Alliance members," she said.

"Maybe." He still didn't like it. It felt wrong.

"We can't research it in depth without tipping someone off," she said.

"Except in the non-networked databases that we have," he said.

She nodded. "It sounds like you have."

"Yeah," he said. "And the only materials I've found have been 'screw-yous' from people who got contacted as they headed out here, and then severed their links so that no one could find them. I found one reference that mentioned a human-only starbase."

"You think that was this one?" she asked. "The review said it had an alien section that was small but sufficient."

"I know," he said. "It's a weird detail, don't you think?"

"Why?" she asked.

"It seems specific."

She turned toward the windows again. Her image looked slightly wavy, as if something was causing a distortion.

"You think it's true," she said.

"I do," he said. "That alien part makes sense to me. Even a human-only base would need an alien section for ships that had malfunctions or refueling issues or needed to stop for some other reason."

"And it would have to be well-segregated to avoid trouble." She rocked back and forth on her flat shoes. That was the closest she could come to going barefoot. Regulations didn't allow it on the ship.

"Yeah," Nuuyoma said. "That would have to be memorable, even after thirty-five years, don't you think? A small alien section, humans only, that sort of thing. It couldn't have been common."

"Actually," Verstraete said, "it is."

Nuuyoma frowned. He hadn't heard of anything like it in nearby regions, and he'd been working the Frontier longer than she had.

Still, he didn't correct her. He had learned that she often saw things he didn't. "Why do you say that?"

"Because," she said, "there's another human-only base not far from here."

Replacing the one that got destroyed? He didn't ask that question, even though he thought it. He wanted to hear what she had to say.

"How long has it been in existence?"

She smiled at him, eyes twinkling. "Thirty years."

He let out a small breath. It took time to build a starbase. "What's it called?"

"It has several names," she said, "depending on the map. The most common one, in a variety of languages, is *Starbase Human*."

"That can't be a coincidence," he said, more to himself than to her.

"I thought it was," she said. "So I did a little digging. It's run by the same corporation that ran the other starbase."

"Is it an Alliance corporation?" he asked.

"That would be too easy," she said. "No. It's a corporation that runs bases all over the Frontier. Most of those bases cater to different species. This is the only one that I could find that catered to humans."

"The corporation isn't human-owned, then?" he asked.

She shrugged. "I'm not one of those researchers who can find that stuff, and I was leery of digging too deep. I don't know how to hide my trail."

"Probably a good call," he said. "So there's a need for this starbase out here. It makes me wonder how many humans fled the Alliance and settled out here."

"Because they didn't like the multi-species aspect of the Alliance?" she asked.

"It still causes issues," he said. "A lot of humans think we shouldn't be subject to alien law."

"We're not," she said. "We're subject to *Alliance* law. We agreed—"

He held up a hand to stop her from launching into one of her favorite rants. "I know, Chepi," he said softly.

She glanced at him—and then laughed. "Gosh. It's like I'm programmed to give that response whenever anyone says anything."

"We all are," he lied. It was part of being in the FSS, though, that need to explain what the Alliance was about and how it worked, and how fair it actually was. He just didn't like ranting about it.

He sighed, thinking about that other base. "I wonder if there's an institutional memory."

"In the corporation?" she asked. "Did you really want to contact them?"

"In the starbase," he said. "Essentially, that's the rebuild, even if it isn't in this exact spot."

She looked around, as if she could see the base with the naked eye.

"Thirty-five years isn't that long," she said. "Someone has to remember something."

"Starbases don't get destroyed very often," he mused. "A lot of people would have died. You don't get over that, no matter how long ago it was."

She stood next to him silently for a long moment. She was clearly giving him time to come up with something.

When he didn't speak, she started shifting position. He recognized it. She didn't like silence. She never had.

"So," she said when he didn't speak. "Are we going to go in as FSS or as some people who are on our way somewhere else?"

"Undercover or official?" he asked. "They both have advantages."

"I don't see any advantage in being official," she said. "Not in a place that's clearly hostile to a lot of things."

"You really believe they hate the Alliance," he said.

She nodded. "If they don't want aliens, they don't want humans who are forced to interact with aliens. And that would mean they certainly don't want someone who is supposed to enforce the laws between humans and aliens."

He hadn't thought of it that way. He might have come to it later, although he wasn't certain. Verstraete had a way of seeing the heart of the matter much quicker than anyone else.

"Undercover it is," he said. He felt a little jaunty about it, even though that would create problems. Because he wasn't sure how to explain to the rest of his team why he wanted to go into a human-only base.

He would come up with something, though.

He always did.

25

Marshal Judita Gomez stood with her right hand clasped over her left wrist, behind her back. She straightened her shoulders, a habit she had just acquired in the last few months. She'd done more sitting around than she had ever expected, so after she felt herself growing flabby and tired, she decided to stand whenever possible.

Before her were the two other main people on this silly quest. Neil Apaza probably hadn't stood up since he boarded the *Green Dragon*. He had become pear-shaped, something that didn't surprise Gomez. One of the reasons he had joined her on this misadventure was because he knew he would no longer pass the physical tests for the Frontier Security Service, and he wasn't willing to put in the time or the effort to get into shape.

Lashante Simiaar hovered beside him. Simiaar was the best forensic director in the FSS, and she had taken a year off to join Gomez. Simiaar had lost some weight on this trip—surprising, since she'd been cooking fantastic meals for them—but she still carried an extra kilo or two. She was tall and broad, and one of the strongest people Gomez had ever met, although she didn't look strong at the moment.

She looked concerned.

Gomez couldn't blame her. They were staring at a floating screen showing a tiny section of the planet below them. Hétique was deeper in the Earth Alliance than any place Gomez had expected when she started following this lead, and a lot more established.

Sixty-six different sentient species called this planet home, even though its land mass was relatively small. Most of the species either lived in the water or in the skies above the planet's surface. They claimed the cliff tops, the oceans, and the lakes—which was why a human colony had been founded on the only arable land long before the Alliance even existed.

That human colony had now spread to three major cities, crammed into a few thousand kilometers, and housed several industries that human-governed societies usually didn't want on their land.

Humans were not the dominant species on Hétique. When three-quarters of the species joined the Earth Alliance, the Alliance determined Hétique was non-human, and not governed by human laws.

Gomez had never even seen the laws for the dominant culture, winged aliens called Tiquis. She didn't want to look those laws up now.

She felt at loose ends these days, because the way she used to conduct a mission—investigating everything there was to know about a planet before she even approached it—did not apply at all now.

She couldn't even really call what she was doing a "mission," nor could she call Apaza, Simiaar, and the senior pilot, Charlie Zamal, her staff. They had worked for her when she ran the Earth Alliance Frontier Security Ship *Stanley*, but she had stepped away from that post for a year, ostensibly to see if she was ready to retire.

She had left the *Stanley* in the capable hands of Elián Nuuyoma, who continued its mission on the Frontier. She missed the constant changes, the unsettled moments when she wasn't certain what she was about to encounter.

Ever since she had left the *Stanley*, she had gone deeper into the Alliance. Before that, she hadn't been in Alliance space—truly deep in Alliance space—for years.

Her ultimate goal now was to get to the Moon. She had information—a lot of information—that she believed the people there would want, and she didn't trust that information to any of the normal channels.

In fact, the longer she had been on this quest, the less she trusted channels at all.

"This planet is *settled*," Apaza said. "I mean, it's completely *established*. I'm not liking this at all, Judita."

They had somehow segued away from last names and titles in their conversations since their first month on this ship. They were colleagues, and Gomez decided they should act like it.

Especially since they kept the support staff on the *Green Dragon* specifically segregated from these main rooms.

The support staff was still pretty impressive. Gomez had hired an extra pilot, who had never been inside the Alliance before and had no family or ties here. She could pilot the ship if she had to—the *Green Dragon* was a medium-sized cruiser, with its own weapons system and a fairly good ability to mask its presence within the Alliance—but she didn't want to pilot the ship at all.

Still, she had learned its weapons systems, just in case, and she had encoded every high-level system to her voice and DNA prints. She did have a navigator and a chief weapons officer, as well as some people that Simiaar simply called "the muscle," glorified security guards who would protect Gomez and her team as long as she paid the guards to do so.

That was the diciest part of this plan—she hated paying people to do their jobs well. She really wanted them to volunteer and do the job because they believed in it. Hiring people to do a job for excellent pay meant they could get bought away if someone else offered them even better pay.

She worried about it, which was why she kept them away from the discussions she had with Zamal, Simiaar, and Apaza.

Sometimes she wished they hadn't come along, either. Oh, they were doing fantastic work, but Gomez felt responsible for them. And the deeper she was traveling into the Alliance, the more responsible she felt.

She worried that this entire mission—quest—trip—whatever she wanted to call it, could cost them their lives.

Especially now.

The floating screen showed the coordinates Gomez had found on an old ship. She, Simiaar, and Apaza had been back-tracing the ship's route from a planet called Epriccom in the Frontier all the way to its starting point inside the Alliance.

For some reason, she had expected that starting point to be some uninhabited part of some remote moon or a difficult-to-reach starbase.

She hadn't expected to find an industrial plant with a footprint so old that it looked like it had been in place for a couple of hundred years.

"Let's see this up close," Gomez said.

Apaza zoomed in on the coordinates. The buildings had a grayish look. They were rectangular and built up several stories. It appeared as though some of the buildings went deep underground, as well.

People swarmed the entire area—walking, talking, sitting in some grassy areas. Gomez supposed she could ask Apaza to go even closer, but she didn't.

"I guess the first thing we do," Gomez said, "is figure out what business this is and how long it's been on this location."

"Already on it," Apaza said.

"From the look of those buildings," Simiaar said, "it's been there longer than we would like."

Gomez looked at her. Simiaar did not look back, which was not a good sign. Usually Simiaar winked at her or smiled or had some kind of snide comment.

This industrial park unnerved Simiaar as much as it was unnerving Gomez.

Gomez shifted slightly. She realized that her right hand had tightened so much on her left wrist that she had twisted the skin. She let go, brought her hands forward, and looked at her left wrist. The skin was an ugly red where her fingers had dug in.

Nothing on this trip had gone as she expected. She had left the Frontier, initially planning to travel alone. Then Simiaar had convinced her not to try this by herself. Simiaar had helped her find the *Green Dragon*.

It had been easy to retrofit a forensics lab into the ship—a good lab, equal to the one on the *Stanley*. The *Green Dragon* had been a science vessel for one of the human Frontier communities—one of the communities that had hidden away from the Alliance—so the ship had all kinds of features that weren't common to Alliance ships.

The lab, the weapons system, even a small area in the cargo bay that changed environments independent of the rest of the ship, and could be locked up tightly. Apaza hadn't known what it was for, but Gomez had, right from the start.

It was used to imprison or kidnap other species and relocate them.

She hadn't removed it from the ship when it was retrofitted because she wasn't sure if she would need to arrest someone.

She could still do that, even though she had taken a leave of absence from her job. She was still Marshal Judita Gomez, a fact she had yet to play up on this trip.

"We're looking at a licensed cloning facility," Apaza said. "It's been on this site for at least two hundred years."

Simiaar looked over her shoulder at Gomez. Simiaar's brown eyes seemed even darker than usual. Was she frightened? Simiaar had expressed her concern about this mission from the very start.

And this mission had started—even though they hadn't known it at the time—nearly sixteen years ago.

With a bunch of clones.

"What does *licensed cloning facility* mean, exactly?" Simiaar asked.

"I don't know exactly," Apaza said. "I assume it means that if you want to clone yourself, you'd go here and get the clone made. It seems strange though. There's more to this facility than just growing clones."

Gomez was noticing that too. There seemed to be too many buildings for someone to simply create clones and have them removed when they had reached term. People took babies out of cloning facilities all the time.

"Are there fast-grow clones here?" she asked Apaza.

Fast-grow clones grew to full size in hours or days. They had severely diminished mental capacity, however, and were usually used for one kind of job, something that would often end in the clone's death. And that was if the fast-grow clones actually had a job to do.

Many of them were fast-grown for medical research reasons, creating certain kinds of enhancements, for example, or seeing what effect new alien environments had on unprotected humans.

"I would assume so," Apaza said, "but I see no evidence of it. I can search, but you didn't want me to do anything that would attract their attention."

"You're right. I don't want to attract their attention," Gomez said. "But let's not assume anything. Surely, you can easily access the history of this facility."

"Well, no," Apaza said. "That's why I'm using the word 'assume.' Nothing is easy here."

"Okay. I'm going to help." Simiaar sank into a chair far from Apaza's magic monstrosity. He had brought his own chair to the ship, and it did all kinds of things that Gomez believed chairs shouldn't do.

Apaza shot a glance at Gomez, which she translated as *don't let her, please.*

"What are you helping with?" Gomez asked, trying to keep her voice neutral.

"'Licensed cloning facility,'" Simiaar said. "I want to see if all human cloning facilities in the Alliance are licensed."

"Eh," Apaza grunted, which meant he hadn't thought of that. He was focusing on this facility. "Okay. Go for it."

Simiaar called up a second screen. It had the forensic lab logo on it, so she was going through her private links, the ones she used to research things in the lab.

Gomez and Apaza had helped her set this up when they first got the ship. Gomez in particular worried that Simiaar would get so deep in her research that she would forget which network she was using and bring attention to the *Green Dragon*, which was the last thing they wanted.

"Yep," Simiaar said. "Every cloning facility inside the Alliance—*human* cloning, which I assume this is—"

"It is," Apaza said, without looking at her. He was doing something else. Both of them made Gomez feel useless.

"So…" Simiaar snapped her fingers in front of Apaza's face. He started.

"Lashante," Gomez said warningly.

"I need his attention," Simiaar said.

"You had it already," Apaza said, sounding annoyed.

"Was the first thing you got on this facility that it was licensed?" Simiaar asked, ignoring his reaction.

"Yes," he said.

"Isn't that weird?" she asked.

He lifted his hands from the virtual keyboard that he was using, and turned slightly in his chair. "Now that you mention it, yeah, that's weird."

"See why I'm helping?" Simiaar asked Gomez.

Gomez didn't feel the need to answer. Instead, she was watching Apaza, who looked a little stunned.

"Why in the world would they trumpet that?" he asked.

"Maybe," Gomez said quietly, "we should find out."

26

NUUYOMA LOVED DOING UNDERCOVER WORK. HE CONSIDERED IT ONE OF the perks of his job. Or he used to. As acting marshal in charge, the regulations suggested he remain with the *Stanley* at all times.

Gomez had never stayed on the ship, and he didn't intend to, either. Besides, there was absolutely no one out this far to enforce regulations. If someone had to reprimand him for what he did out here on the Frontier, then he was clearly doing something wrong.

He did feel a little uncomfortable bringing Verstraete to *Starbase Human.* As the second in command, she should have remained on the *Stanley* while he went undercover, but she was also the only other person who knew the real reason behind this mission.

He had left Deputy Lera Maa in charge of the *Stanley.* Because he'd only had the ship a short time, he hadn't really chosen a third in charge. Instead he'd made his deputies work for the position. He was closing in on a choice, though, and if pushed, he would say that Maa was it. She was not just competent, but she put a lot of thought into everything she did.

He felt secure leaving the *Stanley* in her hands for a few days.

He and Verstraete had taken one of the unmarked shuttles to *Starbase Human.* They could change the registration on the shuttle, which didn't look a lot different from shuttles that traveled from large cargo vessels to starbases with small docking rings.

At the moment, the shuttle's registration marked it as part of a fleet of ships, all of which moved merchandise from one part of the Frontier to another. The fleet didn't exist, but he doubted anyone would probe deeply enough to find out.

He and Verstraete were posing as a couple, primarily because it was easier. They also claimed to be on a short vacation from the ship, here on personal business.

The personal business was his. He'd been clear about that from the moment they bought a suite in the starbase's best hotel. He wanted to talk to anyone who might know what happened thirty-five years ago— the day his father died.

He'd already gone to the base's "historian," a kid who knew a lot about the sector, but very little about the history of the starbase itself. Verstraete had talked to a few of the bartenders and a restaurant owner, trying to track down the oldest businesses to see if something had moved from the original *Starbase Human* to this one. But she hadn't gotten much, either.

Nuuyoma and Verstraete were sitting in the nicest restaurant on the starbase—and the most expensive—sharing a quiet dinner. They hadn't decided how long they would ask questions, and that was something they needed to decide.

But Nuuyoma wanted food other than the kind he could get on the ship and he didn't mind using Alliance money to pay for it (even if he had moved it to an untraceable account). He hadn't eaten well in a long time.

Fortunately, this restaurant wasn't about the view. There actually was no view; it was in the very center of the starbase. Everyone had to walk around it and its multiple entrances whenever they crossed the middle of the base.

The maître d' informed them that the upper levels were for established customers, and she implied that those customers paid a premium for that space. She also implied that Nuuyoma and Verstraete would never qualify for that space.

The maître d' had the same kind of snobbish attitude that so many human employees of upscale restaurants had all over the known universe. They seemed to know that their job was superfluous. It could be done better by an android or a floating menu tray, but the humans were there to show that the restaurant could afford to pay for actual human service, something that so many wealthy people seemed to value for a reason that Nuuyoma never understood.

The snobby maître d' gave Nuuyoma and Verstraete a table in the very center of the restaurant's main floor. The table felt uncomfortable, people walking past, wait staff hurrying by. Nuuyoma felt like he was sitting in the middle of the base's market (unimaginatively called Mercado).

The lack of privacy should have driven him away; it would have driven most people off. But he felt oddly secure here, even having a relatively private conversation. Some of that was because he had spent the last fifteen years on board ships. Privacy was possible, just not something he experienced more than a few times per day.

Both he and Verstraete were tired from asking questions of people who didn't seem to know what they were talking about. He wanted to relax. He had ordered a dish he rarely saw outside of Earth's solar system—ogbono soup served with fufu.

Verstraete wrinkled her nose when she saw it; the soup was thick, orange, and lumpy. The fufu didn't help. He picked pieces out of the fufu, rolled it in his fingers, and dipped it in the soup. The fufu had been made with something that tasted like plantain, although it had been so long since he'd eaten plantain, he wasn't certain. He was certain that the meat in the ogbono soup, which tasted vaguely like goat, wasn't goat, nor was it anything he'd ever eaten before.

Still, the soup, with its chili pepper, wild mango nut, and palm oil base, had all the flavors of home.

Verstraete had ordered some kind of dumpling, deep fried and almost colorless. She also ordered fruit, which actually looked better than anything else on her plate; clearly, the fruit had come from some kind of greenhouse or growing unit on the base itself.

"I say we give this two more days," she said softly.

They were being careful with their conversation, saying nothing that would reveal who they were if someone were listening in, and yet still managing to have a good conversation about the base itself.

"Two days is probably too long." Nuuyoma was beginning to feel that the base was a waste of time. It was clearly a place for transients.

Maybe the information he'd had about the original base was right: no one had survived the explosions.

Verstraete opened her mouth, then closed it and frowned. "We're never going to come this far out again," she said, but she added on their encrypted links, *We traveled months to get here and you want to leave after one day?*

"I'm sure there are other places that might have information," he said, answering both of her points.

"Like what?" she asked, covering her fried dumpling thing with some kind of greenish orange berry he didn't recognize.

"There are a lot of inhabited moons and resorts near here," he said. "Maybe someone had evacuated to them."

She shook her head. "Explosions tend to drive people away."

"No kidding." A man pulled a chair over to the table and joined them.

Nuuyoma was about to protest when he took a good look at the man. He was older—maybe ninety, one hundred—but not as old as some humans could get. He seemed athletic and in shape. He was thin, his face a strange ruddy color that seemed to be part of his age.

His hair—what was left of it—was white and gold; his skull, visible through the thinning hair, was covered with age spots. He had aged oddly. He didn't have a lot of wrinkles, but his skin bulged in some places and looked sunken in others.

He folded his hands on the empty place setting. His hands were big and powerful, but cramped as if he had some kind of affliction. They were also covered with tufts of blond hair.

His gaze met Nuuyoma's, and Nuuyoma started. The man had eyes so startlingly blue they seemed to look right through him.

Nuuyoma's breath caught. He activated one of his chips and commanded it to do a facial recognition search. But he doubted he needed it. He could do this search on his own.

The man reminded him of an old version of the clones who had blown up the Moon.

"Forgive me for intruding," the man said. "I understand you want to know who killed your father."

What the hell…? Verstraete sent on their encrypted private link.

Nuuyoma sent the image of the Moon clones back, but didn't respond verbally. He wanted her to know there seemed to be a connection.

"I've always been confused about his death," Nuuyoma said, letting his voice tremble with a bit of emotion. "I grew up in the Alliance, and there, the maps show that the old starbase still exists."

The man shrugged. "A mistake. They never corrected the coordinates when this base was built. The bases have the same names, you know."

Nuuyoma picked up his napkin and wiped off his fingers. He had to be careful as to how he played this.

"I was never really sure what the old starbase was called," he said. "I found three different names. This base seems to only have one."

The man smiled. His eyes actually twinkled. He had a charisma so strong that Nuuyoma felt the urge to smile with him.

"This base has many names, but only one in Standard." The man's smile widened. "The other names come from non-humans. They hate it here."

"I thought they weren't welcome here," Verstraete said.

The man looked at her. His gaze raked over her, as if he were seeing her for the first time.

"Well, they aren't," he said, "but you can't really bar them. I mean, you can. The starbase is a law unto itself. That's one of the benefits of existing outside of the Alliance, and in this part of space. But barring them just isn't practical. So many ships have mixed crews, and then there are the ships that have to dock for medical or emergency reasons. I know that the base has tried to ban all aliens before, and it simply hasn't worked."

He spoke calmly, as if the policy didn't bother him. Maybe it didn't. It bothered Nuuyoma. But he had grown up in the Alliance, where species mixed and spent a lot of time together.

He valued that about the Alliance.

"Still," the man said, "the people in charge make it pretty clear that the non-humans are here on suffrage."

"Are you one of the people in charge?" Verstraete asked.

The man laughed. The sound made the hair stand up on the back of Nuuyoma's neck. He'd heard that sound countless times before, when he'd been investigating PierLuigi Frémont. Frémont used to laugh a lot, and with great enjoyment. Often, with inappropriate enjoyment.

Nuuyoma took a very shallow but long breath, trying to keep himself calm. He didn't look at Verstraete, to see if she had had a reaction to that laugh.

She wasn't as familiar with Frémont, but some aspects of him were hard to miss.

"I'm not in charge of this starbase," the man said to Verstraete. "I have other interests."

"You came to talk with me about my father," Nuuyoma said, bringing the conversation back.

"You say you don't know what happened to the original *Starbase Human*," the man said. "You do know that it exploded."

"I did see footage." Nuuyoma threaded both horror and sadness into his voice. "The base didn't just explode. It exploded many times."

"Killing thousands," the man said. "They believe no one survived."

"They?" Verstraete asked.

The man shrugged. "Whomever you ask. No one knows for certain."

"Do you?" Nuuyoma asked.

"I know that many people died. I heard rumors that a woman survived, but I've never tried to verify." The man leaned back to signal a waiter. One stopped immediately, as if the man were very important. "Pakora."

Verstraete blinked at him, probably thinking he was giving a command, rather than demanding a snack. Nuuyoma had grown up eating pakora as well, and most of the people he knew in the FSS hadn't. The menu on the EAFS ships was very limited.

Nuuyoma didn't know if the man's order was simply because the food was served here or if he made that particular order just to unnerve Nuuyoma.

The man's very presence was unnerving Nuuyoma. It didn't take a food order to do it.

The waiter had nodded and fled, as if he didn't want to interact with the man. Verstraete's gaze briefly met Nuuyoma's. She found the interaction strange as well.

"You make it sound like you do know something about the old base," Nuuyoma said as the man turned to face him.

"That footage is shocking, isn't it?" the man asked.

"Yes," Verstraete said as Nuuyoma added softly, "You have no idea."

"Oh, I have some." The man snapped his fingers at another waiter and asked for water with lemon. The waiter glared at him, but said that he would bring it as he hurried past.

"You were on the base, then, when this happened?" Verstraete asked the old man.

Nuuyoma closed a fist beneath the table. He wanted to control the questioning, not have Verstraete do it. Still, he didn't communicate to her on the links. Too often, people communicating on links paused too long or looked at each other in the wrong way, letting the people *not* on the links know they were being discussed.

"No," the man said. "But I lost friends there."

"Friends?" Nuuyoma asked. "Not family?"

The question was a risky one. A lot of clones believed the other clones of the same original were family.

The man tilted his head slightly. He was about to say something when the second waiter set down a tall glass of water, with a bright yellow lemon slice floating on the top of it.

The man slid the glass close, his expression changing slightly, as if he had caught himself before he made an indiscretion.

"Not family," the man said softly. "And, truthfully, not really friends. People I knew."

Verstraete nodded. "When so many died, it would be—"

"You know what happened on the Moon?" the man asked, turning his chair so that his back was to Verstraete. He was cutting her out of the conversation entirely.

You okay with him talking just to you? She sent.

Yeah. Record it if you can, Nuuyoma sent back.

"Which moon?" Nuuyoma asked.

"Earth's," the man said.

Nuuyoma shook his head. "I don't care about the Alliance."

"Hmm," the man said. Something in his tone put Nuuyoma on guard. Had the man figured out who they were?

The man sighed. "You've heard of designer criminal clones?"

Nuuyoma frowned. He hadn't expected the man to discuss clones, not this soon in the conversation.

"Yes," Nuuyoma said. "I'm not sure how that relates."

The first waiter slammed down a plate of pakora. The individual pieces were oddly shaped, which meant it had been made from scratch using what looked like cabbage as its main ingredient. The waiter also set down a bowl of tamarind chutney that seemed as pretty and fresh as the fruit on Verstraete's meal.

The waiter moved on without speaking.

The man touched one of the pieces, then moved his hand back as if the fried exterior was too hot.

He pushed the plate away. The food was steaming.

"Clones attacked the Earth's Moon several months ago," he said. "They blew it up the way that they blew up the old starbase."

Nuuyoma blinked. He didn't have to work hard to be surprised. He was surprised that a man who was clearly a clone of PierLuigi Frémont was sitting across from him, telling him that clones had blown up the Moon.

He would have thought the man would want to hide that.

"Clones," Nuuyoma said, as he processed what he heard. "Blew up the starbase."

The man nodded. "It was accidental. They weren't supposed to destroy the starbase. They were supposed to destroy a part of the starbase."

"You know this how?" Nuuyoma asked.

The man smiled. He slid the chutney toward him, then put a hand over the pakora. He looked at his food as if it were more interesting than Nuuyoma.

"I knew about the planning sessions," the man said.

"Were you a part of them?" Nuuyoma asked before he could stop himself. That was a marshal question, not an I-lost-my-father question. But the man didn't seem to notice or perhaps he didn't care.

"In the beginning," the man said. "Before they decided to use fast-grow clones."

"I thought designer clones were created for a particular job," Nuuyoma said. "You're saying—?"

"What I'm telling you doesn't contradict that," the man said. "The job was supposed to be simple: take over the starbase, destroy one small part of it, and keep the people in charge out of the way."

Nuuyoma frowned. He suddenly hated his undercover role. He would ask different questions as a marshal than he could ask now.

So he settled for "What happened?"

"As near as I can tell," the man said, "they did exactly what they were told. They just didn't do it smartly, because they weren't smart. They were fast-grow. They had the brains of children."

"With augmented programming, I assume," Nuuyoma said. "I mean, children can't—"

"Yes, augmented programming. But augmented programming doesn't give anyone the ability to reason." The man actually sounded irritated. He pulled his plate closer and picked up one piece gingerly with his thumb and forefinger. He bit the edge of the piece, then nodded as if he approved, and dipped it in the chutney.

"I'm still confused," Nuuyoma said. "You're saying they were wrong for the job, but they did the job."

"I'm saying that they kept the authorities out of the way by killing them, not by holding them under threat. Then they planted the bombs too close to the jury-rigged physical plant, which then set off some chain-reaction explosions."

"You know this for certain?" Nuuyoma asked. He sounded suspicious. He *was* suspicious. He suspected he would have been suspicious even if he had been searching for information on his father.

"Yes, I do," the man said.

"Because you were there," Nuuyoma said flatly.

The man shook his head. "Because I got a message from my cohorts, saying I should join them in blame."

"Blame?" Nuuyoma asked. "For killing so many people?"

He didn't have to fake the indignation. He felt it.

"For screwing up the mission. We—they—believed it would work with fast-grow. I did not."

"What was the mission?" Nuuyoma asked. "What got my father killed?"

The man popped another piece into his mouth. Then he smiled. "What was the mission?" he repeated.

Something in his tone made Nuuyoma's heart pound. The man didn't ask the one question he'd been expecting: *Who was your father?*

Maybe the man didn't need it. Nuuyoma had a name of someone from the Alliance who had disappeared in this part of the Frontier about the same time, and he was pretending that the name belonged to his father. He had used that name throughout the station.

Maybe this man had heard it.

He certainly had known that Nuuyoma was looking for information on his father's death.

"The mission was pretty simple," the man said. "There was a black market trading off the Mercado in that part of the base. The market made a lot of money in the kind of goods that, well, aren't really goods. More like services. Things the Alliance would frown on."

"You're being deliberately vague," Nuuyoma said.

"Indeed." The man ate another piece, his fingers dark red with chutney sauce.

Nuuyoma's meal had cooled and congealed. He no longer felt the urge to eat any of it. Verstraete had finished her food, however, since she couldn't participate in the conversation.

"All you need to know is that some places out here still use items for currency," the man said. "Things you can't find on a network or in links. Actual physical items. And there were a lot of them on the base at the time."

"It was a theft gone wrong?" Nuuyoma asked.

Seriously? Verstraete sent him, as if she couldn't contain herself.

"It was," the man said. "And considering how much money had been invested in those clones, you can do the math. Figure out that entire mission probably cost ten percent of the take, maybe less. Or would have, if it had succeeded."

Nuuyoma sucked in air. He was stunned. He hadn't thought of the reason for the explosions at all. "And you were part of this?"

And the man was so casually admitting it? That stunned Nuuyoma, too.

"In the beginning," the man said. "Before the fast-grows. I thought they were a mistake."

Ask him how they would have pulled off the theft without them, Verstraete sent.

"You blame the fast-grows for everything that went wrong," Nuuyoma said.

"I blame my cohorts," the man said. "They thought it would be easy. It wasn't, and it killed them."

"They were on the base, too?" Nuuyoma asked.

"They were supervising, until things went wrong," the man said. "Then they tried to get off the base. They contacted me from their ship. Apparently it blew up on the docking ring."

"Apparently?" Nuuyoma asked.

The man nodded. "There are rumors that they made it out, and then their ship exploded."

"Rumors," Verstraete said, probably because she couldn't stay quiet. "No one knows?"

The man let out a small snide laugh. "This place is very far from anything. For things to be observed, someone has to be around to observe them."

"It just seems to me that you're working on some conjecture here," Verstraete said.

The man moved his chair so that he could see her.

"Here's what I know," he said, his words sharp and short, but also soft. "I know that you are both with the Earth Alliance's Frontier Security Service. I know you're searching for answers to the Moon bombing, and I know I have some of those answers. I think we can trade."

Nuuyoma let out a small breath. Had they made mistakes? Probably. He didn't know enough about this sector to know if they had missed something in their prep. Or maybe the base had such fantastic security, they could see through the fake identification he had given the ship.

"Trade what?" Nuuyoma asked.

"My information for the whereabouts of one person," the man said.

"We don't do things like that," Verstraete said.

Nuuyoma held up a hand. The FSS did a lot of things—Gomez used to do a lot of things—that weren't always regulation.

"Let's talk," he said to the old man, "and I'll see what I can do."

27

DESPITE WHAT SHE LET THE OTHERS BELIEVE, GOMEZ WAS GOOD AT RESEARCH as well. She had planned to do a lot of the work on this trip alone, before Apaza and Simiaar had joined her.

"Found the company's name yet?" she asked Apaza.

"It…no." He was looking at a floating screen. "I know what it used to be, not what it is."

Gomez nodded. "Let me try something."

She sat down in front of three non-networked computers in the room. Apaza had initially wanted them in different rooms, away from the networked computers, but the *Green Dragon* didn't have the space for that.

He had a non-networked computer in his tiny room down in the crew quarters—a room he really wasn't using.

Gomez had a non-networked system in her captain's suite, and none of the computers in Simiaar's actual lab were networked, although the one in the entrance to the lab was.

Apaza called these three non-networked systems the half-networked computers, because he claimed that he could access them through a networked system easily.

But you'd have to know they existed to do that, Simiaar had said to him back when the systems were set up.

There is that, he had replied.

So we don't discuss it at all, Simiaar had said. *Problem solved.*

Gomez never thought that really solved the problem, but it was a good half measure, and one she was taking advantage of now.

She called up one of Apaza's virtual keyboards—he thought they were safer than an actual keyboard. Simiaar didn't, which was why the ship carried both—and sat down in a nearby chair.

Gomez entered one of the many databases the group had downloaded before they left on this trip. She had downloaded this database herself, because she had been the only one of the three of them who had access to it.

She entered the coordinates and leaned back as the floating screen vanished for several seconds. With this database, nothing showed on that screen until the requested information showed up.

" 'Licensed cloning facility!' " Simiaar sounded triumphant. "In this context, it meant a facility that the government uses to create its own clones."

"Why would the government need clones?" Apaza asked.

Gomez didn't answer him. He didn't have the clearance to know. And then she smiled at herself. He didn't have any clearance any more. Both she and Simiaar had taken leaves of absence, but he had quit outright.

"Product testing," Simiaar said tightly. "A lot of them work tough jobs that need human involvement, but no one wants to risk original humans."

"Like what?" Apaza asked.

"Some types of mining. Agriculture in some rather dangerous environments." Simiaar shrugged. Gomez knew that movement well. It meant that Simiaar did not approve of what she was discussing, but she wasn't going to say that aloud.

"I thought that's what androids were for," Apaza said.

"No matter how hard we try," Gomez said, "we can't get artificial intelligence to work exactly like human intelligence."

"And why try," Simiaar said rhetorically, "when we have easily available and cheap clones who do think like humans, even though they're not human."

"But they are," Apaza said. "They're—"

"Don't sell me on this one," Simiaar said. "I don't make the rules."

Gomez was glad Simiaar had shut down the discussion. They'd had it before. Simiaar hated the fact that the Earth Alliance did not consider human clones to be actual human beings. Those laws were an outgrowth of ancient practices within the Alliance, an excuse to get work done without recordable loss of "human" life.

"So," Apaza said, "this is a government cloning facility. Does anyone else find that weird?"

Gomez didn't answer him. She was already deep inside her database. The facility no longer had a name. It had a number. There were hundreds of these facilities scattered throughout the Alliance, and that was fewer than the amount there had been when the Alliance was newer and smaller.

A lot of these facilities had existed then to supply bodies—almost literally—to military front lines, places where androids, bots, and military machines did not function well. One of the many reasons that Alliance law still refused to recognize human clones as actual human beings was to preserve the use of those clones in military situations, situations that would have required a lot more safeguards and legal protections if actual human beings (as defined by the law) had gone into battle.

"Judita?" Simiaar said in a tone that implied she had tried to speak to Gomez before. "You know something we don't?"

She knew a lot that they didn't, but she didn't say that.

"The history of the facility," Gomez said, as if she were answering Simiaar's question. "This place has been around a lot longer than two hundred years. It's just been at this location for two hundred years."

Apaza turned in that miraculous chair of his. "How long?"

"I don't know," Gomez said, and by that, she really meant, *I'm not looking that up*. "It's been a government facility from the beginning, and it has made millions of clones for the Alliance."

"I don't get it," Simiaar said. "If that's the case, then how come this place is churning out clones of PierLuigi Frémont?"

"I don't know," Gomez said, "and the information I have here doesn't make it seem that obvious."

The military used cloning facilities closer to the Alliance's borders. There were also some near what the Alliance termed trouble spots, places where humans and some of the other Alliance species did not get along.

But here, near the center of the Alliance, none of that applied.

This facility was being used for something else entirely, and no matter how she approached her background research, she couldn't tell what that was.

Gomez leaned back for a moment and frowned at the screen. As she did so, it went dark, just like it was supposed to.

Something here was even more protected that the usual information she would seek when she was on the Frontier.

"You want me to look at that?" Apaza asked her.

He knew what kind of database she was digging in.

It probably wouldn't hurt to have him do it, and yet she worried about it. Nothing was as secure on this ship as she wanted it to be.

Besides, she'd been inside databases like this one before. Much of the information was unavailable through the standard methods. Either she had to have access to a shadow database or she had to be invited to get the information, often from the place she was trying to find out about.

This cloning facility was being used, and it was being used by the Alliance government, but for what reason, she didn't exactly know.

"Judita," Simiaar said, "what's going on?"

Gomez logged out of the database and shut the entire computer down. Then she stood.

"I need to think," she said, and walked out of the room.

28

"SEND HER AWAY," THE MAN SAID TO NUUYOMA.

I don't think that's a good idea, Verstraete sent.

The man ate another bite of his pakora. He watched Nuuyoma as he did so. He knew they were communicating on their links.

The restaurant seemed unusually loud, or maybe Nuuyoma had started noticing the noise again. People laughing, dishes clanging. He couldn't remember the last time he'd been in a starbase restaurant without non-humans also eating something.

"It's all right, Chepi," Nuuyoma said without looking at her.

No, she sent.

He wasn't going to respond on the links. He had an odd feeling that they'd been compromised. He wasn't sure why.

"There's an open table not far from here," he said, nodding toward it. "Wait there."

"Elián," she said.

He looked at her, his expression serious. He wished he could talk to her on the links, but he wasn't going to. He hoped she understood that he wasn't kidding around.

He didn't want to give her any orders, not aloud and not on the links.

Finally, she slapped her hands against the table, making the man's water skitter across the white cloth. Nuuyoma's unfinished dinner bounced.

She didn't say anything, though. She just stood up and crossed to the other table. As she sat down, a waiter looked agitated and then hurried toward her.

Nuuyoma almost smiled. She was breaking the restaurant's rules, and the system wasn't set up for it.

"All right," he said to the man. "Tell me what's really going on."

The man leaned forward so that his misshapen face wasn't far from Nuuyoma's. "I want to know where Takara Hamasaki is."

"I've never heard of Takara Hamasaki," Nuuyoma said.

"Fair enough," the man said. "She disappeared into the Alliance. I want you to find her."

Nuuyoma did smile this time. "I don't track Disappeareds. My work is on the Frontier."

"There has to be records of her. The Alliance is good at keeping records." The man sounded intent.

"What's your interest in her?" Nuuyoma said.

The man folded his hands together. "She's the survivor."

"Of what?" Nuuyoma asked.

"Of the starbase explosion, what we've just been discussing," the man said.

"I thought you didn't know if anyone survived."

"My cohorts told me she had escaped. Then their ship blew up away from the base."

"So you say," Nuuyoma said.

"I know. I was speaking to them when it blew."

"But they could have been on the docking ring," Nuuyoma said.

"Then why would they tell me they were going after her?" the man asked.

"Why were they going after her?" Nuuyoma asked.

The man leaned back. He let out a long sigh, as if he were contemplating the question.

"Because," he said quietly. "Back then, we didn't want anyone to know we existed."

"We?" Nuuyoma asked. "By 'we' do you mean the theft ring you had put together or the clones of PierLuigi Frémont?"

The man's smile was small. "Both."

"You're clearly not fast-grow," Nuuyoma said. "Why were you created?"

The man's cheeks became even ruddier. "One thing at a time."

"You want to trade information," Nuuyoma said. "You can't be coy with me and expect my cooperation."

The man set his plate on top of Verstraete's. One of the waiters came by and whisked them both away.

"If you want to trade, you need to tell me a few things," Nuuyoma said. He felt like he was talking to a wall.

The man watched him.

"You need to tell me why you want to find this woman," Nuuyoma said.

"She killed my cohorts," the man said.

"Whom you disagreed with and might not have liked," Nuuyoma said.

"That's beside the point," the man said. "You will want to speak to her as well."

That was true. If she was the sole survivor of the explosions, Nuuyoma would want to talk with her.

"If she's in the Alliance, she's out of your reach," Nuuyoma said.

The man shrugged. "It would be nice to know that."

"This happened thirty-five years ago," Nuuyoma said.

"Indeed," the man said.

Nuuyoma sighed. He looked over at Verstraete. She would tell him to ignore this, that it was blackmail and that it wouldn't help anything. But if he could get the information *and* protect the woman (if she was still alive), then he would help solve the Anniversary Day bombings.

"What do I get if I find this information for you?" Nuuyoma asked.

"You will know several things," the man said. "You will know who created us. You will know who manages the DNA now. And you will be able to find the criminals who tried to destroy your Moon."

The echo of Nuuyoma's thoughts almost unnerved him. "Why would you tell me that?"

"It costs me nothing," the man said.

"And why won't you tell me now?" Nuuyoma said.

"Because it's time I handle the final details of my life." The man swept a hand over his body. "I am decaying. My cells are breaking down. The technique used to make me wasn't that sophisticated, and enhancements don't work as you can tell from my face. I would like to settle my accounts."

"By getting revenge on a woman who may or may not have killed two people you didn't like?"

"They weren't just people," the man said. "They were, as some clones call it, my siblings."

Nuuyoma nodded. That detail didn't surprise him. "But you didn't care about them."

"I didn't say that," the man said. "I didn't agree with them."

"And all those fast-grows? Were they your siblings as well?"

The man's smile was even smaller than before. "They were made from the same DNA," he said. "But they were not from my unit. They were failures."

The word *failure* made Nuuyoma start. That was the word Gomez had repeated, the word the clones from Epriccom had used to justify the murder of their other "siblings."

Did that usage go all the way back to PierLuigi Frémont, the original? Nuuyoma didn't know.

"I won't be able to get you real-time information," Nuuyoma said. "I can only search through our databases as they existed about a year ago."

"I know that," the man said. "Death records will exist. Tax records. Addresses, all of that stuff your Alliance does for its members. You will get me close."

"You'll be going into the Alliance to get your revenge?" Nuuyoma asked.

"I didn't say that," the man said. "But what I do want are the actual documents. I do not want you to lie to me about her existence."

"I would like the same from you," Nuuyoma said.

The man nodded, once. Nuuyoma had the odd sense that he had just finalized the deal.

"You never told me your name," Nuuyoma said.

"It's not relevant," the man said.

"Ah, but it is," Nuuyoma said.

The man folded his hands together again. "Here, they call me Luis. I do not use a surname."

"What do you call yourself?" Nuuyoma asked.

"I," the man said.

Nuuyoma shook his head. "If you want to work with me, then you will tell me your name. Your real name. Your given name."

"I have no given name," the man said. "But my peers knew me as One Of One Direct."

"One Of One Direct?" Nuuyoma asked. "What does that mean?"

"The first from the direct line created from the DNA of the original. I am the first made from that line." The man spoke quietly.

"How do I confirm that?" Nuuyoma asked.

"You cannot," the man said. "On some things, you'll have to take my word."

"And on some things, you'll have to take mine," Nuuyoma said.

"Find Takara Hamasaki for me," the man said. "And I will make sure you have everything you need for your investigation."

He stood up. He was taller than Nuuyoma had expected.

"I will meet you here, at this table, tomorrow night. I will only talk with you. You may bring as many friends as you like, but only you will sit at this table. Are we clear?"

"Yes," Nuuyoma said.

The man nodded once. Then he left. Verstraete stood. As she walked over, Nuuyoma leaned back in his chair. He watched the man thread his way through the throng of people.

If what that man said was true—if he was the first clone from the original—then he might not be as old as Nuuyoma thought. PierLuigi Frémont died fifty-five years ago. If he was cloned after death, then that man was only a decade older than Nuuyoma.

The man looked ancient in comparison.

Either that, or clones of Frémont had been made long before the man died.

"Well?" Verstraete asked as she sat down.

"Well," Nuuyoma said. "We have some digging to do."

29

GOMEZ CLOSED THE DOOR TO THE LITTLE INFORMATION ROOM AND STOOD in the corridor for a moment.

Superficially, her choices seemed easy. She could let Apaza search the database. She could let him search all the available databases, which would call attention to the *Green Dragon* and to them.

She could do some more research herself in that database.

Or she could go to the surface as herself, get a tour of the facility, and tell them she was thinking of permanent retirement, and wanted to have a good, secured position inside the Alliance. In other words, she would be asking them for a job.

If she did that, if she went below and identified herself while telling a lie, she put everything at risk. But she had no idea if anyone would investigate her or her story. After all, she had a marshal's badge and she had taken a leave of absence, something high-ranking officials in any secret service did when they were investigating a new position.

She had enough credibility to make this work—if she did it right.

If she did it wrong, then she jeopardized everything she had already done.

She decided to walk while she thought about this.

She used to walk the ship when on the *EAFS Stanley*, but that ship was the size of some cities. *The Green Dragon* was small, lean, and fast, able to pivot in seconds instead of minutes or hours, great in a fight and even better at escaping from a bad situation.

But it meant that walking the ship took her a little over an hour instead of several. Often, she wouldn't make it around the *Stanley* at all, stopping to talk to crew or someone who needed help with a problem or a discovery.

On the *Green Dragon*, the crew stayed out of her way. They let her walk. They understood that she wanted to keep a hard line between them and the four former members of the *Stanley*.

The problem, she realized as she moved, was that she was risking a lot, and yet she wasn't risking as much as she had initially thought she would.

The *Green Dragon* had three distinct levels, with a fourth and fifth that mostly contained equipment. A dummy bubble covered a fake cockpit on the top of the ship. According to the seller (and the material Simiaar researched on the ship), almost every single time a ship in the *Dragon's* class would get attacked, the bubble would get hit first.

That enabled the *Dragon* to target the weapons systems on the attacking ship without receiving a damaging hit.

Gomez liked that feature. Sometimes, when she walked the ship, she walked up to the dummy cockpit and stared at the models inside. It wasn't secure enough to hold environment, and going inside the dummy cockpit wasn't recommended in transit, so she would just look, wishing ships could be designed like this in actuality, because riding in an open-windowed cockpit seemed to combine the best parts of space with that moment of increased adrenaline that she always used to get when she walked into a situation in an unknown culture.

She missed her job. She would love to return to it, if she could.

The upper level housed the quarters. Crew quarters were actually below decks, but since she had hired such a minimal crew, she had given them the larger guest quarters on this level.

She had the captain's suite at one end of the corridor. Simiaar had the second largest suite on the other side of the corridor. Even though Gomez had offered Apaza the third largest suite, he had opted for a room in the actual below decks crew quarters, with a built-in bunk and barely enough room to move.

I'll be spending all my time in the information room anyway, he had said. *I just need a place to shower.*

It had taken her two days to realize that he hadn't said he would sleep down below. He just stored his clothes there, and cleaned up there.

Besides clothing, the only things he had brought on board were equipment (some of it self-designed) and that amazing chair like none she had ever seen. It bolted into the floor, like all regulation chairs did on this ship, but the nanofibers the chair was composed of transformed into a hard wood-like chair if he wanted it or the most comfortable bed she had ever touched.

Apaza had let her examine the chair before she allowed it onto her ship; after it had been bolted in, she hadn't touched it—although she had walked in on Apaza sleeping on it more than once.

She preferred her four-room suite, although she didn't enter it at the moment. She needed the walk. The exercise room on the crew level simply didn't help her think as much as the changing scenery on the ship did.

Her anger at the Alliance wasn't just because no one had paid attention to her reports and requests concerning the events on Epriccom. She figured that things went awry often within all parts of the Earth Alliance. There was simply too much information and not enough people to process it.

Plus, as Apaza told her, much of the information wasn't easily available through links and the usual nets. It took computer specialists with incredible skills and the ability to open some back doors that should have remained locked just to find some of the information that Gomez needed for this (and other) investigations.

After Anniversary Day, she had initially blamed herself for the fact that the information about the Frémont enclave hadn't gone through the proper channels and prevented the attack on Earth's Moon.

And then she started to investigate what went wrong. She decided to start with the injured clones. She was able to confirm that one clone, named TwoZero, had died just after she had seen him. So had the other surviving clones.

They were deliberately erased, as if they had never been.

Other things she had discovered in her early investigation led back to the Alliance, and that was when she realized that she had to investigate off-books, because someone—or many someones—were preventing this information from getting out.

But most of this trip hadn't panned out the way she expected. Gathering information, never easy, was proving terribly elusive—and she couldn't blame Simiaar or Apaza for that.

Some of it was her own fear.

She tried to investigate how TwoZero died, but stopped the moment she realized she would need to use her position as a marshal in the Frontier Security Service to get inside any system.

Apaza was able to get some information, but nothing they needed. Gomez knew if she went back to the prison system in her capacity as the arresting officer for TwoZero, she might set off every possible red flag.

She felt that she had done that before she took the leave. Simiaar believed that the leave of absence actually protected Gomez from the idea that she was investigating anything.

The moment Gomez showed up in any Earth Alliance facility in any kind of official capacity, someone—or those someones—would notice her, and would probably try to kill her.

Her stomach clenched.

She wandered down the corridor, then took the steps to below decks, skipping two entire decks so that she could walk past the cargo area, the crew quarters, and the exercise area. Simiaar's lab was one deck above her, and Gomez didn't want to stop there.

Even Peyla—the Peyti home world—had brought its own share of disappointments. She had tried to talk with Uzven, the Peyti-Eaufasse translator who had mistranslated the initial request from the clone on Epriccom.

Uzven had been deliberately obtuse about the clone's request, later claiming that all clones should have asylum from humans. Uzven had even tried to contact the clone once it was imprisoned.

Gomez had thought fifteen years ago that Uzven was involved in something nefarious. After she had seen the Anniversary Day clones, she believed Uzven was involved.

But Uzven remained cagey to the end, claiming that Eaufasse to Peytin to Standard translations were bound to create errors, that Gomez had been wrong in trying to read any more into the mistakes.

She had disliked Uzven fifteen years before, and she had disliked it again when she saw it on Peyla.

Nothing had changed—not even the amount of information it would share.

The way she saw it, this cloning facility was her last chance to get additional information before she arrived at the Moon.

Either she went into this cloning facility in her capacity as a marshal with the Security Service, or she let Apaza investigate it.

And that was what she needed to decide.

Because if she went in, alone, she might not come out. If she did come out, and then an order came through to stop her, the *Green Dragon* had to escape this area and head to Earth's Moon so fast that no one could catch them.

At some point, she would have to take another risk.

She stopped in the exercise area. Small, built-in holochambers for running and rowing and all sorts of Good-For-You exercises. One small holochamber that could be filled with water so that someone could swim if they wanted to.

She had tried it just once, and decided that it wasn't for her. Simiaar had laughed at her for even trying, and Apaza thought exercise was something the human race should have banned by now. None of the crew used that chamber either, so near Peyla they had drained the chamber, so they wouldn't be carrying the extra weight.

She put a hand on the door to her favorite holochamber. Maybe she should run on the program set up for the mountains of Edgiofor. It was a tough workout and always blocked out her thoughts.

But she didn't need them blocked out.

She needed to figure out if she was taking that last step.

She took her hand off the chamber door and stood for a moment in the small exercise room.

Her tiny team had done a lot of work already. They had found out about the enclave of clones, they had traced the ship that left Epriccom fifteen years ago to Ohksmyte, and they had taken a lot of trace from that ship.

On Ohksmyte they had learned that clones had flown the ship away from the enclave as the enclave was destroying itself, and the ship had been left behind. They learned that the ship was made in the Alliance to distribute to criminals, and instead had been flown directly to the enclave.

They had traced it to the building facility, found other ships that had left and gone into the Frontier, and by all appearances had never been abandoned as they were supposed to have been.

They had even, through Apaza's wizardry and some of the information they had gathered off that abandoned ship, found the registration for the ship that had colonized the enclave and traced that ship's path throughout the Alliance.

Because of that ship, they were orbiting Hétique. All of the information they had found had led them here.

Gomez clasped her hands behind her back and paced the room itself, going around the holochambers and using them like an obstacle course.

It took time to get to the Moon from Epriccom. Months. Traveling in the Frontier took even longer.

She hadn't gathered nearly enough information, but she would wager that the authorities on the Moon—those not involved with the Earth Alliance—did not know anything about the enclave or the fact that there were other clones.

They didn't know about the clone factory here at Hétique.

Maybe all of that would be enough to get their investigation on the right track.

"What are you doing?"

Gomez jumped, startled. Simiaar stood in the doorway of the exercise room, arms crossed.

"I needed to make a decision as to how to proceed with that clone factory," Gomez said.

"You could have discussed it with me." Simiaar spoke softly, then looked over her shoulder, obviously trying to see if anyone was coming down the hallway.

"This is a decision I needed to make myself," Gomez said.

Anger crossed Simiaar's face. She stepped deeper into the room and pulled the door closed.

She said, "It's not just you on this trip, you know. We all get a vote. And I'd like to think I'd get more than one vote."

Gomez felt her cheeks warm. She and Simiaar had been friends forever, and sometimes more than friends. On this trip, they'd managed to spend time together that had nothing to do with a case or with the Alliance or with the FSS.

"I know," Gomez said, feeling a little guilty that she had shut Simiaar out. "But I wanted some time alone first. And if I had decided to go down to the factory, I would have discussed it with you, and then we would have presented it to Neal."

"You might not go?" Simiaar sounded surprised. "I thought this was our last stop before Armstrong."

"It is," Gomez said. "I think we go in clean. The attacks were six months ago. Nothing else has happened. The authorities in Armstrong are probably ready to investigate now. We can help them, maybe figure out what's going on next, and—"

"We end up in the same place," Simiaar said. "You won't be able to return to the *Stanley* any more than I will. There's still a war out there."

"I thought we weren't going to use that term," Gomez said. "Your decision. You said a war scared you."

"It still scares me," Simiaar said. "And we're pawns in it. We can't just go back to the Frontier and pretend like nothing has happened."

Gomez stared at her. Simiaar hadn't done nearly as much on this trip as she had thought she was going to. They had used the lab to analyze the materials they brought from the ship on Ohksmyte, and then they had used it for little else.

Was Simiaar feeling useless now? Feeling like she hadn't been doing enough? Was that why she was surprised Gomez wasn't going to the surface?

"I think," Gomez said slowly, "it might be better if we give the folks in Armstrong our information, and then we all decide how to proceed. We don't know what they know and don't know. We are only guessing."

Simiaar frowned. "Tell me one thing, Judita. If you had on this trip alone, like you had planned, would you be going to the surface tomorrow?"

"Without Neal," Gomez said, "I'm not even sure I would have made it this far. I might have gone into the prisons to find out what happened to TwoZero and his colleagues."

Simiaar's frown grew deeper.

"I'm not sure I would have survived that," Gomez said softly.

Simiaar sighed and shook her head. "That's not what I meant," she said. "I meant are we holding you back? Are you failing to take a risk you would have taken on your own?"

Gomez's hands were still behind her back, right hand around left wrist. And like earlier, the fingers on her left hand were starting to go numb.

She was a lot more tense than she realized.

"I don't know," she said. "Nothing has gone as I planned. Still, we have information for the people on Armstrong, and I want to deliver it in person. I would have wanted that even if I traveled alone."

"You're afraid you won't survive a trip to that factory," Simiaar said.

"I'm afraid that they're going to come after us," Gomez said, "and there's good chance we won't make it."

"Who are 'they'?" Simiaar asked.

"That's the one question we can't answer yet, and it frustrates me," Gomez said.

"Maybe we should poke 'them' and see what happens," Simiaar said. "Maybe they'll reveal themselves."

"And maybe we'll all die," Gomez said.

"Wasn't that the risk all along?" Simiaar asked. "Are you, of all people, getting cold feet?"

"What does that mean, 'of all people'?" Gomez asked.

"Judita," Simiaar said. "You walk into alien cultures with only cursory knowledge of their laws. That's suicide, according to most humans inside the Alliance. You have—by yourself—negotiated truces between cultures, invited the strangest beings into the Alliance, and managed to maintain relationships with some of the most frightening creatures in the Frontier. And now you're afraid that the *Alliance* will come after us, maybe kill us?"

Gomez nodded. Simiaar knew her well. Better than Gomez liked to think anyone knew her.

"We're trying to bring information to the Moon," Gomez said. "We can't do that if we're dead."

"You underestimate Neal. I'm sure he could figure out a way to send something in the middle of this ship exploding or whatever," Simiaar said.

Gomez's heart was pounding. Whenever she had gone to the surface of some new place in the Frontier, Simiaar had remained on board the *Stanley*. The ship, with its huge weapons system and the might of the Alliance behind it, had orbited above, with a full complement of crew.

Gomez had risked dying on those missions, but she had never risked her entire team.

"I don't see what we gain," Gomez said quietly.

"Maybe nothing," Simiaar said. "Maybe we find the one piece to the puzzle that we all need to stop this thing. You can't know until you investigate."

Gomez leaned against the nearby holochamber. Normally, she would have said that to a new crew member.

"We signed on knowing we could die," Simiaar said. "You even had the crew sign waivers that absolved your estate should anything happen to them. You made sure they had valid wills, for God's sake. This isn't like you."

"It's just like me," Gomez said. "I'm used to going in with authority. I'm not used to being a rogue investigator."

"Excuses," Simiaar said. "I agreed with you when you decided not to go into the prisons. I believed you were right when you said that we couldn't get any more from Uzven. But we have a clone factory down there, one that doesn't look right, and that ship—the ship that went to Epriccom *with clones on it*—traveled from here. From *here*, Judita. If you don't investigate this, you're going to force some poor schmuck from the Moon to investigate, and they won't have the experience you do or the ability you have. Nor will they have your rank. They won't get the same kind of access."

Gomez studied Simiaar. Her eyes were shining, her cheeks flushed. She seemed to believe each word she was saying.

"You surprise me, Lashante," Gomez said.

"Why? Because I think we need to finish this thing? Because I think we're the best suited for it? Or because I'm willing to risk our lives?"

"Because you're willing to risk our lives," Gomez said.

Simiaar made a rude, bleating noise. "If you've been paying attention, I've been willing to risk *my* life since I joined you on this harebrained mission. And so has Neal. The only one unwilling to risk lives is you. Time to change, Judita. Because this is our best shot, and you have to take it."

Gomez sighed. She had underestimated all of them. Or maybe she had just realized how much she cared for them. She didn't want them to die.

But they were risking their lives. And what they did with their lives was their choice.

Not hers.

"All right," she said. "We need a really good plan. And before I do anything, we have to talk to Neal. Our information has to get to the Moon, even if we don't."

Simiaar grinned at her. "There she is. Marshal Gomez, I've missed you."

Gomez felt a surge of annoyance mixed with affection. "God, you're sarcastic."

"Yep," Simiaar said. "Brilliant, sarcastic, and *right*. Admit it, you love all those things about me."

"I do," Gomez said—and that, in a nutshell, was the problem. "I really do."

30

At first, Nuuyoma wasn't going to tell Verstraete what the man— One Of One Direct—wanted. But Nuuyoma couldn't keep the discussion to himself.

He waited until he and Verstraete were out of the area of space the starbase claimed for itself. Whether or not it actively patrolled that part of space, he had no idea. But he was taking no chances.

He set the shuttle on a meandering path, not because he thought anyone was following them, but because he planned to return to the base the following day.

And it was that thought that convinced him to tell Verstraete about the full discussion. She needed to know why they were heading back.

He told her in the lounge. The shuttle had a relaxation area filled with wall-to-wall entertainment, yet he'd never used any of it. He liked the lounge because it had the best furniture, and it also had a small, hidden, cockpit-control panel, in case something went horribly wrong.

Verstraete rarely came into the lounge, but she agreed to when he asked her. She sat across from him, wearing her usual off-duty white, hands clasped together over one knee.

He expected her to disapprove of his choice to make a deal with One Of One Direct.

Instead, she said, "How come he can't get this information himself?"

"Maybe he's tried," Nuuyoma said.

"It would seem like it would take very little effort to find out what happened to this woman," Verstraete said. "What are you thinking?"

Because he worried that somehow their communications had been compromised even inside their shuttle, he sent a message along their encoded private links, *New. Ping.*

Which was the *Stanley* crew's code for a new, encrypted, private link that was about to open. This far out away from the starbase, no one could hack the links. At least, he didn't think so, not if the person wasn't already on board.

He knew he and Verstraete were alone on the shuttle.

But that didn't mean someone couldn't have hacked them before they left. At a place like *Starbase Human*, he would expect such activity would be routine.

He had searched the shuttle for any trackers or hacking equipment. He'd found some, but only those that the base had installed. He hadn't found anything else, and rather than reassure him, it had simply made him even more cautious.

Verstraete nodded once, a sign that the ping he had sent her worked.

So he sent a message along the new encrypted link. *Got this?*

Yes, she sent back on the link.

"Maybe I'm not thinking," he said, answering the question she had asked aloud. "I'm going to consider this some more."

But he didn't move, and neither did she. Instead, he sent along the new link, *I'm thinking that we find the information. If this woman's deep inside the Alliance, we send someone to help her, protect her, move her, whatever it takes.*

Seems risky, Verstraete sent.

It is, Nuuyoma sent. *But what if One Of One Direct truly does have information that will help us find whoever is behind the Anniversary Day attacks?*

And what if the information is worthless? Verstraete sent.

It's a risk, Nuuyoma sent.

A risk we might be jeopardizing one woman's life for, Verstraete sent.

If she's even still alive. If she's in the Alliance. If she exists at all.

You think this might be a test? Verstraete sent.

I don't know what it is. I think this man is taking advantage of a situation we've presented to him. He has the chance to find out information he hasn't been able to find out. Or he's just trying to see if we'll negotiate in good faith.

Verstraete stood. She wandered around the room, as if she were looking for a window. *It seems odd to me that he's willing to give us the information. Why hasn't he come forward before this? What does he have to gain?*

We could capture some of his DNA, Nuuyoma said, *see if those claims are true.*

She shook her head. *You know what I don't like? I don't like the way all of these clones of PierLuigi Frémont like to play games.*

Hereditary trait? Nuuyoma sent. *Or something trained?*

That's for the scientists to figure out. She sat back down. *You want the information.*

Don't you? he sent.

Gomez would. Verstraete stood again. *I keep wondering why we have to gamble with people's lives.*

Aren't we gambling if we could learn something and didn't? Nuuyoma asked.

Her pacing sped up. It seemed almost frantic. *I didn't join the FSS to make these kinds of decisions.*

He smiled. *Sure you did.*

Verstraete stopped and looked at him in surprise.

If you wanted an easy berth, he sent, *you would have joined a security service inside the Alliance. You would have been monitored daily, filled out reports, and reprimanded if you didn't follow the rules. You wanted the freedom of the Frontier.*

You seem to know more about me than I do, she snapped, if, indeed, he could describe almost silent communication that way.

Tell me I'm wrong, he sent.

Verstraete sighed. *If this woman dies because of us…*

He nodded. They would feel bad. They would feel worse if the information they got from One Of One Direct was no good. But if the woman died and the information solved the most devastating crime in recent Alliance history? Then he might not feel as bad as he wanted to believe.

We get paid to make the hard choices, he sent.

And to keep them off the record, Verstraete sent as she left the room.

31

THE NARROW STRIP OF LAND THAT HELD THE ENTIRE HUMAN POPULATION of Hétique was billed as temperate, but to Gomez, who spent most of her time aboard ships, the area seemed unbearably warm.

The air was thick with humidity. She could taste it as she made her way from her hotel to the clone factory's industrial park.

She had piloted her own shuttle to the surface, not wanting anyone else involved in this plan. If she got caught, she had only to worry about herself.

Hétique City, nearest the factory, had been the first human city built on the planet. Initially designed for the factory workers, the city had expanded to include all kinds of Earth Alliance facilities, many of which were unmarked, leading Gomez to believe they had some connection to human intelligence services.

She couldn't tell if those services were attached to the Security Division or if they were part of the military, and she didn't want to investigate while she was here.

She was still trying not to call attention to herself.

The hotel she stayed at was approved for Earth Alliance workers. She registered using her badge and her main personal account. Since she was going into the factory without hiding her identity, she wanted to make certain that her behavior remained consistent throughout.

She had even stayed overnight before going to the morning meeting. It felt odd to stay in a hotel. She hadn't done that in a long time, especially one as spartan as this one. It made her long for her suite aboard the *Green Dragon*.

And the food made her long for Simiaar's cooking.

The distance from the hotel to the industrial park was less than a kilometer. She walked it easily, the air so thick that it caught in her throat.

It had rained just before she left—a passing thunderstorm, the concierge told her—and that made the air seem more humid rather than less. The moment she stepped out of the hotel, her blouse stuck to her skin as if it had been glued there.

Her clothing was thin, but professional. Loose-fitting pants, a loose-fitting blouse, open-toed shoes, and no jewelry. Simiaar had thought she should have worn her uniform, but Gomez had vetoed that, reminding Simiaar that she was on leave. The uniform just wasn't appropriate.

Simiaar had said that she wanted Gomez to impress them, but Gomez had the sense that Simiaar really wanted Gomez to remind them that she was law enforcement in the wild Frontier and knew how to handle herself.

Gomez felt that her job spoke for itself.

Simiaar didn't agree, but Apaza did.

And Gomez needed Apaza on her side. He had to concentrate on setting up information dumps that would go directly to the Moon government—or what remained of it—should anything happen to Gomez.

The three of them had spent too much time debating just how to do that. Simiaar had wanted the *Green Dragon* to proceed to the Moon, even if something happened to Gomez.

Gomez wanted Simiaar to change ships as quickly as possible. Charlie Zamal could help them find one. No one would know that the three of them were involved with Gomez.

Apaza wanted a multi-pronged strategy. If Gomez was detained, he believed that Zamal should pilot the *Green Dragon elsewhere*, while Apaza and Simiaar traveled separately to the Moon to give the information they had gathered to the surviving government there.

If Gomez were injured, killed, or never heard from again, then Apaza wanted to send the information to the Moon and vanish himself, maybe even officially Disappear.

If someone or something attacked *The Green Dragon*, Apaza wanted to send the information to the Moon as the attacks began.

And all of them agreed that there should be some kind of failsafe built into the *Dragon* so that if it exploded, the information would be sent automatically.

Apaza had said that was the easiest thing for him to do, and he set it up.

But the other plans were harder to agree on.

Gomez didn't want Apaza or Simiaar involved if something happened to her, but she got outvoted on that. Apaza and Simiaar would travel to the Moon separately if Gomez were detained.

If Gomez disappeared or got killed, then Simiaar would go alone, and Apaza would send the information, heavily encoded, once he had gotten somewhere safe.

Neither Simiaar nor Gomez felt that sending the information as the *Green Dragon* was being attacked was a good idea. Both of them believed that any attacking ship would be prepared to download whatever communications a ship under attack would send out—and maybe even trap that information.

Apaza promised to work on something that wouldn't look like an information packet, but Gomez hoped they wouldn't need that. She felt safe enough with the packet going out as the ship was destroyed.

Otherwise, she believed the information would reach the Moon one way or another.

But as she walked down the cobblestone that someone believed a good idea in place of an actual sidewalk, she found herself regretting not using all of the tricks that Apaza had designed.

Gomez didn't feel good about this meeting, and she finally figured out why.

Most of the people she had passed as she got closer to the industrial park looked the same.

They didn't dress the same—they wore everything from overalls to kimonos, short skirts to long dresses covered in ruffles. But they were the same height and their skin color was a neutral tannish brown, their eyes a bit wide and their noses small.

Even the children looked similar.

If they weren't clones, then they were heavily enhanced.

She tried not to stare at them, feeling a bit dumpy and out of place as she moved.

She left the edge of the commercial area—filled with hotels and restaurants and a few shops—and crossed a green space. Five people worked on their hands and knees, plants in containers beside them, switching out the dying flowers with hardier looking ones.

The ground they had dug up was black and rich. She could even smell the heavy scent of wet dirt.

As she approached the industrial park, the cobblestone spread in three different directions—directly ahead, and off to her left and right. The paths that went left and right butted up against a fence made of the same material.

The fence was at least a meter taller than she was, and appeared to be so solid that she wasn't sure how anyone could break through it.

It did look easy to climb, but she would wager that there was some kind of protective field around it.

The path she was on led to an unmanned gate. She flattened her palm against the lock, letting her badge flare.

"Judita Gomez," she said. "I have an appointment."

She had made that the night before with their personnel office, just like she would have done if she were applying for a job here.

A calm settled over her.

She had missed this kind of risk, missed those moments when she went alone into a place where she had never been and a future that remained entirely unknown.

The gate swung open just enough to let her slip through. Then it eased closed behind her.

Building Fourteen, said an automated voice in her links as a map appeared below her left eye.

Building Fourteen was only a few meters left of the entrance, which made sense. Most strangers would come into the industrial park to either interview for a job or start their first day on the job.

If Gomez had to guess, the buildings to her right housed other services geared toward guests.

The cobblestone continued here, reminding her that Hétique City was a company town, and that the cloning factory had come before any official city government.

Plants, similar to the ones being replaced outside the gate, glistened in the sunlight. Since the rain clouds passed, the sun had come out very bright. Hétique held a similar position in relation to its sun that Earth had in relation to its, but Gomez couldn't remember ever feeling this hot and sticky on Earth.

Nor could she remember the sun ever seeming to be so bright, the light so vibrant.

But it had been a long time since she had been to Earth, and even longer since she had gone into a human-only city with that same feeling of possible danger that she often had on the Frontier.

The map illuminated her way around some stone benches and a lovely little gazebo. A couple sat inside, having a serious conversation, almost as if they had been planted there as advertising for how wonderful and peaceful this park could be.

Gomez glanced at them, and let the details reach her—more tannish brown skin, wide eyes, and long, thin forms. She realized, after a moment, that two people she had assumed were some kind of couple might have actually been brother and sister—or clones with their gender modified.

Gomez shivered. She hated thinking about the way that human beings could be manipulated for profit.

Building Fourteen was wide and rectangular, with a low roof. Greenery that she couldn't identify hung down from the gutters, and she wondered if, from above, this building looked more like a hill than an actual building.

The walls were recessed just enough that she had to walk through vines to get to the door.

It swung open as she appeared.

Judita Gomez, proceed one meter to your right, then turn left.

She followed the instructions as they were sent through her links. She felt better than she had in weeks, as if she had done this before.

And technically, she had, every single time she approached an alien government in the Frontier when someone in that government insisted she come alone.

Regulations stated she should never go alone, but, as she had told Nuuyoma when he took over the *Stanley*, regulations on the Frontier were merely suggestions.

Another door swung open, and this time she entered a sitting area. The temperature had cooled here, and the air was drier. Her damp skin left her feeling colder than the temperature gauge she'd called up in her right eye told her she should be.

"Marshal Gomez." The voice belonged to a man, but Gomez didn't see anyone.

A hologram appeared before her, deliberately clear at first so that she knew she was speaking to someone who wasn't bothering to be in the room.

"To what do we owe this pleasure?" the man asked.

He was thin, like the men she had seen outside, but his skin was several shades darker. His eyes were a light green, making them almost disappear on his face.

"I'm here to discuss a position," she said.

"We haven't advertised a position," he said.

"Of course you haven't," she said. "You never advertise positions. And yet, I heard from a reliable source that you need trained law enforcement."

She had heard that—or rather Apaza had found it deep inside the files that Gomez had found on her database. Anyone interested in working in facilities like this one needed ties to law enforcement.

"Who told you that?" the man asked.

She smiled. "If I told you that, then I might get my source in trouble. Confirm or deny that you're looking for trained law enforcement. I'm hoping to ease into retirement with a cushier job than I'm used to, and if there are no jobs here, then I'll move to my next stop."

The hologram winked out and yet another door opened.

"Come on in, Marshal." The same voice came out of that open door, only this time the voice seemed a little richer. The actual person, apparently, sat inside that room.

Gomez walked inside, and realized that no one sat here. Tables stood to one side, mostly housing screens so that someone could fill out documents or look up information. Gigantic white pillows were pushed against one wall; apparently they were what a person used if she chose to sit.

The floor was covered in thick, green, shag carpet, and the walls matched. The wood trim was dark, making the white pillows the only things in the room that seemed bright.

A man stood in the center of all of it. He was barefoot and wore thin pants that seemed suited to the humid weather outside. His shirt was white and loose. He was younger than she expected, and looked nothing like the people she had seen outside.

His skin was darker—more coffee than tan—and his face wider, his eyes closer together, his mouth broad and curled in a smile. Somehow the combination was charming rather than off-putting.

He waved. "We don't shake hands here," he said. "We're a little conscious of where we leave our DNA."

Then he laughed, as if he had made a joke. Maybe he thought he had.

"I'm Ashraf Guan. I handle initial hiring here, and I'll be honest. I'm interested and intrigued. Interested in you as a possible employee, intrigued that you found us."

That last had a bit of an edge, as if he didn't expect anyone to find them.

Gomez decided to put him at ease. "I use old databases because I'm with the FSS. I'm not sure if the notification I saw is gone now, but I can send it to you, if you would like."

"Please do," he said.

She was prepared for this moment. She had the notice, along with enough of the database so that he could identify where it had come from.

She had had Apaza go over everything to make certain that sending this little piece of the *Dragon's* database did not give anyone here a way into the ship's systems.

"My last few years on the Frontier have been difficult ones." Gomez could truthfully say things like that because *all* years on the Frontier were difficult. If Guan looked at her service record, he would see that she had handled crisis after crisis.

His eyes had glazed just a little: obviously, he was examining the notification she had sent him.

"I'm not getting younger," she said. "I think I would like to stop traveling and settle for a while."

Then he focused on her. "You can retire now. You don't have to do any work. Why apply for another job?"

Gomez smiled, prepared for that, as well. "My friends accuse me of being addicted to adrenalin. They might be right. I liked the challenge of my job with the FSS, but it's starting to wear on me. I still need that occasional adrenaline hit, but I don't think I need to constantly risk my life to do it."

"I'm not sure what you expect here," Guan said. "We are never threatened from outside. We have guards. What we use law enforcement for is training."

She felt a surge of victory. She had gotten him to admit they had placed that notice.

"I'll be honest," she said, "I doubt I would make a good security guard. That's boredom punctuated by terror, and usually better suited to bots and androids—at least in the early phases."

Guan inclined his head toward her. "Indeed."

"What kind of training do you use law enforcement for?" she asked.

He walked to the giant pillows, grabbed two, and flung them onto the floor. "Would you care to sit, Marshal?"

She wasn't sure of the etiquette here. But he had phrased that as a question, so she decided to answer it honestly.

"I think I prefer to stand at the moment," she said. "I don't sit much. My job requires me to keep moving, and that's how I'm the most comfortable."

"Even on your ship?" he asked.

He sank, cross-legged, onto one of the pillows. If she were a standard job applicant, that change in his position would have made her feel uncomfortable. It didn't. She had dealt in situations stranger than this every single day of her career.

"Especially on my ship," she said. "I have to remain in shape for on-site situations. Sometimes I end up running several kilometers, sometimes I have to carry twice my weight. A good thirty percent of the time, my job is physically demanding, and I can't use enhancements for that."

He placed his palms on the edges of the pillow behind him. "Fascinating. I had no idea."

His tone made it sound like he wasn't fascinated at all.

"Sit," he said. "You're making me uncomfortable."

"Oh," she said. "I'm sorry. I didn't mean to do that."

But she had. She needed to see how this place worked, and he was giving her hints of it. The indirect way he had of speaking made it clear that the people who ran this factory did not like to reveal anything easily.

She sat down, keeping her back straight.

"We used to be a military facility," he said, "but military uses for clones have declined in the past century. The factories that work best with the Human branch of the Alliance Military are housed in a different region of Alliance space."

Nice way to tell her that where they were was none of her business. She nodded, mostly to encourage him to continue.

"Here, our needs are different. The more established parts of the Alliance have internal problems that we tend to." He said that as if she should understand what he meant.

She waited. When he wasn't going to say more, she opened her hands slightly.

"Modern Alliance history is a bit beyond me," she said. "I've been on the Frontier for the better part of my life. I'm afraid you'll have to be a little more specific."

"Criminals," he said with just a bit of irritation. He didn't like her. It was becoming obvious. She wasn't at all the kind of person he was used to. "We have a lot of trouble with the Black Fleet operating at the fringes of the Alliance and, yes, within the Frontier—"

She wanted to correct him. The Black Fleet did not operate within the real Frontier. They operated in parts of known space that had rejected Alliance membership, thinking they'd be better off.

In her opinion, they weren't, but she didn't say that.

"Here in the Alliance, in the human-dominated regions, we have another problem. Very savvy crime families who have learned how to operate on the edges of the law in the areas they're based in, and yet they manage to break the laws in other areas. When someone connected to those families get caught, the families disavow them."

Gomez folded her hands together. She hadn't heard of this problem, but it didn't surprise her. Humans had worked on the fringes of society from the beginning of time.

"We have to make cases against them, but first, we need to know exactly what they're doing. These organizations have existed for such a long time that outsiders can't get in, and those that do get in aren't trusted."

Gomez nodded, again to encourage him to continue.

"Which is where we come in. We embed into the operation, and eventually, we make our operative live."

"Embed," she repeated. His vagueness made it difficult to follow him. She thought about that for a moment. Embed, using clones. Who remained inactive until they were needed.

"Yes, Marshal." Something in his tone told her that he thought her a bit slow. "We—"

"Where do you get the DNA?" she asked.

He smiled. "We don't shake hands here for a reason."

She smiled back, even though she didn't want to. In other words, he wasn't going to tell her.

"And you need people like me to train these possible embeds—what, exactly? What law enforcement needs?"

"Something like that," he said, letting her know now that he was being vague. "It depends on the group we're infiltrating, and the age of our embed."

She felt herself grow cold. "You use young embeds, then?" she asked, remembering TwoZero and Thirds.

"Yes, sometimes we do," he said, and there was a challenge in his voice. If she didn't like that, he was inviting her to leave.

"I see," she said. She put her hands on her knees. "I have to ask, given what's happened on the Moon, whether or not these crime family clones are clones of nightmares like PierLuigi Frémont."

Guan raised his chin slightly. He had obviously expected that question. It made her stomach jump, made her wonder if he knew why she was here after all.

"Generally," he said, "we use the DNA of relatives who are not known to be involved in operations—children, cousins, friends of friends— people whom our crime families haven't seen in decades or more. Sometimes we embed a cloned member of one family with another family that has an association with the crime family. It's very complicated."

"You didn't answer my question," she said.

"We try not to use DNA of anyone famous," he said, "and we certainly try to avoid anyone who might be uncontrollable."

"Like a mass murderer," she said.

"Like a mass murderer," he agreed.

"Sounds like you're speaking from experience," she said.

"I have no idea what happened here before I arrived," he said. "But I can tell you that in the twenty years I've been working here, we've never cloned any notorious criminals."

"Good to know," she said, making her voice sound warm. "Because I would have no idea how to train one of those individuals."

"You would need training first," Guan said. "You wouldn't start here. We would decide if we think you're suited to work here, and if you are, we would send you to one of our operations elsewhere."

Gomez noted that he didn't say where. He was being deliberately cagey about that.

"Then you would return here—if they felt your skill set was best used here. Otherwise, we have facilities all over the Alliance to which you might be better suited. Your physical condition alone might be enough to recommend you to our military facilities. At those facilities, they try not to enhance the clones. They try to develop their own innate strengths and weaknesses. Enhancements can be stripped from someone. Innate strengths cannot."

Oh, but they can, Gomez thought, but didn't say. It wasn't relevant to this conversation.

"If you would like," Guan said, "I can help you fill out a transfer application. We can choose where you would do your training, not necessary the place, but the climate."

Her feelings of triumph were leaving. She realized just from his attitude that she would get no farther than this room, and he would oversee anything she did. She couldn't even access systems using her codes and claim she had done so accidentally, as Apaza had wanted her to do.

"How long would the training last?" Gomez asked, casting around for a reason to say no. "As I mentioned, I'm looking to settle down."

"We generally do not bring anyone into this facility without five years of experience in our business. I'm not sure how the military operations work. They might be more amenable to someone with your experience. Maybe…a year or two before you get your posting? But don't quote me on that."

Gomez allowed herself a heavy sigh. "I wish your notification had mentioned that. I had used a good part of my leave to come here. I thought there were opportunities."

"I didn't mean to mislead you, Marshal. There are opportunities. The timetable is ours, however, not yours. I'm sure there are other jobs inside the Alliance which might serve your desire to settle down and your need for the occasional risk."

"I'm sure," she said drily. "I don't suppose you could point me in that direction?"

He swept a hand toward one of the tables. "You could apply—"

"I don't have years," she said. "I would like to settle when I retire, and I was hoping I could do that when I returned to my ship."

He rose to his feet without uncrossing his legs, the sign of someone quite limber. Then he extended a hand so that she could rise.

She remembered his comment on DNA. She smiled at the extended palm, and shook her head slightly.

"Thank you," she said, "but I doubt I'll ever look at such casual contact in the same way again."

He smiled, and let his hand drop to his side. She stood exactly as he had, using her thighs to lift her without bracing herself on anything. She almost felt like slapping out the pillow—or taking it with her. She was suddenly very conscious of the DNA she had left behind.

She looked wistfully around the room. It had no windows and didn't reveal anything. Not even a map of the facility.

She wished she could ask for a tour, but that would seem presumptuous, especially now that she had turned down any possibility of working in this field.

"I thank you for your time," she said.

"If you change your mind, Marshal..." Guan let his voice trail off without promising anything. It was an effective way to leave someone with a good feeling.

She smiled. "I'll remember what you said."

Then she let herself out of this room. The map reappeared under her vision, and she silently cursed it. She couldn't pretend to walk in the wrong direction and see the rest of the facility.

She had a hunch a variety of alarms would go off if she did so.

She contemplated it, though, as she walked out of Building Fourteen. But she wasn't sure what it would gain her.

Right now, she knew, she hadn't attracted anyone's attention. Her cover story could easily pass as truth if she did nothing else, like pretend to get lost.

All that worry about risk, about exposing herself and this little mission, and nothing had come of it.

She felt vaguely disappointed.

Unless Apaza found something while she was here, she had the same amount of information to bring to the Moon as she had had when she left the Frontier.

She had traveled this way with such hope, seeing the possibility of bringing more than news of the enclave to the Moon.

Instead, all she had to offer the authorities there were the bits of information she had gathered in the Frontier, and her ability to investigate.

She suspected that she and Simiaar would be very busy once they got to the Moon. They would be investigating, while others were probably still cleaning up the mess.

She had to be content with that.

But it wasn't the atonement she had been looking for.

She guessed she would have to find that somewhere else.

32

PIPPA LANDAU OPENED THE DOOR OF HER CENTURIES'-OLD HOUSE AND stepped onto the lawn. The air smelled faintly of cut grass and Mississippi River mud. Davenport had just experienced the annual spring flood. Back in the day, the people who lived here had sandbagged the riverbanks to prevent the brown Mississippi water from overrunning the city.

And it didn't always work. Much of Davenport had been built based on the knowledge that the Mississippi would flood periodically. So most of the city was up high, on the bluffs.

Now, the houses had stilts that lifted the buildings above any known waterline. Her house, built above the traditional flood stage, had only used its stilts once in the decades she had lived here. That flood, which happened when her children were small, had been epic, a disaster that would have wiped out the city if modern technology hadn't made city protection possible.

She thought of that flood every time the smell of the Mississippi became overpowering.

And she was thinking of it now.

The grass was wet. She probably shouldn't have had the bots cut it so soon after the heavy rains, but she had. The ground was still squishy, and water soaked into her favorite slippers, making her feet cold.

She wrapped her robe around her waist, hoping the neighbors wouldn't see, and then realized that worrying about her neighbors meant she had become an Iowan.

Tears pooled in her eyes. She wanted to remain an Iowan. A Midwestern teacher of uncertain origin, who raised her family here and put down roots, like she had never thought possible.

When she first arrived on Earth, she had felt like a plant in a hydroponic garden: roots visible in her little glass container, taking in nutrients, but movable—constantly on the alert for the best conditions, the best life, the safest place.

She had found it. Right here. Davenport, Iowa, Midwest, Earth, the center of the Earth Alliance, the place most people ran from.

And she loved it.

Now she was like the garden she planted every spring. Her roots had sunk deep into the rich loam that had kept generations of humans alive in this very spot for hundreds and hundreds of years.

She wiped the back of her hand over her eyes, felt the wet, and made herself take a deep breath.

Then she walked deeper into her yard and looked up.

As she had thought after Anniversary Day, her backyard was not the ideal place to gaze at the moon. The lights of the city were up tonight, which they hadn't been when she went to Prospect Park six months before, unsettled because she had seen the clones that haunted her nightmares.

Only on Anniversary Day, those clones had been alive and entering the Moon's main port in Armstrong, on their way to committing mass murder.

Just like they had done on *Starbase Human*, over thirty-five years ago.

She wrapped her robe even tighter and looked up again.

When she had stood in Prospect Park, the Moon had been full and the night sky clear. The damage to some of the domes had been visible to the naked eye.

On this night, gray clouds skated across the dark sky, threatening even more rain. The weather maps showed thunderstorms that would form over her house by six a.m., which was why she'd had the bots clip the grass.

The Moon was a fingernail, peeking through the clouds at the oddest moment. Even if the damage from the latest attack were visible, she wouldn't have been able to see it, which was why she avoided Prospect Park this evening.

She had a hunch a crowd was gathering again.

The people of Earth—or maybe just the people of Davenport—loved their Moon.

She shivered in the humid air, her neck aching from looking up. She had told herself before she got ready for bed that she wouldn't think about this new set of attacks.

It wasn't human clones this time. This time, the clones were Peyti, and some news sources reported that they, too, were based on a mass murderer—although that hadn't been confirmed yet.

The destruction was less, but there was a lot of collateral damage, and that was what she found herself thinking about, alone in her comfortable bed, window open. Wind shushing through the nearby trees usually lulled her to sleep. She liked the quiet here.

But every time she closed her eyes, she heard the stomp-stomp-stomp of boots overlaid with screams of her friends. She dozed off briefly and the screams became the screams of her children.

She wiped her eyes again.

She wanted to contact them. They were all grown now, with their own families, and their own schedules. She would probably wake them up if she contacted them—and what would she say? That the new attacks on the Moon brought back old memories—memories they didn't even know about?

They had no idea their mom was a Disappeared. They knew she had grown up elsewhere and that her parents were dead, but that had just been part of their lives. Parent stuff. When they questioned her—and they all had—she gave vague answers or told them about going to school at the University of Iowa, how it had felt so different to study in a place that had existed for so long it seemed a part of the Earth itself.

Her children had accepted that.

They had no idea that she had been someone else.

They would feel betrayed when they learned it.

If they learned it.

She wiped her eyes again, wishing they would stop leaking, wishing to whatever god she could locate in the heavens—the made-up heavens—that she had been able to sleep this night. Really and truly sleep.

Because if she had slept, it would have meant that she had put the attacks away, had remained Pippa Landau, whom she had been for so much longer than she had been Takara Hamasaki.

In her life here, she had hardly ever thought of Takara Hamasaki.

Except when she named her children. She had told them she liked the names, but in truth, she had named them for the family she had lost. Takumi had her father's name; Toshie her mother's. And Tenkou was named for the brother she had lost before she had ever ventured to *Starbase Human*.

She had redefined the names so that she could redefine the memories. And, for the most part, it had worked. For more than thirty years, after her travels and her life settled down, she had lived as Pippa Landau.

Eventually, just like the woman in the Disappearance service had promised, Takara had *become* Pippa Landau. Or she thought she had.

But Takara's memories were breaking through. The fears she had held at bay for decades were rising to the surface.

The clouds glided over the Moon. It peeked down at her like a sideways smile, as if it had a secret that she couldn't know.

What if something she knew—something buried deep in her memories—would help the Moon?

Because if there had been a second attempt, there would be a third. And maybe a fourth.

Until they succeeded—whoever *they* were. Until they completely destroyed the Moon.

What if she could have saved the lives lost this day just by revealing herself?

What if she could save more lives?

She wiped at her eyes. She didn't want to leave this life.

She didn't want to reveal herself.

She didn't want to be someone else.

Again.

33

THE SHUTTLE HAD AN ENCRYPTED, PROTECTED VERSION OF THE SAME database that Nuuyoma had back on the *Stanley*. If anyone tried to hack into the shuttle's database, it would destroy itself. It took layers and layers of security codes, DNA links, and other protections just to access the database.

The problem was that the database, just like the one on the *Stanley*, was almost a year old.

To get updated information, the *Stanley* would have to ping the Alliance, then schedule time for a data download. Updating the database was standard for FSS ships near the border, but those deep in the Frontier often didn't update for months, sometimes years. It was risky, and often irrelevant.

Yes, that meant they missed some of the important Alliance news, but what seemed important inside the Alliance often wasn't important outside the Alliance. Particularly when he and the crew were dealing with cultures that had never *heard* of the Alliance.

Nuuyoma decided to do his search on the old database inside his quarters. He had assigned some information to Verstraete, but she didn't seem as willing as he was. He would search, then have her double-check his information.

His quarters on the shuttle were much smaller than the quarters he had on the *Stanley*. Yet in some ways, he preferred the room here. It was well designed, with a bed in one corner, a work table in another, and a state-of-the-art (well, as of last year) entertainment package that could make him believe he was in New Orleans getting laid if he felt so inclined. (He didn't.)

He had been sitting so long that he decided to use a floating screen to get the information he needed. Normally, he would have used voice commands, but he still had that strange feeling that he might have been hacked. He didn't even feel comfortable using the encrypted link because he felt that the link could be back-traced.

So he did things the old-fashioned way, tapping the holographic screen and occasionally calling up a floating keyboard. Typing things slowed him down, but he didn't mind.

He walked and searched and grew in turns frustrated and relieved. Frustrated that he couldn't find a lot of information on Takara Hamasaki, and relieved that he couldn't at the same time.

After hours of searching, he found a lot of references to a young Takara Hamasaki. She'd had an old ship that had broken down a lot before she arrived at the first *Starbase Human*. She had stopped there for repairs, and hadn't left.

Over the years she was on the starbase, she had worked her way into administration, so her name and her image were on thousands of reports and files. Her DNA, encrypted, was also on some files. He used his marshal's identification to download the DNA comparison information.

There was no record of a Takara Hamasaki after *Starbase Human* exploded, except notations in some official records that she had probably died on the starbase, along with everyone else.

However, that ancient and dilapidated ship of hers turned up on sales records on the moon of a planet just inside the Frontier. The ship had broken down (again) and needed repair. Instead of paying for it, the owner had vanished, and the ship got scrapped for parts.

As much as Nuuyoma searched, he couldn't find any more references to Takara Hamasaki. However, he found an internal border security notation that the DNA profile he had found matched a DNA profile of one Suzette Hamdi, who crossed the border into the Alliance shortly after Takara's ship was abandoned.

Hamdi's internal file showed she had gone to Raaala, a city just inside Alliance space. Raaala had just one claim to fame: it had more Disappearance services per square kilometer than any other human-centric city inside the Alliance.

Takara/Hamdi's trail died right there. He could find no more information on her, no matter how hard he looked.

He waved the screen away and stopped walking for a moment. He sat on the edge of the bed and ran a hand through his hair.

Takara Hamasaki had escaped the Frontier and then had Disappeared. That seemed backwards. Most of the Disappeared he had known about or helped track down had either gone to the Frontier when they Disappeared or had gone to the edges of the Alliance.

Maybe his information—his personal experience—was very Frontier-oriented, given his job. He had to take that into account.

The fact remained, though, that someone with Takara's DNA profile and with her ship had gone *back* to the Alliance, and then had vanished. She had gone to a place that had a mountain of Disappearance services.

But someone who used a decrepit ship like hers couldn't afford a Disappearance service. He wondered how she had paid for it, if indeed, she had used one.

It might be another way to track her down. But he wasn't going to search for her. He would wager that One Of One Direct did not have the information from inside the Alliance, because One Of One Direct wouldn't have access to the border and DNA records. So, Nuuyoma could trade that little bit of information for whatever One Of One Direct was withholding.

That relieved Nuuyoma a little. Because he felt as if he wasn't putting Takara in any danger.

Although, he knew, this information could enable One Of One Direct to hire a shady Retrieval Artist to find Takara.

If a Retrieval Artist existed this far out, and if one would work for someone who looked like One Of One Direct.

Nuuyoma sighed, then stood. He had one more task to complete before he had Verstraete retrace his steps.

He opened the floating screen again and started pacing, seeing if he could find information on designer criminal clones that looked like PierLuigi Frémont. *Old* information, stuff that predated Anniversary Day by decades.

He didn't find anything. He wasn't sure he expected to. Criminal activity, even high-end expensive activity, was hard to find through established networks. He wasn't good enough to search criminal sites to see what he could find, nor did he want to.

He would see what One Of One Direct told him. And then Nuuyoma would send what he could find to Gomez. After that, Nuuyoma would consider this particular quixotic task complete.

He'd found something. He hoped that would be good enough.

It was all he could do.

34

No one greeted Gomez as her shuttle docked on the *Green Dragon*. Her interactions with the ship, from the moment she left Hétique, had all been automated.

At first, she hadn't thought anything of it, but as she stepped out of the shuttle into the docking bay, she was stunned to find herself alone.

She had at least expected to see Simiaar. And no one was in the bay's reception area at all.

The *Green Dragon* had three shuttles, all of them big enough for a crew of four if the crew were crowded into each other. Otherwise, the *Dragon* had to land in an official port, something that Gomez hadn't wanted to do on this trip.

She had thought the shuttle practical, and it had felt that way, until she was faced with the emptiness of the docking bay.

The other shuttles were clamped into place. The lights were on low, as they always were when a shuttle came in to dock. Bots scurried to the side of the shuttle she had just left, securing it, and making certain that it had brought nothing on its hull.

She had to go through a cursory decontamination. If Simiaar or Apaza or anyone had been waiting for her, they would have been just outside the actual bay itself, in a little reception area.

190

But she would have been able to see them from the moment she stepped off the shuttle.

And she didn't.

In fact, that little reception area was dark.

Her stomach clenched.

Maybe her visit to the surface hadn't been as harmless as she had thought it had been.

She stepped into the decontamination chamber, half expecting the warm light to find something had attached itself to her. But she was cleared within the standard sixty seconds. She stepped outside, into the reception area, and the lights came up, just like they were supposed to.

The reception area lights were supposed to stay up for at least twenty minutes after the last person departed.

So, not only had no one been waiting for her, no one had been in the area prior to her arrival.

She couldn't take the silence anymore.

Lashante? she sent. *Where is everyone?*

Come to the mess, Simiaar sent back. She did not use a visual or even sound, which was odd. Because Simiaar preferred the human touch, or so she claimed.

Gomez left the reception area and stopped in the cargo bay. A tiny armory hid in a small closet there, known only to her, Simiaar, and the pilot. No one else needed to know that extra weapons existed on this level.

Gomez grabbed a laser pistol, checked to see if it was charged (it was), and then carried it with her to the stairs between levels.

The mess was one deck up. They didn't use it much—or rather, Apaza, Simiaar, and Gomez didn't use it. The small crew did. Which made the gathering even stranger than it had initially seemed.

The mess was directly across from the stairs, taking up a good half of the deck. The smells of coffee and the last meal cooked—whatever it had been—filled the corridor. As she crossed, she smelled eggs, toast, and a bit of soy sauce.

Breakfast.

Her stomach growled. For her, breakfast had been a long time ago. Hétique City did not operate on Earth Standard time.

Gomez slipped into the mess. Most of the crew stood inside, staring at the far wall. Coffee still sat in pots along the counters, as well as donuts and some cold dim sum. Eggs had congealed in serving trays.

Gomez grabbed a donut and scanned for Simiaar. She didn't see her immediately. Instead, her gaze found Apaza, who clutched his personal, gigantic coffee thermos as if it were a lifeline.

Gomez started; she hadn't expected to see him outside of the information room. He was even more pear-shaped than he had been when he started on this mission, and she worried, ever so remotely, about his health.

Apaza shifted slightly, and Gomez saw Simiaar at his side. Simiaar was watching the screens, as well.

Gomez threaded her way through the crew. Normally, they would have nodded at her or said hello or welcome back. She would have greeted them, as well.

Instead, they were focused on the screen, too.

Gomez looked up, saw some flying cars passing over buildings, and Peyti everywhere, with their masks off and clutched in their long fingers. She knew if she scrolled through her links she could find sound, but she didn't.

Instead, she stopped beside Simiaar.

"What the hell is going on?" Gomez demanded.

"They tried again," Simiaar said softly.

"Who tried again?"

"God, if we knew who, we could stop this, couldn't we?" Simiaar snapped, which was wholly unlike her.

"Back me up here, I've been traveling," Gomez said.

Apaza glanced at her, his face lined with worry. "Someone attacked the Moon again, only this time, the word is they might have used Peyti clones."

Gomez cursed softly, heart pounding. "Is anything left?"

"They seemed to have caught it in time," someone said from behind her.

"The Peyti were using bombs built into their masks, and the bombs didn't work if the environment got changed from Earth Normal to Peyti Normal. Some kind of failsafe." Apaza clutched his coffee thermos even tighter. "But anyone with those Peyti when the environment changed from Earth Normal to Peyti Normal died."

"They have no idea what the body count is yet," Simiaar said softly. She looked over at Gomez. "Did we miss this?"

Gomez was staring at the screens. The images made no sense to her. Various Peyti faces, buildings she didn't recognize, people standing near sectioned domes.

She was startled. She hadn't expected the Peyti.

The Peyti, who considered violence a last resort. The Peyti, who always questioned any addition to the Alliance if the addition had a culture based on violence.

Her brain was having trouble processing this.

"The commentators I'm listening to are reeling," Apaza said. "They all thought the first attack was blowback against some human policies, and now this with the Peyti, it doesn't make sense."

"Peyti clones," Gomez repeated. "The cloning facilities generally don't mix clone types."

"What does that mean?" Camilla, the secondary pilot, asked.

"It means that the businesses are human-only or Peyti-only," answered Jiang, the third pilot. That meant Charlie was alone in the cockpit.

Gomez wondered if that was a good idea.

"Uzven knew, didn't it?" Simiaar asked Gomez. "The bastard just didn't tell us."

Gomez looked at her. Uzven, the Peyti translator who had screwed them up so badly on Epriccom more than fifteen years ago.

"Uzven trains the Peyti in human customs," Simiaar said, practically spitting the words. "I bet it trained these clones."

Gomez wasn't so certain. But Uzven had been a problem from the moment she met it. It would be so easy to believe Uzven had something to do with this. But Uzven might simply have been a cranky, difficult Peyti. She'd met dozens of those. They always believed they were superior to humans—and in some ways, they were.

Gomez shook her head. "We don't know anything yet, Lashante."

"This is a nightmare," Simiaar said. "I can't imagine what those poor people are going through."

Neither could Gomez. But one thing was clear. These attacks were focused on the Moon itself, for whatever reason.

That piece of information was probably important.

The fact that these attackers had used clones as weapons again was important as well, although she wasn't quite sure how that factored in.

And with more people dead in yet another attack, the investigators on the Moon would be tied up with another emergency.

She turned away from the screens and looked at her small crew.

"We're heading to the Moon as fast as we can," she said. "Obviously, it's one of the most dangerous places in the Alliance at the moment, and I won't look askance at any of you if you want to leave. There are human cities here on Hétique. I'm sure you can find your way home if you don't want to travel with us."

What the hell are you doing? Simiaar sent. *If they don't believe in us, they might report what we're doing.*

Gomez didn't care. And she wasn't going to handhold Simiaar at the moment.

The crew was looking at her, faces gray with shock. A few people had tears in their eyes.

"I'm afraid, however, that you'll have to make your decision now. We're leaving Hétique's orbit in less than an hour. I want to thank you all for your help—"

"What can we do on the Moon?" asked Floriano, who grew food for the kitchen. "I mean, we have jobs here, but you're planning to stay once we get on the Moon, right?"

"I'm not planning anything at the moment," Gomez said. "Things have obviously changed. And we have a ship. If the Moon government needs us to track things or investigate things, then we might have to travel to do so."

"And if we don't?" Floriano pressed.

"Then I'm sure there will be plenty for you to do."

To Gomez's surprise, that sentence came from Apaza. He sounded almost angry.

"Like what?" Floriano asked.

"Clean-up," Sionek, who handled the cargo bay, said.

"Rebuilding," said Hana, whom Gomez had brought in to handle the weapons systems on the ship.

"Taking care of the dead," Simiaar said, and the conversation stopped.

Everyone looked at her. She shrugged.

"Think it through," she said. "They lost millions in the dome collapses. And now they have collateral damage from their attempt to stop this second attack."

"What a nightmare," Floriano murmured.

Gomez nodded. She glanced back at the Moon images on screen. Yellowish atmosphere swirled around an enclosed room with a single window. A human hand slapped against the window and then slid down, out of view.

She shuddered.

Gomez turned back to the crew. She had no idea how many people had just seen that.

"Let me repeat," she said. "Anyone who wants to leave, can."

Floriano was shaking his head. The rest of the crew stood very still. No one seemed to be bolting for the door.

"You're right," said Hana. "They need a lot of help."

"There're not a lot of us, but at least we'll be fresh faces," said Sionek.

"And we'll be a little more emotionally stable," said Jiang.

"Speak for yourself, my friend," said Camilla, and everyone laughed, breaking the tension.

Then, as quickly as the levity appeared, it dissipated.

"Thank you," Gomez said, and eased out of the mess. She had a lot to do.

More clones, but of a different species. More killing. More attempts at destroying the domes.

And yet, she knew all of this was coming from inside the Alliance.

She needed to review the material she had gathered and see what she'd missed.

She had a feeling the pieces were there.

She just had to put them together.

35

NUUYOMA AND VERSTRAETE RETURNED TO THE RESTAURANT THAT EVENING. Verstraete took a table near the entrance. Nuuyoma had reserved the same table he'd had the evening before.

At first, he thought the snotty maître d' wouldn't give him the table. But after a bit of arguing, she relented.

The restaurant was full. People—humans—sat in tight groups of three and four, having intense conversations. As the maître d' took Nuuyoma to his table, he noted again how strange it was to see a human-only restaurant. It made him uncomfortable on a very deep level, as if he were heading into a dark place.

Conversely, he loved the smells of Earth-based spices and herbs. Cinnamon and nutmeg, garlic and ginger, pepper and more pepper. The scent of baked bread combined with the smell of cooked fish. All of those smells would have to be isolated in some restaurants with mixed clientele since the scent of some of the human spices could kill certain aliens. Most mixed restaurants opted for some kind of manufactured "cooking" smell that had been designed to appeal to all customers (and probably appealed to none).

The maître d' sniffed as she pulled back his chair and made a production of handing him the bound menu. Everything about this place was an affectation. The bound menu—on this level, at least—had a screen inside. He was told that the upper floors had actual paper menus, which were not just expensive, but wasteful.

Nuuyoma scanned, even though he knew he was going to order ogbono soup with fufu. He hadn't had a chance to finish yesterday's order. This time, it didn't matter what One Of One Direct said to him; he would finish the meal.

He had ordered a pineapple lime drink, no alcohol, and received it—with a bit of fresh pineapple attached to a stir stick—by the time One Of One Direct appeared.

One Of One Direct limped, which Nuuyoma hadn't noticed before. His skin tone seemed even paler than it had the day before.

One Of One Direct glanced at Verstraete, then sat down heavily across from Nuuyoma. "Have you ordered?"

"I'm waiting for you," Nuuyoma said.

One Of One Direct reached out a hand and grabbed the nearest passing waiter, nearly making her stumble into a table of diners.

"I'm having rigatoni with meat sauce," One Of One Direct said. "*Real* meat. From an animal source. Got that?"

"That's all we serve, sir," the waiter said.

"Yeah, sure," One Of One Direct said. "And my friend here will have…?"

"Ogbono soup with fufu," Nuuyoma said, hoping the waiter didn't take the word "friend" seriously.

"They have four hundred items on the menu," One Of One Direct said, "and you order the same thing twice?"

Nuuyoma shrugged. "I know what I like."

"Hmmm," One Of One Direct said. Then he looked at the waiter. "I want whatever he's drinking, as soon as you can get it to me."

"Yes, sir," the waiter said, sounding sullen. It amazed Nuuyoma that One Of One Direct could make anyone sullen within such a short interaction.

One Of One Direct let go of the waiter's arm.

"You don't like me, do you?" One Of One Direct said to Nuuyoma.

"I don't know you," Nuuyoma said.

"You're predisposed to hate me," One Of One Direct said.

"You're trying to pick a fight," Nuuyoma said. "Why is that?"

One Of One Direct sighed, then glanced at Verstraete. "I suppose you don't have any information for me."

"Actually, I do," Nuuyoma said.

One Of One Direct swung his head back toward Nuuyoma so fast that the table wobbled. Clearly, One Of One Direct was surprised.

"You probably know some of this," Nuuyoma said, "and I don't think you know the rest of it."

"Did you bring me documentation?" One Of One Direct sounded a bit too eager.

"On some of it," Nuuyoma said. "Some of it is eyes-only for Alliance Security employees."

One Of One Direct let out a small snort, as if that were expected. "Okay, tell me."

"I'll start with the information that I think you already know. If you're satisfied with it," Nuuyoma said, "then you tell me some of the information you'd mentioned. If I'm satisfied with that, I'll tell you more of what I know. And you'll tell me some things."

One Of One Direct's eyes narrowed. He clearly didn't like Nuuyoma taking over the conversation. Still, One Of One Direct didn't argue.

"All right," he said.

The waiter set down One Of One Direct's drink. Nuuyoma waited until she'd walked away before he began. As he did, his gaze brushed across Verstraete. She was watching closely. She almost looked nervous.

"We discovered that you were right," Nuuyoma said. "It appears Takara Hamasaki survived the explosions on *Starbase Human*. Her ship broke down just on the edge of the Frontier, and she abandoned it."

"There's no guarantee that she was the one who abandoned it." One Of One Direct's voice thrummed with frustration. That alone told Nuuyoma that One Of One Direct had found the ship information, but had been unable to go farther.

"That's correct," Nuuyoma said. "But she did. And before I tell you how I know that, you get to share with me."

One Of One Direct leaned back in his chair, balancing it on two legs. He kept one finger on the table, as if that helped him remain centered. He studied Nuuyoma for a moment.

Nuuyoma got the sense that One Of One Direct hadn't quite expected to be in this position, that he had expected to get some confirmation from Nuuyoma and then leave without saying anything.

Nuuyoma waited. He could wait all night if need be.

The waiter came back with his ogbono soup. It smelled fantastic. He tried not to think about One Of One Direct's comment about "real" meat. Nuuyoma had no idea what else tasted like goat besides goat. So he was going to assume that was the meat in the soup.

He rolled some fufu between his fingers and dipped it in the soup. One Of One Direct watched him. Nuuyoma would happily finish this meal, even if One Of One Direct never spoke to him again.

One Of One Direct sighed. "I was created by a conglomerate that you would consider criminal. It was called Cloni."

"Was?" Nuuyoma asked.

"Ah," One Of One Direct said. "We trade information back and forth."

"That's a name you could have made up," Nuuyoma said.

"But I did not."

"At least tell me where it was based," Nuuyoma said.

"Not far from here. On LeirSky."

"Where's LeirSky?" Nuuyoma asked. He had familiarized himself with the planets and moons around *Starbase Human*. He hadn't heard of LeirSky.

"It is an industrial base that orbits the planet Leir," One Of One Direct said. "It's huge, and has many industries like cloning—although Cloni is no longer there."

So the information was easy to give out, and had little consequence. It was as if they were playing a game, and they were starting with their least valuable cards.

"You can check this information," One Of One Direct said.

"I am," Nuuyoma said, and then sent the name of Cloni and the industrial base LeirSky to Verstraete to confirm.

"Your woman cannot join us," One Of One Direct said, as if he knew what Nuuyoma was doing. Of course he knew. He would probably do the same thing under the same circumstances.

"I know," Nuuyoma said, "but she can research for me while you and I talk."

Nuuyoma did not correct the phrase "your woman." He knew that One Of One Direct was trying to irritate him.

One Of One Direct snorted again, then shook his head. The waiter returned, this time carrying a plate of noodles covered in steaming red sauce. She set the plate down so quickly that Nuuyoma thought she almost dropped it on One Of One Direct.

The scent of tomatoes, oregano, and garlic wafted across the table.

Yes, Verstraete sent. *Cloni was a cloning conglomerate known for designer criminal clones. It made millions, maybe billions, thirty years ago before it was bought out and moved.*

"Has she confirmed?" One Of One Direct asked.

Apparently Nuuyoma was letting himself get a bit glazed as he got information through his links. He needed to retrain himself so that he didn't do that.

Nuuyoma dipped more fufu into the soup. He ate the piece slowly, reveling in the spice and texture. Then he wiped his fingers on the nearby napkin.

"I found no record of Takara Hamasaki after the explosion of the first *Starbase Human*," he said.

One Of One Direct flushed. "You promised—"

"At least by name," Nuuyoma said. Then he frowned. "You're very interested for a man who claims he waited decades to find out this information."

"I've been trying to find her for a long time," One Of One Direct said. "Your arrival gave me an opportunity."

Nuuyoma nodded. He wondered if he could use that volatility.

Then One Of One Direct frowned. "You said, 'at least by name.' Does that mean you found her another way?"

"Yes," Nuuyoma said. "Now you give me more information."

"That's not enough," One Of One Direct said.

"It's what you get," Nuuyoma said. "You didn't give me much either."

One Of One Direct pushed his plate aside. His fingers brushed the pineapple juice glass, but he didn't pick it up.

"After the spectacular failure of the fast-grow clones on the first *Starbase Human*," he said, "Cloni got bought out."

"I know that much from my partner's quick research," Nuuyoma said. "It probably won't take her long to find out who bought out Cloni."

"Oh, but it will," One Of One Direct said. "Because there are dozens of shell companies between the buyer and the corporation that bought Cloni."

Nuuyoma dipped more fufu. He didn't even look at One Of One Direct. Nuuyoma just continued to eat until One Of One Direct sighed heavily.

"All right," One Of One Direct said. "The buyer is your precious Earth Alliance."

Nuuyoma's stomach clenched. He made himself move slowly so that he didn't seem surprised. "You know that how?"

"I have tracked all the shell companies," One Of One Direct said. "I will give you that documentation if you tell me what happened to Takara Hamasaki."

That sounded like a fair trade. Still, Nuuyoma sent another message to Verstraete. *Are you finding who bought Cloni?*

He didn't look up as he sent it. He just continued to eat.

I'm finding a lot of corporate family trees, she sent back. *I'm not sure how much work I should do while I'm sitting here.*

That was probably as much confirmation as he would get. Nuuyoma took the last of the fufu and sopped up the remaining soup. After he'd eaten it, he said, "I found Takara's DNA signature. I cannot give that to you because it was on classified documents only available to Security inside the Alliance. But the signature appeared more than once."

One Of One Direct's blue eyes seemed even brighter than they had been when Nuuyoma met him. "Tell me where she went."

"You told me that you could point out who manages PierLuigi Frémont's DNA now, and I'm not settling for 'the Alliance,'" Nuuyoma said.

"You'll have to," One Of One Direct said. "There is no direct line Frémont DNA on the market."

"What about clones of clones?" Nuuyoma asked. "You're leaving a lot of DNA here right now. I could scoop it up and sell it."

"You could," One Of One Direct said. "And I guarantee that the buyer would be a front for the Alliance."

Nuuyoma felt his face heat. "You're telling me the Alliance tried to destroy Earth's Moon."

"I'm telling you that the only place you can buy Frémont DNA and therefore make Frémont clones is inside the Alliance. Through the Alliance."

"I don't believe you," Nuuyoma said, even though it sounded true. It was the same circular information that had led Gomez to take a leave of absence from the *Stanley*.

"Cloni still exists," One Of One Direct said. "Last I heard, all of the Frémont DNA goes through that company. Figure out what they do with the Frémont DNA and you will find your killers."

Nuuyoma's heart was pounding. Would it be that easy? Of course not. If someone inside the Alliance had turned this cloning company into an assassin mill, they would protect it.

"You make it sound so simple," Nuuyoma said.

"It is simple," One Of One Direct said. "Cloni has stayed small, and no one pays attention to it. It pays its taxes and reports what it needs to."

"How do you know this?" Nuuyoma asked.

"Because, unlike personal records, business records are easily available in the open net. The benefits of free trade." One Of One Direct sounded sarcastic. "Still, I'll give you all of the documentation. And there is a lot of it. Now, tell me about Takara."

Nuuyoma took a deep breath. He had to play this right to get the documentation, because he didn't have nearly as much information as One Of One Direct did.

"The DNA signature appeared on the border between the Frontier and the Alliance two months after the destruction of *Starbase Human*,"

Nuuyoma said. "The name attached to the signature was different, but the DNA matched on all levels."

"She went back inside the Alliance?" One Of One Direct asked.

"Yes," Nuuyoma said.

"I want to see the documentation," One Of One Direct said.

"I can give you the name she used and the information she publically declared going through customs," Nuuyoma said. "I cannot give you the DNA."

One Of One Direct's eyes narrowed. Something in them made Nuuyoma want to slide his chair away from the table.

"You said you could help me," One Of One Direct said.

"I did," Nuuyoma said. "I also said I would give you everything that I could legally give you. I cannot give you information that can be easily traced to me. Her DNA signature could be traced to me."

One Of One Direct cursed. "Give me what you have."

Nuuyoma sent the documentation he had prepared through the public links. It didn't matter who saw it; anyone could get public border-crossing information.

One Of One Direct put his chair down on all four legs. His eyes glazed over as he stared at the information. For once, he didn't seem to be playing coy.

Nuuyoma pushed his own plate aside. This time, One Of One Direct's plate was the one that held congealed food. That was a good sign.

"All right," One Of One Direct said after a moment. "I will send you all of my documentation if you swear to me you will tell me where she went inside the Alliance."

"I can do that," Nuuyoma said.

One Of One Direct tilted his head. "You're being awfully agreeable for a lawman."

"I am," Nuuyoma said. "Lucky for you you're dealing with a marshal and not someone who works inside the Alliance."

One Of One Direct snorted a third time, then shook his head. "I'd heard that the Frontier Security Service had its own rules. I hadn't believed that until now."

Nuuyoma's private links pinged. He wasn't really surprised. He had had a feeling all along that One Of One Direct had hacked most of his links.

Nuuyoma opened the message and found thousands of pages of documentation, all of it corporate security trees, sales documents, and business histories. He forwarded it all to Verstraete.

Confirm that this concerns Cloni, he sent along with the download. *I know you can't go through all of it now, but let me know I'm dealing with what One of One Direct promised.*

Okay, she sent back.

One Of One Direct looked over at her, then back at Nuuyoma. "Does this mean we should order dessert?"

The sarcasm would have worked if One Of One Direct had eaten his meal. He hadn't.

Nuuyoma smiled. "Just give it a minute."

He expected One Of One Direct to say that he didn't have a minute, which would have let Nuuyoma know that the information was false. But One Of One Direct waited, just like Nuuyoma did.

They sat in silence for more than ten minutes. Finally, Verstraete sent, *This all looks legit to me.*

"All right," Nuuyoma said.

One Of One Direct started. He had clearly been thinking of something else.

"Here's what I know about Takara Hamasaki. It seems like very little, but give this some thought before you respond," Nuuyoma said.

One Of One Direct's expression hardened.

"Takara went to Raaala as soon as she entered the Alliance. The name she was using was Suzette Hamdi. Both Takara Hamasaki and Suzette Hamdi never appear again on any records. *Anywhere.* Nor does the DNA signature that I had been tracking."

"So," One Of One Direct snapped. "You have no information."

"I asked you to think about this," Nuuyoma said. "No one's DNA signature vanishes, particularly if they must travel throughout the Alliance or get medical care or even if they die. Unless…"

"You can't change your DNA signature," One Of One Direct said. Then he frowned. "At least, not without help. And then only on the materials you use for identification. She Disappeared?"

"Raaala is known throughout the Alliance as the place most non-corporate humans go to Disappear. There are more Disappearance services per capita there than anywhere else in the known universe."

He might have exaggerated just a little. He wasn't sure about the known universe. He was certain about the Alliance itself, though.

One Of One Direct whistled. He ran cramped fingers over his blotchy forehead.

"I checked with every Disappearance service on the Frontier," he said softly, as if he were speaking more to himself than to Nuuyoma. "I never found her."

That was a lot of searching for something One Of One Direct claimed to be doing on a whim. That tightening in Nuuyoma's stomach had grown worse. He was lucky that she had successfully Disappeared. Because One Of One Direct had been very serious about finding her.

"Tell me where she is now," One Of One Direct said.

"I don't know," Nuuyoma said. "I'm not a Tracker or a Retrieval Artist. I don't have the tools to trace a Disappeared, particularly one who Disappeared successfully. Plus, she's inside the Alliance, and I'm not."

And fortunately, neither was One Of One Direct.

"Now I at least know where to start." One Of One Direct pushed his chair back. He started to stand, but Nuuyoma caught his wrist.

"Not so fast," Nuuyoma said. "You know who created the original clones. You're one of them. Tell me who did this."

One Of One Direct looked at Nuuyoma's hand, but Nuuyoma didn't let go of One Of One Direct's wrist. One Of One Direct sighed.

"The direct line was created with DNA given to Cloni by PierLuigi Frémont before he founded Abbondiado," One Of One Direct said. "The clones who attacked the Moon are not from my line at all. They were created from a different line, one that came from an Alliance source. Apparently, the clones from the direct line are failures, at least according to everything I've heard. Fast-grow clones from this line do not have the capability to work within instructions, and the slow-grow clones…"

He shook his head.

Nuuyoma tightened his grip. "What about the slow-grow clones?"

One Of One Direct smiled. "We're more concerned with building our own lives than doing the bidding of some mighty master."

Nuuyoma frowned. One Of One Direct sounded awfully certain.

"How do you know this?"

"Because," he said, "my line originally supervised the Frontier clone colonies that trained the slow-grows that eventually attacked your Moon. My siblings quit when ordered to destroy any clone that did not follow the rules exactly. Or rather, some of my siblings quit. After many of them were slaughtered along with their charges."

One Of One Direct shook his hand free. His face was flushed bright red.

"The propaganda coming from the Alliance states that the Frémont clones have a natural tendency toward murder. I can say categorically that we do *not*. The tendency toward murder was trained into clones by non-clones, people who have some kind of horrid agenda. They don't see us as human, so we can be destroyed at will."

His voice was shaking.

Nuuyoma was barely breathing. This man, angry, captured the attention of everyone around him. They were all staring at him, and One Of One Direct didn't seem to care.

"We are human," One Of One Direct said. "We are living beings. We do not deserve to be treated this way. My siblings objected. They saved many of the clones—whom I will not help you find, because they've gone on to real lives here on the Frontier. Find whoever owns and is running Cloni. Those people are your monsters."

Nuuyoma let out a breath. "Yet you want to get revenge on Takara Hamasaki."

"I want to find her," One Of One Direct said. "She is the only one who knows what happened on that base. She has answers. And I'll admit, there's a part of me that wants her to pay for all the lives lost. But I have never killed anyone. That's why I pulled out of that mission in the first place. I doubt I will harm her."

"Doubt is a weak word," Nuuyoma said.

"Yes," One Of One Direct said. "I never claimed to be strong. You assumed it, because of who my original was."

He spun and stalked away. The restaurant's patrons watched him go. Nuuyoma did too.

He let out another breath. He wasn't sure he believed One Of One Direct, on any of it. Nuuyoma knew he didn't believe One Of One Direct about the man's lack of desire for revenge.

But it didn't matter.

What mattered was the information Nuuyoma had received. Information he would look through. Information that he would send, through encrypted messages, to Gomez.

Information he would never, ever, send to the Alliance.

Not just because One Of One Direct had implicated the Alliance *again*. But because Nuuyoma no longer knew who to trust inside the government he worked for.

He could trust Gomez.

He knew she would use the information correctly.

And he was glad.

Because he wanted nothing more to do with this.

He wanted to return to patrolling the Frontier, just like he had been trained to do.

36

Iniko Zagrando had been traveling for nearly ten days when he finally heard about the attacks the human media had started calling the Peyti Crisis (and oh, boy, did he hate that name. He thought it completely misrepresented what had happened on the Moon just a few days ago).

Zagrando had allowed himself a single, short download of information as he went deeper into the Alliance itself. One download, just to make certain he wasn't heading into some kind of disaster—only to discover that his trip was even more important than it had been when he fled into the Alliance.

Zagrando stood inside his space yacht's entertainment room. This yacht, which he'd bought just before he went AWOL from the Earth Alliance Intelligence Service, had every bell, every whistle, every single luxury known to human kind.

It had been built outside the Alliance so it didn't fit Alliance specs at all. The doors were in the wrong places; the corridors were less than 1.5 meters high and curved, so that humans of normal height had to crouch as they walked; and the amenities—the amenities startled him every moment of every day.

Including the unnecessary rooms, like the entertainment room. He could just as easily have watched the news he had missed from the Alliance inside the captain's suite—which also had its own entertainment room, galley kitchen, and a bathroom like none he'd ever seen before—but he didn't.

He had to keep himself in shape, because he knew at some point, he would probably be fleeing for his life—maybe even on this ship.

A month ago, he'd been an undercover operative for the Intelligence Service. He'd worked for the service most of his adult life, primarily undercover as a police officer, then as a detective in Valhalla Basin. He'd been in Valhalla Basin on a long and dirty operation, collecting information on Aleyd Corporation, when his handler, Ike Jarvis, had pulled him away.

Not really pulled Zagrando away so much as forced him out of the job. Jarvis had used a fast-grow clone of Zagrando to fake Zagrando The Detective's death so that the real Zagrando could do all kinds of jobs outside of the Alliance.

Only, in the last ten days, Zagrando had been mentally reviewing those jobs, wondering if he had been working for the Intelligence Service or if he'd been working for Ike Jarvis.

Zagrando suspected he'd been working directly for Jarvis. In fact, Zagrando believed the last operation he'd been on had had a different mission than what he'd been told.

Zagrando had been told he was trying to find the source of the Pier-Luigi Frémont clones that had bombed the Moon six months before. He'd tracked down suppliers of designer criminal clones, and even set up a buy with another operative two weeks ago.

The other operative had blown the operation in such a way that if Zagrando hadn't given her to the criminals they were meeting with, he would have been murdered.

He fled with the millions in buy money and his life. Then, when he informed Jarvis that the operative had blown the operation, Jarvis had panicked, demanding Zagrando go back for her.

That had been the last straw. At that moment, Zagrando had known that Jarvis had set him up. Zagrando resigned, severed his connection with Jarvis (who never knew about this space yacht), kept the money as payment for all that retirement and back pay he would never receive, and then headed into the Alliance.

Not to get his job back. Not even to report Jarvis.

But to let the people on the Moon know Zagrando's suspicions. He guessed that Jarvis hadn't wanted him to find who made the clones of PierLuigi Frémont, but to discover if tracking the source of those clones was easy.

Zagrando could categorically say it had not been easy, and he was pretty convinced he hadn't found the source at all—at least, not until Jarvis and the other operative had tried to kill him.

Then Zagrando rethought everything. He had time on this trip to review every single mission he'd been on—and Jarvis's bizarre insistence that Zagrando not inform anyone in the Intelligence Service what he was doing.

In fact, Jarvis had told Zagrando that his cover was so very deep, he didn't dare report in to the service at all.

Good little soldier that Zagrando was, he had followed the instructions to the letter.

Just before he crossed the border into Alliance space more than a week ago, Zagrando had realized that Jarvis had used Zagrando The Detective's fake death not just to convince Valhalla Basin authorities that Zagrando was dead, but also to convince the Intelligence Service that Zagrando had died, as well.

Zagrando had made one last download of information, using some old Earth Alliance codes that he had to investigate himself on the public Alliance government boards, and he found his death listed as a member of the Earth Alliance Security Division. The death date listed was the date of his clone's death in Valhalla Basin.

Zagrando had felt even more vindicated in keeping the money (although the cop part of him, the ethical part of him, still had trouble with the fact that he had stolen something. Each time he had to reassure himself that the money had already been stolen—by Jarvis. But that didn't always help).

Zagrando had found a rather shady business in a scruffy starbase that destroyed his Earth Alliance identifications, his badge, his chips connecting him to the Earth Alliance government—everything that had once made him Iniko Zagrando.

He had bought an entirely new identity before crossing into Alliance space. Then, once he was here, he bought another one, and then one more, figuring if anyone wanted to trace him, they would have to work at it.

The only thing Zagrando didn't change was the space yacht, and that was only because he couldn't find anything like it on the market.

This thing was huge, built for a crew compliment of thirty, and a maximum of sixteen passengers. He rattled around the yacht like a ghost—which, in most definitions of the word, he was.

He spent his time exercising, planning his escape should this yacht be attacked, and retracing his own steps over the last three years, seeing if what Jarvis'd had him investigate offered clues to the Anniversary Day bombings.

Zagrando felt like he had seen whispers of those clues, but he also felt like he didn't have enough information to understand what he was seeing.

He hoped he would be able to work that all out when he arrived in Armstrong—when he got his audience with the people who were investigating the attacks.

He had an in; at least, he hoped he did.

The one other thing he had done along the way, at a space station where he knew his work couldn't be traced, was look up a Retrieval Artist who lived in Armstrong, a Retrieval Artist named Miles Flint.

Zagrando had met Flint years ago, on Valhalla Basin. Flint had come in search of his ex-wife, only to discover her missing. She had been kidnapped and had left a child behind, a daughter that Flint hadn't known he had.

Because the daughter was a clone of the original child, who had died as a toddler.

Flint could have left the clone behind. He had no legal obligation to take care of her. He hadn't created her—his ex-wife had, and his ex-wife had died as a result of her kidnapping.

But Flint had taken the clone, adopted her, and made her a legal human being with the same rights as everyone else. He had shown compassion in a way that Zagrando hadn't expected—indeed, in a way that Zagrando hadn't believed existed any longer.

Now, he was going to rely on that compassion to get him into Armstrong. Even if Flint didn't know who was leading the investigations of the Anniversary Day bombings, he would know who to contact.

All Zagrando had done in that single, brief, look-up was see if Flint still lived on the Moon and still worked as a Retrieval Artist. As of a few days ago, he had.

Although Zagrando now worried that he would have to check again.

The so-called Peyti Crisis had occurred days ago, and a lot of information was just coming to light. Zagrando actually sat on one of the comfortable chairs in the entertainment room and let the various recap news accounts wash over him.

Hundreds of people, maybe a thousand or two, had become collateral damage. The Office of Moon Security, apparently the only thing left structured like an all-Moon government, had ordered that the Peyti who had initiated the crisis be segregated, and then their environment changed from Earth Normal to Peyti Normal. That environmental change had defused thousands of bombs, but had killed any humans within range, leaving the Peyti perpetrators alive.

Zagrando had initially watched the coverage in disbelief, thinking perhaps someone had spoofed the entire Alliance. The Peyti were the most peaceful, non-violent people inside the Alliance. Peyti lawyers, on the other hand, were the most feared lawyers in the entire Alliance legal system because of their incisive minds and their take-no-prisoners attitude. They could manipulate Earth Alliance law to their own ends in ways that humans and other Earth Alliance lawyers could only emulate.

So, the idea that a group of Peyti lawyers had turned on the Moon simply seemed like a tasteless joke.

For a few minutes, Zagrando had scrolled through the mountains of data he had received from that download, thinking perhaps something had gone awry, that he had downloaded a bunch of particularly nasty satires instead of actual news reports.

When he finally realized that he was watching actual news reports, he got up and paced the small room. His brain couldn't handle the idea that the Peyti would turn against the Alliance like that.

However, it had taken a while for him to get all of the facts, and the one fact that was distributed in the days following the event that no one seemed to think worth mentioning in the more recent updates was that the Peyti lawyers were all clones of a Peyti mass murderer named Uzvekmt.

That detail made Zagrando sit back down again.

In fact, it made him shut off the reports while he thought about them. More clones. Another mass murderer.

Slow-grow clones, too, which meant that this plan—whatever it was—had been brewing for years.

Like Zagrando's seemingly aimless wanderings in the three years since he went deep undercover for the Earth Alliance.

After a fast-grow clone of him had been murdered right before his very eyes.

None of this could be coincidental. None of it.

Including his search for the Frémont clones, who had been impossible to find. Even the criminals he had met with on Jan hadn't said they had access to slow-grow Frémont clones. They had implied that they could get clones trainable for homicide before his partner, the operative he had left behind, had focused their attention on designer criminal clones specializing in thievery instead.

Zagrando's handler had gotten his answer, and then had decided that Zagrando was useless to him.

And the panic that Jarvis showed once Zagrando resigned told Zagrando that he had a lot of information that could lead to whoever the people behind these attacks were.

In no way did Zagrando believe that Jarvis was a mastermind of something this big. The man was venal and cruel, and not nearly as smart as he thought he was.

Jarvis wasn't a long-term planner so much as a reactor, someone who followed circumstances rather than trying to direct them.

The more Zagrando had reviewed his past three years, the more he realized just how much of a pawn he had been—a pawn in some kind of shadow game he hadn't known he was playing.

When he got inside Earth's solar system, he would contact Flint. He needed Flint's help to get into the Port of Armstrong. Zagrando firmly believed that someone—probably Jarvis—would have flagged the space yacht or put Zagrando's description into law enforcement networks in the space ports all over the Alliance.

Only now, with the so-called Peyti Crisis, Zagrando wasn't sure that Miles Flint still lived. For all Zagrando knew, Flint had been collateral damage in those attacks.

Zagrando had no way to double-check that information. He could search the current download, but he wasn't sure anyone had the names of all the dead.

He didn't dare execute another information download. He kept the yacht in its masking mode and didn't ping any nearby systems. He had worried about the two downloads he had done—one outside the Alliance and the other inside—but felt he couldn't do without them.

Still, they made him feel traceable.

Zagrando had to think that Jarvis and the people he was working for were searching for him and doing everything they could to find him.

Because he was a threat to their organization. If he weren't, they would have given him another assignment after Jan and sent him on his way.

Instead, they had tried to kill him.

They would try again.

He needed Flint, but if he couldn't get Flint's help, he would need to find someone else who could help him enter the Port of Armstrong without calling too much attention to himself or his ship.

He needed to search his memory and the databases he had for the name of the lawyer who had helped out Flint and his daughter. Because that lawyer had been from the Moon as well, and she might be able to smooth Zagrando's way through the port.

Or not. She was a lawyer, after all. And he wasn't sure how a lawyer would be willing to bend the law to let a man who no longer existed onto the Moon, particularly after the two disasters the Moon had experienced just this year.

He could only hope that Flint had survived, and that Flint would be willing to help him.

Zagrando could only hope that this trip wouldn't be in vain.

37

THREE SLEEPLESS NIGHTS LATER, PIPPA LANDAU PACKED. AT FIRST, SHE packed every single fancy outfit she had—dresses, shoes, slack and blouse combinations. Then she unpacked them and grabbed utilitarian clothes—black pants, comfortable sweaters.

Finally she closed the suitcases and collapsed on the hardwood floor of her bedroom, exhausted and alone.

If only her husband were still alive. She would sit across their kitchen table from him and say, *Ray, I'm in a hell of a mess.*

He'd smile at her and reach out his big, callused hand. *Pips, you're never a mess.*

What would he have done if he had known that she had lied to him every day of their lives together? What would he have said?

I love you anyway, Pips.

Or...

I asked for one thing and one thing only, Pips—Takara—whoever you are. I asked you to always tell me the truth. And you never have. Ever.

She leaned against the bed. Their bed. The bed she hadn't been able to bear replacing for ten long years.

Maybe it was good that Ray was dead. She wouldn't have that conversation.

She had decided not to have that conversation with her children, either. Twice, she had nearly pinged Takumi's links. If she told anyone, it would be him. He was the executor of her estate, her firstborn, the one she trusted the most.

He would have kept her secret if she asked. He would have never told his siblings. He would have defended her to the death.

After he assimilated the news.

Because Takumi was like his father. Volatile and loving, quick to anger and just as quick to forgive. Brilliant and strong and reliable.

Pippa drew her knees to her chest.

When she had Disappeared so long ago, the Disappearance service warned her that returning to her old identity would—at best—ruin her life. At worst, it would result in her death.

But it would also have all kinds of impacts on the money she earned, the things she owned, the relationships she had. The final identity she received—and she went through six under the service's aegis—was legal, at least in the Alliance.

Her marriage was valid, her property ownership valid, her will valid.

Unless she admitted that she had once been someone else. Then everything could be challenged. Depending on the laws of the place she ended up, she might lose everything.

Or her children might.

Or they might be subjected to the justice she had escaped.

She sighed and picked at the throw rug, which had bunched up near the foot of the bed.

Only she hadn't escaped justice. She hadn't run afoul of any aliens. She hadn't committed a crime against another species.

She had been the sole survivor of a horrific experience. She had been chased by a ship filled with people who wanted her dead, and she had managed to kill them.

But it had taken time—and they might have had a chance to warn someone that she had escaped.

From that moment on, she had proceeded as if her life were in danger. The Disappearance agent she had contacted had told her that was a good thing—that the only people who had long lives had the kind of caution she had exhibited.

The Disappearance service had recommended the full Disappear—and they had no incentive to do so, since she had no money at all. She had gone in as a poor client, hoping to get a grant.

She hadn't gotten it.

Instead, she'd had to spend the first five years of her Disappearance working for the service. Terrifying Indentured Servitude, one of her colleagues called it.

Indentured Servitude, because she had to work off every bit of her fee, mostly in helping other Disappeareds get to ships or get a hotel room or find a job.

Terrifying, because if she had failed in any way, she would have been sent back to the Frontier, her name restored, and maybe—just maybe—she would have died there. Because maybe, just maybe, if she had screwed up badly or committed more crimes or harmed one of the other newly Disappeared, the Disappearance service might have let her presence in the Frontier be known.

That had never been stated, but the threat had been implied. And she had felt it every day of that five-year period, always feeling like she was being judged and always worrying she was coming in short.

Afterwards, she had fled as far from the Frontier as she could go. Earth, where Disappeareds rarely ended up. Earth, with its strict laws and its ancient history.

When she was pregnant with Takumi, she had gone to a lawyer in Chicago and hired him for one hour's worth of advice. She had paid him in cash, and she had never told him her name.

She had met him outside of his office, so that nothing inside his office could identify her. She had colored her hair, changed her eye color, and used a short-term vanity enhancement to darken her skin. She wore lifts inside her shoes, and clothing so unlike what she usually wore that her friends wouldn't have recognized her—*Raymond* wouldn't have recognized her.

She had told the lawyer she was a long-time Disappeared, just starting a family, and she wanted to know—she *needed* to know—if her deception were discovered, what would happen to her husband and her child?

The lawyer had quizzed her, asking all sorts of questions about the set-up of her new identity. Finally, he concluded that her children would be subject to nothing—no untoward laws—nothing. Her husband would probably be fine as well, because as far as the lawyer could tell, she had broken no Alliance laws.

But he was uncertain about the status of her estate. Not that she would lose the money in it, but whether or not anything she did under the Disappeared identity would matter if her deception were uncovered.

And he used the word *deception*, which made her shudder.

She had deceived everyone, but if she hadn't, she would be dead now. She wouldn't have met Raymond, she wouldn't have married or become pregnant with Takumi, she wouldn't have had an estate.

She had left the lawyer in tears, just as frightened as she had been when she visited him, but more determined than ever to make sure that no one knew Pippa Landau was a Disappeared.

And now—

Now she couldn't sleep because someone—that same someone who had destroyed her life on the Frontier—was destroying the Moon. She had information—very old information, but information nonetheless— and telling anyone about it would put everything she had worked for in her entire life at risk.

She had toyed with sending an anonymous message along her links, but she would be sending it to the authorities on the Moon, and honestly, she was no good at encoding or hiding her tracks.

Not anymore.

Her information was decades out of date.

She would screw something up.

Plus she wasn't certain if anyone would pay attention.

If she went to the Moon, she could force them to listen to her, force them to take her seriously, force them to make her sacrifice worthwhile.

Maybe, if she did it right, it wouldn't be a sacrifice.

Maybe, if she found the right person to talk with, she would remain safe.

She leaned her head against the bed's softness.

Her heart was pounding so hard, it almost felt like it would come out of her chest.

But she had to make this trip.

Somehow.

She stood back up and looked at her suitcase.

The clothes were wrong. Everything was wrong.

She had to be sensible. She had to think it all through.

And she had to do it right.

Even though no one in her family realized it, they were all counting on her.

And maybe, just maybe, the Moon was, too.

38

ODGEREL FINISHED THE LAST OF HER NOODLES AND SET THE CONTAINER down on the bench beside her. She tilted her face toward the sun, feeling its warmth on her skin.

She didn't get long breaks from her job at the Earth Alliance Security Division Human Coordination Department, so she snuck away for lunch whenever the weather was nice. She always went to Beihai Park because it was so large, and that made her hard to find, even when someone tracked her through her links.

On this day, she sat on a red bench in the Hao Pu Creek Garden. Behind her, trees swayed in the wind. Children ran past, laughing, as a group of tourists gathered with their guide not too far from her chair.

She loved Beihai Park. Its age appealed to her and made her remember that Earth had centuries—millennia—of history before it became part of the Earth Alliance. Many of the gardens here had existed for centuries, including this garden-within-a-garden, still considered one of the best of the existing imperial gardens in all of China.

If Odgerel had it to do over again, perhaps she would be a garden architect or a historian, someone whose work echoed through the ages, instead of carving a bit of a future for humanity inside the ever-expanding Alliance.

With the edge of a chopstick, she scooped the last of the sauce from her Zhajiangmian, enjoying the hot sauce combined with garlic. There hadn't been enough cilantro in the dish for her, but she would remedy that the next time she ordered.

If she remembered.

She so rarely remembered anything about her day-to-day existence anymore. It felt like her mind was always elsewhere, thinking about other people's problems and other people's lives.

She wrapped her black skirt around her knees, then waggled her toes. She had kicked off her sandals, but she kept them beneath her feet in case she had to slip them on quickly. Her white blouse felt almost too heavy in the warm sun, but she did not care.

At some point soon, she would have to turn her links back on. She had the emergency links on, of course, but she shut off all other links— including family links—during lunch.

It was the only uninterrupted time of her day.

The slap of sandals against the ancient path made her sigh. That didn't sound like children at play. That slap sounded like someone running at great speed.

And even though she had no reason to connect the sound to her, she knew whoever it was had been looking for her for some time.

"Um, Ms. Odgerel...I mean, Odgerel, sir, I'm sorry to interrupt you, but..."

She didn't open her eyes. That whisper of a smile lingered. Just the confusion with her name told her who the man was. The latest member of Earth Alliance Security Division Human Coordination Department had just come over from the West, where two names were common.

Oh, who was she kidding? Two or more names were common for humans within the Earth Alliance now. So much in the Alliance, at least on the human side, ended up following Western traditions.

Which meant that her ancient Mongolian name seemed strange and out of place, even in a universe where strange and out of place had become the norm.

A hand brushed her shoulder.

"I'm sorry, sir, Odgerel, sir," the voice said.

She couldn't remember his name, either. Something common, at least in the West. And old-fashioned common, the kind of name that the West had seen throughout human history.

Charles? James? Thomas?

Mitchell. That was it. Mitchell Brown.

Now that she had his name firmly in place, she felt like she could safely open her eyes. She did, slowly, and she was glad of it, because his face was only centimeters from hers.

His hazel eyes were bloodshot, and his caramel-colored skin was pockmarked.

"I'm not deaf, Mitchell," she said calmly.

"I'm sorry," he said. "I'm sorry to interrupt you. I just—you know—I needed—"

"Of course, you needed," she said. "Is it an emergency?"

"No," he said.

She suppressed a sigh. Young and eager and stupid. Why did they always appoint the stupid ones?

"You're a little close," she said.

"Right," he said and leaned back. He was a tall man, thin in an intense way, the kind that suggested he regularly forgot to eat rather than had a metabolism that worked overtime. He shoved his hands in the pockets of his black pants, then pulled them out and smoothed his ill-advised pink shirt.

He glanced around, then moved the remains of her lunch without asking her if she was done. He sat down next to her.

"They told me that lunch was the best time to get you alone," he said. "So I..."

She didn't listen to the rest. Of course, someone had told him that lunch was a good time to find her alone.

It was a kind of hazing ritual the older staff members in the division practiced on the newcomers. Odgerel had asked them to stop, but they never did. And they never took credit for forcing a brand-new idiot into the old routine.

Maybe if she yelled. But she wouldn't have received this assignment—and held it for two decades—if she were the kind of woman who yelled at the smallest thing.

"You were misinformed," she said. From the look on Brown's face, she had interrupted him. She did not apologize. "Lunch is my private time. I have repeatedly asked that no one interrupt me unless there is an emergency."

"Oh, jeez, sorry." He bounded up as if the bench had suddenly become scalding hot. "I didn't know. I'll just—"

"You're here," she said. "And I'll wager you spent most of this past hour searching for me, didn't you? Because lunch is nearly concluded."

His face flushed. "I did. I'm sorry—"

"So stop apologizing, sit down, and tell me what was so important."

"You sure?" he asked.

She resisted the urge to roll her eyes. Instead, she patted the bench. A group of teenage girls approached down the walkway, laughing and pointing at something behind Odgerel. She did not turn around, although Brown's gaze flickered in that direction. He smiled momentarily, then the smile faded as his gaze met hers.

He nodded, the flush growing, and sat down like a recalcitrant child.

The girls passed, giggling and talking so loudly that Odgerel could barely hear herself think.

She waited until they were several meters away before continuing.

"Well?" she asked, knowing it sounded imperious.

She used to hate that quality in herself. As she got older, she embraced it. She had an affinity for the lost empires. That was one reason she came to Beihai Park every day, one reason why she had insisted the Earth Alliance Security Division Human Coordination Department be housed near the Forbidden City.

She wanted the EASDHC employees—at least the human ones—to know what they were defending. Civilization had existed here for a very, very, very long time. Things humans took for granted, like paper and silk, had all started in this nation, on Earth, before any human ever went to space. Long before. So far back that most humans never even studied these civilizations at all.

She had. She believed in their import.

And she believed in protecting them against alien incursions. She still started when she saw Disty sitting cross-legged on the rails overlooking Beihai Park's lake or eight-legged Sequev stomping their way across the beautiful arched bridges.

Brown was staring at her. Apparently her invitation to speak had made his brain freeze.

"Mitchell," she said, "please forgive me, but I have finished my lunch and I was going to stroll back to the division offices. If you would like to talk with me, you have only ten minutes or so before I begin my journey back to work."

"Oh, right," he said. "Sorry. You must think me an idiot."

She did not answer that. Instead, she felt a pang at the loss of privacy, that lost moment when the sun would caress her face.

"You're familiar with the situation on the Moon, right?" he said, then shook his head. "Of course you are. That's all anyone talks about, whether or not the attacks will start here. Everyone's acting like it's terrorism or y'know, some kind of coordinated attack on the Moon. Y'know, a crime or something."

It was a crime. One large crime that masked several small crimes. But she didn't correct him. She had worked personally with the head of the Earth Alliance Security Division Human Investigative Department to dispatch investigators to the Moon after the Anniversary Day bombings. She made certain that there were Earth Alliance investigative staff in every devastated city, and she had lost some staff members in the Peyti Crisis, as the media called it.

She folded her hands in her lap. Anyone who knew her well would see that as a sign of impatience.

"If you do not believe this is a crime, what would you call it?" she asked.

"It's a crime," he said. "Clearly. But there's a lot of chatter about it, coming from the Moon itself, and that chatter scares me."

Since *she* scared him, she didn't know if his fears were something to be alarmed about. But again, she said nothing.

"Some of the local officials—and some of the people who are acting heads of this and that—are calling the attacks 'a war on the Moon.'"

She let out a small breath. She hadn't seen that.

"What do you mean by local?" she asked.

"Sorry," he said, obviously still unsettled by the trick the other staff members had played on him. "I mean, Moon-based officials. The folks in charge. The *remaining* folks in charge."

Inwardly she winced at his correction, not because he made the correction—it was accurate; so many on the Moon were dead—but because he had to make it. For clarity.

"How many references have you found?" she asked.

"Just a few, three weeks ago, mostly in private, link-based conversations," he said. "But after the Peyti Crisis, it seems to be a meme. *Everyone* mentions it. Usually in this sort of way, 'Why would anyone declare war on the Moon?'"

Why indeed? It was a good question, and one she had not looked at from that angle. It was not the normal way she approached anything. She headed the Security Division. Her office coordinated all of the human parts of the security forces, from Frontier Security to the Earth Alliance Police Force.

She thought of protection and crime, not about war. If one group in the Alliance wanted to declare war on another group, then the diplomats had to sort it out. Or the various military divisions.

Not hers.

"This meme, as you call it, alarms you," she said after a moment.

"Yes." Brown said.

"Should the Moon officials not think they are at war?" she asked, then realized she had probably phrased the question incorrectly. "After all, they are under repeated attack."

"But they don't know who is attacking them, and neither do we," he said. "And some of the arguments I've seen, they lead me to think this isn't a crime at all, nor is it isolated to the Moon. I think these people, they have a point."

Odgerel looked at him. She had assumed, because he had fallen for the hazing, that he was stupid. She had also assumed that, because he was the latest appointee in a string of relatively incompetent appointees, that he was similar to them. And finally, she had assumed, because he apologized too much, that he always made mistakes.

She had probably assumed incorrectly. Now that he had relaxed into the subject he had intended to discuss, his eyes glimmered with intelligence. He seemed stronger than she realized, and most people did not seem strong when they met with her. They allowed her power to reflect their weaknesses.

"You felt the need to tell me this privately," she said, "and outside of our offices. May I ask why?"

He took a deep breath, then glanced over his shoulder. Those movements told her more than any words would. Either he had not been in Beijing long enough to learn to trust anyone or he believed no one worthy of his trust.

"I read data differently than a lot of the staff," he said. "It's one of the reasons I got promoted. I make leaps—"

"Of intuition, I know." She remembered him now. She had seen his results in various documents. He had headed a small division near the Outlying Colonies and had managed to dissolve two criminal syndicates that had operated out of the Outlying Colonies since the days when the Colonies were at the edge of the known universe (and were actually colonies), instead of places squarely inside of Alliance territory.

Odgerel had asked for him a year ago, and then forgotten about the request. She often forgot about requests because so many of the people she requested did not want to return to Earth (if they had ever been to Earth at all), believing the "action" happened at the edges of the Alliance rather than in its very heart.

"The attacks are focused on the Moon," Brown said, "but they use resources from all over the Alliance."

Odgerel nodded. She knew that.

"Because of its proximity to Earth," he said, "the Moon is considered a human place. If you ask anyone from the Outlying Colonies about the Moon, they would tell you that *only* humans live there. They do not know about the large alien populations or the way the port brings in species from all over the known universe."

"The perception is correct," Odgerel said softly. "Humans govern the Moon, just as the Disty govern Mars. There are human enclaves on Mars, but they are not the center of Martian life."

He frowned a little. "The enclaves are the center for the humans on Mars."

Odgerel noted that piece of information. He was human-centric as well. That did not disturb her. She encouraged that among her staff. Even though the Earth Alliance Security Division handled security for the entire Alliance—humans and aliens—her wing only focused on humans (or focused as much as it could).

When humans had to interact with other species, she watched the line between whether the interaction belonged in the Human Coordination Department or went back to the Security Headquarters for reassignment in the Joint Department (Humans and other species) or into a strictly alien department (such as the Peyti Coordination Department).

Watching that bright line was part of her work, seeing where the impact on humans was and whether or not her people could deal with it without involving aliens at all.

She actually encouraged the reluctance of her staff members to involve aliens. She liked to keep human issues human, because she knew that deep down, humans cared more about themselves than they cared about any other species.

"Nonetheless," Odgerel said. "Your point about Mars is a side issue. You were making a much larger point."

Brown nodded, then watched as a group of earnest children walked by, name badges flaring in a square on their lapels. A school group. So many came here. She liked to watch them as well, and to remember that the future started with them.

Always, the future. And keeping that future safe.

"The human point is an important one," he said. "The first attacks used human clones—and clones of a type that would scare humans, if they know their history."

Odgerel nodded. She knew that. It was one of the most discussed points whenever the Anniversary Day bombings became the topic of conversation in the overall staff meetings.

"But the attempted bombings last week," Brown said, "those used Peyti clones of a mass murderer not known to humans. Had the murderer been known to humans, the Peyti clones could not have hidden in plain sight for decades."

Odgerel shifted slightly in her seat, turning her body toward him. He was making points she hadn't considered.

"So, if the attacks were designed to scare humans," he said, "they would have used other clones of human mass murderers. This is something bigger, and something much more complicated."

Odgerel leaned her head back, considering. He was right.

And she had missed it, precisely because of her focus on the human angle inside the Alliance.

"And here's the other thing," Brown said. "These attacks used slow-grow clones. The Peyti clones lived on the Moon and integrated into society there. These attacks were planned for *decades*. I've spent my life combatting criminal enterprises, and none of them has a decades-long view of their work."

Brown leaned just a little closer to Odgerel, and the movement didn't bother her. He had engaged her mind in a way that no one had for some time.

"That's been my experience, as well," she said. "Criminal enterprises may have plans that last a few years, but never decades. No leader can expect to maintain control that long."

She truly had been looking at these attacks incorrectly. It irked her to think how wrong she might have been.

"And if the leader does expect to maintain control that long," Brown said, "he won't tell someone his plans, because it would be easy to thwart them. But these plans? The ones that led to the attacks on the Moon? Just to raise and train the clones would take a large staff, and a lot of investment up front."

"Which is something else criminal enterprises generally do not do," she said as she thought aloud.

She looked at the nearby pagoda. Ironically, it was surrounded by a tour group that had two Peyti, a couple of Imme, and a handful of humans wearing clothes too bulky for the weather.

"A war on the Moon," Odgerel said softly.

"No," Brown said. "The Moon is the gateway to Earth. And Earth is the heart of the Earth Alliance. If you want to destroy the Alliance—"

"You destroy Earth," she said quietly.

That was an old adage of the Alliance, which came from the early years. The Earth was under threat so often back then that its defenses became rigid, and the Earth became difficult to travel to. It still was.

If someone wanted to go to Earth, they had to go through the Moon first. And even then, getting to the Moon did not mean that someone could travel onto Earth.

The Moon's ports were relatively open; the Earth's were closed.

"You think this is a proxy attack," Odgerel said. "The Moon substituting for Earth."

"I'm not sure," Brown said. "But I think 'war' is a much more accurate term than 'crime' for those attacks."

Odgerel almost nodded, but caught herself in time. She needed to think about this.

"I scan the reports from the Military Division," she said. "I have not seen any credible threats from communities outside of the Alliance. The Alliance has grown so big that no single culture can attack it. No one would consider trying. If cultures do not approve of us, they do not do business with us. They do not travel through our space. But they don't attack us. What would they gain?"

Brown shrugged. "It's not my area of expertise. But I do know human history."

She looked at him. He had caught her attention.

"In the past, in places like this and in the West—all over Earth—empires rose and fell. They fell because of hubris, yes. We were taught that quite young. But sometimes the fall was initiated from outside. When a group saw the cracks in the empire, saw the places where the right amount of pressure applied in the right way would make certain the empire would collapse."

"I know the history, as well," she said. "Generalizations do not help."

"Please forgive me, ma'am, but don't dismiss this. Guerilla warfare has existed throughout human history, and the warfare often looked just like this. Hit a pressure point, then hit it again, and in tiny ways that would reverberate throughout the government."

Odgerel looked at him. "I understand that. What I don't see is why anyone would attack the heart of the Earth Alliance. There is no profit in it. Destroying the Alliance would destroy billions of lives and more money than anyone can conceive of. The peace we have lived under for most of the life of the Alliance would disappear, and relations between various species would collapse. So, what would someone gain in destroying the Alliance?"

"I don't know." Brown shook his head, then bit his lower lip, and glanced at the tour group near the pagoda. The leader, a slight woman with long, dark hair, was gesturing wildly. "I think we have to look, though. We can't assume that because we believe something is good, others do as well."

Odgerel let out a small breath. She had been making that assumption, hadn't she? And history had shown over and over again that what one group believed were benevolent conditions, other groups did not.

"Do you believe it's important that we're looking at clones who have done this?" she asked.

"I don't know," Brown said. "I think we need to discover who believes they're being harmed by the Alliance, and who feels strongly enough to take action to destroy the Alliance in order to alleviate that harm."

"I'm sure that the Political Department has information about dissident groups," she said, "and the military will have information about those outside of the Alliance who want to destroy it."

"They've had that information for years," Brown said. "But is the Earth Alliance Military Division using it to investigate the Moon? And really, can the military legally investigate inside the Alliance? Conversely, can our Political Department investigate adequately? I think we should get the information from them and then coordinate the investigations, maybe through our Investigative Department."

So that was why he wanted to talk with her alone. He was, in effect, suggesting something that would cause all sorts of interagency rivalries, and he was smart enough to know it.

"It's not as simple as that," she said. "The divisions are territorial. We don't share information easily."

"Even when the fate of the Alliance is at stake?" he asked.

"Prove to me that it is," she said, "and then I can run interference for you."

He shook his head ever so slightly, head down. His shoulders rose and fell as he sighed.

She could actually see him make a decision.

"I came here," he said, "because I had heard you were a risk-taker, someone who would go against the internal Alliance mechanisms if necessary. I don't think we have the time to 'run interference.' I think we have to get these organizations to work together. We need to share information, and we need to filter it through the prism of who wants to harm the Alliance and who has the means. We need—"

"I'm aware of what we need," she said quietly. "I can do none of this without proof."

"I can't get you proof without the cooperation of the Military Division and our own Political Department," he said.

"Then you are not as creative as your work record implies that you are." She stood, smoothed her blouse, slipped on her sandals, and picked up the container for the noodles. She left him, without bidding him farewell.

The tour group was walking from the pagoda to the gardens. One of the Peyti looked over its shoulder at her. Their eyes met.

She felt a shiver run through her.

She had never liked aliens.

She liked them even less now.

39

The convention center inside Garner's Moon went on for kilometers. Deshin owned both the center and the moon, although he rarely came here anymore. One of his corporations rented the facility out on an almost daily basis. In fact, they'd had to cancel the contract for a trade show of black marketeers just so that he could hold this meeting.

His accounting staff told him the hit would cost him millions. He didn't care about the money. He had more than enough money to last his lifetime, Paavo's lifetime, and the lifetime of Paavo's great-great-great-grandchildren, even if they worked hard at spending all of it. Deshin was more worried about clearing out the trade show attendees before his cohorts arrived.

Fortunately, his staff had managed to cancel the trade show, and they had managed to clean up the convention center, closing off the non-human wings and getting rid of the dining and bathroom accommodations set out for a wide variety of aliens who could handle Earth Normal.

Deshin's staff had asked if the trade show could continue in another part of the gigantic center, but he had said no. He instructed his staff to inform the trade show attendees that a show which paid considerably more would be taking the space.

He knew he hadn't lost the black marketeers' business. They would be back within a month. There weren't many safe places inside the Alliance to hold a trade show geared toward the black market.

The thing that Garner's Moon had that no other place inside the Alliance had was a complete guarantee of safety from external attack. Even if someone found out that a meeting was being held in the Garner's Moon facility, that someone couldn't bomb the facility out of existence. The moon was too well made for that.

He had built Garner's Moon early in his career, when he thought he had money to burn. At the time, he had needed the underground conference space and a safe location to conduct business inside the Alliance but away from Earth's Moon.

Garner's Moon was probably the safest place he knew of inside the Earth Alliance—at least for him.

Garner's Moon joined nearly two dozen other moons orbiting Szokla, the uninhabitable planet below. In all the years Szokla had been part of the Alliance, no group had ever discovered life on it, no matter how life was measured.

The moons—satellites, really—were too small to sustain life, and none had their own atmosphere. Deshin's technicians had believed that no one inside the Alliance would see the appearance of another moon orbiting Szokla.

Back then, Deshin had believed that the Alliance noticed everything, and he thought his people—or someone—would have to come up with an explanation for Garner's Moon. But no one had ever noticed, and the moon never showed up on star maps.

He later learned that when the Alliance deemed an area impossible to settle, the organization rarely bothered to revisit it.

Garner's Moon had seemed like a good plan in the beginning, but he soon learned why no one else of his acquaintance had developed anything like it. Initially, Garner's Moon had nearly bankrupted him. It had also killed the architect, a dear friend. Deshin named the moon for him in a sad sort of tribute.

Eventually, though, Garner's Moon had turned a profit, even with the improvements Deshin had had to continually make in the first decade. Now, it was one of the most lucrative properties he had. He just didn't want to go through that kind of financial stress ever again.

Even though he rarely visited Garner's Moon, it was still geared to him. He had his own private dock for his ships and an apartment that had all the ostentation that he and Gerda now avoided.

He and his team had settled into the owner's apartment complex the night before. The people he had invited—humans all—had shown up throughout the day.

The fascinating thing about Garner's Moon—at least to Deshin— was the fact that no one ever thought of it as his. If the people he had invited had realized they were coming into the heart of one of Deshin Enterprises's most lucrative businesses, they wouldn't have come.

But so many groups had used Garner's Moon over the years that it had felt natural for the invitees to attend, as if Deshin had rented the space for his own private conference.

This meeting would only use one small corner of the convention center, so technically, his staff had been correct: he could have left the black market trade show alone.

He hadn't, though, because everyone he had invited was wanted somewhere within the Alliance, and everyone he had invited did not want to be considered as a "known associate" of the other people who were attending.

Deshin hadn't seen some of these people in more than ten years. He had hoped he would never see some of them again. But he saw no choice this time.

The first meeting—maybe the only meeting—would be over dinner. He had invited the representatives of eight families. Eight people, plus their entourages, security details, and factotums. Maybe a thousand people would end up inside the convention center, although only the eight invitees would be inside the luxurious private dining room.

Not even their security details were allowed. If people didn't like the arrangement, they didn't have to come. And yet, all eight had said yes.

The security details would have their own isolated rooms overlooking the dining hall. They wouldn't be able to hear any audio, and the tilt of the isolated rooms—leaning over the floor below at a 20-degree angle—made reading lips almost impossible.

He also insisted that links were shut down for the duration of the meeting. Recording chips were disabled, and everyone who left the room would be searched by Deshin's people and the convention center's automated system to make sure no recordings would leave with them.

Deshin, on the other hand, would be able to hear and record every word. The private dining room had a state-of-the-art recording system, one that Deshin and a few others on his security team could link into. He knew from experience no one would test his links to see if they remained on—and if they tried, he would find a way to bar them from the meeting.

Three members of his security team had access to any message he sent from the room. The message would go from his links to the recording system, and out to them.

If he had news he needed to act on immediately, he had the available system.

He could also mentally scream for help if he needed to.

Deshin had excellent chefs who cooked for the high end trade shows, and he used those chefs for this gathering, accommodating all the different eating styles of his guests. He did not allow any servers, so the food sat on sideboards around the room, labeled by cuisine. Each serving bowl and plate had a sensor. When they were empty, they slid through the wall unit and down a narrow shaft into the kitchen below. More food got sent up through a different unit.

Deshin's security team had allowed all of the other security teams to inspect the food delivery systems before the meals would be served. Some of Deshin's guests also had tasters, and Deshin gave those guests a choice: they could either watch everyone else eat or let their tasters sample in the kitchens before the food made its way to the sideboard.

Deshin wanted absolute privacy. He knew what he was going to ask this gathering, and just the fact that he was having the meeting could get them all in trouble.

He hadn't told any of them what this was about, only that they needed to act in concert to stop an ongoing threat. He told them all he would explain in depth when they met.

He arrived in the dining room one hour before the meal was to begin. He had already been to the kitchens. He had approved the wine for those who drank alcohol. He had approved the clearers for those who drank in excess.

He sampled the foods—at least from the cuisines he could tolerate—and he approved the presentations. He made certain that there were visible poison control kits at every single seat at the table, even though he knew that anyone who would worry that Deshin wanted to poison them would bring their own kit.

Before he had arrived at the kitchens, he had spoken to the high-level security staff—the one that could handle a trade show of assassins without losing a single life—and he made certain they had ways of safeguarding every aspect of this meeting.

Then he had his own personal staff back up the Garner's Moon staff.

By the time he double-checked the dining room, he knew that internal threats had been neutralized—at least as best as possible. He assumed someone could stab someone else in the neck with a fork or a chopstick. He figured some risks were necessary.

He stood at the head of the table and looked down its length. There was no decoration, only napkins and placemats that marked each place. The attendees would choose their own utensils and their own serving plates. If they preferred to eat out of bowls using bread or their fingers, so be it. If they would rather use chopsticks and small plates, that was fine as well.

Deshin was being accommodating, at least on the cuisine. When it came to the conversation, however, he was demanding.

He made certain that everyone could hear everyone else, even if they were whispering. He set up seating arrangements so that friends and current business partners did not sit next to each other.

Here, at least, he would use that ancient advice that while friends should be close, enemies needed to be closer.

After all, almost everyone he had invited had, at one time, been his enemy. A few still might count themselves that way.

They were, at the very least, competitors.

He would try to cut through that.

Because they had a common enemy, one they had allowed to remain unguarded for too long.

It was time to go after the Earth Alliance.

And he wanted to do it in a very specific way.

40

Mother, you have never been to the Moon.

Pippa Landau stood in the departures lounge inside the Port of Chicago. Not that the port was actually in Chicago. It was west of Chicago, on a big patch of land that had once housed towns like Oswego, Yorkville, and Sandwich. It was flat here, with lakes and rivers that had been diverted or that went under the port itself.

She had driven there, stunned as always to see a dome on Earth—a gigantic, glasslike dome that would open to accept or send out ships. Even they became visible in the blue, blue sky as she got closer, some ships no bigger than her hover car, and probably no safer.

Her son Takumi was right: Pippa Landau had never been to the Moon. As far as he knew, she had never been off Earth, not once in her entire life.

It's just a conference, she lied. *I'm looking forward to it.*

Actually, her stomach was in knots so tight that she was amazed she had been able to eat during the last week. The closer she got to the port, the more frightened she became.

She felt like two different people: the girl who had known how to pilot her own ship, and the woman who had no idea what differences between spaceships were.

She'd had to research her flight—something she hadn't done in forever—and then she had to consider what kind of commercial vessel

Pippa Landau would take, not the kind of vessel that Takara Hamasaki would take.

She had to acknowledge that she was a teacher now, a middle-aged Midwestern woman whose first grandchild had been born just the year before, a woman who would be terrified of this trip, because it was something new.

She *was* terrified of this trip, but not because it was new.

She sank into a chair near the gate. She set her bag on the floor beside her. The bag was filled with three days' worth of new clothes, all nothing like clothing that Pippa Landau would wear to class or even around the house.

She had cut her hair and had made her eye color match the color of her blouse for the first time since she married Raymond. She couldn't entirely ditch her Pippa Landau persona because she was traveling under that name, but she didn't want to be entirely recognizable, either.

Maybe that was foolish. Maybe the entire trip was.

But she had finally settled on a way to travel.

She glanced around the lounge. Right now, it was nearly empty. The ship wouldn't leave for another two hours. In her very distant past, she would never have arrived this early for a flight.

But she was a school teacher on the trip of a lifetime; of course, she would arrive early.

Besides, arriving this early gave her the chance to talk to her son, without anyone else really knowing what she was doing. She had left messages for her other two children during their busy times at work, and then blocked their links as if she were already on the flight.

But she knew she had to talk to one of them, and she had chosen Takumi because he would be the one to handle things if she didn't come back.

She couldn't tell him that, of course. She had decided not tell him anything about this trip, taking that old lawyer's advice, keeping her true identity secret until the last.

Maybe she would have to publically reveal it on the Moon, but she doubted that. She wanted to get in and get out, to do her duty, and maybe make her nightmares go away.

Mother, Takumi sent, *these days, the Moon is not somewhere you go for a conference.*

She felt her face color as her son said that. Of course. She hadn't thought through her lie.

All right, she sent. *I misrepresented it, sort of. When I teach, I teach personal responsibility.*

Yes, Mother, he sent. *I know.*

Fortunately, she couldn't see him. She didn't want him to know how she looked as she was traveling. She didn't want the questions. So she had lied (had she ever lied this much to her children before?) and said that the departure lounge didn't allow visual links.

Her children had never traveled off Earth, so they had no idea what was allowed and what wasn't. They were Earthbound, and she was happy for it.

In some of Takumi's questioning, she could feel the underlying thrum of fear that the Earthbound had for the rest of the Alliance. Space travel was expensive and dangerous. The distances were long and difficult. And the aliens crowded every single non-Earth place, making the chance of breaking Alliance law even greater.

She had heard that swill from the moment she arrived in Dubuque. When her kids were in school, they had come home repeating it—even when she quizzed them about the other species in their classrooms. Apparently, to her children and so many others, "aliens" were not the children of non-humans whom they had grown up with. Aliens were the species they'd never seen or the ones that made the news, like the Disty with their Vengeance Killings or the Wygnin, coming in to steal children in the night.

Raymond used to disabuse their children of these notions, but Pippa had remained quiet, deciding that on one level, the ignoramuses who taught her children were correct: space was dangerous, and her children never needed to travel there.

Well, she sent to her son, making up the lie as she went along, *one of the organizations I belong to is holding a conference that's rather hands-on, letting us help rebuild the Moon. I think it's a good cause—*

Mother, let someone else do this, her son sent. *We have no ties to the Moon.*

It's the greatest humanitarian crisis of our time, she sent, and that part was true—at least in this solar system, it was. The Earth's solar system hadn't seen this kind of mass loss of life from a non-organic cause in decades. *If I'm going to teach my students to respond with compassion, then I'm going to have to allow them to travel to places like this. In order to organize a return trip later in the year, I have to attend this conference now. I have—*

Now? Takumi sent. *Mother, hundreds of people have just died up there. Again. It's the wrong time to go.*

I'm sorry, Takumi, she sent, and hoped the links picked up her rather sad tone, *but right now is the* best *time to go. If there's going to be a third attack, it won't happen for weeks, maybe months. Just like the second attack. Everyone will be vigilant. I think right now is the absolute best time to go, and if I don't like the measures the Moon government is taking in the wake of these two crises, then I won't bring my students later.*

Mother, there is no Moon government. There never really has been—

You know what I mean, Takumi, she sent.

It's not fair that you've contacted me as you're about to leave, he sent. *I'll reimburse you for the ticket. We need to discuss this before you go.*

Takumi, she sent. *The conference starts tomorrow. I can't wait.*

Mother—

I love you, darling. Give kisses to that little girl of yours, and your beautiful wife. She was about to sign off when she added one more thing. *And don't worry your siblings. They have enough on their plates at the moment. I'll be back in no time. You won't even miss me.*

That's not fair, Mother—

She signed off as if he weren't sending anything at all. Then she blocked any reply with an automated response, saying that her ship was boarding.

It wasn't, of course. There wasn't even a notification above the exit, saying that the trip was about to start.

She stood up. Her stomach wasn't as knotted as it had been.

Maybe she had just been frightened of telling her children what she was going to do.

She was on her way now, even if she hadn't yet boarded the ship.

She was going to do what she believed to be right.

And then she could go back to her anonymous little life.

Once and for all.

41

THEY TRAIPSED IN, ONE BY ONE, LOOKING SMALLER THAN USUAL. DESHIN hadn't realized until the eight guests he had invited to this little meeting had actually showed up for it how much their bodyguards added to their own aura of invincibility.

They sat around the table, four men and four women. The only person he had never worked with before was the one whom he had to struggle to stop staring at. Sonja Mycenae.

She looked like her clone's older, tougher, meaner sister. She had stunning, copper-colored skin and matching brown eyes. Her dark brown hair was cut short, accenting the angle of her jaw and the curve of her neck.

She wore a black tank top that revealed every muscle in her torso as well as the aureole of her breasts and a pair of tight, black pants that looked like they'd been glued to her legs. Only her shoes weren't practical. She wore black sandals that, in Deshin's opinion, did not offer enough protection against injury to her shapely feet.

She saw him looking at her, and she gave him a sardonic grin. He nodded in return, wondering if her mother had ever told her that he had hired one of her illegal government clones, and that that particular clone had ended up dead.

He couldn't ask. Aurla Mycenae had died five years before in a failed raid against the Earth Alliance. And because of that, frankly, he was surprised that Sonja Mycenae had shown up at all.

"Food first?" Nartay Cyzewski asked. He was a round man with chubby red cheeks and bright green eyes. He kept his perfectly shaped skull shaved, revealing tiny ears and a gigantic birthmark on the back of his neck that he obviously refused to enhance.

Deshin smiled at him. They had worked together on a construction project near the edge of the known universe, and had nearly come to blows over the financing. They had worked out an understanding and, of all the people in this room, that made him the person Deshin was the most comfortable with.

"Food first," Deshin said.

The group went to the various food stations. No one asked a single question; obviously, they'd listened to the briefing and knew how Deshin would run this meeting.

He took a stir-fry, made of vegetables grown inside the conference center, and a drink made of fresh berries. He doubted he would eat much of this, but he didn't want to be the only one not partaking.

He set his plate at the head of the table, grabbed chopsticks, and sat down, scooting his chair back slightly so that he could watch everyone else fill their plates.

Sonja Mycenae finished second. She took exactly the same food he had, then met his gaze as she found her name card at the seat to his right. Her food choices were a challenge and a message: *I don't trust you, so I'll eat what you do.*

Everything about her startled him. He was surprised that she had once worked as a nanny, even if she had given it up after her mother died. He couldn't imagine anyone hiring this woman to care for children.

Although he had hired a facsimile of her.

The others sat down, some carrying more than one plate, others balancing their plates over a wine glass. Layla Kee carried a glass and an entire bottle of wine to her place first, then added six small bowls, each filled with things that looked lumpy and unrecognizable. She, too, had chopsticks.

Deshin waited until everyone was seated before he spoke. Some in the group had already finished eating by the time others had sat down. The others ate as slowly as they had gathered their food.

"Thank you for coming," Deshin said. "I'm sure all of you are aware of what's been happening to the Moon. I also know that these events have had an impact on your businesses."

"Half my employees can't get to the Moon these days," said Gahiji Palone. He was the only person who had filled his plate with all meat. He was eating a large rib of something or other with his bare hands. Some brown sauce stained his well-trimmed gray beard.

"Why can't they?" asked Bibi Steeg. She was delicate and pale, her hair silver, her eyes almost clear. The only things she had taken were some yogurt dish with raisins and almonds, pita bread, and some weak tea.

"Half his employees are Peyti," said RaeAnne Ibori. She was tiny as well, but nothing about her was delicate. In fact, she looked like she could fight everyone in the room while finishing her meal.

"Why would you hire aliens to work for you?" Steeg asked Palone.

"They're smart," he snapped, then yanked some flesh off the bone with his teeth.

Deshin grabbed his glass of juice and held it as if he were going to make a toast. He couldn't let this meeting get out of hand, but he felt just how hard it would be to keep these eight people under control.

"As you can probably guess," he said, speaking over Steeg, who seemed to want to continue her argument with Palone, "these attacks on the Moon have had a dramatic impact on my bottom line."

He was exaggerating. The attacks hadn't yet had an impact, and he suspected that, if the attacks stopped, his bottom line would grow rather than decrease. The impact had been more emotional than he wanted to admit—the loss of life, the loss of friends and colleagues, and the loss of that sense of protection that living in the center of the Earth Alliance used to bring.

"The authorities on the Moon aren't getting anywhere in their investigations," Deshin said. "I've had some of my best people on this as well, and there are some connections that I don't like."

"What does that mean?" Mycenae asked. She leaned close enough to him that he could smell her vanilla perfume.

"There are some Alliance connections to these attacks," Deshin said.

"Meaning what?" Cyzewski asked.

"Meaning that either lower-level officials are working in concert or they're covering up something," Deshin said.

He explained as much of his investigation to them as he felt safe doing, telling them about his search for the designer criminal clones of PierLuigi Frémont, the hunt for the explosives, and the fact that several trails dead-ended in Alliance connections.

He ended with, "I invited all of you here because we have one thing in common."

"Besides the loose way we do business?" asked Locan Robuchon, and then he burped. He shoved aside a plate covered mostly with chocolate covered sweets.

Deshin gave Robuchon a sideways look. Deshin didn't conduct loose business in any way, and most of the others in the room didn't, either.

But no one corrected Robuchon.

"I invited you," Deshin said, "because we've all had Alliance-made clones infiltrate our organizations, sometimes with extreme ill effects."

It took a lot of self-control not to look at Mycenae. Her mother's raid on the Alliance facility had started because every single member of the Mycenae family had been cloned, and Aurla wanted it to end. She had pretended disinterest when Deshin had told her about the Sonja clone he'd discovered in his organization, but he later found out that afterwards, Aurla Mycenae had launched an aggressive campaign against Alliance clones that had nearly destroyed her organization.

"We just kill them," Mycenae said flatly. "We find them, we slaughter them. We record it and send the information back to the source."

This time, Deshin did look at her. Her expression was cold, her eyes glittering with rage.

"Yeah," Ibori said to Mycenae. "Isn't that how you took over the family business? After you proved yourself by killing, what, twenty-five different versions of yourself?"

Mycenae turned toward her.

"They're not me," Mycenae said. "They're not versions of me. They're blobs of flesh that don't deserve life. And I killed seventy-five clones, not just of me, but of my family members, as well. I'm the one who is rebuilding the Family Mycenae after my mother let this thing with the Alliance make her crazy. Trying to stop the Alliance is crazy. Using tools at our disposal to find and destroy clones is the best use of our resources."

Deshin felt the hair rise on the back of his neck.

Cyzewski's gaze met Deshin's over Ibori's head. Deshin recognized the look on his old colleague's face. Cyzewski was scared of Mycenae, and not because he feared for his life. Instead, he feared that her desire for vengeance made her reckless.

"You said that you send information back to the source," Deshin said to Mycenae. "What do you mean by that?"

"We found out where they were making the clones," Mycenae said. "My late brother sent someone in to destroy all the Mycenae DNA, but of course that didn't work. The DNA is backed up off-site."

She grabbed her berry juice, then leaned back in her chair, her gaze still on Deshin's, her look challenging.

"You do realize," she said, "that the Alliance has collected DNA on all of us."

He didn't "realize" it. He had worried about it, and suspected it, but he didn't know it for a fact. And he wasn't sure she did, either.

"How do you know that?" Steeg asked Mycenae.

Mycenae gave her a withering glance. For a moment, Deshin thought Mycenae wouldn't answer the question. Then she said, "You know, people pay me to get this kind of information."

"The government has a DNA collections division," Palone said. "It puts everyone in there."

"Everyone?" Kee asked.

"There's a criminal division," Palone said. "But think about it: how else do they confirm your identity when you travel?"

"I don't know," Kee said. "I don't let the Alliance confirm my identity."

Deshin set down his juice glass. Mycenae mirrored his movement. He didn't know if she was deliberately trying to annoy him or if she was just focused on him.

"I don't get it," Robuchon said to Mycenae. "If your brother wasn't able to destroy the DNA, and you think it's stored elsewhere, how do you find the clones?"

Her back was to Robuchon. She rolled her eyes at Deshin, as if they were co-conspirators. He didn't respond.

"We know where the clones are made," she said. "We know how they're distributed. We have set up clients who demand Mycenae clones. The clones show up at that location, and we kill them. It's easy."

"But expensive," Kee said.

"We don't worry about money," Mycenae said.

Deshin made a mental note of that. Because if the new leaders of the Mycenae family didn't worry about money, that meant the entire empire would be for sale in a few years.

"I want to know how the clones are transported," Palone said.

"Depends on the size of the order," Mycenae said. "And the point of the clones."

"They're selling clones as well as distributing them like secret agents?" Kee asked, as if that had just become clear to her.

Mycenae shrugged. "I didn't design the business model. I actually think someone inside the clone factory is selling them without government knowledge, but honestly, I don't really care."

"Well, you should care," Cyzewski said, "because if you're only killing the ones you buy, you're missing all the ones owned by the government."

Mycenae tilted her head and looked at him sideways. The look chilled Deshin. She wasn't entirely sane.

"I told you," she said. "I'm not sharing everything."

"Where is the clone factory?" Deshin asked.

"Not all of them are inside the Alliance," she said.

"We know that," Ibori said. "The one you're working with."

Color suffused Mycenae's cheeks. "I'm not working with them."

"You're paying them money and keeping them in business," Ibori said. "I think that's working with, not working against."

"Enough," Deshin said.

The room got quiet. Everyone looked at him. If he handled this next part wrong, then everything would fall apart.

"I have a question," he said to Mycenae. "You said there are a lot of clone factories. I assume you mean that there are a lot owned by the government."

"Yes," she said.

"Are the ones making clones of us and infiltrating our organizations inside or outside of the Alliance?" he asked.

"Where would you put them?" she asked, bracing her elbow on the table, putting her chin on her palm, and looking directly at him.

"I would put them inside the Alliance, close to government facilities," he said. "It's easier to protect. I'd make other types of clones, military or manufacturing, near the edges of the Alliance."

Mycenae grinned. "Mr. Deshin gets it in one. Are *you* working for the government?"

He felt a surge of anger run through him, even though he knew making him angry was what she had been trying to do.

Maybe the anger came because he had been working with the government on the bombings, even if that working "with" had been through the Retrieval Artist Miles Flint.

"If I were," Deshin said, "I would know where the facility is."

"You're looking for the place building those assassin clones, aren't you?" Maurizio Eto spoke up for the first time. He was the oldest man in the room. He had eaten nothing and touched nothing. He had simply watched everyone as the discussion played on.

He was asking the question of Deshin.

"Yes," Deshin said. "I'm looking for the assassin clones."

"You need a facility that handles both human and alien clones, then," Eto said.

"There is none," Mycenae said. "No cloning facility handles both."

"One does," Eto said. "It is exactly as you described, Luc. It is not far from some major government facilities, and it has existed for more than a century. It is on Hétique."

"It is not!" Mycenae snapped.

Three others in the room glared at her. Eto didn't even bother to look at her.

"We have been watching that facility for some time. It is also the source of some of the small ships that a decade or two back found their way into the black market. We've been worried about attacking the facility on our own, especially given what happened to Aurla—"

"She wasn't attacking that!" Mycenae said. "She wasn't that dumb. She was—"

"—but," Eto said, clearly ignoring Mycenae. Apparently, he had decided she was worthless. Deshin was beginning to agree. "—if we approach that facility with all of our forces together, we might be able to destroy it."

"Is that worthwhile, given that the DNA is stored elsewhere?" Palone asked.

Deshin turned his chair slightly, so that Mycenae didn't block his vision of the others.

"They're attacking us," Deshin said. "Even if they continue making more clones of us elsewhere, this will slow them down. And it might just take out the folks inside the Alliance who are making those assassin clones."

"Lots of ifs, Deshin," Steeg said.

Deshin nodded.

"I see no benefit in this," Mycenae said.

She had gotten on his last nerve. He gave her his coldest look, and she actually shrank back just enough.

"The benefits are simple. Best case, we stop them from cloning our families. But like you, I doubt that will happen. Also best case, we destroy those who are making the assassin clones. I also doubt that will happen."

"See?" Mycenae's bravado had returned. "No benefit."

"However, if we succeed, we will slow them down. If the attacks on the Moon are being caused by a rogue element inside the Alliance, then that rogue element will be on notice. They'll know we're after them. The Alliance itself might think the attacks on the Moon have moved to other parts of the Alliance—"

"And they'll come after us," Mycenae said. "You don't know what that's like. They took out half my family—"

"Correction, little girl," Eto said quietly. "You took out half your family. The Alliance may have killed your mother, although I doubt it."

He looked at Deshin and raised his eyebrows. Deshin got the message: *Don't trust Mycenae.* As if he were dumb enough to trust her at all.

"You just want to continue killing," Ibori said to Mycenae, "and we're going to take away your excuse."

Deshin liked the *we're.*

"To go on with your list," Eto said as if Mycenae hadn't spoken up at all, "we might force the Alliance's hand. They might have to stop the clone infiltration of our businesses."

"At least the way they're doing it now," Robuchon muttered.

Deshin shrugged a shoulder. "I think if we work together and strike at them, we'll accomplish a lot."

"Count me out." Mycenae slid her chair back and stood up. "I'm leaving this dump. You people are crazy."

She stomped her way to the door and walked through it.

"Are you going to let her go?" Kee asked quietly.

"We all decide that," Deshin said. "I can prevent her ship from leaving if we believe it necessary. But if we come up with a good plan to go after that clone factory, she might be useful."

"What makes you think that, Deshin?" Palone asked.

Deshin smiled. "She'll tell them who attacked them. And why."

"And they'll come after us," Kee said.

"They're already after us," Eto said. "We just make sure the press and the rest of the Alliance know that we're doing this for noble reasons, right, Deshin? We make it clear we're going after the assassin clones because the Alliance lacks the will."

"And because the Alliance made them," Cyzewski said, grinning. "Suddenly, we're the good guys."

Everyone laughed. They knew they wouldn't be the good guys. But they also knew that distrust for the Alliance ran deep in many circles, and this plan might strengthen their standing in those circles.

Only Kee didn't laugh.

"You're playing a dangerous game, Deshin," she said.

"I always have, Layla," Deshin said quietly. "I always have."

42

THE FOLLOWING MORNING, ODGEREL HAD JUST ARRIVED AT THE HALL OF Imperial Peace when she received a message along her links. She tried not to think of the irony. If she got a message through her links before she got to work, it often meant there was some kind of threat to peace—at least to her peace.

On lovely days like this one, with the sun whispering through the trees, she left her apartment early so that she could walk through the Imperial Garden on her way to the office. The Imperial Garden, which always seemed so rejuvenating to her after she walked through Tiananmen Square and into the Forbidden City. The garden was different every day—new flowers blooming, new plants pruned—and yet it had a feeling of eternity that eased her troubled spirit.

She thought of ignoring the message, but did not feel as if she had the luxury on the way to work. Everyone knew that she ignored all but the most important emergency during lunch, but very few knew about her walk to the office on days like this.

She stopped near an ancient cypress tree. The crowd was thin at this time of the morning, mostly locals and no tourists, but she didn't want to monitor the aliens and tour guides while she was responding to a potential crisis.

She opened the message.

I would like to speak with you outside of the office about my assignment. The message came from Mitchell Brown.

She sighed and sent him her location. She understood his caution.

He appeared near her, breathing hard. He had run again, and apparently slowed down as he entered the Gate of Heavenly Unity. Someone had probably reminded him to show respect.

She thought of taking him to the statues of the Xiezhi. The mythological creature had been a symbol not just of justice and law, but of civil service. She doubted Brown knew any of that, so the reminder would be wasted on him.

He stopped beside her, his clothing mussed, his face covered with sweat.

"Sorry," he said, beginning that annoying apology again. "I'm just finding all kinds of strange stuff. You wanted proof that the Alliance is in danger, and I don't really have that, but—"

She put a finger to her lips.

He stopped talking.

"Speak slowly and quietly," she said.

He nodded, then took a deep breath.

"What I have," he said, speaking slower than he had before, but still not slowly, "are some strange coincidences. Like the only place that the DNA for both mass murderers exists, as far as I can tell, is in Special DNA Collections of our own forensic wing. An accusation from a reputable law firm that Alliance ships fired on a transport that housed a Frémont clone that had been imprisoned during the years of planning for the first Armstrong attack, and—"

"You are saying that you find suggestions that within the Alliance, forces are gathering that would destroy the Alliance." She raised her head, and gazed at the nearby rockery, plants poking their ambitious heads through openings in the stone.

Breathe, she reminded herself. *Remain calm.*

"Yes, sir, I am," he said, "and that's with just a quick search. I also found a lot of dissident groups and some long-standing political groups from within the Alliance that believe all kinds of dumb things, like—"

"I'm aware of the levels of stupidity that can exist in any governmental endeavor," she said. "None of this is proof positive, like I asked for."

"Sir, forgive me," he said. "But my gut sense is that something is happening, and it's happening with the help of a branch of the Alliance."

"You mentioned the Special DNA Collections Unit in the Forensic Wing," she said. "You realize that is under the Security Division's auspices."

"I do, sir," he said. "That, plus the fact that this Frémont clone died the moment he was released from prison by a judge's order, sends some suspicion toward the Security Division."

"If that is the case," she asked, "how do you know you can trust me?"

His look was almost comical in its surprise. "Sir?"

"I lead the Human Coordination Department of the entire Security Division. You are implying that I do not know what happens under my watch?"

Brown swallowed visibly, his Adam's apple bobbing. She could see the calculation in his face. Did he say what he truly believed and insult his new boss? Did he risk his entire career by making a wild, unsubstantiated claim that might harm thousands of jobs? Or did he bob and weave and make nice until he had some kind of verifiable information?

"Sir, I'm sorry," he said, and she felt a deep disappointment. So much for finding an employee who would face her head on. "But I think we need the help of all the other divisions and we need it fast. What I'm finding makes me uncomfortable, but it doesn't give us the proof you want. I'm not sure the proof would be easy to find. I mean, you're making an assumption here."

She tried not to smile. He was taking her on, and in a way that she approved of. She let him continue.

"You're assuming that we're up against the usual stupid types, the folks who don't understand how government works or why the Alliance exists or what benefit it brings. I learned something when I was chasing criminals. The folks at the bottom—the thieves, the murderers, the thugs—they were often stupid. But the people who ran the networks? They were usually twice as smart as those of us pursing them. Our arrogance led to many mistakes. Once we stopped thinking of ourselves as superior, we actually made progress."

"That is the second time you have used the word 'arrogance' around me," she said.

"Yes, sir." If there had been a moment when he should have apologized, this was it. And he did not.

"You believe we are making the mistakes of the arrogant," she said.

"Yes, sir." He kept his gaze on her. The only thing that betrayed his nervousness was a visible, rapid heartbeat in his neck.

"You believe that we have missed a lot of opportunities to solve or prevent these crimes—"

"Acts of war, sir, I truly think they are acts of war."

"To prevent these acts, criminal or warlike," she said. "We have missed the opportunities not because they were impossible to find, but because in our arrogance, we did not look for them. We are, in your words, being diligent against enemies we do not have while failing to protect our Alliance from the ones we do have."

"Yes, sir. Exactly, sir."

She made a soft sound. She had been thinking of that since she saw him the day before. That was one reason she had taken the long walk this morning, hoping to find peace in the Imperial Garden.

She had found tranquility here, but no peace. Peace was not something she could simply command into being, no matter how much she wanted to.

"Please, sir," he said, "I'd love to have more help on this. Not just from within our division, but from the other intelligence and investigative units."

"And if our division is as corrupt as you say, then what is the point?" she asked.

He suddenly seemed less agitated than he had a moment ago.

"The point, sir, is that we make this top-secret, need-to-know, high clearance. We choose the people we know we can trust and we do the investigative work quickly and quietly."

"And if we find traitors in our midst, Mitchell?"

He swallowed again. "I don't know. I guess we either use them to find more traitors or we prosecute them to the fullest extent of the law."

"The fullest extent of the law," she said, *"Alliance* law, is draconian, put into place after the Disty joined the Alliance."

"Vengeance killings?" he asked, surprised.

She shook her head. "Vengeance killings look tame in comparison. We haven't applied the fullest extent of the law to treason and traitors in hundreds of years for a good reason. Are you still certain you want to pursue this?"

Brown ran a hand through his hair, then looked over at the Hall of Imperial Peace. He probably had no idea what the building was or what it stood for.

"If I'm right, sir," he said slowly, "then these traitors are the masterminds of attacks that have cost millions of human and alien lives. Disty Vengeance Killings are brutal, yes, but perhaps, when facing this type of organized mass murder, we leave all options on the table. Including whatever it is that's worse than slaughtering a single murderer for revenge."

Brown was much more bloodthirsty than she had expected. Her respect for him went up again.

"So be it, Mitchell," she said. "We'll do this your way. Let us hope that what we find is something less dramatic than what you envision. Because if you're right, then we will be making examples of these traitors, and the next two years inside the Alliance will be some of the most controversial this organization has ever seen."

His gaze met hers. His expression seemed calm for the first time.

"Not if we handle this right, sir," he said. "Not if we handle it right."

43

Two hours later, the rest of the group left the dinner meeting. They had decided on a strategy to attack the clone factory on Hétique, and they had agreed upon a plan to deal with Mycenae. She would leave after the rest of them did.

Deshin moved to his apartment inside the convention center. Before he made certain his staff had heard the conversation in the private dining room, he wanted to be in the safest part of the center. Like the private dining room, Deshin's apartment was set up so that no one could hack into it.

Still, he set up extra protections as he walked, knowing that Mycenae, among others, might try.

He opened the door to the apartment to find Keith Jakande waiting for him in the center of the entry. Jakande was a strong man who looked bigger than he was. He was also Deshin's head of security—the best person Deshin had ever had in the job.

Deshin trusted him just a bit more than he probably should have.

As Deshin entered, Jakande said, "We got—"

Deshin held up a finger to silence Jakande, then double-checked to make certain the door was not only closed but all of its protections were turned on.

Then Deshin moved Jakande through the large living area, past the kitchen, and into a corridor. There, Deshin opened a panel, revealing one of six secret rooms inside the apartment.

The room smelled faintly of old air. Deshin turned on the room's environmental controls, put a hand inside so that his security chip could measure the quality of the air, and then, when it turned out to be fine, stepped inside.

Jakande joined him.

This room was small, barely big enough for the two of them. Deshin had designed this part of the apartment before he met Gerda and before they had Paavo. This was a one-man room, built for survival. There were features Jakande didn't need to know about, features only Deshin's old friend Garner had known, features that—since Garner was dead—only Deshin knew.

The panel closed, and a dull gold light turned on. It cast an unfortunate glow over Jakande, turning his dark skin sallow.

"Well?" Deshin asked.

Jakande grinned. "We checked. Eto was right: there is a cloning facility on Hétique, right near Hétique City. That crazy Mycenae girl might also be right. There's no evidence of alien clones anywhere near that facility, at least now. But decades ago, when those Peyti clones were designed? The facility was handling some Peyti work."

Deshin nodded. "Good work. I want to see all you have on the facility before we join in this little parade I started."

Jakande looked surprised. "I thought we were leading this."

Deshin shrugged. "We might. We might not. It depends on what our informants find. I assume we already have some ships in the area...?"

"Yes," Jakande said. "We'll have information shortly."

"Good," Deshin said.

"Why wouldn't we want to participate?" Jakande asked.

Deshin smiled. "There's organizing and then there's participating. I value our people, Keith. It might be too risky to get deeply involved."

"Your nasty friends will notice if you don't send a ship or two," Jakande said.

"I know," Deshin said. "I never said we wouldn't send a ship. I said we might not participate."

Jakande grinned. "You can be pretty devious, sir."

If Deshin hadn't been devious, he wouldn't have built a business that spanned the known universe. But he didn't say that.

Instead, he said, "It's always best to not only know who is useful, but what they're useful at, and whether or not you're better using, or leading."

"You'd rather use," Jakande said.

"Oh, no," Deshin said. "I've spent all day leading this small group. It might just be time for the troops to take over."

Jakande's smile faded. "You're anticipating a large loss of life."

Deshin suppressed the urge to nod. "We'll contain the attack to the cloning facility, and we'll do it when the human work force is at its lowest daily point."

"Still," Jakande said. "There might be hundreds working in some place like that."

"Yeah," Deshin said quietly. "They make and discard clones. We'll show this little group that we value life as much as they do."

Jakande shuddered. Then he asked, "Is that everything?"

"For the moment," Deshin said. "Let me know when the images come in."

"Yes, sir," Jakande said, and let himself out.

Deshin kept the panel door open, feeling a cool breeze and fresher air enter the small space.

He had forgotten: Jakande hadn't worked with Deshin as Deshin set up his business. Jakande was used to a more genteel Deshin, the Deshin who had a stable, long-time marriage to a good woman. The Deshin who loved his son.

Jakande knew that Deshin had a dark history, but a dark history was easy to ignore when it was only history.

Deshin would keep an eye on Jakande. If the man got squeamish about any of this, he could be replaced. Or left behind.

Or forgotten.

Deshin had done a lot of forgetting in the past.

There was nothing to stop him from doing it again.

44

ZAGRANDO HAD JUST CROSSED INTO EARTH'S SOLAR SYSTEM WHEN THE space yacht jerked and then stopped. The stop—a full stop—lasted less than five seconds, but the state-of-the-art cockpit informed him, not just with little holographic warning signs rising off all of the boards, but across his internal links as well.

Oddly enough, Zagrando felt a thread of relief. He'd been expecting something like this for more than a week. He hadn't been stupid enough to think that, just because he had reached the center of the Earth Alliance, he would be safe.

If anything, he was in even more danger.

Zagrando tapped one of the warning signs that appeared above the board. It flared, which meant he could send a message to it.

What the hell is going on? he sent.

The yacht didn't respond.

He had never called her by name, although she had a name: *Day's Reach.* He had no idea what the name meant, and he didn't care. He had scrubbed it from the yacht's exterior—which was not a hard task. The name *Day's Reach* only appeared when some port pinged the yacht or needed additional information.

It took three layers of actual official behavior to get to the name at all—making him harder to trace.

Maybe that was why he had never called the yacht by her name.

What's going on? he sent again.

And again, no response.

That was a bad sign. It meant she didn't feel like she could respond. He had set all the security features on this space yacht at the highest level, which meant no easily traceable communication during a crisis.

Which, apparently, this was.

Fortunately, he had been in the main cockpit when the crisis happened.

He shielded the cockpit's controls so that they couldn't be accessed from anywhere else on the yacht.

The second cockpit, on a different deck, was coded only to his DNA, combined with his warm and living body. If blood wasn't coursing through his veins, then his skin, his DNA, his entire body, wouldn't gain anyone access into that cockpit.

He'd bought the yacht for that feature combined with all the other defensive capabilities. He'd known someone would try to get him eventually; he also knew that his brains alone wouldn't keep him alive.

He had the same training that the people who were coming after him had. In fact, Ike Jarvis had done most of Zagrando's undercover training.

The big challenge, since Zagrando started running from Jarvis himself, was to think outside that training, in a way that Jarvis would never consider.

No one knew about this space yacht except the woman that Jarvis had partnered Zagrando with on that fateful last mission. And from Jarvis's panicked tone in their last conversation, she was most likely dead.

The space yacht changed course—and the course change did not come from Zagrando. More warning beacons went up until he shut off all except the one on the console in front of him.

He tapped on a live holographic representation of the yacht's exterior. It appeared above the console, his beautiful big space yacht, bought with more stolen money so far outside the Alliance that he had never seen a space yacht like it.

Beside it—or, rather, all over it—was a larger ship, made of a black material so dark that it almost blended into the darkness around it. Only the slight reflection of faraway stars gave it away—that, and the fact that it seemed to displace everything around it.

He'd seen ships like that hundreds of times before. They belonged to the Black Fleet. Only the Black Fleet didn't operate deep inside the Alliance. It couldn't—at least, not obviously, like this ship was.

Not that it mattered. Someone—or something—had copied the Black Fleet's design and sent the ship after Zagrando. Jarvis had finally located him.

And if Zagrando didn't act quickly, he would die.

45

W<small>ITHIN FIFTEEN MINUTES</small>, J<small>AKANDE HAD RETURNED</small>. D<small>ESHIN HAD BEEN</small> fielding messages from the eight, all of whom wanted to leave. Deshin was stalling them until he had all of the information.

He knew some of them would send ships ahead; he just wanted to control the operation as much as he could.

Keeping the eight on Garner's Moon would slow things down, just a bit.

He had made himself some coffee and had just finished making a burger for dinner with the fresh meat the staff had stocked in his fridge when Jakande contacted him through the links.

You need to see something, sir, and I want to show it to you privately. I'll be right down.

Unlike other members of his staff, Jakande did not ask Deshin to leave the door open or loosen the security protocols. Jakande would never ask for anything like that.

It was one reason Deshin knew that his contact was Jakande. It still didn't make Deshin lessen the security codes, or even tell Jakande to let himself in.

But it did reassure him a bit.

Deshin's stomach growled. He hadn't eaten much at the so-called dinner, just enough to put his guests at ease. Even then, a few of them only picked at their food and Eto hadn't eaten at all.

Deshin had been around people like Eto for so long that he wasn't insulted. In the same circumstance, Deshin wouldn't have eaten, either.

He put the well-done burger on a bun, added guacamole (also from the fridge) and a bit of salsa, as well as some fresh lettuce and a fresh tomato.

He had just taken a bite when the door chirruped, announcing someone's arrival. At the same moment, Jakande sent a message along his links.

It's me.

Deshin did not reply. He set the burger down and walked to the door, calling up the security images from the corridor. It looked like Jakande but, as per Jakande's insistence on this trip, Deshin also did a DNA check.

When it came back positive, he still didn't have the door open automatically. He moved to the side where no one could knock Jakande out of the way, shoot inside, and then force a way inside.

Then Deshin ordered the door to open.

Jakande slipped in. His skin still looked sallow.

"My guests are restless," Deshin said. "If that's what this is about, then I've been handling it. We can—"

"It's not that," Jakande said. "Can we go somewhere to view some footage?"

Deshin frowned. "How protected should we be?"

Jakande shrugged. "It's our conversation I'm most worried about."

Deshin didn't want to go into another private room, especially the close one where the quarters were a bit tight.

"Did you bring the footage or are you going to download it while we talk?"

"I have it," Jakande said tightly.

Deshin nodded and led him to the entertainment room off the kitchen. "I just made myself a burger. Would you like one?"

"No," Jakande said, "and I don't think you do, either."

Deshin looked at him sharply. Jakande stood in the doorway of the entertainment room. "Something wrong with the food?"

"No," Jakande said. "Let me show you this, and you'll understand."

Deshin reluctantly left his burger behind. He closed the doors and changed the security in the entertainment area so that it blocked all links, including emergency links.

Then he turned to Jakande, and said, "Show me."

Jakande rubbed his fingers together, activating some chip that had the footage in it. A small holoimage rose to eye level. It showed an Earth-like park—grass, trees that Deshin didn't recognize, and a path. In a sandy area, children played.

The children—two boys and five girls—appeared to be about three. The girls were laughing, and both boys were looking in the direction of whatever was making the recording.

Deshin's breath caught.

"Where is this?" he asked, even though he knew the answer.

"The information was incomplete," Jakande said.

"*Where is this?*" Deshin asked.

"This is the clone factory." Jakande's voice was soft. "It's not just a single warehouse or something. It's an industrial park, and in the center are dormitories, two schools, and playgrounds."

Deshin looked at Jakande, who was studying the image. "How did we miss this?"

"We got the information from Sonja Mycenae," he said. "She doesn't care what she kills."

That was true, but it wasn't what Deshin meant. "You told me this was a clone factory."

"It *is*," Jakande said. "They make and ship off clones all the time."

"Fast-grow clones," Deshin said.

"And slow-grow as well." Jakande took a deep breath, stealing himself. "What we didn't expect was that they raise a lot of the slow-grow clones until they're needed for some operation. I'll wager that some of the clones who've infiltrated the organizations represented here today were raised in this facility."

Deshin felt the blood leave his face as the import of what Jakande told him sank in. "How many children are we talking about?"

"Mycenae would argue that they're just clones," Jakande said.

Deshin didn't care what that crazy woman would argue. *"How many children?"*

"We don't know. Hundreds, judging by the footprint of the facility."

"And they live onsite."

"Yes," Jakande said.

Deshin cursed. He turned away, his right hand gathered in a fist. He wanted to hit something, but refrained from doing so.

"We can order the others not to attack," Jakande said.

"Sure," Deshin said, his back to Jakande. "And that'll be as effective as a fart in the wind."

"Surely, they'll understand—"

"Maybe one or two of them will," Deshin said. "But most of them agree with Mycenae. The children won't even be human to them. They're clones, nothing more."

"But if we tell them we're not going to do anything—"

"It'll make no difference," Deshin said. "Some of them probably have ships already heading toward Hétique. They will want to get there ahead of us, to steal what they can before it all gets destroyed. We can't stop them now."

Deshin felt ill. Jakande had been right: what little Deshin had already eaten sat heavily in his stomach.

Jakande didn't look at him.

The image remained.

"There's more, isn't there?" Deshin asked.

Jakande nodded. He tapped his fingers together again and the image enlarged until the boys' facial features were clear.

Their faces were identical, which was no surprise. But the face itself, Deshin would have known anywhere. Round, dark brown hair, intelligent eyes.

Paavo.

46

ZAGRANDO KNEW HE HAD ONLY A FEW MINUTES TO PROTECT HIMSELF, or he was going to disappear into the maw of that gigantic ship and no one would care, no one would find him, and no one would ever know.

The ship held his yacht in place. The ship could have just as easily opened its cargo doors and pulled the yacht inside. It hadn't.

The Black Fleet would have. They would then have picked the yacht clean of all valuables, disassembled it for parts, and made it appear as if the yacht had never existed, either.

Yet more confirmation that he wasn't facing the Black Fleet.

Someone wanted him to believe he was, because he would respond differently if he believed pirates were trying to take his yacht.

It was an old trick used by the Earth Alliance Intelligence Service. Make someone think they were being pursued by a different enemy, and plan for that response. Members of the Earth Alliance Security Division had all received training that encouraged operatives to invoke some kind of standard behavior, and then to respond accordingly.

Zagrando wasn't going to behave as if he were being attacked by the Black Fleet. In fact, he was a bit insulted that Jarvis believed Zagrando would fall for this trick.

Zagrando might not have been inside Earth's Solar System for years, but he still remembered how things worked. And the Black Fleet couldn't get near this part of the Earth Alliance, certainly not with a ship that large.

He hadn't planned for Jarvis to come after him in a Black Fleet replica ship, but he had planned for Jarvis to come after him, somehow.

And he'd even expected Jarvis to use a much larger ship.

The yacht shook again, more warning signs rising, complaining that its hull had been breached.

It had taken the Alliance ship longer than usual to open the exterior entrance.

Zagrando blessed the saleswoman on Goldene Zuflucht, who had convinced him that a yacht built outside the Alliance would serve him better than anything built inside the Alliance.

She had said: *Earth Alliance specs make ships easier to board. Out here, we prefer non-standard luxury ships. They're safer.*

And it appeared she was right—about everything.

Including being boarded.

Boarding the yacht was a stupid move if this yacht had been under attack simply because it was a luxury vessel. Better to take it apart far away from the spot where it was captured, in privacy. Hell, the rich owner (Zagrando) could even be sold back to his family (if he'd had any). Kidnappings had become lucrative these days.

But boarding the yacht was a smart move if someone were coming after Zagrando. By now, Jarvis had realized that Zagrando had stolen the money designated for buying designer criminal clones.

Normally, an agent would let the money go. But Jarvis couldn't. Not only had that operation been off the books, but the money had come from somewhere else.

And that money had been millions.

Even if Jarvis wanted to write it all off, he couldn't.

He had to find out where the money was before he killed Zagrando.

Still, even with the small advantages Zagrando had, Jarvis held the bigger advantages. He had a team, probably a large one. He had a larger ship, one with actual firepower.

He knew Zagrando's training, and the way Zagrando thought.

And weirdly, he had killed a version of Zagrando before, so he wouldn't think twice about doing it again.

Zagrando had to act fast if he wanted to stay alive.

Zagrando had practiced dozens of maneuvers since he had bought this yacht. He'd always planned for a larger ship to grab this one. And he had known he would be at a disadvantage.

Now he had to put those practice sessions to use.

He had to do things quickly and accurately. He hoped he had trained himself so thoroughly he could do much of this by rote.

First, he transferred all of the control to the second cockpit. He knew that whoever had boarded the yacht would come to this cockpit first. This cockpit was the only one visible on the schematics. No published design of this yacht showed the second cockpit.

Plus, as the saleswoman had shown Zagrando weeks ago, the second cockpit had layers and layers of protection that prevented it from showing up on most scanners.

Particularly, Alliance-made scanners.

Zagrando forced that thought from his mind, his fingers racing. He touched a dozen different controls, but did nothing with them. His touch was simply to throw off any scans the invaders used, things that might show the invaders how to access the equipment.

The logical thought would be that the last things he touched were the things that made the equipment work.

Then he called up a virtual link, attached to the second cockpit and accessible for only a few minutes. Using it, he set up a shadow cockpit right here. If the invaders came into this cockpit, they would waste a good fifteen minutes touching panels and hitting controls that did not exist at all.

But the shadow control panel he set up would show them that they were making progress. He would use it to buy time.

Next, he changed the sound recording settings inside the cockpit to make any playback run backwards. He hadn't spoken in the last several hours, so there was no way that the invaders could know what he had done.

He hit the last command just as the virtual control panel ceased to function. He hoped it all would work.

Then he went to a hidden wall panel and used a voice command to open it. The command was in Peytin, a language he simply could not speak well. One of the Peyti ambassadors Zagrando had met early in his intelligence days had laughed at his pronunciation, telling him no one sounded as bad as he did.

Zagrando hoped that was correct. It would be a second failsafe if the backwards recordings didn't work.

The wall panel slid open to reveal three laser pistols and a laser rifle. He wrapped the belts for two of the pistols around his waist, and then strapped the rifle over his chest. He disarmed the last pistol's safety, switched the pistol into *ready* mode, which kept it charged up, and left it inside the panel.

Then he activated the panel's self-destruct system. It wouldn't blow unless his life signs vanished from the yacht's controls. If his heat signature vanished, if it was clear he stopped breathing, if someone took him off the yacht, this panel would explode, and the explosion would be compounded by the pistol.

An image sent by the yacht herself floated across his vision. Invaders crowded into the airlock.

As he suspected, they were human. If he had access to the cockpit controls, he would be able to do some kind of identification. But he couldn't. Not here.

At the moment, he didn't recognize any faces, but he saw movement from the other ship. Only four people had entered the airlock—which was all it held.

More waited on the other side.

Waiting to board.

He had no idea how many would come for him. He only knew that there would be more than he could handle on his own.

His heart rate increased. He had never felt quite this alone before.

He had never *been* this alone before. No partner, no back-up, no government behind him.

He was on his own.

He let himself out of this cockpit and hoped to hell that the masking program he'd set up would hide his life signs from the invaders.

He had three stops to make before he could get to the second cockpit—and maybe, just maybe—an escape.

47

"THEY STOLE MY SON," DESHIN MURMURED.

He stared at the image floating above the entertainment room floor. The image was a bit see-through, allowing the paneled wall to create a ghostly backdrop to the two cloned faces of three-year-old boys who looked exactly like Paavo had looked five years before.

"They're not Paavo," Jakande said.

Deshin looked at Jakande. Jakande hadn't been working for him when the clone had been his son's nanny. Did Jakande ever know the details of the clone infiltration?

Deshin wasn't certain.

"I know," he said flatly. "I worried that they had stolen Paavo's DNA. Now I know that they have."

"We can figure out a way to make sure they'll never use those clones or others like them to infiltrate—"

"I know," Deshin said. Strangely enough, he wasn't thinking about someone looking like Paavo infiltrating his organization. That was years in the future. No one would mistake these young boys for his son.

Besides, he could set up an identification system that would immediately rule out any clone. Not through DNA, but through the old links that Paavo's biological parents had illegally installed in his brain when he was an infant. The scarred-over links were unique to his boy, and always would be.

Deshin walked around the image. The children had put him off before he had put an actual, beloved face on them. But now that Jakande had shown him clones of Paavo, Deshin knew he couldn't be part of anything that would result in the death of children who were biologically the same as his son.

He wouldn't be able to live with himself.

He *had* softened up.

Once he had been able to live with anything.

"Who do we have in the vicinity?" he asked Jakande.

"I checked before this," Jakande said. "Otto Koos was nearby. I figured you'd want him to run our part of the op, so I sent him and a team in that direction."

"Good," Deshin said.

Koos, Deshin's former head of security, had redeemed himself by taking care of the person who had sent the clones who had infiltrated Deshin Enterprises, as well as the clones themselves.

Ever since, Deshin had used Koos for secret ops inside the Alliance. Koos was discrete, talented, and ruthless.

"We need a lot of cargo ships," Deshin said. "This operation has changed."

"Excuse me?" Jakande frowned, clearly surprised.

"We're not going to destroy the clone factory," Deshin said.

"But you said we can't stop the others," Jakande said.

"We can't," Deshin said. "I also said a bunch of my colleagues would try to steal what they could before the attacks hit."

"Yeah," Jakande said. "You said they'd take the DNA."

"And other valuables," Deshin said. "But they're not going to steal what we will."

Jakande's frown grew deeper. "The Paavo clones?"

"Too specific for a quick in and out," Deshin said. Besides, doing that didn't satisfy the sense of horror he felt at those schools, those dormitories. "We're going to take every clone we can, starting with the youngest, and working our way to the young adults."

"And do what with them?" Jakande asked.

"Make them legit," Deshin said. "We're going to make them legit."

48

THE NARROW CORRIDOR'S LIGHTS DIMMED AS ZAGRANDO MOVED, THE opposite from the way the lights in a standard space yacht functioned. In standard Alliance configurations, lights dimmed or went out after people left a corridor, not as they entered it.

He had gotten used to crouching through the low-ceilinged corridors as he went from section to section. His thighs had become a lot stronger than they had been, and his back had become accustomed to the angle.

Just this one change alone would tire his pursuers.

He hoped it would slow them down as well.

He opened a person-sized side panel, and went down one deck. The panels in the corridors were built for bots and for actual living servants because this truly was a luxury yacht, just not one of the yachts for rich Alliance teenagers.

Zagrando made it to the cargo level. He moved quickly. This was one of the most dangerous parts of his trip to the second cockpit, but he absolutely had to do this.

He could feel the time ticking away. Right now, a group had either huddled near the airlock door *inside* the yacht, or they were already going through the lower deck corridors, searching for him.

He was only two decks up.

His mouth had gone dry.

He slipped into the armory. The armory, like most places on the yacht, was coded to his DNA, and his DNA only. No one could get in, not even if they had copies of his DNA. Even a clone couldn't open anything, because it would have either shortened telomeres and/or a marker inside its DNA, differentiating that DNA from his.

He loved that about this yacht.

The armory was tiny, little bigger than the average crew cabin on an average human-designed Alliance ship. He opened the tiny weapons bay, and saw all six torpedoes. That wasn't a lot, but it might be enough to help him escape. He had to touch them as he gave them the command that would let them know that any launch sequence had to come from the second cockpit.

He slipped his middle finger into the groove on each of the six torpedoes, felt them heat in response to his touch, and then he closed the panel.

He half expected to turn around and find someone staring at him, but he hadn't so far.

He ignored the other weapons. Some were truly terrifying—an actual crossbow and some vicious looking swords—but most were standard Alliance-grade guns. He set all the laser pistols and laser rifles to the *ready* mode, but left them behind, just as he had in the main cockpit.

Then the yacht sent him a map with heat signatures. Eight invaders so far, all crowded in the corridor near the main entrance.

It wouldn't take them long to fan out.

He set up this armory to blow, just like he had set up the control panel in the cockpit one deck up. It was to do so after the torpedoes launched.

Not before.

He eased out of the armory, and headed to the cargo bay, half expecting the door to slide open and reveal even more invaders.

But the bay was empty.

It took one minute to set the explosives he had rigged weeks ago near the cargo bay door.

Twelve invaders now, and they had fanned out. He studied the map, saw that if he hurried, he might be able to make it to the second cockpit. He would have to forgo setting the explosives he had placed in the yacht's galley and entertainment areas.

He slipped into another side panel, went up three decks, emerged—

—to find Ike Jarvis standing directly in front of him, laser pistol pointed right at him.

49

Jakande clearly didn't understand what Deshin intended to do with the clones once he had them. Deshin already had a plan. It would take a lot of setup on his part, but he didn't have to do it until he got the clones away from Hétique—and that would be a trick in and of itself.

"We can't kidnap hundreds of children," Jakande said.

"We're not," Deshin said. "We're stealing hundreds of slow-grow clones."

"Still," Jakande said. "That's a major operation and it'll take planning, and even if we succeed, what'll we do with them?"

All good questions. Deshin hadn't had much time to think about this, but one reason he had become head of Deshin Enterprises was because he could think so well on his feet.

"There are a couple of places we can take them," he said. "I'll worry about that for the moment. But we need to execute this plan fast."

"What plan?" Jakande asked. "I don't see a plan."

He actually sounded panicked.

"I'll work with Koos," Deshin said. "He's been around a long time. He can remember when we've done similar operations—"

"Sir, I don't think you're thinking this through," Jakande said, then went gray as he realized exactly how critical he sounded. "I mean—"

"I know what you mean," Deshin said.

"I don't think so, sir." Jakande spoke fast as if he wanted to get the thought out before he made another verbal error. "These are *children*, which means that if they're under ten, they'll need supervision, and if they're under five, they'll need a lot of supervision. You'll have mercenaries do that?"

Deshin looked at Jakande over the images. Another good point, and one Deshin hadn't completely realized. Especially with the infants.

"I guess we take caretakers out of the schools and dormitories as well as the children," Deshin said. "We'll figure out what to do with the adults later."

"Sir—"

"Just find me Koos," Deshin said. "I'll talk to him. We did something similar in the past. If I remind him about it, he'll know what to do."

Jakande shook his head slightly. "If this doesn't work—"

"I'll know we tried," Deshin said.

Jakande stared at him, as if he wasn't sure who Deshin actually was any longer. "Do you want to talk to him here?"

"No," Deshin said. "I'll go to my office in the conference center."

"The others might track your communications," Jakande said.

"That's all right," Deshin said. "They expect me to go in early. They'll be doing the same thing. We just have a different target. Go. I'll join you in a minute."

Jakande snapped his fingers together and the image vanished. Then he opened the door to the entertainment room and let himself out. After a moment, the apartment let Deshin know that Jakande was gone.

Deshin sank into one of the nearby chairs. Children. Whom he probably couldn't rescue.

But he would try.

Timing would be everything. He would need to get those children onto those cargo ships just as the attack forces showed up. The ships would have to leave *before* the bombs hit, so that no one would associate his cargo vessels with the attacks.

Then he frowned. He would need more ships, waiting nearby. He would have to dump the initial ships.

And he would have to participate in the attacks as well, maybe even lead them, just to keep the timing under his own control.

He cursed again. It had seemed like such a good idea a short time ago. Go in, attack the clone factory wherever it was, get some revenge.

He had learned at the beginning of his career that revenge was often one of the most costly things a man could indulge in.

Apparently, the lesson hadn't taken.

But it would now.

50

"YOU'RE DONE, INIKO." JARVIS'S VOICE WAS DEEP AND GROWLY, THE SIGN of an enhancement gone wrong.

Zagrando's heart pounded. They were in a narrow corridor, neither of them standing upright. Zagrando had just come out of the armory after setting everything to blow.

What worried him was this: Jarvis hadn't shown up on Zagrando's internal map. No heat signature, nothing, not even now. For a moment, Zagrando wondered if Jarvis had accessed his links, and the man pointing a laser pistol at him was just a hologram.

Zagrando had to act as if Jarvis were real.

Because if he was, then Zagrando had another problem.

How many other invaders had already arrived and weren't visible on his scans?

Zagrando tried not to let how unnerved he was show on his face. The training, which had hurt, was coming in useful now. If he acted calm, he would be considered calm.

He slid a finger behind him, commanding the panel to close.

It did, just as Jarvis shot at him—low, like Zagrando expected. Jarvis shot to wound, but not kill.

The shot missed, and Zagrando backed up, out of Jarvis's line of sight, heart pounding, but glad for the confirmation:

Jarvis needed to find that money before he killed Zagrando.

Zagrando could use that.

He could still see the edge of Jarvis's shoe, but didn't know how long that would last.

Zagrando shut off all contact with the space yacht after sending a shadow signal up one more level. As the hookup with the yacht winked out, Jarvis remained. If the shot hadn't convinced Zagrando that Jarvis was real, then the fact that Jarvis hadn't disappeared with the links did.

Still, Zagrando didn't like severing the contact. He couldn't figure out where invaders were without the yacht, but if he stayed hooked up to the yacht, then someone might track him through the yacht's systems.

Then Zagrando pulled out one of the pistols he carried, set it on high, and hoped to hell he wouldn't have to use it.

He backed away, moving as quietly as he could until he reached the next access panel. He went down two decks, squeezing through a space that he barely fit in.

Before he opened the access panel on that level, he sent out a silent prayer to all the gods he had never believed in, hoping against hope this would work.

He pushed the control, and the panel slid open.

No one waited for him in the corridor.

He scurried along, touching nothing, pistol in front of him, feeling blind without his links, lonely without a partner, and just a little worried that he had missed something important.

51

Odgerel's office had no desk. It had no furniture, not as most people would define it. She had large, multicolored pillows on the floor, several rugs covering the tile, and some thick mats for stretching. Four decorative screens divided the room into sections.

Her favorite screen reproduced the famous Qing Dynasty painting, "One Hundred Horses." She loved the piece, not only because its browns, greens, and blacks pleased her, but because of what it symbolized. The artist, Lang Shining, had been born in Italy, but his work became beloved by Chinese emperors. To her, the screen represented the hope that if humans could blend their cultures long ago, then humans and aliens could do so now—with the human becoming dominant, of course. Like the Chinese were dominant in this painting.

The other screens were also reproductions of famous old works, and all of them had a message—at least to her. The screen closest was a version of *Emperor Taizong Receiving the Tibetan Envoy* from the early years of the Tang dynasty, *Peach Festival of the Queen Mother of the West* from the Ming Dynasty, and *The Jade Rabbit Explores* from the early 21st century. Of all of them, she liked the moonscape the least, but her eye went to it now, looking past the moon rover to the grayish surface of the Moon itself.

Back then, who would have known that the exploration would lead to such a vast and complicated civilization, one with so many moving parts even she could not understand it?

Odgerel sat cross-legged before *The Jade Rabbit Explores*, the large, pale pink pillow soft beneath her legs. She needed to unite the various Division and Department heads without making any of them feel threatened. She decided she would start with her old friend, Gāo Ya Dé. He headed the Earth Alliance Military Division Human Coordination Department Intelligence Service, and she could trust him to speak frankly to her.

She waved her right hand, activating the screen hidden in the center of the Jade Rabbit rover.

A brief, yellow-coded image appeared on her screen. It was the usual warning screen, one that prevented outsiders from entering the secure divisions in the Earth Alliance government.

Any contact initiated by her or someone with the codes to her screens in this single room would immediately bypass those screens.

After a moment, Gāo appeared. He had put on weight since she had last seen him, making his already-round face seem moon-shaped. He had an ill-advised mustache that accented how pale his once-brown skin had become. His eyes, dark and inquisitive, remained the same.

"Odgerel," he said, with unfeigned pleasure. He bowed enough that she could see the top of his head before he continued. "I have missed you."

"And I, you, Ya Dé," she said. "It has been too many years."

"And too many light-years," he said, with the boyish smile she remembered. "I have a staff meeting in progress. I assume I must dismiss them?"

"Only for a moment," she said, and then she waited. She did like this part of her job: the fact that others—no matter how highly ranked—catered to her.

His face disappeared, and an Earth Alliance Military logo replaced it. She waited while he dismissed his staff, using those moments to make sure her breathing was regular and her heart rate remained even.

Then Gāo's face filled the screen once more. Behind him, she could see the edges of a starscape. He had changed locations, perhaps to a room with a view of space.

"Now," he said warmly, "how may I help you, Odgerel?"

She let her hands rest on her knees. "You have, of course, heard of the latest attacks on the Moon."

"Yes." His eyes glittered. From his tone, she could tell he thought the attacks had nothing to do with him.

"I am hearing disturbing chatter, and I must consider it." She paused, making certain he knew that she was choosing her words carefully. "I am hearing that these attacks are not criminally based, as we first thought, but are aimed at something larger."

"What could be larger than destroying cities on the Moon?" Gāo asked.

She waited. She did not want to insult him. He needed to come to his own conclusions. Then he would own the ideas.

"No one would attack the Alliance," Gāo said. "No one has the military power to attack us. Everyone who has tried has failed. We've never encountered a larger military in the known universe."

She waited and watched. He frowned, as he thought about this.

"You think the attack is coming from within?" he asked.

"I am sure, Ya Dé, that you have kept a close eye on dissidents," she said.

"Dissidents, yes," he said. "We follow all sorts of dissidents. Generally, they dislike their own governments, not the Earth Alliance. The Intelligence Service's Joint Unit follows those that seem to span species, and—"

"I'm aware of the structure," she said softly. She didn't need him to explain the sections that most divisions in the Earth Alliance had. Each alien species had its own wing of not just the military intelligence service, but also of the military prisons and, oh so many others. Just like each division had its own overall human overseer. She had to meet with her compatriots three times a year, generally off-Earth, which annoyed her greatly.

"I'm sorry," Gāo said. "Of course, you're familiar. I'm so used to explaining the intricacies to subordinates."

Sure he was. She kept the disbelief off her face. She had a sense that he had started to make those little unnecessary speeches that some people in command resorted to. They often believed their subordinates were ignorant, rather than trusting them.

Almost like she had done with Brown the day before.

"Dissidents," Gāo repeated. "Have you discussed this with your political branch? They send us updates quite often. I believe between us, we're tracking two million different groups—and those are just human."

"Humans against the Alliance?" Odgerel asked.

"If we get that kind of specific, then maybe half are what you're looking for." Gāo tapped a finger against his lips. "There are, literally, a million suspects, Odgerel. And that's not even the problem."

She would have thought it a problem. In fact, she did think it a problem. She had no idea how they would find the particular needle they were searching for in so many large haystacks.

"What is the problem, then, in your estimation?" she asked.

"Organization," he said. "Dissidents rise because of events, and events, by their nature, are short-lived."

Odgerel frowned. She thought about that for a moment, felt the truth of it.

"Perhaps we are using the wrong word," she said. "Dissidents were once of the community, right? Then they decide that they do not agree or something happens to take them outside of the community."

Gāo stroked that ill-advised mustache. "It's simplistic, but we could say that."

Had he always been so pedantic? So caught up in being right? She had known him when they were both young, and while they had stayed in touch, they had not had a long business conversation in—well, perhaps ever.

"So, let us discuss instead, groups that have never wanted to be part of the Alliance," Odgerel said.

"Humans?" Gāo asked. "Because we began the Alliance, and I doubt there are any human-only groups that have opposed it from its start. At least that I am aware of. Perhaps your political branch knows of some."

She nodded. She would check.

"As for others, you know that non-human groups are outside of my expertise," he said.

He was actually trying her patience. She hadn't had someone try her patience like this in a very long time.

"Perhaps," she said, sounding as reasonable as she could, "you could check to see what human opposition groups have existed for several decades."

"After the—what are they calling it? Peyti Disaster?—are we certain that the groups are human? Because the evidence suggests a joint group."

As if Gāo had seen the evidence. He hadn't really been paying attention. That much was clear, just from his inability to name the most recent disaster that had hit the Moon.

"We don't know anything," Odgerel said, and it pained her to say that. "I will be talking with your cohorts in the other divisions."

Or someone would. She didn't want to talk to all—what was it? At least 1,000 branches of military intelligence—on her own.

"But," she said, "I would like you to examine this for me, see if you can find anything."

Gāo nodded. "You do think this is human-based, don't you."

It wasn't a question.

"I do not know," she said. "Until recently, we have looked at this as a Moon-based problem that we are providing back-up and assistance for. We see the criminals as very dangerous."

"Yet you're talking to me," Gāo said.

"I am," Odgerel said. "One of my newer staff members reminded me that the Moon is the gateway to the heart of the Alliance. Plus, we must ask who gains if the Alliance goes away."

"No one," Gāo said quickly.

Odgerel bowed her head slightly in acknowledgement. "That was my first reaction as well. And I have learned to mistrust those automatic vocalizations. They come from my assumptions, not the assumptions of someone who is bent on harm."

Gāo took a deep breath. "It would help if we knew how to focus the investigation."

He was once again asking, in a sideways manner this time, if the culprits were human.

As if she knew everything. If she knew everything, she wouldn't have to ask his help.

"The initial clones were human," she said, because he clearly hadn't followed this closely. "The second batch were Peyti."

"So we have no idea," he said.

"The Moon suffered an explosion years ago. The authorities at the time believed it connected to the Etaen crisis." She also hadn't given this as much thought as she would have liked. "Some corporations have hired Etaens to teach guerrilla warfare—how to get tiny weapons into large ports, for example, to cause a crisis that would then make the corporations' products and services desirable."

Gāo let out a small breath. "You don't think a corporation tried to destroy the Moon."

"I don't think anyone wanted to destroy the Moon," she said. "I think the attacks against the Moon's domes will benefit several corporations, particularly those that offer construction contracts."

Gāo shook his head. "Some of those corporations had branches on the Moon."

"Yes," she said, "and some of those corporations routinely do things that would, on their face, harm the corporation. For example, many have Disappearance services, so that any employee that accidentally crosses an alien government can avoid jail time. This violates Alliance law. It also risks the lives of employees."

Gāo's lips thinned, pulling on that mustache and making his face look puffy.

"Attacking the Alliance makes no sense from any corporation's perspective," he said. "The corporations, in particular, benefit from the Alliance's existence. It enables the corporations to do business in places that normally would be closed to them. And we both know that corporations are about profit, not about politics."

"Unless politics interfere with profit," she said.

"But the Moon's governments were too loose for that," Gāo said. "They were only just uniting."

He shook his head.

"I need your help," she said. "I do not think on these large political scales."

She was astonished at how easily the lie came, even to her old friend.

"I would like to know about long-standing dissident groups, organizations that have been a thorn in your side and in the side of the Alliance for generations. I would also like to know about opposition groups that have existed for more than a century."

She kept her voice calm. Gāo watched her, a slight frown on his face.

"I would also like to know if you are seeing positive chatter about the Moon attacks—groups that believe them good," she said.

He didn't appear to be listening closely. He was still thinking of something.

"Odgerel," he said, "you realize that attacks on this scale cost a fortune. There would be a financial trail."

"Yes," she said.

"I could see which organizations have the largest coffers," he said.

"That would help," she said. "Although we could pull in our forensic accounting division, if you would only point us in the right direction."

Gāo shook his head slightly.

"I don't like this, Odgerel," he said, and she felt a stab of worry. He didn't like that she had contacted him? Had he seen through her efforts to get the agencies to help her, outside the system?

"If," he said, "this is an organized campaign, from a group inside the Alliance bent on destroying the Alliance—"

She straightened her back as subtly as she could. Something in his tone told her to brace herself.

"—then we don't have much time. Because they have put a long-standing plan into action, and that means—if they're thinkers, which you believe they are—they will continue on this plan until it succeeds. They will have contingencies. They will know what's coming next. And we do not."

She nodded, relieved she had gone to Gāo after all.

"That's my concern," she said.

"Finding them, in the vastness that is the Alliance, will take time," he said. "If you're correct, we do not have time."

"Unless," she said, knowing she had to be delicate here, "we use *all* of our resources. Together."

He smiled at her. "You have already thought this through, my friend."

She smiled in return. "Some of it. But most of it, I have no clue how to implement."

"So you came to me," he said, "not for friendship, but for my military mind."

She inclined her head sideways. "I came to you for friendship," she said, "*and* your military mind. We need to work together, all of the divisions of the Alliance."

He let out a small sigh. "I don't know if that's ever been done."

"And," she said, because she didn't know either, "we have to investigate without tipping off the attackers. If they're part of a long-standing organization, they might have spies of their own inside the Alliance."

He nodded. "I'll see what I can come up with."

Odgerel clasped her hands together and bowed slightly. "Thank you, my old friend."

He let out a small sigh. "Let us hope we're wrong, Odgerel."

"Yes," she said, and signed off. Then she let out a sigh of her own.

She did not believe they were wrong at all.

52

SOMEHOW LUC DESHIN HAD FOUND SEVEN CARGO SHIPS WITHIN SPITTING distance of Hétique. The man was a damn miracle worker. One of the ships had even arrived before Otto Koos's cruiser.

Koos had brought the cruiser and a team of fifty. It wouldn't be enough to cover the grounds he saw before him on imagery, but those were all the team members he could trust to think first and shoot later. The shoot-first group had stayed behind on this mission, and Koos knew he would miss them.

Deshin had left a lot to Koos's discretion. Deshin had deliberately not told Koos if there was an acceptable percentage of survivors from this little mission—not among Koos's team, but among the children they were going to kidnap.

Koos didn't expect to kill any of them, but given the numbers he was seeing—nearly five hundred, counting the adult handlers, he expected to leave a good three-quarters behind.

Deshin would probably sell the kids when he got his hands on them, so Koos made the call among his own people: babies and toddlers first, under-fives second, and under-tens third. The rest? Bonus.

He'd been monitoring the space around Hétique. Dozens of ships that he didn't recognize were already showing up. Deshin had told him to expect a good hundred vessels within twelve hours. That had been six hours ago.

And those hundred vessels, Deshin had said, didn't count the ships that Koos would find in orbit around Hétique, with their teams already on the ground.

Deshin figured at least four of his colleagues would send teams to steal from the facility before the attack, and judging from what Koos saw, that number was probably an understatement.

The only good thing was that the other teams had gone in dark. They had sent shuttles to Hétique City's private space port and used landing strips that were designed for quick, secret trips by those wealthy enough to afford clones.

Koos had brought ten shuttles so small they could land anywhere. The problem usually was that they often destroyed ground cover.

Here, it wouldn't matter. The ground cover would be bombed to hell and gone within the next 48 hours. Whatever damage he did would be minimal compared to the damage the attack ships would do when they arrived.

Koos was landing with the first crew. If this were an ordinary mission, that would be a terrible choice. The commander should never lead from the front.

But he had a feeling this mission wouldn't work out, and he wanted to make the on-the-ground call, not someone else. He wanted to tell Deshin personally that they couldn't get anyone out, and why.

Deshin had ordered the mission to happen at night, which had delayed the landings two hours. Normally, Koos would have found a way to surreptitiously evacuate the facility, but he didn't have time to do any of that.

Besides, he figured out that the other teams were keeping the locals engaged.

He'd had no idea until he piloted his own small shuttle over Hétique City. Lights everywhere, and, as he closed in, he saw people running in the streets, screaming, shooting laser rifles at anything that passed overhead.

He had to rise up several meters and turn on his shields to avoid it all.

He flew over the gates to the facility—industrial park, really—and saw that the doors were already open. One lone guard was shooting at people who were running in. Fires burned in the buildings up front, and a lot of black-clad figures showed up on his scanner as a negative image until he switched to infrared.

As Deshin had predicted, none of those black-clad figures were anywhere near the children's facilities.

Koos landed on the grassy area in front of a playground. The four other small shuttles that came on this part of the mission landed in the widest areas they could find, as close to him as possible.

He grabbed his own laser rifle as he got out of the shuttle, leaving a copilot inside. His partner, Piet Nawotka, slid out the other side, rifle in hand, another along his back. Nawotka also had several smaller, flash-bang weapons, just in case they were needed.

Four other teams of two joined them, and they spread across the courtyard. Koos had decided on the dormitory first. He knew the doors would be barred, with everyone barricaded inside.

In the short few hours he'd had to do research, he'd realized that most of the security in the factory was near the gate and in the buildings with the actual equipment, including the buildings that were currently on fire.

No one expected attacks on the schools and dormitories, so the security here was minimal.

He hoped that the specs were right, but he was prepared for them to be wrong.

The night vision he could access with his chips told him a good dozen people were spread out near the two closest entrances. Which was fine with him, because he wasn't going in a door.

He was going in the side windows, one floor up from the basement safe room—where he was certain the staff had moved the babies.

53

Z AGRANDO ROUNDED THE LAST CORNER.

Jarvis waited for him in front of the second cockpit door.

The panel nearest that cockpit was closing now.

Apparently, Jarvis was familiar with the layout of this space yacht.

Jarvis smiled. It seemed like a warm, welcoming smile, but Jarvis had never been warm or welcoming.

He said, "Let me in, Iniko, and then code everything to me. Give me the yacht and the money, and all will be forgiven."

Zagrando shot him.

Jarvis expected the move and dove to one side.

The only advantage Zagrando had was that Jarvis didn't want to kill him.

Shots rained through the corridor—not from Jarvis or Zagrando. Someone else was here, and Zagrando did not have the opportunity to get out of the way.

There was no *out of the way*.

More shots. He couldn't see the shooter, but the air smelled of burnt wall. If Zagrando focused on the second shooter (shooters?), he would open his back to Jarvis. But if Zagrando focused on Jarvis, the shooters might kill him.

Only they, like Jarvis, were under instructions not to kill him.

Zagrando shot at them, shooting higher than they did. He didn't care if he killed them.

And then a burning pain ran through his left foot. He glanced down—no amount of training prevented that reaction—and saw a laser burn through his left shoe. Son of a bitch.

He'd been hit.

He swore, turned around fast, shot, and managed to kill the man behind him—the dumbass was bent toward him, giving Zagrando a clear head-shot.

A shot hit him in the right foot and Zagrando would have collapsed if he hadn't braced himself against the curved wall.

This time, he didn't look at the shooter. He knew that shot had come from Jarvis.

Zagrando blanketed the area near Jarvis with shots, all along the floor and wall, not caring if he damaged the yacht. His eyes ached from the laser light reflections in such close quarters.

No one ever recommended shooting like that. It temporarily blinded everyone.

Zagrando didn't care. He kept firing until he heard an *oof* and a thud and hoped to hell it was Jarvis.

Zagrando stepped forward and his legs buckled. His feet couldn't hold him up. The pain was unlike anything he had ever felt before.

For the first time since he started this thing, he wondered—really deep down—if he would survive it. He had always known he would die, always known he would die *badly* given his work, but he hadn't expected it now.

But no one shot at him anymore. Zagrando's nanohealers repaired his eyes just enough that he could see shapes.

Jarvis was hunched on the floor near the entrance to the second cockpit.

Zagrando would have to crawl over him to get to it.

Jarvis didn't move, but Zagrando shot him again anyway for good measure—or maybe for that helpless clone of Zagrando that Jarvis had taken such pleasure in killing all those years ago.

Jarvis was clearly dead, but that didn't mean Zagrando was in the clear.

In no way could Jarvis have run an op like this on his own. He had backers. He had supporters. And he had someone on his side powerful enough to hide the theft of a Black Fleet replica ship and to allow it to operate inside the Alliance.

Hell, inside Earth's Solar System.

Another shot careened down the corridor from behind Zagrando. He didn't dare get hit again. He would probably faint from the pain. Jarvis's people, whoever they were, would use clearers and nanohealers just to keep Zagrando alive so that they could get the financial information out of him.

He started to crawl, then realized that—weirdly—crawling required the use of toes and ankles, so he fell to his stomach, back to a position he had used in training decades ago, but never since.

He pulled himself along by his arms, moving his hips to gain some traction, and moved a lot faster than he had a moment ago.

He finally reached Jarvis as more shots started. Even if the shooters had equipment that protected their eyes from temporary laser blindness, the equipment wouldn't be good enough to let them see detail. They'd see a man leaning upright, nothing more.

And Zagrando could use that.

He slipped in behind Jarvis's body, propped him up against the corridor wall, and made the body face the shooters.

Then—and only then—Zagrando opened the second cockpit door.

54

THE SOUND OF BREAKING WINDOWS CARRIED ACROSS THE COURTYARD—
and that was when Koos realized just how quiet this part of the compound
was. The screaming, the sirens, and the explosions were more than a kilometer away—distant enough to seem unrelated to what he was doing.

No one screamed inside the dormitory, and his nine team members worked
in silence. Except for breaking the windows, they'd made no noise at all.

He climbed in. The room he entered was dark, and no one was in
it. There were several empty cribs and a scrunched blanket on the floor.
The air smelled of baby powder tinged with burning rubble.

He signaled his team, then went to the left. The building specs he'd
found on the net were accurate. Apparently no one thought this place
would be raided. There was no real security at all.

He let Nawotka go down the steps first, but Koos went second, the
rest of the team behind him. The basement smelled damp, along with a
slightly acrid stench that he recognized almost immediately.

Pee. And as he got farther in, poop as well.

The environmental system on this level wasn't designed to keep up
with a multitude of dirty diapers.

He rounded a corner, only to find Nawotka had stopped. An arch-
way appeared in front of him, and bluish lighting revealed ten adults and
behind them, babies strapped into carriers.

A few of the babies were crying, but someone had placed noise re- ducers on the carriers. It was nearly impossible to hear the wails.

Two of the adults had laser rifles trained on Nawotka. His rifle was up as well, but he hadn't taken a shot.

You said no killing, he sent to Koos. *Now what?*

Koos ignored him. Instead, he stepped to Nawotka's side and trained his own rifle, not on the adult woman in front of him ready to shoot, but at the nearest baby.

It looked at him with big, fascinated eyes.

"You shoot us," Koos said as calmly as he could, "we shoot the babies."

What the hell? Nawotka sent. *You can't do that.*

Koos didn't answer. This strategy was a risk. These babies were clones, and if their caretakers thought of them as commodities, then the caretakers would shoot at Koos.

But he was gambling that adult humans would react to babies as babies, even if their DNA designated them inferior.

He gambled that the caretakers would take him seriously, and they'd drop their weapons.

He had no idea what he would do if they called his bluff.

He stared at the woman holding a laser rifle on Nawotka. She stared back.

Then she slowly set the laser rifle down.

"Put your weapons down," he said to the remaining caretakers, as more of his team showed up beside him. "Now."

The woman nearest him was shaking so hard he was suddenly wor- ried her rifle might go off anyway. He grabbed it and pulled it from her, handing it to one of the men behind him.

"What are you going to do with us?" someone asked.

"We're taking you with us," Koos said.

"What about the babies?" someone else asked.

"We're taking them, too," he said. "Is this all of the babies in this building?"

"Babies?" asked the woman in front of him, the one who had held the rifle. "Why?"

"Because if I find more, I might just shoot them to get them out of the way," he snapped.

"Yes!" she said. "Yes! There are no more babies."

Ten adults, twenty infants, five small shuttles that could normally handle three adult passengers plus a copilot each. He could take two adults, and that would leave room for the babies—if nothing happened to the shuttles on the way out of here.

"You're all coming with us," Koos said. "And you're bringing the babies."

"W-Where?" the woman asked.

"Just shut up and follow instructions," he said, and felt a small thread of relief.

The first part of the mission was underway, and while it wasn't easy, it was better than he had hoped for.

If only the rest went as smoothly, he could report to Deshin that the entire mission was accomplished.

The entire impossible mission.

Koos doubted that would happen.

But he would try.

55

ZAGRANDO HALF EXPECTED SOMEONE TO SHOOT HIM FROM INSIDE THE second cockpit. But as the door eased open, the interior remained dark.

He braced himself for Jarvis getting up somehow and racing in with him.

But Jarvis didn't move.

The shots continued, and something sparked ahead of Zagrando. He hoped that shot hadn't hit anything important.

He used the edge of the door to pull himself inside, then let the door slide shut. More shots hit.

He only had a couple of minutes—three at most.

This thing was set up to withstand pirates outside the Alliance, not an Alliance vessel or Alliance shooters equipped with powerful Alliance weapons.

He pulled himself up onto the only chair and slammed his palm on the console.

The stupid second cockpit recognized him and greeted him with some dumb chirpy message that he had always meant to change.

His fingers were shaking.

He had to time everything perfectly, and he could feel shock setting in. He needed to get the second cockpit to separate from the space yacht just after he released the torpedoes.

He had designed this maneuver so that the pilot of the gigantic ship would focus on the torpedoes and not notice that the yacht had split into two pieces.

Of course, if the pilot of the gigantic ship had the yacht's specs—and of course he would; how else could Jarvis have found Zagrando?—the pilot might be expecting the separation.

Zagrando would have been.

But he didn't think anyone would expect the explosions.

He hoped they wouldn't because the splitting process wasn't easy and it wasn't fast. The little bullet ship that the second cockpit turned into didn't have its own weapons system, either.

At least the bullet ship was quick—once it separated from the larger yacht, anyway.

Despite the need to hurry, he made himself concentrate, take his time, do this absolutely right. He created a mental bubble around himself, almost as real as the bubble the yacht could built with its shields (which had proven worthless, since he'd been using the damn shields when the damn gigantic ship had taken over his yacht, but oh, well, he couldn't think about that. He didn't dare think about anything else—he had to focus, because his brain was going, his body was shivering now, and the nanohealers were trying, but they weren't succeeding in keeping at bay the physical reaction to his injuries, which had to be a lot more severe than he thought…).

Five steps. He had to execute five steps.

The door to the second cockpit glowed red. Whoever was out there wasn't fooled by Jarvis's body—or maybe they had been for that silly minute, but they weren't any longer.

Five steps.

Step one: Zagrando had to activate his identification (finished. Oh, yeah. He had already forgotten that).

Deep breath. *Concentrate.*

Step two: Activate the separation protocols.

Step three: Shut down the environmental controls in the yacht.

He did steps two and three together, wishing he had shut down the environment before the invaders had started to burn their way into his secondary cockpit. Now they would just focus on getting in, and he couldn't remember if they were wearing environmental suits or body armor that turned into environmental suits and…

Concentrate.

Step four: Set the speed at which the bullet ship would travel (fast as possible).

Done.

Step five: Finalize.

He slammed his palm against the console. *Finalize, finalize, finalize.*

A voice—the bullet ship's voice—told him the procedures, but he couldn't concentrate on those. He had to give himself something to clear his head or make the pain recede or deal with his feet.

He looked down. His pants had burned away, and his skin was red and black and crusty, almost like magma he had once seen on a volcano on a job, and it felt like magma too, steaming and hot and—

He staggered to the medical supplies, then said *screw it,* maybe out loud, and demanded that the medical assistant appear, and hoped to hell the assistant worked in this part of the ship and wasn't tied to the yacht.

It was a feature, an automated doctor that took care of a person with minor medical issues or major ones if they were common (please, let laser pistol burns be common) and the yacht would assist.

The assistant appeared—a woman, hair pulled back, lab coat, nice face, and she said, *Oh, dear.*

And he said—or maybe he thought through his links at the damn second cockpit—*I can't pass out. Tend to me. Let me get us out of here.*

I'll do what I can, she sent. She didn't seem hopeful. *I'll just do what I can.*

56

Two hours later, Koos had just fired near the boots of an unruly teenage boy clone when the emergency sirens went off. It took him a moment to realize those sirens were inside his links, and they weren't sirens, but alarms he had set.

The attack ships he had been anticipating had finally arrived.

He was standing inside the school cafeteria. Maybe a dozen teenagers were holding him off, mostly with knives and cleavers. Two boys actually had laser rifles, although Koos had no idea where they had come from.

He had lost track of how many trips his people had taken but they followed Deshin's instructions—babies first, toddlers second, under-fives, under-tens. The children who really couldn't act for themselves were already scattered among the cargo vessels, and one of Deshin's other ships had shown up to guard everything, which was good, since ships were starting to crowd the space around Hétique.

The fighting in Hétique City had gotten severe, and most of the buildings inside the industrial park were burning. The air was thick with smoke, but the screams of the dying had stopped maybe thirty minutes ago.

Koos had a team of six with him, and they were facing off the teenagers, who had watched most of what was happening.

These kids weren't trained for combat, but they were scared, and large enough to do some damage.

The alarms inside Koos's head were making him nervous, but he didn't shut them down. He couldn't. But he could feel the seconds ticking away.

"An attack on Hétique is about to start," Koos said. "It'll be from orbit, and it's going to destroy this entire compound. We only have a few minutes to get out of here. Either you let us rescue you or you die."

"You're lying!" one of the boys yelled.

"You don't have time to figure that out," Koos said. "Either you trust us and live or you stay here and die. Your choice."

Then he signaled his team. They were leaving with or without this batch of kids.

The three team members nearest the door backed out of it, then started to run. The remaining three did the same.

Koos looked at the teenagers, all staring at him with terrified expressions, and then he backed away from them.

The alarms were making his head ache.

He pivoted and ran for the shuttles. As he did, he saw other teenagers coming out of the bushes.

His heart sank. If all the kids came out of the cafeteria and joined these kids, there were too many for the shuttles.

He couldn't pick and choose. There was no time.

"Get on board!" he yelled, waving his arms.

His team had the shuttle doors open. Fortunately the teenagers were thin. They could cram into the back until the shuttle hit its weight capacity.

Koos reached his shuttle, climbed in, watched five boys and two girls press inside, and then he closed the door. The other shuttles were doing the same.

Voices he barely recognized were screaming at him through the links.

The attack's about to start.

Where the hell are you?

Some of the teenagers from the cafeteria were running toward the shuttles.

He started it up. He was going to pilot hybrid—he set the automatic pilot for evasive maneuvers that he could override if he saw something that the sensors didn't catch.

The shuttle started to lift off, but it couldn't rise. It wobbled.

Weight limit breached.

His heart constricted. Was he going to have pick which teenager to throw out?

Then he saw that other teenagers clung to the back of the shuttle. One kid had jumped onto the front.

"God! Let him in! That's Derek!" yelled one of the girls in the back.

Koos's mouth was dry. The other shuttles had the same problem. They were covered in teenagers who had probably been messaged by the ones inside.

Turn on your shields, Koos sent to his entire team.

Shields weren't recommended in atmosphere, but they would wipe away any intruders.

He flicked his on, and the kid on the front of the shuttle screamed, then slipped off.

Not that Koos heard the scream. He saw the kid's mouth open, the terror on his face, the hopelessness in his eyes.

The shuttle went up, followed by the remaining four.

Laser fire rose from the surface—someone was shooting at the shuttles. Some kind of automated, large gun started shooting from the top of a building in Hétique City. Finally, the authorities there realized that the entire area was under attack.

Maybe when they saw the hundred attack ships approaching the planet.

The air was filled with smoke and laser fire. The shuttle bobbed and weaved its way up and out, shots occasionally zooming past it.

Koos was braced for the sound of an explosion as he lost a shuttle, but nothing exploded so far.

The girl behind him was sobbing.

"How could you leave them behind?" one of the boys yelled. "They're people, you know."

"We know," Nawotka snapped. "If you had cooperated instead of fighting us, we might've gotten another group of ships to the surface."

"Shut up," Koos said to Nawotka.

"You gotta go back!" the boy yelled.

"We're not—"

"Shut. Up. All of you." Koos focused on the piloting. The bickering continued behind him.

Pay attention, he sent to Nawotka. *We're not out of this yet.*

Koos was heading toward one of the last cargo ships in orbit. The attack ships were lining up. He could see them on his screens, in the guidance system he'd set up in his own vision, and in his mind's eye.

He knew what it was like to be in one of those forces. You never even saw the ground. Just the targets.

He reached the cargo ship. Its bay doors were open, and he slid inside. Two other shuttles slid in right behind him.

One of the girls reached for the door. "Let us out."

He looked at her over his shoulder and realized, with a sinking feeling, that these kids had never been in space. No one had educated them about atmosphere and environment.

One more shuttle wobbled its way in, a long scorch mark down its middle.

He searched for the last shuttle on his equipment, saw it, saw some kind of fire weapon pursuing it, watched as the weapon hit and the shuttle exploded—

He closed his eyes, forgetting that he had the same images on his vision, watched the bits of shuttle expand like a flower in the remaining red light.

Bits of shuttle and bits of his team and bits of teenagers.

He shut down the internal vision.

Close the doors, he sent to the pilots of the cargo vessel. *This is everyone.*

All that hope he'd had after getting the babies, the feeling like he might be able to accomplish this mission completely, gone now.

He'd done more than he'd thought was possible, but not nearly enough.

Plus, he'd seen that kid's eyes as he fell off the shuttle.

Hopelessness. Terror.

Koos would be seeing that as long as he lived.

But he would be living.

He'd done the best he could—and Deshin would have to deal with that.

Just like Koos would.

57

THE YACHT'S AUTOMATED DOCTOR BENT DOWN, EXAMINED ZAGRANDO'S legs, and then gathered tools. She had limited capabilities of touch. She could do some things to heal and not others. Some she might have to ask him to do, and he was in no shape to comply.

But he didn't tell her that. He figured she probably knew.

Besides, being healed was the least of his worries. He needed to remain alert, at least until the bullet ship separated from the space yacht.

He moved back to the second cockpit's single chair, worked the console, saw the separation was happening, and looked at the door.

It didn't glow red anymore.

In fact, if any of those invaders were near it, they would be experiencing the separation as if they were on the edge of an open door with no airlock.

One of the first things he had done after he bought this ship was redesign the separation sequence—and he had designed it so that no one would be protected as the second cockpit became another ship.

He had figured that if he ever had to separate the yacht and the bullet ship, he was being invaded; and no one outside the second cockpit was someone he wanted to protect.

Good for him, thinking ahead. Yay, him.

And then, with those thoughts, those cheery thoughts, he realized that his judgment had become impaired. He was acting like he did when he was drunk.

I gotta think clearly, he said or maybe thought or sent to the doctor.

I know, she said/sent/whatever. *It's all I can do to keep you awake.*

Great. He made himself focus—again, ignoring the probing feeling in the wounds, the great bursts of pain that shot through him at irregular intervals (okay, he couldn't ignore that).

He called up a holographic image of the exterior so he could see what was going on.

The gigantic ship was swallowing the yacht, which meant if this damn second cockpit didn't launch soon, it would launch inside the other ship, and the other ship probably had measures set up for that, which meant they had measures to handle his explosions, which meant he was caught no matter what he did—

And then he cursed.

He had planned for five steps, finished five steps, added the doctor, but he had been wrong from the start. He hadn't needed five steps.

He needed six.

He had to release the torpedoes. If the yacht went inside the gigantic ship, he was screwed no matter what, and he couldn't let that happen, so if he got caught in the blowback of his own explosions, so be it, he'd let that happen, he'd let it all happen—

Concentrate.

He fired the torpedoes, all of them, not caring if the bullet ship escaped.

Everything blacked out—including the doctor—and for a moment, he thought *he* had blacked out, and then he realized the blackout was the separation. He had separated, the second cockpit had separated, the *bullet ship* had separated and he needed the systems back online so it could move, move, move—

Lights, power, everything returned, including the doctor who told him she couldn't work like that and he ignored her as best he could even though she was poking at his injured legs, and then the image showed up, the gigantic ship, the yacht, the bullet ship—and balloons of red hitting the hull of the gigantic ship, and the yacht got sucked inside.

But the bullet ship didn't.

It caromed (okay, not caromed but hurried—moved, went at top speed—)
Concentrate.

It took more work this time. But he saw it. He saw the yacht disappear into the bay of the gigantic ship, and he counted—he made himself count down the time to the destruction of his beautiful yacht, even though nothing was happening, even though he was failing—

Big, gigantic explosion, rocking the giant ship. (Maybe a series of explosions, maybe the weapons and the explosives going off in sequence.)

He couldn't focus on those details.

Because he didn't have a lot of time.

That gigantic ship, that gigantic *Alliance* ship, would contact other Alliance ships unless they knew they were running an illegal op for Jarvis, unless they were *only* coming after the money to cover their respective asses.

And even then, they might just say that this little space yacht had attacked them out of the blue, and they needed to destroy the person who had destroyed their ship, and they might have convinced someone in the Alliance to come after him.

He needed to get the hell out of here.

And he needed help doing it.

He cursed himself again.

Not six steps.

Seven. Seven steps.

He needed to get to Armstrong, in a no-name ship, without identification.

He needed someone to help him enter Earth's Moon—

In the center of the Alliance.

Right after a second major attack.

He'd escaped only to trap himself in Earth's Solar System.

He was screwed, and he had no idea what to do.

58

The upper level cargo deck smelled of fear. Babies wailed, little children watched everything with wide open eyes, and a handful of overwhelmed evacuees already slept on top of pillows someone had scrounged up.

The ten adults Koos's teams had brought on that first trip were the only full adults on this cargo vessel, although more had arrived on another, with the toddlers. He was grateful that the toddlers were on a different ship. The under-fives were tough enough, with their overwhelming energy and their fear.

That last group he'd brought had fourteen- and fifteen-year-olds, and he'd pressed them into babysitting service. He needed them to deal with the younger kids, at least until he could figure some of this out.

The adults wanted answers and he wasn't giving any, except to say that they'd all been rescued.

He had instructed the staff not to give them answers, either. No one was to identify the name of the corporation running the ship or the parent company of that particular corporation.

Deshin didn't want anyone to know he had taken the clones, and Koos's job was to make sure no one would get any information.

Particularly since he was going to dump the adults at the nearest starbase. He already had staff there, hiring actual nannies and gathering supplies.

This was the largest operation he'd organized for Deshin in years, and they'd done it in less than twenty-four hours.

"You need to tell us what's going on," said one of the teenage boys Koos had rescued in the last group. That group still had a bit of bravado.

"Yeah," a couple others said nearby.

"Why were we being bombed?"

"What did it mean?"

Koos looked at all of them, a sea of somewhat matching faces, and sighed heavily. He needed to say something. So he was going to tell them what he could.

He raised his hands above his head and clapped.

The room grew silent—except for the crying babies. Apparently, the sound covers on the carriers weren't up to the task.

Then he realized that several of the crying babies were being held by adults and teenagers—probably not for the baby's comfort, but for the adult's comfort.

"I'm the person in charge here. I ran the operation, and I'll tell you what I know. Please don't ask questions until I'm done." He cleared his throat. He had to raise his voice to speak over the crying.

All of the teenagers stood. A few put their arms around the younger kids, who were also watching him.

Koos felt like this was a tougher task than getting them out of the industrial park.

"I don't know much about the mission, okay? I was contacted a day or so ago with the news that the industrial park was going to be attacked. My team was sent to rescue as many of you as possible—"

"Why didn't someone tell us you were coming?" the adult woman who had turned a rifle on him demanded.

"Please," Koos said, "no questions. I don't know why this method was chosen. Probably expediency."

He would have to be careful. His mixture of lies and the truth need-ed to sound convincing.

"We got as many of you out as we could. The attack started just as the last group left. We lost two rescue shuttles—and no, I don't know who among your friends was on them."

Two of the teenage girls wrapped their arms around each other. One of the boys stifled a sob. Apparently, they knew.

"We're going to make a stop in a few hours to get supplies and some hired help for the younger children and babies."

One of the adults let out an audible sigh. Koos took that as encouragement.

"You adults will have a choice at that moment. You can leave the ship. We will give you enough money to get back to your families in Hétique City. We can't send you farther than that. I have no idea what condition the area will be in when you return. That's your problem, not mine."

He knew that sounded harsh, but he had no choice. A few of the adults put hands over their mouths.

"Can't you find out what's going on there?" that annoying woman asked.

"No," Koos said. "It's not my concern."

He stared at them, willing someone else to challenge him. No one did.

"You need to let us know your decision when we arrive. If you decide to stay, you must remain on the ship."

"Where will the ship go?" one of the adult men asked.

"I'm not going to tell you until we've left the starbase." *And not even then,* he thought but didn't say. "We're in the business of saving lives today, and the last thing we want is for one of the adults who leave us to tell the people who bombed your home tonight where we're going."

Some of the teenagers were nodding. Good.

"Then how can we make a decision as to whether or not to leave?" the annoying woman asked.

"I don't care," Koos said. "You will make your decision. Once we leave the starbase, we'll have food and water for all of you, a comfortable place to sleep, and the right amount of care."

"What happens when we get where we're going?" one of the teenage boys asked.

"I have no idea," Koos said. "My job was to rescue as many of you as I could as quickly as I could. I was told to start with the youngest and work my way to the older children. I did that. We saved as many of you as we could. I know expecting you to be grateful is probably a bit too much, but I will tell you one thing. Not one of you would be alive now, without us. Clear?"

The room was silent for a moment. Then the annoying woman spoke in a near whisper. "Not even the babies?"

"Not even the babies," he said. Then he looked directly at her. "And you know why."

He met as many eyes as he could. Then he nodded once and stepped back.

He left the cargo bay and waited until the doors closed before leaning against the wall of the corridor. He was exhausted, and he still had a lot to do.

He hadn't lied about one thing: He had no idea what Deshin would do with all of these children.

The man had never taken children before, and he had an aversion to clones. This was completely atypical behavior.

But Koos had learned early in his career with Deshin not to question what the man did.

Koos would simply be glad when this assignment was over.

And he hoped nothing like it would ever come up again.

59

THE STUPID DOCTOR WAS FORCING ZAGRANDO TO DRINK WATER. SHE'D hooked up some kind of solution into his arm, hydrating him, and re- placing—oh, he didn't know what. He didn't care.

He needed to think.

Behind him, the gigantic space ship that had tried to destroy him was falling into pieces. More explosions racked it, and he wasn't sure how that happened, but it had. The laser pistols? Stuff they carried?

He couldn't think about it.

His next problem was what was waiting for him ahead as he ca- reened toward Earth's Moon.

His calculation was pretty simple: He'd get there in less than two hours. This damn bullet ship was well named. And once he got there, no one in authority would let him into the Port of Armstrong, or any other port.

The news reports he had seen said that the Peyti weren't getting in, and that meant anyone suspicious wasn't getting in, and he sure as hell was suspicious. In the old days, he would have asked to get onto the surface and then let them deal with him, but these weren't the old days, this was post-Anniversary Day, post-Peyti Crisis, and he didn't know anyone—

Except a Retrieval Artist.

Except Miles Flint.

God, Zagrando's brain was working slowly. He had planned to contact Flint anyway.

He needed to do so now.

Flint had given him a back-up link long ago, when Detective Iniko Zagrando of the Valhalla Police Department had worked with Miles Flint, father, to adopt his clone daughter.

Zagrando had to pray that the link still worked.

He sent: *Miles Flint, this is Detective Iniko Zagrando. I need your help.*

Nothing. Of course there was nothing. Why would he expect anything? The universe was making this hard, and of course it needed to get harder. He needed—

He yelped. The pain that shot through him would have made his eyes water if there were any water left in his body.

Sorry, the doctor sent. *You need real medical attention.*

No kidding, he thought but didn't say, at least he hoped he didn't say it or think it or discuss it.

Maybe he could contact that lawyer, Celestine Gonzalez, if she were still alive. Lots of lawyers died during the Peyti Crisis, all in meetings with the Peyti, and for all he knew, she was one of them—

My sources tell me Iniko Zagrando is dead.

Zagrando let out a shuddery breath. A happy, shuddery breath. He had gotten a response. On these back links.

Detective Iniko Zagrando is dead, he sent. *But Iniko Zagrando isn't. I was working undercover for Earth Alliance Intelligence. You can check that with Celestine Gonzalez, but do so fast, because I'm coming in hot, and I need some serious help...*

Zagrando realized that Flint had checked out in the middle of that contact, that he hadn't heard the entire message. It echoed, like unsent messages often did. Maybe Gonzalez was dead. Maybe he couldn't contact her.

Maybe Zagrando had made a huge error, contacting Flint.

Maybe the authorities were already listening in and—

What do you need?

Flint was back. The man was nothing if not efficient. And Zagrando blessed him for it.

He yelped again, hoped that sound didn't go through the links, and made himself breathe one more time. He was dizzy. He didn't want to be dizzy.

Please get me clearance with Space Traffic Control. I have information you need.

He had no idea why he thought Flint could help him with something that official, but a whisper of a memory told him it was okay to ask.

That won't be easy, Flint sent back. *We've had some serious—*

I'm coming in hot, Zagrando sent. *There are factions in the Earth Alliance who don't want me to talk to you people. Please, do what you can. Please.*

God, he was begging now. He'd never been a begging man.

Send me the relevant information, Flint sent. *I'll see what I can do.*

It wasn't much of a promise, but it would have to do.

Thank you, Zagrando sent. He gripped the edge of the console to keep from passing out. *Thank you so very much.*

60

DESHIN SANK INTO A CHAIR IN HIS SUITE. HE HAD TAKEN ONE OF THE newer space yachts from Garner's Moon and brought most of his team. He was heading to one of his compounds near the Frontier. It would take nearly a month to get there, especially since he had to stop to pick up a few experts and an entire cadre of lawyers and accountants.

Koos had rescued about four hundred children, of all ages, more than Deshin had been told were even on the property. Not all of the children were young; some were teenagers, which would be a problem.

Deshin had already drawn up a plan, which he would need his people to implement. He was going to adopt out the children. He would give them legitimate birth certificates, and he would make certain they would go to human families scattered around the Alliance. No children with the same DNA profile would go to the same area.

The adoption service would be for-profit, but mostly to cover expenses. Or maybe it would be non-profit—some kind of war orphan thing. He would leave that to the lawyers and accountants.

He didn't want to lose money on this venture, but he didn't want to make money, either. He didn't believe in trafficking in human beings.

He realized that, under Alliance law, these children weren't human beings, but he didn't care. They were to him. If he had thought of them as property, he wouldn't have gone to all the expense to save them.

Expense and loss of life. Two downed shuttles, with at least six people on each, maybe more.

He hadn't known anyone who had died—his organization was so big he couldn't know everyone—but he felt it.

No one would have died if he had known that the Alliance had been raising slow-grow clones on site.

If he had done his research.

And if he hadn't felt like he needed to do something, anything, to deal with the clones attacking the Moon. He had figured that finding where the Alliance made clones would help.

And he had figured that going after the secret clones based on criminals would be best. It would stop everything.

He wasn't sure now if it would stop anything. He had been bent on vengeance, and in the process, he had made the kind of mistake he hadn't made since he met Gerda.

Of course, he hadn't consulted with Gerda on this, and he wouldn't tell her now.

He would clean up his mistake—as best he could, anyway.

He ran a hand over his face. He hadn't slept in more than a day. He'd managed to choke down some food before the mission. He knew he needed more.

Gerda would yell at him for not taking care of himself.

She would be appalled at what he had done.

He wasn't entirely appalled. He knew that two different groups inside the Alliance would understand why Hétique City and the clone factory were destroyed.

The Security forces would know that the clone factory was targeted by some of the larger criminal organizations, working together, and maybe this would finally stop their infiltration of the families.

But he hoped that the masterminds behind the attacks on the Moon would understand why this factory had been chosen and not some other Alliance clone factory. Those masterminds had to assume that someone knew about the Peyti clones being grown here, all those decades ago.

Deshin toyed with sending a message to Miles Flint. But any message Deshin could think of was one that admitted guilt.

And while Deshin was bothered by what he had done, he wasn't about to admit guilt. He had survived a long time by avoiding any admission of anything.

He was going to avoid this, as well.

He'd left Flint with enough information to track those clones, and maybe he had diverted the attention of the masterminds away from the Moon.

Deshin leaned his head back. He needed that sleep. And that meant he couldn't think about the Moon any longer.

His family was off the Moon until the crisis was over. And he had a new business to start that would take all of his attention.

Maybe he would move his base of operations away from the Moon, away from the Alliance itself.

He felt a deep sadness at the thought.

That would be a decision for another day. Right now, he had work to do—and a lot of it.

And maybe, by the time he finished all of that, the Moon crisis would be completely over and he could go home.

He closed his eyes and thought of Gerda and Paavo.

He was such a fool sometimes.

Home was where his wife and child were, not some arbitrary place.

When he was done setting up the new business, he *would* go home—to his family.

Where he belonged.

61

EVERYTHING BLURRED AND SCRAPED IN HIS MIND.

At some point, Zagrando had slipped from the chair to the floor. He'd ordered a shadow console to appear close to his hands—or maybe the bullet ship doctor had.

She kept talking to him, exhorting him to stay awake, telling him she was giving him this and that to stimulate his brain, but his brain didn't feel stimulated.

It felt like his brain was melting.

Only he knew that couldn't happen.

Someone or something was communicating with his ship, and the doctor told him to communicate back. Identification, ship's code, all kinds of information.

He couldn't remember any of it, couldn't really remember what he had called this little thing. It didn't have the same name as the space yacht, and even if it had, he wouldn't have wanted to state it.

He couldn't have stated it, not now.

He sent to Flint, *They need stuff. I don't know what—*

And he couldn't remember if Flint responded.

The trip seemed to take forever and it seemed like the trip was over quickly. Every now and then, he'd have a moment of clarity, and he realized that he was truly injured, maybe dying. The burns were more than a yacht's doctor program could handle.

Zagrando had a new goal: stay alive until he could talk to someone.

He really hoped Flint would be near his ship when he arrived.

If they let him into the Port of Armstrong.

If they didn't, maybe he would trust the links.

Maybe.

But the voices swirled around him, demanding identification, sounding official. A hologram appeared above the shadow console, showing dozens of Space Traffic Control ships surrounding his, escorting him.

Zagrando hoped that was a good thing. He hoped it didn't mean someone from the Alliance was going to get him.

He hoped this would work.

Flint might have mentioned a name for Zagrando to talk with, or maybe Zagrando had just imagined it.

He didn't know.

In the hologram, there was one of those fake lines that showed the edge of Moon-policed space. He had gone into it—how long ago, he didn't know—and then…

The next thing he knew, the hologram showed a dome, and a port opening, and his little ship settling over an area to land. The voices said he was approved for some terminal or other, and he closed his eyes.

Approved. Terminal. Dying. Of course. The doctor told him his death was approved.

That didn't surprise him.

The next thing he knew, hands were on his shoulders, shaking him. Voices above him.

"…never seen anyone look like this…"

"…shot up really bad. Wonder how long his feet have been like this…"

"…be able to save the legs…?"

He was floating now. They had him on a cushion of air. He opened his eyes, saw human faces, saw uniforms with insignia that had a dome and a word in all caps. He didn't know what that word was—what language it was in—and then it came to him. An acronym for Port of Armstrong Space Traffic Control.

He grabbed someone's arm, and a face (male?) looked down on him. "Flint?" he asked, or rather, whispered. It was hard to talk.

"He approved you. But we're arresting you all the same. It's procedure. If you get cleared by a higher-up, then you'll go free. You can talk to him, though. He'll be here soon."

Zagrando nodded—or rather, he hoped he nodded. Flint. Here. Zagrando could tell him anything.

"Need...to...be...awake...then..."

"We'll see," said the man. "You need medical attention."

"Need...to...talk...first...life...and...death."

"No kidding," the man said. "You're going to have to fight hard to survive."

"No..." Zagrando had to be really clear. "Talk before...surgery... or...medicine...life...and...death...for...Moon."

The man looked at his companions. Zagrando realized they were no longer on his ship, but in a place he didn't recognize, with a movable ceiling and clanging sounds and something that smelled faintly of warm metal. The port. That was the terminal. Not that *he* was terminal.

"Please," Zagrando said, knowing he wasn't clear-headed, and he needed to be. "Flint. Please."

"He just arrived outside. He'll be here as quickly as he can," the man said. "In the meantime, we'll get you to medical here in the port. They can help you."

The man was probably lying, but Zagrando could hang on until Flint made his way through the building.

Zagrando was strong. He had made it this far.

He would make it another hour or two.

He smiled.

He had succeeded.

It might not look like success to anyone else, but in his universe, a universe of spies and double agents, of thieves and murderers, getting this far wasn't just success.

It was a miracle.

And somehow, he had pulled it off.

The thrilling adventure concludes with the eighth book
in the Anniversary Day Saga, *Masterminds*.

The fate of the Alliance hangs in the balance as the masterminds
behind the Anniversary Day bombings trigger the final stages of a plan
decades in the making. A plan that will bring about the total destruction
of every dome on the Moon.

As Moon Security Chief Noelle DeRicci struggles with the overwhelming scope of the investigation, Retrieval Artist Miles Flint races
to save the life of a man from his daughter Talia's past. A man with vi-
tal information regarding the identity of the masterminds who planned
the Anniversary Day bombings. And deep beneath the surface of Armstrong, a dome engineer makes a chilling discovery that could crack the
investigation wide open.

If only he can get someone to believe him.

Turn the page for the first chapter of *Masterminds*.

SEVENTY YEARS AGO

1

THUMP. THUMP. THUMP. SHUFFLE. DRAAAAAG.

Jhena Andre huddled in her bed, covers nested around her, her favorite doll cradled against her chest. She woke up, heart pounding, afraid someone was in her room—and someone was—but then she heard him mutter, and she realized—*Daddy!*

She wanted to go back to sleep, but she couldn't. Daddy sometimes came to her room to make sure she was okay. Sometimes he just held her. Sometimes he stared at her from the door.

Her room was the best room in the house. He painted the walls—Daddy wanted to be an artist Once Upon A Time, before It All Went Down which Jhena knew meant the day that Mommy died and everything changed. Greens and golds and touches of sunlight, bits of color. The tall grasses waved and glistened. Sometimes the sky turned gray and rains fell, but not for long. Then the sun came out and the grasses gleamed. The air fresh—Daddy said it smelled like fresh-cut grass—but Jhena thought it smelled like green.

Daddy's paints made everything come alive, except Mommy.

Jhena's brain skipped—that memory everybody wanted to know or not know, the memory everybody told her to forget or not forget, the memory of the day It All Went Down. All she had from that day was Daddy and her favorite doll. Her favorite doll didn't have a name because Mommy said they'd name it together, and smiled, and never smiled again.

Jhena pulled the doll close, and listened to the rustling. The air didn't smell green. It smelled like sour hot chocolate and sharp sweaty smell Daddy got when he got scared. He hadn't taken her special cup from the room. He always did or the bots did or someone did, because in the morning her special cup always got clean, and ready for that night's chocolate, which she drank while Daddy read stories and she looked at the swaying grasses on the wall.

Thump. Draaaaag.

Daddy was taking stuff out of her closet. Her stomach started to ache.

Then Daddy swore, and Jhena sat up.

He turned around so fast she thought he was going to fall down. One hand out, catching the wall, disappearing in the grasses kinda—shadows of them always crossed skin but not really shadows. Echoes sorta. The grasses couldn't be on skin unless they got painted there, and Daddy said that nothing should get painted on skin.

"Jhen," he said in a voice she'd never heard before. Like he wasn't ready and he was scared but he wasn't scared of her. "Baby."

Then he sighed, and she thought maybe she heard another bad word, but she wasn't sure.

He waved a hand, and dawn started in the grasses. The light in the wall was her nightlight. She thought maybe a minute ago there was a full moon—the night-time light—but Daddy changed it. That orange glow meant get up, even though her eyes felt sandy and the clock she hid under the edge of her night table had a 2 as the first number not a 6. She knew the difference.

She was a big girl now.

"Oh, sweetie, I didn't want it to go this way." He looked scareder than he had before, like she was the daddy and he was the little girl and he'd been doing something wrong.

Jhena pulled her doll close, clutching the blankets. The light was just enough to see his familiar face, all twisted in something like a frown, his black hair mussed, and his brown eyes wet like they'd been the day It All Went Down.

"Daddy?" Her voice sounded tiny. She didn't want it too, but she wasn't sure she should be loud. The day It All Went Down Daddy picked her up and held her and shushed her and she was afraid he'd shush her now.

"I'm so sorry, baby," Daddy said. "I didn't mean for this to happen. If I thought it could happen again, I would have stayed in Montana."

Then Daddy grabbed something from the floor. Her duffle. He tossed it on the bed.

"You gotta stay here, baby, and be really really quiet, okay? My friends will come for you. They'll take you to Aunt Leslie. You remember Aunt Leslie, right? She'll take care of you."

He leaned over, all sharp sweat and cologne. His arms went around her and he squeezed too hard.

She said, "Don't wanna go with Aunt Leslie. Wanna stay with you."

"You can't, baby. I screwed up. Again. I screwed up again. I'm so sorry." He ran his hand through her hair, kissed her crown (*My princess*, he usually said when he did that), squeezed even harder. "I love you. I love you more than life itself. Can you remember that much, at least? That I love you."

Her heart was pounding. "I love you too, Daddy. Take me with you."

"No, honey. I can't. You'll be okay. I promise. Aunt Leslie—she's a good woman. She'll raise you right."

Raise? Daddy was raising Jhena. Daddy was raising Jhena alone ever since It All Went Down.

"Daddy—"

He put a finger over her mouth, shushing her. Then she heard the door close, the house telling someone that Daddy and Jhena were in the bedroom.

He stood up. "You stay here, okay? They'll come back here, and they'll take you to Aunt Leslie."

"Wanna stay with you," Jhena said, tears falling now.

"I want to stay with you too," he said. "But we don't always get what we want, honey. God, I wish I wasn't the one to teach you that."

He ran a hand over her head, cupped her chin, said, "I love you," and then walked out of her bedroom, his back framed against the hall light, his shoulders square.

He didn't look back.

But she kept looking at the space where he had been.

Looking and seeing nothing.

At all.

The thrilling adventure concludes with the eighth book
in the Anniversary Day Saga, *Masterminds*,
available now from your favorite bookseller.

ABOUT THE AUTHOR

USA Today bestselling author Kristine Kathryn Rusch writes in almost every genre. Generally, she uses her real name (Rusch) for most of her writing. Under that name, she publishes bestselling science fiction and fantasy, award-winning mysteries, acclaimed mainstream fiction, controversial nonfiction, and the occasional romance. Her novels have made bestseller lists around the world and her short fiction has appeared in eighteen best of the year collections. She has won more than twenty-five awards for her fiction, including the Hugo, *Le Prix Imaginales,* the *Asimov's* Readers Choice award, and the *Ellery Queen Mystery Magazine* Readers Choice Award.

To keep up with everything she does, go to kriswrites.com. To track her many pen names and series, see their individual websites (krisnelscott.com, kristinegrayson.com, krisdelake.com, retrievalartist.com, divingintothewreck. com, fictionriver.com). She lives and occasionally sleeps in Oregon.

Made in the USA
Middletown, DE
01 September 2017